THE DEVIL'S

ALCHEMISTS

◆ ◆ ◆ ◆ ◆

A. R. HOMER

Llumina
Press

This is a work of fiction. Names, characters, places, and incidents are either a product of the author's imagination or are used fictitiously. Any resemblance to actual events, locales, or persons, living or dead, is entirely coincidental.

ISBN: 978-1-59526-503-6

Printed in the United States of America by Llumina Press

Library of Congress Control Number: 2008905969

To Carol

Without whom this book would not have been possible

PART ONE

"He who fights with monsters must take care lest he become a monster."

—Nietzsche, *Beyond Good and Evil*

Ravensbrück Labor Camp.

Hannah Goldmann peered into the darkness. The prison cell had no windows. No light entered the small room. There was neither day nor night, only the impenetrable gloom. The stale smell of a score of unwashed bodies hung in the fetid air. A few of the women had bare wooden bunks; most, like Hannah, lay on the unforgiving earth floor of the prison cell. The blackness engulfed them all.

Yet Hannah fought to see. She conjured a blackboard in her mind. A large blackboard, like the one that stood behind Heisenberg in the lecture room at Leipzig University when she had been one of his students. For a moment, images of her fellow students fought their way into her mind. Probably all dead on the eastern front by now. She pushed their ghosts aside. The blackboard. Only the blackboard in her mind mattered. And the chalk.

The chalk flowed across the blackboard, scratching out the symbols. She started with the basics – Meitner's proposition on nuclear fission. The equations didn't stop her mind turning to Meitner. The first woman professor at Berlin University. And, like all the women in the prison cell, a Jew. Meitner had fled to Stockholm in neutral Sweden before the Nazis could get her. Escaped.

Hannah became angry with herself for letting her concentration be disturbed. The blackboard. Only the blackboard. The chalk scratched once more across the board. She stopped and checked the previous equation. Her breathing quickened. If that were true, then....

The woman alongside her on the floor turned over and coughed. It was the gasping cough of dying lungs. The chalk hesitated, but, without mercy, wrote the next equation. And the next. The symbols almost ran away from her. Suddenly, in the darkness, there was a gleam of light. Her eyes ran over the symbols on her blackboard. She smiled. He had missed it. Heisenberg had missed it. A rat scurried along the wall, looking for food that wasn't there. Hannah ignored it, seeing only her triumph on the blackboard. The Nobel Prize winner had missed it! Heisenberg, who had made appropriate noises when she and other Jewish scientists had been thrown into the camps, only to back off when

1

the Nazi circus masters had cracked the whip – he had missed the crucial point.

Her eyes ran over the blackboard again, and a third time. She could find no flaw; she was right. It was possible to create a new element, beyond uranium.

The blackboard vanished as the key rattled in the lock and the door flew open, flooding the room with unaccustomed light. The women's hands leapt to their eyes, trying to recapture the once-hated darkness, begging sleep to reclaim them. There was no escape; the guard's night stick banged against the door. *"'Raus! 'Raus!"* He kicked at the nearest body on the floor. "Roll call. Wake up, you Jewish bitches!"

The women stirred, searching for their shoes and any vestige of dignity left them. The night stick rattled again on the door and the guard began to shove the women out into the yard.

Hannah tried to recapture the blackboard and her triumph, but they had gone. There was only the harsh light and the guard's night stick. And the fear.

Frederikshavn, Denmark.

The message. Jørgen Sørensen's hand clutched in his pocket at the piece of paper with the unintelligible cipher as his boots clattered on the wet cobbles. It was so important that Marius Johansen, head of the regional Resistance cell, had gone himself to Copenhagen to bring it to Frederikshavn for transmission. The young Dane pulled up his greatcoat collar in a vain attempt to stave off the early morning storm that had suddenly burst upon the town. He looked up at the clock at the base of the steeple of Frederikshavn Kirke. Eight o'clock.

The message. It was better to send it from an out-of-the-way place like Frederikshavn, a port on the eastern coast of Jutland, Marius had told him. But even here the face of the despised enemy was everywhere. Jørgen crossed the street to avoid a handful of German soldiers. He recalled when they had arrived, back in 1940, just after his twenty-sixth birthday. The invaders had been lenient, almost friendly then, but Jørgen had loathed them from the start. He kicked viciously at a discarded cigarette packet in his anger. The presence of every single German in Denmark's streets, cinemas and beer halls made him seethe.

Jørgen was angry, too, at his own countrymen. Until recently, they had gone along with the occupation because Denmark had been treated with kid gloves by the Nazis. King Christian was still on the throne and there was still an elected government, even though it kowtowed to the Nazis. So far, Denmark had been spared major shortages. His countrymen still had decent food on their dinner plates, and Jørgen could understand why they had been lulled into complacency. But their bellies seemed to determine their politics, and that infuriated him. He had heard it was a different story in the other occupied countries, and Churchill had called Denmark 'Hitler's pet canary.' It stuck in Jørgen's craw. It hurt his pride.

Marius had brought the message to Frederikshavn for security reasons, he had said; the Germans were too damn good on radio detection in Copenhagen. Jørgen turned down Skippergade, pulling his coat tight as the rain lashed down. The bus came around the corner and he ran to the stop.

After the Nazis had invaded Russia, there had at last been some signs of resistance. The brakes of the bus screeched; he got in line, boarded, and squeezed his tall frame into a seat. Small efforts – graffiti, posters – first signaled that things were beginning to move. Underground newspapers telling the truth about the Nazis –*Land og Folk* and *De Frie Danske* – were expanding their circulations and influence. A massive demonstration had broken out when the Danish government had been forced to sign a treaty against the Soviet Union.

The message was burning a hole in his pocket; it was so important not even Marius knew what it said. The bus swung south to the working-class area where Jørgen lived. And where the radio transmitter was hidden. He wiped the condensation from the window and watched yellow-washed houses with red-tiled roofs rush by. The Germans were beginning to drop their uneasy friendliness as the resistance increased.

The message. Jørgen knew the Resistance was trying to work out a deal to get weapons from the English MI6, but what was so damn important that even a big shot in the Resistance like Marius wasn't let in on the secret? Jørgen looked out the steamy window and recognized Mrs. Gronborg's butcher shop on the corner. Only another two stops. He stiffened as a German truck full of soldiers drew alongside the bus. A soldier looked at him, and he was relieved when the truck turned down another street. The soldiers were probably on their way to Bangsbo to work on the Atlantic Wall – the immense fortifications they would hide behind when the allied nations invaded. Jørgen hoped with all his heart it would be soon. The brakes squealed as the bus stopped and Jørgen got up from his seat, nervously checking his pocket to make sure the message had not dropped out.

He stepped down from the bus and glanced around as he made his way through the downpour and up a side street to a grimy brick building. He bounded up the creaky steps two at a time to the top floor, unlocked the door, tossed his wet coat on the floor, and fastened the aerial outside the window of the small room.

"Well, here we go," he said to the radio transmitter as he took it out of the case. "Let's hope the German radio surveillance patrols are all out having breakfast." He smoothed the piece of paper flat and began to copy the code. Carefully, letter by letter.

Bletchley Park, England. MI6 Office.

The man removed his wire-framed glasses and looked out the window at the well-watered lawns of Bletchley Park. The rain poured down and he yawned in boredom as he sat at his desk. His job, deciphering and forwarding the messages that came from agents all over Europe, wasn't exactly unexciting, but he was ready for a change.

He put his glasses back on and looked through the sheets of paper carefully laid out on his desk. Requests for arms drops, reports on German troop movements, details of Messerschmitt production figures. All useful stuff, he thought as he sorted them into piles for their intended recipients. But he'd seen it all before.

He picked up one from Denmark, where he knew nothing in particular was happening. The message was, no doubt, another plea from the Danish Resistance for arms. It would be a dull repetition of all their other requests, but it had to be deciphered.

His eyes narrowed as he decoded. Either the Danes were mad or there'd been some mistake. He checked his de-encrypt again. There was no mistake.

He pressed a button on the desk. Within seconds, a courier entered.

"You'd better take this one to the Director." He reached in his desk for a security bag. Before slipping in the message, he read it once more.

Last week, Germany's leading physicist, Nobelist Werner Heisenberg, paid an unexpected and clandestine call on his former mentor and fellow Nobelist, Dr. Niels Bohr, at Bohr's home in Copenhagen. Purpose of meeting ambiguous. Implied message clear: German scientists now working on bomb of enormous power. Single bomb capable of destroying London.

Kaiser Wilhelm Institute for Physics, Berlin.

"I need clear answers to my questions, gentlemen." The many eyes in the conference room turned to the uniformed figure at the head of the table. Reichminister Albert Speer, Minister of Armaments and Munitions for the Third Reich. Suave, handsome, not yet forty, he exuded authority. Every man at the table knew he exercised power in an off-hand but incisive manner. Above all, he had the ear of Hitler.

The sunlight of a hot summer day came through the large windows of the conference hall. Around the table, apart from Speer and the high-ranking representatives of the military, sat the cream of German physicists. Most were member's of Hitler's elite 'Uranium Club,' the Nuclear Physics Research Group formed shortly after German scientists had become the first to split the uranium atom a few years earlier. Behind them sat Maximilian Heldorf, a nuclear physicist from the Institute of Theoretical Physics in Göttingen, his SS uniform standing out in a room full of civilian suits.

Werner Heisenberg, at only forty-one, was the unchallenged leader of the Uranium Club. The Nobel laureate laid out his papers in a precise manner and ran his fingers through the blond hair that sat atop a high forehead.

Speer leaned forward and placed his hands flat on the table. "Before I ask my questions, gentlemen, let me summarize the situation. The war is at a significant juncture and it's imperative that this year's campaign in the east be successful." There were murmurs of agreement around the table.

Speer looked around the room. "I'm sure you realize that time is of the essence. Against the Reich are now arrayed the huge forces of the United States and Russia, not to mention the British Empire. The

5

Führer knows that time is not necessarily on our side and has decreed that all weapons projects must produce positive results within nine months." He waited until the murmurings around the table died away. "So I ask you, gentlemen, what has nuclear physics got to offer? Can this fission thing lead to an atomic bomb?"

There was a silence around the table, followed by a rustling of papers.

"Maybe." The answer came from Heisenberg. "In theory it is possible. The basic science is relatively simple."

Speer laughed. "Then if it is simple, we should have no problem understanding." The military brass alongside the Reichminister shared his laughter. "Please go on."

"Bring two masses of fissionable material together," Heisenberg punched his right hand into his left palm, "and neutrons are released. These neutrons cause more atoms to split, giving rise to more and more neutrons, causing—"

"A chain reaction?"

Heisenberg tried to hide his surprise of Speer's knowledge. "Yes, a chain reaction, releasing vast amounts of energy. Unlike any seen before."

Field Marshal Milch, Goering's Deputy Commander of the Luftwaffe, broke the silence. "I've heard that such energy, in the form of a bomb, could destroy a large city."

"Without a doubt." Heisenberg shrugged. "London would be wiped out." The high-ranking military officers leaned forward with interest. "Everything within five kilometers of the blast would be vaporized, and other blast effects would be even more widespread."

A muted whistle came from Milch's lips, but Speer remained unmoved. "My dear Professor Heisenberg, I'm always skeptical when scientists tell me that things work in theory. But what will happen in practice? Can we make this wonder bomb?"

"Yes." Heisenberg furrowed his brow. "But first, we'd have to obtain the fissionable material – from uranium, for example."

"And how much do you need to make a bomb?" Speer's question came instantly.

"We'd need about this much." Heisenberg cupped his hands in the air. "About the size of a pineapple."

Milch's eyes widened. "We wouldn't even need a heavy bomber."

"Excellent!" Speer smiled broadly. "There should be no problem. The mines we now control in Bohemia-Moravia can supply the uranium."

Heisenberg grimaced. "Unfortunately, it's not quite so easy. The uranium in those mines is natural uranium. It can't be used for bombs. It's a combination of two isotopes, but only one, Uranium-235, is capable of sustaining a chain reaction. But it exists as less than one per cent of natural uranium—"

"Am I right to assume that this, this—what did you call it?"

"Isotope."

"—that this isotope that you need to make the bomb can be separated out of uranium?"

"Yes, but it is very difficult."

"But it can be done?"

Heisenberg squirmed on his seat and opened a folder. "We've been looking at several ways to separate—"

"Spare us the technical details, Professor Heisenberg. So, it can be done?"

"Yes, but—"

"Yes, but what?" The raised voice of the usually-unflappable Speer made the scientists look anxiously at each other.

Heisenberg struggled to regain his composure. "Herr Reichminister, you mentioned that the Führer wants a positive result on all new weapons projects within nine months." He closed the folder resignedly. "In nine months, even if we devoted all our resources to the work, I'd be very surprised if we had enough pure U-235 to fill a thimble."

Speer could not hide his dismay. "A thimbleful? Is that all you scientists could come up with?"

Heisenberg picked up the folder and passed it to the Reichminister. "You'll find all the analysis and conclusions in this report."

Speer looked disdainfully at the folder and passed it to an aide. He picked up his cap from the table and stood up. "At the moment, from what you've told me, I'd get a better result by giving all you scientists a rifle and sending you to the Russian front."

There was a prolonged silence. "A joke, gentlemen, a joke!" Speer put on his cap and walked from the room, the forced laughter ringing in his ears.

• • •

As Speer waited for his chauffeur to open the door, a voice called for his attention. "Herr Reichminister! Herr Reichminister! I need to speak to you."

Speer turned to see Max Heldorf, the scientist in the SS uniform, come toward him. "You had ample opportunity to speak at the conference Herr Heldorf." Speer climbed into his car. "And now I must be on my way."

"But you must give me some time, Herr Reichminister." There was an insistence in Heldorf's voice that annoyed Speer, who leaned forward to tell his driver to go.

"Heisenberg may be wrong."

Speer started at Heldorf's insinuation. "Why didn't you speak up at the conference?"

"Because of something more important." Heldorf's voice barely carried above the sound of the car engine. "Because Heisenberg is not to be trusted."

Speer thought for a moment. "Come see me at Horcher's Restaurant after dinner on Monday evening. Nine o'clock." He tapped on his chauffeur's shoulder and the tires of his staff car hurled the gravel into the air.

New York City.

Heads turned as Christina Lindgren walked down Broadway. Perhaps it was her uniform, a novelty in the early days of the Woman's Army Auxiliary Corps: on Christina, the fitted jacket and flared skirt seemed to defeat their utilitarian design and instead emphasize her feminine contours. Or maybe it was the bounce in her step, the blond, upswept hair tucked under her cap, or her glowing complexion and blue eyes that elicited more than one low whistle, unheard above the din of the raucous city.

High above her head, a grinning GI on a Camel Cigarette billboard blew smoke rings out over Broadway. As she threaded her way down the street, the bleating of the traffic, cries of street vendors, and buzzes and bangs of new buildings taking form made her wish she were back in Providence, Rhode Island. She had seen enough of New York that day to hope that whatever reason caused her to be summoned here – a mystery that made her uneasy – would not involve a transfer to this concrete and glass loony bin.

She turned down 44th Street, gazed up at the Art Deco building that thrust its arcs and zigzags into the blue Manhattan sky, and double-checked the address against the one in her instructions. Before going in, she glanced at her reflection in the window of the revolving door – she was proud of her WAAC uniform. She'd enlisted a month before, just after her twenty-eighth birthday. With the war six months old, she'd felt she had to do something for the country that had adopted her after she had arrived with her parents from her native Sweden some ten years earlier.

Inside, the champagne-colored marble walls and black marble floor of the high-ceilinged lobby afforded cool peace and helped restore her composure. In a back corner, a fresh-faced sergeant manned a gray Army desk that was incongruous in the sleek lobby. As she approached, his eyes wandered over her tight-fitting uniform, then hastily shot back to look her in the eye as she cleared her throat to get his attention.

"Can I see your I.D., miss?" The sergeant reached for the card that Christina held out for him. "Ah, Technical Leader Lindgren."

"I'm here to see Major Stevens."

Her eyes followed his forefinger as it ran down a list on his desk.

She wondered what was going on. Only the week before, she had been doing the work she had done since enlisting – translating Swedish and German diplomatic and technical reports into English. Then her supervisor had taken her aside to meet a man who had rigorously tested her Swedish. Swedish, of all things – her native tongue. And then he tested her in German, as if the translations for which she had been praised didn't speak for themselves. It was too much, and she had complained. That's when the letter appeared, telling her to report to the office in Manhattan. Was it because she had complained? Her unease acquired a tinge of concern and her instincts told her to go, that she might be walking into something she'd regret.

"Yes, here you are on my roster. Two o'clock – you're right on time. I'll give Major Stevens a call and tell him you're on your way." He pointed to the elevator.

She checked her instructions for the number of the floor. More and more she felt she should leave, but a perverse curiosity drove her on. The operator slid the elevator doors open. As she stepped into the gaping car, she felt another pang of apprehension. "Twenty-eighth floor please." The operator shut the doors.

A Train. Thuringia, Germany.

Clackety-clack. Clackety-clack.

The monotony of the wheels counted the miles to the destination. He knew that it was a final destination, yet he perversely wished for it to arrive.

Clackety-clack.

The smell of urine hung heavily in the air, smarting the eyes, catching the back of the throat; there was no escape from the all-pervading stench. Albert Weiss tried to move his cramped leg. His tall, muscular build belied the years he had spent in university lecture halls, but the trials of the past decade were written in lines on his forehead. He tried again to move his leg, but there was no room. Over eighty Jews were crammed into the foul cattle car, eighty souls cast down into an abyss of hell. All dignity had gone; they were reduced to the savagery of animals.

"It's my turn, it's my turn!" A woman clad in a torn dress that had once graced the salons of the Unter den Linden elbowed her way through the heaving throng of misery, pushing others aside.

Clackety-clack.

Albert averted his eyes as she lifted her dress and squatted over the bucket that served all eighty.

"Can't you see it's full, woman?" A disembodied voice came from the darkness. She ignored him, her hissing stream spilling onto the already-sodden straw on the floor of the swaying car.

Albert retched, but nothing came. There had been no food since they had left Berlin six hours earlier. Only a few swallows of foul, brackish water. *Clackety-clack.* He wiped the spittle from his unshaven chin.

He looked down at the figure crouched at his feet, curled on his boots like a large fetus. "Rebecca, are you all right?" It was a stupid, fatuous question, but, in his hopelessness, he could think of nothing else to say. There was a brief, desperate squeeze at his ankle. He looked down and saw the mass of gray that had once been her jet-black pride. He bit his lip. Already an old woman. *Clackety-clack.* And not yet forty.

He peered through the slats of the car and saw, in the fading light, the land he knew: the forests of Thuringia. Albert knew where the train was headed. He had overhead a guard back in Berlin. First to Jena. He uttered the name, which came from his lips like a sigh. Jena. The memories of his student years in the city some twenty years before tried to deny his current misery. Jena. The broad avenues, St. Michaels Church, the University, the Griesbach gardens where he had met Rebecca. How they had….

And then the guard in Berlin had thrown back his head and laughed and had said, "And then on to Buchenwald." Albert shuddered.

"O, God, why have you forsaken us?" The voice came from a bearded mouth that had once held sway in Berlin's grandest synagogue.

Albert ignored the self-pitying cry. He had no interest in God. He remembered his mother beating him for not going to synagogue. When he had first begun to study physics, he had tried to construct a proof to show conclusively that God did not exist. He listened to the sobbing and wailing that came as a background to the stench. *Clackety-clack.* He no longer needed the proof.

Jena.

Now he had no wish to see it again. Yet, like all the miserable wretches on the car, he was waiting for Jena....

Clackety-clack.

From the back of the cattle car came a clatter as someone fell. "Look out, you fool!" There was consternation, a shuffling of feet. "Oh, God, he's dead!"

"That's the third since we started out." There was a sob in the woman's voice. "Why can't they stop the train?"

"Stop the train! Stop the train!" There was a half-hearted call from some of the prisoners, a cry that soon died away, unheard. *Clackety-clack.* The train did not stop.

As the train continued into the evening, Albert's thoughts, unbidden, drifted to the engineer, up in the cab, checking the steam gauges, his hand on the throttle. Surely he knew what he was doing, pulling almost a thousand souls of despair to an inevitable doom. Or was he, too, merely waiting for Jena? A drink in a bar, the comforts of his wife and bed. Yes, he was waiting for Jena.

Clackety-clack.

Jena could not be far, Albert thought, but he sought to distance the city, to put off the arrival. To postpone it until there was a new world, a new world in which he could awake, free from the nightmare. Suddenly, everyone lurched; some stumbled and slid down to the rotten straw as the train lost speed. The rhythm of the engine changed, the relentless steam blew a slower breath, the cadence of the wheels beneath their feet eased to a lesser beat. The buffers clattered together.

Albert peered through the slats of the cattle car. They were pulling into a siding, the gathering gloom dispersed by powerful floodlights. The train ground to a halt, the wheels screeching on the rails. He saw army guards move along the train, unlocking and opening the doors to each truck, one by one. He saw bodies tossed from the cars, willing Jewish hands throwing out their dead. Some tried to get down from the trucks, but were beaten back. The doors were closed and locked again, stifling the cries of despair.

The guards came to the door of Albert's car. The bolts rattled and the doors slid open.

"My child is ill, my child is ill." A young woman pushed herself to the doorway, holding her infant.

"Back, back, you Jewish slut!" A German soldier smashed the butt of his rifle against her legs. She screamed and fell, clutching at the child who slipped from her grasp. She picked up the baby and crawled through a forest of legs to the back of the truck.

An officer came forward, a clipboard in his hands. Albert saw the young man's finger run down a list of names.

"Is the Jew Albert Weiss in this car? Albert Weiss?" The voice was strident; there was a muttering behind him, and Albert was aware of several pairs of eyes inside the car fixed upon him. He saved their consciences from the guilt of betrayal.

"Yes, I'm Albert Weiss."

The muttering stopped.

"Get down from the car. You are to be separated from the others for a special work detail."

Albert peered into the harsh glare of the floodlights. He could see only the outline of the officer, black against the light and the swirling steam.

"Get down from the car, Jew Weiss!" The voice was harsh, insistent.

Albert felt the clutch at his ankle. "Go, my love, go. At least one of us will be saved." He looked down at her imploring face.

"I have my wife here. I won't leave her!"

One of the soldiers climbed into the car.

"Go, Albert, go!" He felt his wife's hands push at his legs. The soldier manhandled Albert to the edge of the door.

"I won't leave my wife!"

The officer laughed. "Don't worry, Jew. Her name is on my list, too. Bring out the Jewess Rebecca Weiss!"

Albert tried to grasp what was happening, but he felt the butt of the soldier's rifle between his shoulder blades and fell heavily onto the ground by the side of the track. He struggled to his knees, looked up and saw his wife scrambling down from the car. His mind fought to make sense of it all.

A voice came from the car. "My name is Rosenblatt. My name must be on your list!" There was desperation in the call.

"And me. I'm Fishbein!"

"Lock the cars!" The officer barked. The doors crashed together and the soldiers slid the bolts. The cries became louder. "And Lippmann! Check for my name!"

Albert got to his feet and reached out for his wife. Bewilderment and fear danced together nervously in her eyes. He shrugged his shoulders; he could not answer her unasked question.

"You two – come with me!" The officer nodded and soldiers formed up as escort. They began to walk away. The engine whistle blew and the train shuddered as the driver tugged on the throttle. The pistons heaved, the steam screamed its escape and the cars clattered into motion.

Albert turned to look over his shoulder. The desperate cries died as the train sped away into the night.

Clackety-clack. Clackety-clack.

New York City.

The major, a tall man with dark wavy hair and a Clark Gable moustache, was waiting in the hall to greet Christina as the elevator doors opened; they exchanged salutes. "Hello, Miss Lindgren. I'm John Stevens. Please come this way."

He led her to a door at the far end of the corridor. There was no name or any indication of organization on the frosted glass. She hesitated as he opened the door for her, and he sensed her anxiety.

"Don't worry. Please go in." He wore an encouraging smile as his outstretched arm motioned her inside. She entered a small office pervaded with the odors of tobacco and coffee. The furnishings were sparse: a small desk cluttered with files, a telephone and a full ashtray; a chair behind the desk and one before and an old cupboard that had seen better days, atop which sat an off-center photograph of the president and his dog, Fala, in a cheap frame.

The whole scene looked tawdry and did nothing to allay her anxieties. She turned sharply to the officer. "Look, I need an explanation. What's going on?"

Her outburst took him aback. "Sorry?"

"I was told I was to attend an interview with—," she pulled the letter from her purse, "—the U.S. Army Department of Special Linguistic Services." She looked contemptuously around the dilapidated office. "This doesn't quite fill the bill, Major Stevens. What's going on?"

"I can understand that things don't appear as they're supposed to be." His tone was apologetic. "I ask only ten minutes of your time to talk about Sweden, Miss Lindgren." He saw her eyes widen at the mention of her native land. "After then, if you're still unhappy," he shrugged his shoulders, "then you can call it quits and go. No questions." His hands came up in a gesture of surrender. "Can I get you some coffee? Please sit down. I'm sorry our office is so spartan."

As she eased herself into a folding wooden chair, he opened the old cupboard, which contained a thermos. "Milk and sugar?" She nodded and he filled her cup.

"First of all, Miss Lindgren, let me assure you that we are what it says on the letterhead – the U.S. Army Department of Special Linguistic Services." He placed her cup in front of her on the desk. "The name's a mouthful, I know, but it's a new department." He caught her disparaging look. "Sorry about the mess – we only moved in last week." He gathered up some files. "It's only until our full budget is approved."

She sipped her coffee and put down the cup. "What I'm really interested in is what the Department of—," she looked down at the letter on her lap, "—of Special Linguistic Services really does." She raised an eyebrow. "More to the point, what exactly am I doing here?"

"One thing at a time, Miss Lindgren." He held out his hands, palms facing her. "We do exactly as it says – we provide the Army with special language services. We translate foreign language technical and diplomatic papers."

She didn't like it. Things didn't add up – the tacky office with no name on the door, the need to bring her here from Providence, Rhode Island, when there were surely plenty of translators in New York. She leaned forward. "But I've been doing just that – translating foreign language technical and diplomatic papers – for the past two months." There was an unusual shrillness in her voice.

Christina shifted to the edge of her chair. "Exactly what is going on, Major Stevens?"

Sturmbannführer Heldorf's Apartment. Berlin.

Max Heldorf drew the straight razor diagonally across the shaving soap on his cheek. His hair was so blond that, even at thirty-five, his beard hardly showed. He barely needed to shave again, but tonight he had to look his best. A difficult task lay before him; he had to convince Speer of his plan. He wondered if the Reichminister would be hostile to him, a member of the SS. After all, there was no love lost between Speer and the SS leader, Reichführer Himmler.

Heldorf had often wondered how he had managed to end up in the SS. There were not many physicists in the Schutzstaffel; he chuckled to himself.

He rinsed and dried the razor, sharpened it on the leather strop, and put it away.

It had probably all started when he was a boy, growing up in the small town of Lierstedt. He had loved to read and learn, and his study of mathematics and science had convinced him that all entities strive for perfection, often to the detriment of other, less perfect entities. Wasn't this the basis for Darwin's theory of evolution? People and their nations should be no exception.

He rinsed the remains of the shaving soap from his face and toweled it dry.

When he had arrived at the University of Leipzig in '28, he had heard Professor Karl Haushofer lecture on *Lebensraum*, the 'living space' into which a great nation had the right to expand so that its people could prosper, and it had reminded him of his boyhood theories about the struggle for perfection. The principle seemed logical and far from radical; hadn't the United States sought its own *Lebensraum*, guided by the doctrine of Manifest Destiny, as it expanded into the territory of others?

He brushed his hair with the silver-handled brush his mother had given him.

It was too bad about the Jews, of course. But as was true in the best interests of any society, some groups had to fall by the wayside. Sacrifices had to be made for the greater good; it couldn't be helped.

He looked at his face in the mirror and ran his hand over his smooth skin. He felt good.

Unbeckoned, the image of Hannah Goldmann came into his mind and the smile fled from his face. All his certainty about the Darwinian order of things was called into doubt. The face in the mirror was, in his mind, replaced with hers. The sensual mouth, the wide-set deep brown eyes that had tormented him. His thoughts leapt back again. Like himself, Hannah had been a student of Heisenberg in Leipzig in '31. Her analytical skills had drawn Heisenberg's praise, and Heldorf remembered how he had envied her.

The smile returned to Max's face in the mirror. Despite her undoubted ability, she hadn't been arrogant. Sometimes distant, perhaps, but never arrogant.

Max put on his tunic, looked in the mirror and realized that, after so many years, he was a different man. But Hannah had been more than a friend to him. He recalled their long discussions about nuclear physics. And then he remembered her long black hair on the pillow.

He picked up his hat and brushed the peak.

Then had come the time in '34 when she suddenly disappeared from the university. Everyone knew why.

Heldorf put on his cap, checking to make sure that the death's head badge was centered correctly.

It had been a long time ago. He had fallen in love with a Jew.

New York City.

Major Stevens stubbed out his cigarette and stood up. "All right, Miss Lindgren, let me explain." He opened a folder on the desk. "The work you've done so far is excellent. But it's all standard protocol – official communiqués, technical papers, magazines and such." He paused and looked at her, his eyes narrowing. "Let me come clean with you – the key word in the name of our department is 'special.' Some of our communications don't always come through official channels."

Christina sensed that he was watching her every reaction.

"And sometimes we, shall we say, actually collect these unofficial communications."

"You mean spying, major?" Her direct question made him stiffen for a moment.

"No, no, I wouldn't use that word." He smiled. "Too dramatic. Let's just call it Intelligence." She declined his offer of a cigarette and he lit one of his own.

"Is that where I come in? Spy—" She corrected herself with a hint of sarcasm. "Collecting Intelligence?"

He ignored her implications, sat down, and opened a file. "Let's see. Christina Lindgren. Born Gothenburg, Sweden, 1914. Naturalized

American 1937." He looked up at her. "Do you still have relatives in Sweden?"

"I have an uncle who still lives in a little village near where I was born." She answered naturally, eager to know where he was leading.

"You studied languages at Gothenburg University." He looked back down at the file. "English. And German." He closed the file. "I must say your English is perfect."

"Thank you. Except that now it has an American accent."

He laughed. "I wouldn't have noticed. And the German?"

"*Sehr gut*, but unfortunately there's not too much chance to practice it in Providence nowadays." She leant forward. "My Danish is passable, but my French—"

"The Swedish – and the German – will do fine." There was a pause as he looked down at the file, as if weighing some issue.

She felt anxious. "Can I change my mind?" She saw him look up sharply. "It's just that I'd like a cigarette after all."

"Sure." He looked relieved as he offered the pack and flicked his lighter.

She drew deeply. "So where do I fit in," the smoke drifted up from her lips, "with the collecting of unofficial information?"

"It's not as dramatic as you think." He spoke in a matter-of-fact manner. "The task is simple – and without danger to you. You'll go to Sweden – we'll arrange things. A German will come from Berlin. You'll meet him as if he was an old friend and he'll give you a file." He was off-hand, as though he were asking her to take the subway to Coney Island. "You'll take the file and deliver it to the American embassy in Stockholm."

Christina sensed that something was not quite right. "A German? Aren't they the enemy?"

The major smiled. "Yes, but this particular German is bringing something we think will be useful to us."

"You mean he's a spy?"

He appeared not to have heard her. "I forgot to tell you – this job pays well. One thousand dollars."

Christina's eyes widened. One thousand dollars. The boat, the beautiful sailboat she dreamed about owning one day flashed through her mind. But the doubts returned. The job involved risk. Someone who was supposed to be a major in the U.S. Army sitting in a makeshift office was offering her a thousand dollars to pick up a file from a German and walk around the corner to the American embassy. It didn't make sense.

"But this German – he's a spy?"

"Good heavens, no." Stevens chuckled as he lit another cigarette. "He's just a courier. Once you've delivered the file, we get you out of there and back to the good old USA. And one thousand dollars."

The offer was tempting, but Christina felt he wasn't being straight with her.

"But why me? Surely you've got dozens of people already in Stockholm who could do the job?"

"Not with your language skills." He sipped at his coffee.

"Look, major, I wouldn't be honest if I didn't say that the job doesn't add up. There's something else, isn't there?"

"Okay, I'll level with you." He put down his cup. "We do have people on the ground in Stockholm, but, apart from the fact they don't speak German, they're also known."

"Known?" Christina's brow furrowed.

The major got up from his desk and walked around it to face her. "Sweden is a neutral country, Miss Lindgren."

She felt talked down to, as though she were in a classroom, but let him continue.

"In its capital are many observers from many countries, including our own—"

"Observers?" she interrupted. "I'm not stupid, you know. Don't you mean spies?"

He looked down at the floor. "I prefer the term 'agents.'" He sat on the corner of his desk. "The point is that these observers – agents, if you wish – get to know each other's faces."

"So that's it," she couldn't help smiling as she realized what he was saying, "you want me to be a fresh face!"

He returned her smile. "Not to put too fine a point on it, yes."

Alarm bells rang again. She was out of her depth. She saw danger. And then she saw the thousand dollars.

Stevens returned to his chair and said nothing for a while as he watched her reaction. "Miss Lindgren, I can see that you're worried, but I can promise that there's no danger to you." He caught her distrustful look. "It's simple. We get you into Sweden – we'll arrange everything – and when you've done the transfer – perhaps within a day, maybe two – we get you out and bring you home. Probably a week, ten days – no more." His eyes fixed hers. "And one thousand dollars."

Her first reaction was to cut and run, but she found it difficult to turn her back on a thousand dollars. "I need time to think." She stubbed out her cigarette. "Can I have some time?"

"Sure." The major got up and poured himself another coffee. "But not long. Three days, maybe four." He held the coffee pot in her direction; she shook her head. "The exchange is expected to take place by June 20th. And we need a week to train and brief you fully."

He watched her over the brim of his cup, almost seeing the thoughts running through her mind. The risks, the dangers, seeing her native land once more. And a thousand dollars.

"Look, it's up to you. When we met, I said you can walk away, and I meant it." He pulled a pencil from his pocket. "However," his fingers reached for a pad, "if you're interested, why don't you call me?" He wrote down a phone number, tore off the sheet and pushed it across the desk.

Christina picked up the paper, folded it and placed it in her purse. The major came around to the front of the desk. "I'll show you to the elevator."

"No, it's okay, I'll find my own way." She smiled at him, trying to deny the conflicting thoughts that were battling inside her head. She turned in the doorway. "I'll be in touch." She left and closed the door.

Another door opened: one to a connecting office behind the major's chair. "John, she's just the ticket!" The colonel rubbed his hands together. "I saw her in the corridor when she was on her way in and I listened to everything on the intercom. Tall, blond, Nordic – von Rastenberg will be putty in her hands." He pulled out a cigar from his breast pocket. "And she speaks all the lingoes perfectly." He paused the lighter at the end of his cigar. "Do you think she'll take the job?"

"Maybe, sir." A whimsical smile came to the major's lips. "For a thousand dollars, I'd take it myself if I could speak Swedish and German. Except I don't look like von Rastenberg's late wife. But you never can tell with a broad. And I feel that Miss Christina Lindgren is one tough cookie."

"But she's absolutely perfect for the job, John. There's only a chance in a million of her cover being blown." He pulled on his cigar.

"And if she should happen to fall into the wrong hands," he pulled again and blew a large smoke ring, "perish the thought, of course—"

"Perish the thought, sir."

"—there's no way she could be traced back to the Office of Strategic Services."

Horscher's Restaurant, Berlin.

"This way, *mein Herr*."

Sturmbannführer Max Heldorf followed the waiter between the tables of Horscher's Restaurant, the select establishment where the Nazi elite came to dine. The music of the orchestra was almost eclipsed by the lively chatter that rose from the smoke-shrouded tables. "This time we'll show the Russkies." Heldorf affected a smile to disguise his rage. These leeches would show the Russians nothing; they would sit on their fat asses in Berlin while soldiers who had somehow managed to survive the previous icy winter in Russia would be shedding blood on the eastern front.

Could the war in the east be won, he wondered? The heady days of the blitzkrieg, when the whole of Western Europe except Britain fell within weeks, was now but a distant memory. Russia was a different story; so far, hundreds of thousands of Germany's best soldiers had been lost in that bleak wasteland. He stood aside as a woman with a fur stole draped across her bare shoulders passed by; he could not help thinking what a soldier on the eastern front would have given for a fur in that previous, horrendous winter.

The waiter made an expansive gesture with his arm. "This way to the Reichminister's private room, *mein Herr*."

Heldorf straightened his tunic and adjusted his tie. Now that the United States, with all its manpower and industrial might, was in the conflict, Germany had only one way to win the war: to produce a weapon so powerful it would bring all the enemies of the Reich to their knees within the space of a week. Germany had to develop an atomic bomb.

Heldorf knew that Heisenberg could not achieve such a task; he knew the Nobel laureate lacked the will. The SS man had pushed the Gestapo to pursue a secret investigation and he now knew that Heisenberg had moral qualms. A National Socialist should not have moral qualms; all morality had to be thrust aside to develop the bomb. Of course, Speer would share this view, but he needed to be convinced of the plan. Heldorf's plan. A plan that defied logic.

He knocked on the door and entered the mahogany-paneled private room.

"Ah, Heldorf!" The Reichminister pushed away the remains of his *Jägerschnitzel* and dabbed his lips with his napkin.

"Heil Hitler!" Heldorf clicked his heels and rigidly extended his arm.

"Heil Hitler." Speer brought up his arm slowly. He knew the protocol, but was weary of the ritual. "Some refreshment?" Without waiting for an answer, Speer filled a glass and handed it to him.

"You asked to talk to me, Heldorf, yet at the conference, despite every opportunity, you didn't say a word. Why?" Speer took a sip but watched Heldorf closely over the rim of his glass.

"May I speak freely, sir?"

Speer sighed and glanced at his watch. "I thought that's why you were here," he said with some impatience. "It's about Heisenberg, isn't it? You don't like him very much, do you, Heldorf?"

"It's not a question of like or dislike. It's a matter of commitment to the cause."

Speer raised an eyebrow as he pulled his dessert in front of him. "I know Heisenberg isn't a member of the Nazi party, but I do believe he's a loyal German nationalist. After all, he had a chance to defect to the United States during a visit before the war, yet he returned to Germany." He closed his eyes as he swallowed a piece of the pastry. "You know, Heldorf, nobody does *apfelstrudel* better than Horscher's."

"I'm sure it's excellent, *mein Herr.*" Heldorf waited for the Reichminister to finish his dish; the strains of a Strauss waltz from the restaurant's orchestra came faintly through the door.

The SS man cleared his throat and returned to his argument. "Heisenberg, *mein Herr,* owes his allegiance not to Nazi Germany, but to another nation, another Germany, a Germany long gone – the Imperial Germany of his youth. Heisenberg chose not to defect because he believes the old Germany – his idealistic Germany – can be saved."

Speer put down his fork and turned his head abruptly. "Saved? What are you saying? Saved from whom? Are you implying—"

"Precisely, Herr Reichminister. Saved from the Führer. From National Socialism. From us."

"That's preposterous!" Speer pushed back from the table and threw his napkin on top of his plate. "Heisenberg is our leading nuclear physicist. He's heading all our research."

"Permit me, *mein Herr* " Heldorf put on his glasses and pulled a dossier out of his briefcase. "I'll ignore his reluctance to sign manifestos for the Führer, and even rumors of his love for the Jews. But let me tell you he's been discussing the problem – the so-called moral problem – of the bomb since the start of the war. We have evidence that he's discussed it with several of his colleagues."

"Heldorf, although I'm relatively new to the position of Reichminister for Armaments, I am aware of some of the background." Speer frowned and drummed his fingers on the armrest with impatience.

"But there's more." Heldorf pulled another sheet from the file. "Late last year, Heisenberg visited the renowned Danish physicist Niels Bohr in Copenhagen. Bohr told the Americans – and our sources are impeccable – that Heisenberg gave him a diagram of a nuclear reactor-bomb."

Speer furrowed his brow. "Of that, I was not aware. And if it's true, it's treason! He told me only a few days ago that he was unable to build such a weapon."

"If I may read a little more from my intelligence report, Herr Reichminister?"

Speer nodded.

"According to our agents, Heisenberg proposed to Bohr that neither we nor the Americans should build a bomb." The SS man closed the file. "Presumably for moral reasons."

"Let me see those reports!" Speer pulled the file from Heldorf's hand. "If your information can be corroborated, then the man's a traitor." He flipped through the papers and snapped the file shut. "I should have him arrested."

Heisenberg's apartment. Berlin.

"Of course, Franz, so much depends upon the supply of heavy water from Norway—"

"Really, Werner," Elisabeth Heisenberg sighed and shook her head in mock umbrage, "rather than bore us with physics as our after-dinner conversation, perhaps you and Franz would like to go to your study," she took a last sip of wine and put down her napkin, "and leave Trudi and me to talk about real things." She pushed her chair back from the table and stood up.

"It was a delightful meal, Lisbet." Trudi von Rastenberg got up from her chair. "You must tell me where you got the veal for the schnitzel – my butcher has little to offer but poor cuts of pork. And I must apologize for my brother; I think it was Franz, not Werner, who brought up the subject of physics."

"I'm sorry, Frau Heisenberg," Franz von Rastenberg stood up to make the pretence of a formal apology, "but you know what it's like when two scientists get together."

Lisbet threw back her head and laughed. "I've had almost five years of scientists getting together." She clapped her hands. "Now, off to the study with both of you! Unless you want to stay and discuss fashion with Trudi and me!"

Books populated Heisenberg's inner sanctum. They lined the walls, rose in towers on the floor; an open book lay face down on his favorite chair. Only the framed photograph of his children on his desk and the bouquet of pink roses arranged by Lisbet that morning attested to a world outside physics.

"Lisbet is such a charming hostess. You're a very lucky man, Werner."

"Can I offer you some port, Franz?" Heisenberg reached for the decanter and poured two glasses. "Yes, I'm well aware that I'm a lucky man. But next week she and the children will be moving to our house in Bavaria for the rest of the summer; frankly, I'm worried about their safety here in Berlin."

He removed the book from his upholstered armchair and settled into it with his port. "I must say, I'm going to miss my wife terribly." As soon as the words were out, Heisenberg wished he hadn't spoken. Von Rastenberg had lost his own wife, Elsa, six months before in a streetcar accident; they had been married only two years and she had been expecting their first child. Heisenberg tried to change the subject quickly. "Tell me, Franz, how are things going at the heavy water plant in Norway?"

"I went there two weeks ago." Von Rastenburg's voice lacked animation. "The plant superintendent told me production is excellent."

"You go there regularly, don't you?" Heisenberg ran his finger around the rim of his glass distractedly, making it sing.

"Yes, every few weeks or so." Von Rastenberg's thoughts were elsewhere; his glass was untouched and his eyes studied the carpet.

"Franz, something's wrong, I know. What's the matter?"

Von Rastenberg spoke quietly. "It would have been our anniversary next week, Werner, our third anniversary." He looked up and tried to smile, but it came out as a grimace.

Heisenberg leaned forward and patted his friend on the shoulder.

Von Rastenberg reached for his glass and downed it all. "In any case, life goes on." He sat up and rubbed his hands together vigorously, as if to signal a change in his mood. "Tell me, Werner, what's the latest with the program?"

"Program?" Heisenberg smiled wryly. "What program?"

Von Rastenberg looked perplexed. "The program to build a uranium machine – a nuclear reactor." His voice became almost a conspiratorial whisper. "Perhaps an atomic bomb."

Heisenberg smiled. "Franz, you were at the meeting with Speer. You heard what we told the Reichminister about our inability to construct an atomic bomb."

Heisenberg stared absentmindedly at the roses before turning to von Rastenberg. "Franz, we've been colleagues – and friends – for a long time." He put down his glass. "Can I be honest with you?"

"Insofar as it is possible nowadays, Werner."

Heisenberg nodded at his friend's implied warning. Of course, he was right. The Nazi party had fear working for it. Spies were everywhere, listening for the slightest opposition to the regime.

"Do you believe, Franz, here," he tapped on his chest, "in the deepest part of your heart, that we should build an atomic bomb and place it in the hands of *that* man?" He pointed to the obligatory picture that hung on the wall, as it did in almost every German house.

Von Rastenberg hesitated. "But don't you want Germany to win the war, Werner?"

Heisenberg thumped his fist on the arm of the chair and shook his head. "Franz, you don't understand me. I love Germany. It's my country, my home." He breathed deeply. "I was offered professorships in the United States in '39, but I came back to Germany. To my home." He pulled out a handkerchief and mopped some beads of sweat that had appeared on his brow.

"But that man," he shook a finger at the portrait, "that man has betrayed Germany." He turned and fixed von Rastenberg with a piercing look. "I repeat my question, Franz. Do you think it right that we should develop a bomb that can vaporize a city, a bomb that can kill tens of thousands of people, and put it in Hitler's hands?"

"Werner, I've never seen you so emotional. Calm down." Von Rastenberg lowered his voice, as if the very walls were Gestapo spies. "But I'll answer your question – it's no, a thousand times no."

Heisenberg exhaled his relief. "I think I always knew as much, Franz." He reached over and touched the back of von Rastenberg's hand.

"So, Werner, what are you proposing we do?"

"Perhaps we don't have to do anything. Because of what I said at the conference, Speer believes we can't manufacture enough fissionable material to arm a bomb."

Von Rastenberg leaned forward and looked intently at Speer. "Werner, do you really believe that?"

Heisenberg ran his fingers through his thick blond hair. "I believe, as I said at the conference, that the thermal diffusion method for extracting isotopes that we have tried would take years to yield sufficient material to make a bomb." He looked pensive. "Of course, there are other ways to obtain fissionable material." He gave von Rastenberg a sly smile, then slapped his thigh and stood up. "In any event, the huge moral question is taken out of our hands. No fissionable material, no bomb. More port, Franz?"

Heisenberg refreshed their glasses. "We should concentrate on what we have asked Speer to support – work on a uranium machine as a supplier of electricity, perhaps to drive submarines." He walked to the end of the room, placed his glass on the mantel of the fireplace, and turned around. "Now, Franz, I want to ask you another question. Do you think the allied countries are trying to build such a bomb?"

Von Rastenberg raised his eyebrows. "Perhaps. They have the scientific talent. Think of the physicists who left us in the thirties. There's Szilard, Bethe, Franck—"

"Not to mention my old pupil, Edward Teller," Heisenberg continued the sad litany of Jewish physicists who had fled after the Nazis had passed the Nuremberg race laws in '35, "and the Italians, Fermi and Segre."

Von Rastenberg whistled. "Well, that's certainly talent enough – even not counting their home-grown star, Oppenheimer."

They fell silent as they realized the potential that Germany's enemy had for building an atomic weapon.

At last, Heisenberg spoke. "Franz, I believe...," he cleared his throat as he collected his thoughts, "I believe we have a duty to send a message to the scientists in the United States."

Horscher's Restaurant. Berlin.

"If I may say, sir," Heldorf decided to declare his hand completely to Speer, "having Heisenberg arrested could be the wrong course of action."

The Reichminister furrowed his brow. "Wrong? You have just shown me that the man may be guilty of treason."

"Suppose, as the evidence suggests, that Heisenberg has told his American friends that he will deliberately sabotage efforts to develop the bomb. That he will hoodwink leading political figures," Heldorf paused to let the effect sink in, "into thinking that an atomic bomb is not possible."

Speer leaned forward with keen interest. "So, if he's arrested—"

"Precisely, Herr Reichminister. If he's arrested, the Americans will think we have discovered his ploy. And, perhaps, believe that Germany is now on the right path to develop a bomb."

"I see your reasoning, Heldorf. And then the Americans would have strong motivation to build a bomb of their own." Speer leaned back and cradled his chin with his hand. "But I'm still inclined to arrest him."

"But—"

"Do you think the Americans can develop an atomic bomb?"

"Possibly. They have the resources. And the scientists." He forced a bitter laugh at the irony. "German scientists who left our country. And they have the materials. And all the power of a huge industrial state."

Speer shook his head slowly as he thought through the situation. The music had stopped in the restaurant beyond the door and there was a burst of laughter. "But what are you suggesting, Heldorf?"

"We can build the bomb ourselves."

The Reichminister stared blankly into Heldorf's eyes for a long while, then rose and walked over to the window. "Heldorf, I do believe you are out of your mind. How can we possibly build a bomb when Heisenberg, Hahn and all the other top physicists at the conference say it cannot be built?"

"I think I have proved that Heisenberg has no wish to develop the bomb."

"But how can you go against all the greatest scientific minds of the Reich?"

"Not all the greatest minds were at the conference, Herr Reichminister."

Speer chuckled. "Did we forget to invite someone?"

The SS man ignored the jibe and pressed on. "Yes, there are other, perhaps better scientists. But they didn't make the invitation list."

Speer looked puzzled. "Why ever not? Who are these people, Heldorf?"

Heldorf replaced his glasses, pulled another sheet from his file, and read. "Albert Weiss. Professor of Physics at Jena until he was sacked from his position. Artur Steinitz, a gifted atomic theorist." His finger ran down the list. "And Ernst Schlegel, one of Heisenberg's top students until 1933—"

"But why weren't these scientists at the conference?"

"Because, Herr Reichminister, most of them are in concentration camps." Heldorf brought his hand to his mouth and cleared his throat. "Because they are all Jews."

Heisenberg's apartment. Berlin.

Von Rastenberg put his glass down and shifted to the edge of his seat. "You think we should do *what,* Werner? Send a message to the scientists of the United States? Werner, what on earth are you saying?"

Heisenberg sat down and faced him. "I think we must. To tell them that we, as German scientists, will not develop the atomic bomb."

Von Rastenberg was aghast. "But, Werner, men are rotting in Gestapo cells for having committed lesser offences."

Heisenberg looked at his friend and laid his hand on his shoulder. "Think about it, Franz. It might be our one chance to save Germany. If the Americans know we're not building a bomb, we weaken any incentive on their part to build one for retaliation. You do understand the power of such a bomb, don't you?"

"Theoretically," von Rastenberg gazed at the ceiling as he thought, "equivalent to anything between ten and twenty kilotons of dynamite. Maybe more."

"Imagine what such a bomb could do to Leipzig, Dresden," he spread his hands wide, "or Berlin."

"But if we tell the Americans we're not developing the bomb," von Rastenberg squirmed in his chair, "it would be tantamount to telling them we know we can't win the war."

Heisenberg smiled wanly. "Franz, the war is already lost. The whole industrial might of Russia and the United States is ranged against us. It's just a question of time. You know that. Speer knows that. Even the Army General Staff knows. Only Hitler and a few of those sycophants around him believe otherwise." He emptied his glass. "If we can prevent an atomic bomb in the hands of Germany's enemies, we may be able to save Germany from utter destruction."

"But what you're proposing is terrifying, Werner! What makes you think that even if we tell the American scientists that we won't develop the bomb they'll stop their own research?"

"We don't." Heisenberg nodded his acceptance of the argument. "We can only appeal to their moral sense."

"I don't know, Werner. Giving out the secrets of our atomic research is a very dangerous ploy."

"No one knows that better than I do, Franz. I already tried it once before and failed."

Horscher's Restaurant. Berlin.

"*Juden? Juden?*" The usually-implacable Reichminister Speer stood dumbfounded, mouth agape. "You are asking me to release Jews from concentration camps? Have you taken leave of your senses?"

Fear that he had gone too far slithered in Heldorf's stomach. "I know it sounds strange, *mein Herr*, but—"

"Strange?" Speer lifted the decanter from the table and poured himself a large cognac. "It is unthinkable!"

Heldorf paused, waiting for the storm to pass, and then spoke slowly and deliberately. "I have thought it through at great length, *mein*

Herr. With these Jewish scientists," he waved his list of names, "it may be possible to build an atomic bomb."

Speer sat down and eyed Heldorf coldly. "Putting aside the enormity of your suggestion, Heldorf, may I have the temerity to ask how?"

"First, we ask them to review Heisenberg's report." Heldorf took a copy from his briefcase and laid it on the table in front of Speer. "I personally believe that Heisenberg is using this report to mislead us." He tapped on the folder. "But I must be honest and say that I, myself, do not have the theoretical expertise to unravel it. That's where the Jewish scientists come in."

"You think they could find errors where the whole of the Uranium Club have failed?"

"The Uranium Club is entirely in Heisenberg's pocket."

Speer peered at the ceiling, his analytical mind racing. "And suppose your Jews can find nothing wrong with Heisenberg's report?"

Heldorf shrugged his shoulders. "Then I shall be proved wrong. And you will know that there can be no atomic weapon to win the war."

"And if they do find a flaw?"

"Then they will have found a way to do what Heisenberg claims he can't – extract enough fissionable material from uranium to make an atomic bomb."

Speer furrowed his brow and shook his head. "Your scheme is harebrained, Heldorf. How could I – how dare I – explain it to the Führer?"

Heldorf realized he was forced to play his last, most dangerous card. "Might I suggest the ultimate heresy, sir?"

Speer fixed him with a harsh gaze and did not reply.

Despite Speer's stunned silence, Heldorf persevered. "Might I suggest that you tell the Führer nothing?"

"Nothing?"

"Well, you could tell him of Heisenberg's pathetic results. But, of my proposals, nothing."

Speer shook his head. "Your plan is outrageous. I don't think I can contemplate it."

Heldorf pressed his case. "Look at it this way, sir – from your own point of view, you cannot lose. If my plan doesn't work," he looked down at the floor, "then I'll become, shall we say, a footnote in history, and the Jews will be returned to the camps. No one will be the wiser. On the other hand, if the plan works, you'll win the Führer's eternal thanks by delivering to him the ultimate wonder weapon." Heldorf rapped his knuckles on the table to emphasize his point. "Either way, you cannot lose, Herr Reichminister."

Speer thought deeply, determined not to be pushed into a hasty decision. "If what you say is true, do you really think you can produce this bomb without the help of Heisenberg and his people?"

Heldorf spoke confidently. "By definition. If the Jews disprove Heisenberg – which means they find a way to produce a sufficient quantity of fissionable material – the rest is relatively easy. Even Heisenberg has admitted that. You can leave Heisenberg and his Uranium Club to carry on fiddling around." He smiled at his own thought. "And they'll continue sending their treacherous messages to the enemy that Germany will not build the bomb."

The Reichminister smiled. "I see your point, Heldorf. And then the Americans will perhaps slow down or even abandon any efforts of their own to produce an atomic weapon."

"Yes, *mein Herr*. Think of the possibilities. If we do develop the bomb – perhaps harness it to the developing rocket technology – why, London, perhaps New York...." He lifted his hand and snapped his fingers. "Poof!"

"Before we get carried away, Heldorf, aren't you forgetting one important point?" He pointed to the list of Jews. "I somehow don't think," his voice became heavily sarcastic, "that our Jews will be predisposed to help us. After all, they are, as you say, in concentration camps."

"That problem can be overcome." Heldorf opened the dossier on the Jews. "My research shows that all these scientists, every single one, has a father, a mother, a sister – several relatives – who are already in a camp, or waiting for the Gestapo to knock on the door."

"Are you suggesting that—?"

"Yes, we give their relatives safe conduct visas out of Germany." He looked hard at Speer. "And there are no tricks, we carry it out. That way we get their trust. But in the beginning we give visas to only one relative: where there is a mother and a father, we let only the mother go; where there are two children, only one. We get their cooperation, and then keep a threat hanging over them."

Heldorf's anxiety grew as Speer's frown deepened. *"Mein Herr,* if you're concerned that the enemy will learn of the death camps through the released relatives—"

"That's not a concern. The enemy already knows about the camps and has chosen to do nothing." Speer continued to weigh Heldorf's proposal, swirling his cognac in the snifter.

Suddenly he put his glass down and pushed it away. "Despite my reservations, Heldorf, I'm prepared to let you conduct the first phase of your project." Speer picked up a briefcase that sat on the floor and pulled out some stationery which bore his official letterhead. "After all, as you say, I have nothing to lose." He pulled a fountain pen from his pocket and wrote briefly, finishing with the flourish of his signature.

"Here, Heldorf," he put the paper in an envelope, sealed it, and passed it over, "this will give you the authority to pull those people from the camps."

Heldorf reached for the envelope. A great sense of relief coursed through him. He had already gambled and, on his own authority within the SS, ordered the Jewish scientists to be brought from the camps.

Speer reached for his cap and made for the door. "Report back to me in two weeks." He fixed Heldorf with a cold stare. "No later." Speer turned and was gone.

Heldorf took off his glasses and collected his papers, trying to ward off the growing fear in his stomach. He looked down at the list of Jews. If they failed, he knew that their days would be numbered. He shook his head. Not to mention his own.

Heisenberg's apartment. Berlin.

"Werner, what are you saying? When did you try to give away our secrets?" Von Rastenberg was confused and shocked at Heisenberg's words.

Heisenberg lowered his voice and looked around to make sure that the door was still closed. "Do you remember the conference I went to in Copenhagen?"

Von Rastenberg nodded. "You were there just a few weeks ago."

"Well, I took that opportunity to visit Niels."

Few were on a first-name basis with Niels Bohr, the Danish physicist who was the father of the theory of atomic structure. Bohr had been Heisenberg's teacher, mentor, and long-time friend. But Bohr was a Jew, and Germany had been occupying his country for two years.

"Margrethe served a lovely dinner, and afterward I asked Niels if he and I could take a walk on the Langelinie. I wanted to discuss something with him, but I didn't want to talk to him in his house – it occurred to me that it might be bugged."

"What did you want to talk to him about, Werner?"

"I told him that I felt physicists of all countries, no matter which side of the war they were on, should agree among themselves not to work on an atomic weapon for reasons of morality."

A low whistle came from von Rastenberg. "Oh, my God, Werner; what did Dr. Bohr say?"

"I think he was stunned. He said he wasn't sure such a weapon was feasible and asked me if I thought an atomic weapon could be built."

"And you said—"

"I said I knew it was possible because we were working on it."

"But, Werner, that's—"

"What I meant to say was in theory we know how to build an atomic weapon but in practice it would be a massive technical effort, just as I told Speer." Heisenberg closed his eyes and rubbed his forehead. "Goddamn it, Franz, the conversation didn't go as I had intended. Niels became agitated; he seemed to take my words as a threat, or maybe as a sort of trick. In any event, he asked me to leave."

Von Rastenberg scowled. "Werner, this isn't good – this isn't good, at all. If Dr. Bohr conveyed what you just said – that Germany is working on an atomic weapon – to the enemy alliance, they would doubtless redouble any efforts to develop an atomic weapon of their own."

Heisenberg grimaced. "I'm well aware of that. I failed to get my point across, I know. That's why we've got to get another message out, this time to the scientists of the United States."

"I don't know what to say, Werner. I'm a physicist, not a military strategist."

"But do we really have a choice, Franz?" Heisenberg went to his desk, unlocked a drawer, and pulled out a piece of paper. "Look, here's the message I've drafted." He handed the paper to von Rastenberg. "Franz, you pass through Sweden regularly en route to your visits to the heavy water plant in Norway. All you have to do is stop over in Stockholm and pass a message to a contact. I've already arranged for the contact, who I expect should be there shortly." He looked earnestly at his friend. "Will you take the message?"

From the darkened city outside, the sirens began to wail, at first a gentle call, then shrieking in their demand.

"Damn!" Heisenberg gathered up his papers. "It's an air raid." Lisbet's face appeared in the doorway. "We've got to go to the cellars." She disappeared in the same instant.

"Quickly, Franz. Lisbet will take the children." They paused in the doorway, Heisenberg's demanding look repeating his request.

Von Rastenberg looked uncomfortable. "Let me think about it, Werner. I need time."

"Time is not on our side, Franz."

On the Road to Jasenovac Extermination Camp, Yugoslavia.

Hannah Goldmann no longer cared. The floor of the truck battered against her bruised body as it jolted along the rutted track. One of the other women crammed into the truck fell on top of her. She did not complain. Nothing mattered anymore.

She struggled to find the solace of her imaginary blackboard, but the image would not come. The heat was intolerable. And the thirst. Earlier in the day, the sun had made an oven of the inside of the truck, roasting the souls of the two score women. The jolting of the vehicle tossed them all from side to side, as if playing with the dice of fate.

There was a voice. "Papa, papa." The truck rumbled on, ignorant of the plea. The voice became louder. "Papa, papa, help me!"

Hannah saw the image of her own father. The day the men had come.

The voice came again. Now it called feebly, drained of hope. The woman's father could not help her. Neither could Hannah's. Hannah remembered the day they had come.

She and her sister, Rachel, were home for Passover. There could be no visit to the synagogue; the Nazis had long since burnt it to the ground. But it was a time to be together, to be family. Her mother was ailing, but her father had insisted that they come together for the Seder.

The truck lurched, bringing a piteous chorus of groans from the women.

Her father had been a proud man, his pride shining through fierce brown eyes. But the eyes had become dulled, all pride lost by the time

*the men had come. They had come for so many before. She and her fa-
ther had seen many friends disappear. The Nazis had said they were
being resettled in the east, but only fools believed the lie. There were
never any letters. No one ever came back.*

*And nobody had done anything. Not the rabbis. Not the cantors.
Nobody.*

*A few days before they came, her father had spoken to her. "Han-
nah, this world is a vile, cruel place, and our country is in the hands of
monsters." He had looked fearfully about the living room, as if Nazis
lurked in every corner. "But your life is important. You must do everything to survive." He had cupped Hannah's face in his hands.
"Anything. You must survive. Promise me."*

The truck stopped and there were voices. Hannah stared blankly ahead
as she recalled her promise. It was a promise she could no longer keep.

*It was early in the morning when they came, their boots clattering
on the courtyard as they jumped from their trucks, the air full of shouts
and menace.*

*Hannah's father had roused his daughters. "Quickly, get dressed.
Get out the back!" He had hustled them to the door. "Go to your
friends, hide in the forest – anywhere – get away!"*

"But, Papa," Rachel had said, "what about you?"

*"I cannot leave Mama." He had kissed them both and pushed them
through the door.*

"Right, you Jewish scum, get down from the truck." The tailgate
clattered. "Welcome to the camp of Jasenovac. End of the line. For all
of you." He guffawed an ugly laugh.

*After her father had pushed her through the door, Hannah began to
run. She had covered fifty yards before she realized Rachel was not
with her; she had turned, breathless, to see her sister heading back to
the house. Rachel reached for the door, looked around to glance at
Hannah, then disappeared. Hannah started to run back toward the
house but stopped, her mind in turmoil. Her promise to her father had
rung in her ears. Do anything. Survive. What had he meant? Anything?
Even sell her soul to the devil? She took one last look at the house and*

fled, her legs flying as they never had before. She did not stop to wipe the tears from her cheeks.

"'*Raus* – get into line!" She felt the butt of a rifle dig into her ribs and gasped in pain.

Hannah hadn't kept her promise; she'd been caught in a random search a month later.

With the other women, she fought her way through the bottomless mud into the barbed-wire compound. She looked up at the gates. Had her family come this way? Guard dogs barked and a sweet, sickly smell hung in the air.

Despair seized her. There was no God. Not even a devil to whom she could sell her soul. She hadn't kept her promise to her father.

Heldorf's Office, Berlin.

S turmbannführer Max Heldorf caught his reflection in the glass that protected the photograph of Hitler and adjusted his tie. The soft, herring-bone tweed suit, double-breasted with wide lapels, looked back at him incongruously, almost with innocence. He laughed. High-ranking SS officers did not wear herring-bone tweed suits. He felt almost naked without the field-gray uniform and the cap with the death's head insignia. Strange, he thought, as his eyes ran over the different image. He no longer appeared as an exalted member of the master race; more like an insignificant government bureaucrat.

It was the role he had to play that day. A quiet, unassuming role as he interviewed the first of the Jews.

He sat down at his desk, put on his glasses and opened the file. Albert Weiss. Born Weimar 1901. Graduated in Physics summa cum laude from the University of Jena 1923. Ph.D. 1926. Thesis on Atomic Structure of Heavy Metals. Professor of Physics, Jena 1930.

Heldorf turned to the personal details. Weiss had married Rebecca Braun 1930. Two daughters: Naomi, born 1931, Miriam 1932. Heldorf closed the file and considered the irony. At the peak of Weiss's career, the Führer had come to power. Weiss's happy days had come to an end.

After the passing of the Law of the Regulation of the Civil Service – a law to exclude Jews from all public offices – Weiss had been forced out of the university. There were a few sympathetic voices, but the murmurs had quickly died away in the prevailing political wind. Weiss had been stripped of his professorship.

There was little more in the file. Weiss's life had, in effect, come to an end. Janitor at a university in 1936. Denounced by an administrator at the university after Kristallnacht two years later. Held in various camps. Shipped to Buchenwald by train two days ago. From which train Heldorf had ordered his release together with that of his wife.

Heldorf closed the file. He knew the task that faced him. He had to persuade Weiss to join his team – his team to produce enough fissionable material to power an atomic bomb. Doubts pushed into Heldorf's mind. If he failed with Weiss…. He shook his head. The project would fail. Weiss would be the acid test. If he could win him over – with bribe or threat it did not matter – then others would follow.

He got up from the desk and looked at himself again in the reflection. He had been right to cast aside the SS uniform; there was no need to alarm Weiss. Heldorf breathed deeply. Everything depended on the next half-hour.

He picked up the phone. "Show Herr Weiss in."

Frederikshavn, Denmark.

The young boy was sitting in the fishermen's shelter looking out over the harbor and the sea beyond. Jørgen came out of the Danyard where he worked and made his way along the quayside toward him. Every day after his clerking job at the shipyard he came to the harbor to check his sailboat. Peder was always there, gazing out over the sea, like the mermaid in Copenhagen harbor. Every day the boy came to watch the ships coming and going. And always with his dog.

Jørgen stopped and lit a cigarette. Everyone knew Peder, but, like Jørgen, they knew little of him. Jørgen guessed he was eight or nine, even though he was small for that age. He was looked after by Sara Gronborg, a Jewish widow who lived over her butcher shop near the harbor. Peder had shown up in town one day, dirty and in rags. No one knew where he had come from, but Sara had taken him in.

His appearance was striking. A huge mop of silky, blond hair sat atop his head, with roughly-cut bangs that hung over his blue eyes. His sparse, skinny frame sprouted meager arms with slender fingers that gently stroked his dog. But everyone knew that Peder was strange. He didn't go to school. The teachers had long given up on him. Unable to communicate, they had said.

Jørgen stamped out his cigarette. Peder spoke only when spoken to, and then slowly, in a hesitant voice, as if talking was a great labor. Yet he had special talents: his fingers would put pencil to paper to draw the birds that swooped across the town. The birds would disappear from sight, but Peder would recreate them on his pad in remarkable detail. And he had a phenomenal memory: he would recite the names of every ship that came and left the harbor, and the times of their arrival and departure.

Jørgen approached the shelter. The boy knew he was there, but there was no acknowledgement. It was his eyes that Jørgen found fascinating. They flicked side-to-side, up-and-down, looking everywhere except at anybody who tried to talk to him.

Yet those eyes would fix the gaze of Soldat. Soldat was the boy's dog, a German Shepherd who always followed Peder. No one knew where Soldat came from. A stray, some said. Jørgen thought of the irony. Like the boy. Both strays.

Peder ran his hand down the length of black fur that lay like a saddle on Soldat's honey-colored coat. The German Shepherd turned his head and panted, his lips curling up in what seemed a smile. The dog's nose looked as if it had been dipped in an inkpot, black patches above his eyes, like truncated eyebrows, giving him a pensive, concerned look. The boy and his dog gazed at each other as if they could read the other's thoughts

"Many ships today, Peder?"

The boy continued to stroke his dog. "Eleven." In a monotone voice, he gave the names and times of the ships. He did not look at Jørgen. He raised his eyes to gaze at a seagull, climbing above. His hands caressed the dog again, then reached for his drawing pad.

Berlin. Heldorf's Office.

"My wife! My wife! Where is my wife?" Weiss burst into the room like a wild animal. Heldorf saw the fire of rage in his eyes; for a moment he thought the Jew was going to attack him. He controlled his reaction, getting up slowly, his eyes fixing Weiss's. The guard rushed in flourishing his gun, but Heldorf made a simple gesture, waving him away.

"She's fine, Professor Weiss." Heldorf smiled. "Please relax. We wish you no harm." He watched closely as Weiss's labored breathing eased. "Your wife is in a different facility, no doubt enjoying a bath and the provision of new clothes." Heldorf ran his eyes up and down Weiss's new suit. "As I see you have done."

The wind had been taken from Weiss's sails, but Heldorf could still see the potent mixture of rage and fear in the Jew's eyes.

"I guarantee that you'll see your wife – Rebecca, isn't it? – as soon as our meeting is over." He saw that Weiss longed to believe him, despite his fear. "Please sit down." He waved a hand toward the chair in front of his desk. He held the Jew's eyes as he pulled a silver case from his pocket. "Cigarette?"

Weiss made the expected show of refusal. Heldorf knew it was nothing more than a gesture. Weiss grabbed suddenly at the case, accepting Heldorf's light before drawing deeply on the cigarette. Heldorf noted the weakness. He had to know everything about the man who sat opposite him. Everything that drove him, every weakness, every fear, every foible, every nuance of his soul.

"Who are you? Why have you brought me here? What do you swine want of me?"

Heldorf felt that Weiss's reaction was pathetic, typical of an *Untermensch*, but he had to curb his instincts and prejudices. Tell yourself Weiss isn't a Jew, a voice in his head insisted. The project must succeed. Tell yourself he isn't a Jew. He's the leader of your project team.

"So many questions, Professor Weiss." He smiled. "And I will answer them all. But first I must ask if you have been treated well. Your new clothes fit you well."

The anger did not abate. "We were on a cattle car, treated like animals, and now you want to talk about fashion. Why am I here? And who are you?"

Heldorf leaned back in his chair. "My name is Maximilian Heldorf. I am the Chairman of the German Physical Science Research Council." He saw the interest in the Jew's eyes – a flicker, no more, but it was there. "Like you, I'm a scientist. A physicist."

"So, what do you want of me? It's been a long time since I did any serious physics." Again there was anger in his eyes. "I was thrown out of the university nearly ten years ago. A professor. Thrown out, just like that!" He snapped his fingers. "For being a Jew." He lingered on the last word.

"But your paper on quantum theory was excellent!" Heldorf switched tack, intent on pulling Weiss back into discussing science. He pulled a copy of Weiss's paper from his file. "You developed Niels Bohr's work, didn't you?"

Weiss's eyes lit up at the mention of the famous physicist. "I couldn't hold a candle to Bohr." Weiss crushed out his cigarette. "But in terms of quantum theory…."

Heldorf listened intently as Weiss outlined his theoretical findings. There was a brief pause as the Jew looked anxiously at the cigarette case on the desk. Heldorf quickly pushed the case and lighter within Weiss's reach. He lit up and continued describing his past work. Heldorf was pleased. Now the Jew was talking like a scientist, divorced from the political world that had engulfed him. He waited for Weiss to finish.

"Very interesting. Would you like to get back into physics, Professor Weiss?"

Heldorf saw a moment of hope suddenly swamped by disbelief. "Herr Heldorf, don't play silly games with me. I'm a Jew." He was breathing heavily. "A son of Abraham. A kike. Such people don't practice physics in Germany." Weiss scowled and stubbed out his half-smoked cigarette as though preparing to leave. "I don't know what you're aiming for me to do, but whatever it is – sabotage, espionage, something else that requires a physics background – whatever it is, I won't do it."

Jasenovac Extermination Camp, Yugoslavia.

In the hut, Hannah sorted through the clothes with the other woman. She did not know her name and they did not speak. Coats in one pile. Shoes in another. Undergarments were to be stuffed into sacks. They were not told where the clothes came from; they did not ask. But Hannah knew.

Two other women came to collect the sacks every hour. They never spoke as their skeletal bodies struggled with the bundles. The other woman looked at her briefly, then returned to the clothes.

The other woman was a newcomer; she had replaced Gisela two days ago. Gisela had been a friend, insofar as there could be a friend in the hellhole that was Jasenovac. Hannah recalled her face. Gaunt, pale skin drawn as tight as a drum over her shaven skull, yet always a grin, despite the horrors that surrounded her.

Hannah looked out of the hut's solitary window. Acres of sodden mud stretched to the barbed-wire fence; the early summer rain was still falling. At the far end of the camp stood two large buildings. When they had arrived, they were told they contained delousing rooms: people were to be cleansed before resettlement in the east. Beyond the buildings, a tall chimney stack rose into the damp sky, and all day long it belched smoke. And everywhere, the sweet, sickly smell that stuck in the nostrils, the smell of roasting flesh that brought unwelcome saliva to a parched mouth.

Hannah shuddered and spat on the floor.

Berlin. Heldorf's Office.

Heldorf waited for Weiss's outburst to die away. "I don't need you for espionage or sabotage – I need you to do research. I have authority for a special project. Top secret. Soon you can be in your own laboratory again." He watched closely as hope and disbelief battled across Weiss's face.

"A laboratory?" Weiss pictured the one he had dominated in Jena, the laboratory in which he had been admired, respected. "What's this special project?"

Heldorf felt a moment of triumph, but he refused to rush his seduction. "All in good time, professor, all in good time."

Weiss became defensive again. "It's a trick, isn't it? Some form of trap. What's the catch?"

"Catch?" Heldorf laughed. "There's no catch. In fact, there's a reward for resuming research."

Weiss raised his eyebrows and Heldorf played his trump card. "Your wife will be given an exit visa to a neutral country – Portugal," he saw Weiss start, "as soon as you start work on the project."

Ten years of despair had robbed Weiss of his ability to hope. "No, it's a trick, a trap. You grind us down, treat us like animals, then dangle something too good to be true as a taunt. How can I trust you?"

Never grateful, these Jews. Heldorf stifled his feelings. Just think of the project. The project was everything. "It's natural that you distrust me, Professor Weiss, after all that's happened." He opened a desk drawer and took out an envelope. "But I want you to know that I'm acting in good faith." His fingers pulled out a document from the envelope. "Here's the exit visa for your wife." He placed it deliberately in front of Weiss.

After a moment's hesitation, Weiss scooped up the document. Heldorf watched closely as Weiss saw the photograph of his wife, his eyes widening when he saw the authorizing signature. "How did you get—"

"Enough questions for now, Professor Weiss." Heldorf picked up the visa. "Your wife could be in Lisbon by next week if you agree to work for me."

Weiss shook his head. "How do I know it's not some elaborate trap? That Rebecca won't just be shipped to another camp?"

Heldorf resisted a growing anger. "Because, quite simply, Professor Weiss, your wife will write to you. Her letters will confirm my promise."

There was still doubt on Weiss's face; Heldorf decided to play another card in his game. He picked up a second envelope and shook out its contents. "Here are two more exit visas for Portugal." He waited for Weiss's reactions as he looked at the photographs of his daughters.

"Naomi and Miriam! Where are they? I haven't seen them in three months. Are they safe?" He looked imploringly at Heldorf.

Heldorf picked up the visas. "They're quite safe." He looked at the photographs. "Your daughters are most beautiful."

Weiss's heart lurched at the word 'beautiful.' He cursed again his powerlessness to protect them from brutes who would value their beauty for the wrong reasons. "And they'll go with Rebecca?" He could not hide his anxiety.

Heldorf decided to display his complete hand. "I've been totally honest with you, Professor Weiss, and I'll continue to be so. Your daughters will not go with your wife now." He saw the disappointment on the Jew's face and continued quickly. "I'm sure that you will realize, as a man of the world, that I need some insurance for, shall we say, my investment. Both your daughters will be released when you've completed your work for me. And then you will go." He watched as Weiss began to grasp the crux of the deal.

Heldorf felt he could see the conflicting emotions running through the Jew as his fear of the Nazi state wrestled with his love and concern for his wife and daughters. His hands were shaking.

"Would you like another cigarette, Professor Weiss?"

The Jew pounced on the case. "What's the nature of the work you want me to do?"

Heldorf offered him a light and smiled.

Jasenovac Extermination Camp, Yugoslavia.

A guard at the door of the hut looked in at Hannah and motioned with his rifle to continue sorting.

Gisela had been an innocent or a fool, or both. She had always worn a grin, always had the belief that she would survive, that she would escape. "Soon we'll be resettled," she had said. "I've heard the word."

Hannah recalled the hopeful dark eyes, large in her shrunken face. "But Gisela, the clothes you're sorting – don't you know where they're coming from?"

"Of course," Gisela had shrugged. "They're the old clothes of the people who've been resettled. We all get new clothes for resettlement."

Hannah sighed as she picked over blouses still bearing the aroma of their erstwhile wearers. "Who told you this nonsense, Gisela?"

"It's not nonsense. He told me." She nodded toward the guard at the door.

"But Gisela—"

"You want a cigarette?" Gisela had looked around furtively as her hand plunged into the neckline of her red blouse.

"A cigarette?" Hannah looked at Gisela's prize, a half-smoked cigarette. "How on earth did you get it?"

Gisela grinned. "From him." She nodded toward the guard. "I do...," she lowered her eyes, "...well, you know, I do things for him."

Hannah had blanched. Gisela had sold her body for a few pathetic cigarette stubs.

"Just think." The grin had returned. "I'll be getting new clothes and I can get rid of this old red blouse at last."

Gisela had disappeared the day before.

Hannah picked up another blouse, and suddenly her fingers felt on fire. The blouse was red. She tossed it aside, angrily.

"You, Goldmann." The guard prodded her ribs with his rifle. "The Commandant wants to see you."

Hannah followed him, her eyes lingering on the red blouse.

Berlin. Heldorf's Office.

Heldorf pulled another folder from the drawer of the desk. "You're aware that a neutron can split the fissionable uranium isotope, Professor Weiss?"

"Yes, of course – it was the discovery of Otto Hahn three years ago. I remember that when I first heard the news, it occurred to me that if the fragments resulting from the split of the atom themselves emit neutrons, and if enough neutrons are emitted, a chain reaction would occur."

"A chain reaction!" Heldorf was pleased. Weiss was no longer talking like a persecuted Jew, but as a scientist. "You are aware of the work of Fermi?"

"Only from papers I read some years ago. He bombarded uranium with atoms and seemed to observe the creation of new elements—" Weiss stopped suddenly. An idea of what Heldorf's plan might be crossed his mind. He tried to push the idea away. "But, of course, I'm rusty." He shrugged his shoulders. "I'm sure that you know, Herr Heldorf, that I've been unable to do research for many years."

Heldorf saw that Weiss did not attempt to hide the accusatory look in his eyes. In that moment, he, Heldorf, was personally to blame for the loss of Weiss's scientific life over the past decade. He feared that he would lose the Jew, that the project would die before it was born. He had to make good the ten years that Weiss had lost. He pulled another sheaf of papers from his drawer and thrust them across the desk.

"Here's a paper by Niels Bohr on the mechanism of nuclear fission. And here are all of Fermi's published papers up to 1940. Anything later we don't have." He looked across at the Jew. "Fermi now works for the Americans." Heldorf knew he had to be honest. If he were caught in a lie – any lie – then Weiss might opt out, whatever the offers regarding his family. He opened another folder and laid it in front of Weiss.

"What do you think of this? It's a method for separating out the fissionable U-235 isotope from natural uranium." He ran his finger over the diagrams and formulas. "It uses a thermal diffusion process, in which uranium hexafluoride is subjected to high temperatures to separate the isotopes. Designed by the finest scientific mind in Germany."

He watched as Weiss pored over the diagrams, shaking his head. Weiss the scientist, not the Jew.

"And do you know, Professor Weiss, that this is the work of a Nobel Laureate?" He laughed. "Problem is, it's not very efficient!"

The Jew looked up from the diagrams. "It's Heisenberg's work, isn't it?"

Heldorf smiled. Weiss might be rusty, but he knew his stuff. "It really doesn't matter. The key question is can you find a way to separate out U-235 that *is* efficient?" He waited to see if Weiss would rise to the bait.

Weiss continued to look at the diagrams. He was beginning to get a grasp of Heldorf's objectives. He looked up at Heldorf. "To be honest, at this moment, I'm not sure. Perhaps. It's possible. But it'll need a lot of research – research that won't come cheap or easy."

Heldorf was undeterred. "There won't be a problem with resources." He smiled. "Let's just say I have connections."

Weiss pushed the papers aside. "And I'll need help. I can't do this work alone."

"Obviously, you'll need others. You may ask for whomever you wish." He pulled a list from his pocket. "But you cannot have any name here." He passed the paper to Weiss. It was a list of Heisenberg's friends in the Uranium Club, the doyens of German science who had tried to fool Speer.

Weiss glanced at the list and shrugged. "It's difficult without some of these names. But there are scientists who can do the work." His eyes narrowed. "But they're all Jews. And most of them are in your camps." He paused and looked at Heldorf. "If they're not already dead."

"Then give me their names at once." Heldorf picked up a clipboard; he had already anticipated some of the people.

Weiss's eyes ran down the list in his mind. "Ernst Schlegel, a brilliant scientist. Artur Steinitz – a theoretical physicist without equal. Georg Silberstein – one of the best experimentalists. And we must have Sol Friedberg, a gifted chemist. He's a bit old now, but he was always one of the best in his field."

The Jew continued with his list. Heldorf ticked the names off on his own list and was pleased that he had foreseen nearly all of Weiss's requirements. He thought that Weiss might be padding his list a bit – there were one or two scientists who didn't really have the necessary credentials – but he said nothing. That he had the key people was all that mattered at that moment.

"I'll make arrangements for these people to join you." Heldorf put down the list and got up from his desk. "And now, perhaps, Dr. Weiss, you would like to see your wife?"

"Wait, there's one name I'd forgotten. How could I? The expert on beta decay."

Heldorf picked up his list again. He was surprised that, in his research, he had missed someone. "And who is this man?"

"It isn't a man. She's a former student of Heisenberg. Her name is Hannah Goldmann."

Heldorf turned sharply at the mention of the name. The black hair cascading on the pillow; he saw again the deep brown eyes.

Frederikshavn, Denmark.

Jørgen shaded his eyes as he peered across the waves. About ten yards from the shoreline was a breakwater, a huge mound of rocks piled into the sea to prevent erosion of the shore. Peder had climbed to the topmost rock.

At the end of the rock a heron sat quietly, its plume rippling in the breeze. Peder edged toward the bird, and Jørgen thought he heard a gentle murmur coming from the animal's mouth. The heron reacted only with a slow movement of its head, fixing Peder with its yellow beads of eyes.

Jørgen felt anxious as Peder moved closer to the creature. Herons weren't vicious, but the boy might be in danger if attacked by the long sharp bill. The boy looked at the bird and slowly moved his hand toward it. Was Peder, who shunned human company, seeking companionship with a bird? Were the eyes that never sought his now locked on the heron?

Peder's hand rested lightly on the bird's back, gently stroking. The heron did not stir.

"Peder, maybe that's not a good—" Jørgen's shout destroyed the spell of the moment.

The bird lurched and quickly took to the air, its strong wings beating, its long legs stretched out behind. It circled twice and then a third time over Peder's head. The boy raised his hands and watched, his eyes following the creature until it was no more than a dot between sky and sea.

Berlin. A modest apartment.

"Albert, what's happening?"

Weiss could feel his wife's fear as she clutched him. "Rebecca, don't worry." He ran his fingers through her hair.

"But I don't understand." Her eyes were flooded with tears. "One day we're on a train to hell, and now this…" She waved her hand around her room, sparsely furnished, but warm with a comfortable bed.

"I prayed hard to God." Despite the circumstances, Weiss, the atheist, could not resist his joke.

"Don't talk such nonsense, Albert." Rebecca broke from his grasp and pushed him away. "How can you joke at a time like this?" She sat down on the bed. "And don't take the name of God in vain."

Weiss sat down beside her. "Rebecca, you're going to be free." There was a hint of pride in his voice, as if he, himself, had wrought the miracle.

"Free?" His wife screamed the word. "How can one be free in this godforsaken country?"

"My precious, you're not going to be in this country much longer – you're going to Portugal."

Rebecca looked at her husband of twelve years as if he were a madman. "Now I know you've taken leave of your senses. Have you been drinking?"

Weiss ignored her question. "No, it's true. You'll leave tomorrow. I've struck a deal with Herr Heldorf."

"What deal? Who is Heldorf? Will you be coming with me?"

"One thing at a time, Rebecca." He lit a cigarette. "Heldorf wants me to do some special scientific research for him—"

"Research? You haven't done research for years—"

"Hear me out, for God's sake." He stopped, angry at himself for being angry. "I'm sorry, Rebecca, I didn't mean to snap at you. Let me explain."

"Albert, I, too, am sorry." She dropped her eyes. "But I'm so frightened."

"I understand, but you don't have to be frightened anymore, my love." He spoke earnestly, although he, also, had doubts. "Heldorf wants me – and other Jews – to do this special research. He knows he can't force us to do it with threats, so he's offering inducements. I've seen the visa that will get you to Portugal."

"But you can't trust these people, Albert. You've seen what they've done."

"You want I should refuse? And they put us both back on the train?" Weiss rose and walked up and down the room, trying to control his anger.

"How do you know it's not a trap? That they won't just send me to a camp?"

Weiss sat down at the table and put his head in his hands. "To be honest, my love, I don't. But it's our only chance. And Heldorf said that Naomi and Miriam can join you – when I've finished the work."

"Naomi and Miriam?" She leapt up from the bed. "They're all right?" The mention of her daughters brought a glimmer of hope to her tired eyes.

"Heldorf assures me that they're well. He's shown me the visas for them to join you."

"My God," Rebecca's eyes lit up. "Together with my girls again. We haven't seen them since—" She stopped suddenly. "But what about you? Will you be with them? Have you got a visa?"

"Yes." Weiss smiled as he lied. If his work was successful, he would know such secrets that Heldorf would never release him. "I shall join you. We'll be a family again."

She held a picture in her mind of the four of them together, but her doubts pushed it aside. "But we don't really know that he's not going to ship me to a camp instead."

"He said that you could write to me." He pulled a piece of paper from his pocket. "This is the address."

She took the paper, folded it and tucked it into the cuff of her blouse. "I still can't trust these sadists. How do we know they won't take me to a camp and force me to write something good to fool you?"

"I've thought of that. Come, *Bubbeleh.* " He gently guided her by the arm and they sat on the edge of the bed. "You need to insert some sort of code into your letter – a number, say. If I see that number, I'll know that they've kept their promise, that you're safely out of Germany.

"A number? What number? What should I use, Albert?"

Weiss thought for a moment and took Rebecca's hand. "Do you remember our very first night out together?"

Rebecca beat back the welling tears. "In 1925. We went to a concert together at the Jena *Volkshaus.* Beautiful music, by Bach." She smiled as it all came back to her. "It was the most wonderful night of my life."

He gave her hand a squeeze. "They performed Bach's Cantata Number 82. Put the number 82 in your letter – 82 people on the train,

82 days until Rosh Hashanah – just make something up. As long as I see the number 82 somewhere in your letter, I'll know that you're safe."

"Eighty-two," Rebecca repeated. "It brought us luck once, perhaps it will bring us luck again."

Berlin.

She was a Jew. Sturmbannführer Heldorf had to put aside all memories of the brief time he had spent with her so many years ago. He stared down at the file on his desk; the face in the photographs looked back at him. There were three – profile, full-face, and three-quarters views – and it pained him to look at them. They had cut off her hair, her long, lustrous black hair, but her wide brown eyes and proud jaw declared courage and defiance.

Heldorf dreaded meeting her again. He'd thought dealing with Weiss and the others would be difficult, but it had been child's play compared to what lay ahead. Her eyes looked up at him again. He remembered where they'd met, outside Heisenberg's lecture hall in Leipzig University. She'd had the nerve to challenge the Nobel prize-winner on an aspect of his theory and had been upset when the great man put her down. Later, outside, she'd dropped her books and—

Heldorf slammed his fist down on the desk. No. No more. He turned the photos face down. She was a Jew. He opened the file. The basic data he had known for some time. Hannah Goldmann. Born Weimar 1912. Thirty years old – a year younger than himself. Graduate in Physics at Leipzig. About to be installed as an assistant professor when she had been thrown out of the university in '34.

And then nothing. Heldorf flipped through the papers. Nothing until her arrest earlier in the year and her removal to Ravensbrück. From where he must now pull her out, because Weiss said the project could not go forward without her.

He picked up the phone. "Get me the Camp Commandant of Ravensbrück." There was a long pause on the line as the call was placed. Yes, she had given Heisenberg a run for his money, he chuckled.

Stop thinking about her! He struggled for self-control. She was a Jew. He tried to distract himself with a cigarette, watching the smoke billow around the lamp on his desk. Smoke from another time came to his mind. It was after they had—

"Yes, this is Sturmbannführer Maximilian Heldorf. Under orders of Reichminister Speer, I need to arrange for the transfer of one of your prisoners, a Hannah Goldmann.....Yes, I'll hold while you check." He began to reach for her photograph, but pulled his hand back.

"Yes, I'm still here....What do you mean she's no longer there? She's been moved to Jasenovac?....Yes, I know that's a death camp! Look, you must order her immediate release into my care or you shall hear from Reichminister Speer personally! Yes, immediate release – tonight, preferably, tomorrow at the latest. And if she's still alive, make sure she's cleaned up and fed a decent meal before you deliver her!"

He slammed the receiver down and held his head in his hands. He reached over, turned Hannah's photos face up, and studied them in silence. Had he loved this woman? Had he loved this Jew?

RAF Airport in Leuchars, Scotland.

The unheated transport plane which had brought Christina Lindgren across the Atlantic was hardly the Pan American Clipper she had expected, but the small aircraft on the tarmac that was to take her to Sweden inspired no confidence at all. Nor did the grizzled pilot, who looked as if he had been flying since the last war and was not the dashing RAF flying ace she thought manned all English aircraft.

"Isn't she beautiful?" The pilot must have mistaken Christina's open-jawed shock for a look of awe. "She's a Mosquito – built of wood, you know," he said proudly. "I fly her twice a week to Stockholm to deliver the diplomatic pouch." He extended his arm toward the steps that had just been rolled into place. "The steps are a luxury for our honored guests. After you."

Christina put her foot on the first step, pulling up the pant leg of her oversized flight suit so she would not trip. She took another step tugging at the other pant leg, the parachute strapped to her back almost causing her to lose her balance. At the top she peered inside. "Where do I sit?" she asked, scanning the cramped interior.

"There's only one passenger seat. It's in the bomb bay."

Christina gulped. "We're going to be dropping bombs?"

"Good Lord, no. We fly unarmed."

Christina clambered into her seat as the pilot followed and took his place in the cockpit. "Isn't flying unarmed dangerous?" she called to him. "Shouldn't we have something to defend ourselves with?" Earlier in the day, she had been shown a map with their route, which would take them to neutral Sweden by flying over Nazi-occupied territory.

He turned around to answer her. "It's true we're often spotted by German anti-aircraft batteries on the west coast of Norway, but you needn't worry, miss. My Mosquito here, she's hard to swat." His broad smiled revealed gaps in his teeth.

Christina guessed she was not the first upon whom the pilot had inflicted his witticism. She did not return his smile as she wondered whether it was too late to bolt. "What do we do if we're shot at?"

"Simple. We just climb higher. The flak tops out at about twenty thousand feet, so if we're above that, we're fine."

She did not find his perpetual smile reassuring. Twenty thousand feet. Four miles up in the air in a wooden plane.

"That reminds me," he got up and squatted his way into the bomb bay, "I need to show you how to hook up your oxygen supply. If we have to go up, you'll be needing it. See—," he pointed to the sides of her flight helmet, "—there are earphones built in. Wait a minute," he said, adjusting her helmet, "yours aren't positioned properly. I need to be able to tell you over the earphones when to hook up your oxygen if it comes to that. See, right here's your oxygen bag."

"And if we're hit while we're ascending, before we're out of range of the flak?"

"Good question." He reached under her seat and pulled out a package. "Here's a stick of flares. If we're hit badly, I'll open up the bomb bay and you'll have to jump out." He tapped the front of her flight suit. "Here's the rip cord you'll need to pull to open your parachute. Don't forget to take these." He held up the flares. "They'll help them find you in the dark." He moved back into the cockpit.

Her heart now in her throat, Christina began to have second thoughts and started to get up. But the door suddenly slammed shut and the engine began to roar. As the plane taxied she was thrown back into her seat.

Twenty thousand feet. A thousand dollars pay. She did a quick calculation in her head as the plane gained altitude. That came to a five cent profit for every foot she'd be above the cold North Sea.

The thousand dollars had better be tax free.

Berlin.

She was alive, and she was in the next room. Heldorf knew that meeting her would take all the finesse and courage he could muster. He shook his head as he again looked at her file. Nothing. For Weiss and all the other Jews, he had found a lever. A father, a mother, some family. In Hannah Goldman's file there was nothing. No evidence of a marriage, no children. Both parents killed in an action that took place during the collection process. Sister also likely dead.

Heldorf knew he had no sanction against her. He could not threaten a relative to make her join the team. He paced the floor. Unless. Unless he could find another threat. The idea had come to him the previous night, and he wondered how he could think of such cruelty. To be used on a woman he once had loved. He got up, smoothed out the creases in his SS uniform, and walked toward the door.

Hannah Goldman looked up as he entered the room. She was pale and thin with hollows in her cheeks, and was wearing a freshly-laundered dress several sizes too large with a kerchief tied at the back. For a moment, there was a brief smile on her full lips that vanished when she saw the uniform; her eyes narrowed to slits of hatred.

"So you've become a member of the master race, Max." The words came dryly, from someone whom life had hurt much, but now could hurt no more.

"Hello, Hannah." Heldorf ignored the remark. "I'm pleased you're here. Are you being treated well?"

She threw her head back; her laugh was short and caustic. "Much better than at Ravensbrück, although I never had a chance to try the room service at Jasenovac. Here, at least, there are no rats." She sniffed the air and looked at him. "Or are there?"

Heldorf smiled to hide his anger. He knew he must not lose his temper. "I trust your room is comfortable? I'm sure it's better than your previous accommodation."

She shivered at the memory of the smoke-belching stacks at Jasenovac. He saw the shudder and decided to seize the advantage, to keep her on the defensive.

"Hannah, I need your help."

"Is that why you've brought me here?" The anger had returned to her voice. "To *help* you?" She lingered on the word sarcastically. "Are you sure it wasn't to—"

"That's enough, Hannah." He spoke sharply. "What happened between us many years ago is of no concern to me now." He fought to convince himself that he spoke the truth. He sat down and continued quickly, anxious to change the subject. "You know Albert Weiss?"

"Albert?" Her eyes widened. "Albert's still alive? I would've thought, by now, that you bastards—"

"Professor Weiss is safe and well." He knew he had to retain the initiative and keep it. "In fact, he's insisting that you be on his team."

"Team?" She rose to the bait, as he wanted. "What team?"

Heldorf took a list from his pocket. "His team consists of Georg Siberstein, Artur Steinitz, Ernst Schlegel, Sol Friedberg…" He watched the disbelief come to her face as he continued. Her jaw dropped as he finished the list.

"What the hell is going on? What are you Nazi bastards doing with a team of Jewish scientists?"

Heldorf sensed anxiety beneath the façade of bravado; he was getting the upper hand. He opened his cigarette case and offered it to her. She shook her head. Perhaps she'd changed. He remembered a time she'd lit a cigarette after they'd—

Stop, an inner voice said. Focus on your goal.

"You're aware of fission?" His question got under her guard and hit the intended target: Hannah, the scientist.

"Yes, of course. I've read Lise Meitner's paper. Imagine – a brilliant scientist like Lise Meitner, the woman who discovered nuclear fission, and you geniuses throw her out of Germany."

When he had mentioned physics to Weiss, the scientist had taken over, but with Hannah it was still the Jew who had spoken. And the woman. She wasn't making it easy for him; he decided to float the bait. "Dr. Weiss believes it's possible to harvest fissionable material, and he says that success depends upon your being on his team." He waited for her pride to feed on his words.

"And why have you gathered a team of Jews to do this work?"

There was doubt in the intense dark eyes that looked at him piercingly. He turned away, unable to stare her down.

He tried another ploy. "Because no one else can."

"What?" She gave an ironic smile. "Not even Heisenberg and his star-studded Uranium Club?" She gave a sarcastic chuckle.

"No, they cannot. Do you remember that time when you challenged him on a small aspect of his theory—" Heldorf stopped. He had started down a path he didn't wish to travel.

It was too late. Her memory recalled the day. "Yes, it was when the great professor put me down. It was the day I met you outside the lecture hall afterwards—" She halted suddenly and lowered her eyes. She, too, didn't wish to tread the path. She recovered quickly. "But let me tell you he is still wrong." She recalled her imaginary blackboard in the prison.

"Perhaps this is your big chance to get back at him."

She raised her eyes slowly. "Maybe. But why do you want to harvest fissionable material?"

The unexpected question knocked him off balance for a second. "We need to find new sources of energy." He could feel he was stumbling with his answer. "To power our submarines."

Hannah stood up and fixed him with her eyes. She spoke slowly, deliberately. "You're trying to make an atomic bomb, aren't you?"

Heldorf fumbled for an answer and realized he had no option but to tell her the truth. "Yes." He saw her eyes flash. "And it cannot be built without your skill."

He expected her reaction, but was surprised by the vehemence. She flashed her eyes. "Never!"

Frederikshavn, Denmark.

The bell on Sara Gronborg's kosher butcher shop door jingled cheerfully as it heralded her next customer. A tall, large-boned woman in her middle years, Sara had a proud bearing and a ready smile. The lines at the corner of her soft brown eyes made her eyes smile, and the dark brown braids that encircled her head gave her a proud, almost regal air. She looked up and smiled. "Ah, Gerda, how nice to see you. How are you? How's your knee?"

"Can't complain. It's as arthritic as ever, but it still gets me around. And how are you?"

"I'm just fine, thank you."

"And little Peder?"

"He's very well, too."

Gerda Rosenfeld, older than Sara by almost a decade, rested her parcels on the counter and heaved a weary sigh. Much of her wiry gray hair had managed to elude her untidy bun that day, and a perpetual scowl, the occupational hazard of having passed on much gossip over the years, was etched on her face. "You know, Sara, your taking that child in was a *mitzvah*. It was a pure act of kindness, right from your heart." Gerda placed her hand on her bosom.

"Oh, no, really – it's a pleasure to have Peder around. Especially since I never had children of my own, and when I lost Jacob last year…" The shop had kept Sara busy during the day. Despite the Nazis in their midst, the small Jewish community of Frederikshavn had remained vibrant and business was good. All Danes were on meager rations imposed by the Germans because the Nazis took a good portion of Denmark's meat supply to ship back to Germany; yet she was still able to get some good pieces for her customers. But while she was occupied during the day, until Peder arrived, her evenings had been bleak with loneliness.

Gerda would not be sidetracked. "It was a *mitzvah,* I tell you, to take in a child no one else wanted." Gerda tugged on her faded cotton print dress that had become snug around her torso. "And you not even knowing where he came from." Gerda looked around the shop to make sure they were alone. "Tell me, Sara, is Peder Jewish?"

Sara chuckled. "If you mean to ask is Peder circumcised, the answer is, well, Peder is not Jewish."

"But he's a bit, well, you know, different, isn't he, Sara?"

"Peder's a special child. He rarely speaks. He's afraid of things that others take for granted – he's afraid of other children, for example, and he doesn't have a single friend his own age – but he's fearless in so many other respects. And there's his artistic ability – he can draw anything he's seen – even from memory. And he has an affinity with animals, almost like he speaks their language. His dog, Soldat, is his real friend." She adjusted her apron. "Anyway, what can I get you, Gerda?"

Gerda looked longingly at a particularly fine cut of beef, then looked away quickly. "Nothing too good. I don't believe in using good cuts of meat in the *cholent* I make for Shabbat. I prefer to use more beans and potatoes in the stew – Stefan used to say it tasted better that way."

Gerda's husband, Stefan, had died a number of years ago, and she now made ends meet by keeping a few scrawny chickens. She continued to scrutinize the case of kosher meats. "Perhaps you have a few scraps in the back? Maybe a little suet – something just to give my *cholent* a bit of flavor?"

Sara thought of the pile of scraps she had set aside for Soldat. "No," she lied, "I'm clean out of scraps. But how about some of this?" She pointed to the beef Gerda had originally eyed.

"No, I don't think—"

"Please, you'd be doing me a favor to take it off my hands – I ordered too much of it." Another white lie; it was her most popular cut.

"Well, no, I don't—"

"You know, Gerda, I really could use a half dozen of your chickens' fine eggs. Somehow they taste better than other eggs."

Six eggs for a fine cut of beef – they both knew it was an uneven swap. But it was one that allowed Gerda to hold her head high. "Well, all right, but don't give me too much." She watched Sara slice off a good-sized piece.

Sara wrapped the meat in brown paper and tied it with string. "There you are, Gerda."

"Sara, you're a good woman. May you live to be a hundred."

Sara raised her eyebrows. "I don't know, Gerda. Is that a blessing or a curse? Isn't there an old saying – live long, die alone?" They both laughed.

Gerda took the package of meat, then put it back down on the counter with the rest of her parcels. "One more thing, Sara." She again glanced around the shop conspiratorially. I don't want you to think I'm sticking my nose in where it doesn't belong...."

"Yes, what is it, Gerda?"

"You should know that Peder's been hanging around down at the harbor with one of those hooligans."

Sara frowned. "What are you saying, Gerda? What hooligans?"

"You know, the young man who seems determined to get us all into trouble with the Germans. I saw him rip one of their posters off a wall when he thought no one was around, and someone down the street said he handed him a newspaper once which he immediately burned because he was afraid—"

"Calm down, Gerda. What's this man's name?"

"Jørgen Something."

"Jørgen Sørensen? I don't think he's a hooligan, Gerda. Perhaps he's a bit brash, but he's been kind to me. After Jacob died, he used to come over and help me with the store after his work. That's how he knows Peder."

Gerda screwed up her lips. "Well, he may have been all right then, but mark my words he's a bad egg now – why does he need to rock the boat? I've heard stories that would curl your hair about what's happening in other countries where the Germans have decided to squat. I don't like the Germans any better than you do, but we've got it pretty good here now, and, all things considered, it's just not a good idea—"

"Gerda, the Germans may call themselves Denmark's protectors, but you know as well as I do how life has gone downhill "

"I don't mean to make trouble, Sara." Gerda picked up her packages and prepared to leave. "Just a word to the wise. I'd keep Peder away from that Jørgen hooligan if I were you."

Berlin.

"Hannah, I don't think you understand the seriousness of your situation."

He had hoped to avoid the ultimatum he was about to deliver, but there was no option.

She gave a brief sardonic laugh. "I spend three months in Ravensbrück and two weeks in Jasenovac and you think I don't know how serious it is?" She paused and sighed deeply, as if resigned to her fate. "Send me back to the camp. It'll be better than making a bomb for Hitler and his murderers."

"Your situation is much more serious than that." He paused, watching as her eyes flicked anxiously left and right. Her mind raced, trying to understand his meaning. He remained silent to allow fear to begin to seize her. Finally, he spoke. "You need to know that I've struck a deal with Dr. Weiss and other members of his team."

"A deal?" She didn't understand. "They did a deal with you? Jews did a deal with the SS?"

"Yes, and it's a very favorable deal for them. They work on the project, and their relatives get visas to a neutral country."

She laughed uneasily. "But it's a trap. They're fools. How could they believe you?"

He smiled. "Because it's true." He picked up a folder from the desk. "Here are the visas. Of course, some of the relatives will not leave until the end of the project." He watched her face, stunned, as she looked at the visas. "But some leave for Portugal tomorrow. Frau Weiss is already there."

He waited as her mind grasped his intention.

"But you can't use that with me. I don't have any relatives. You've killed everyone in my family."

"I'm afraid there's no way out for you, Hannah." His cajoling tone was replaced by coldness. "Weiss insists he can't do this work without you, and I have to believe him. So if you don't agree to work with the team, I'll have to call them all to a meeting to tell them the deal is off. Their family members won't leave for Portugal and they'll all be shipped back to the camps." He picked up his cap and went to the door. "You'll be present at that meeting." He paused in the doorway. "And I'll have to tell them that it was your refusal to work for the team that caused this unfortunate turn of events."

His stern gaze locked with her defiant stare for several moments before he left and closed the door behind him.

Frederikshavn. Resistance Meeting.

Gunnar held both of the skeleton's bony hands over its lower pelvis and said in a falsetto voice, "Mercy me! I think I'm a bit underdressed for this nasty Danish weather!" Jørgen rolled his eyes as Gunnar wrapped his red scarf around the shoulders of the skeleton.

The Resistance cell meeting was in a doctor's office, and Gunnar was clowning with a model skeleton that dangled by a wire in its skull in the corner. For security reasons, each time the cell met the starting time and venue changed; the previous meeting had been in a garage, the one before in the bacteria room at the Frederikshavn Serum Institute. Jørgen leaned on a white cabinet and looked at his watch: ten minutes before the meeting was supposed to start. Everyone was there except Marius, their leader, who was never late but who was also rarely early.

Gunnar – short, somewhat stocky, and with disheveled hair in need of a barber's shears – was the new man in the cell; Jørgen thought he was trying too hard to gain acceptance. Gunnar was now waving the skeleton's hand at Svend, who laughed heartily and patted his large stomach. "Gunnar, please ask your bony friend what medicine she's taking; I could use some – my wife says I'm eating too much pastry."

Erik, perched on the edge of the examination table, smiled at Svend's self-deprecating retort. Jørgen knew Erik appreciated unassuming people like Svend. Erik had been his friend since boyhood. Jørgen looked at him with fondness; in the harsh light of the room,

Erik's red hair looked darker and his skin and green eyes paler than usual. He caught Jørgen's glance and grinned, tilting his head toward Gunnar and shrugging.

Lars sat on a low stool, his head buried in a dog eared copy of *De Frie Danske,* the underground publication. Jørgen had known Lars for almost as long as Erik, but he worried about him. A bit too raw and naïve, Lars sometimes seemed in over his head in Resistance work. Jørgen felt protective of him, as though he were Lars's elder brother. He had bailed him out of sticky situations on a couple of occasions. Maybe, Jørgen hoped, Lars would give up sabotage when he settled down with Inge, his pretty blond girlfriend.

The other two members of the cell, Jan and Wilhelm, Jørgen didn't know very well; they tended to keep to themselves. At the moment, they were pondering the anatomy of the human foot, depicted in full color on a wall poster.

Jørgen checked his watch again. He wished Marius would show up; Marius did not suffer fools gladly and his arrival would put an immediate end to Gunnar's annoying attempt at comedy. Jørgen had great respect for his cell leader. Marius was cold and distant – no one knew who Marius's friends were, or even if he had any friends – but he was dedicated, organized, and shrewd. Moreover, he had demonstrated formidable bravery in a number of operations.

Marius had selected Jørgen to be trained by the British Special Operations Executive. Jørgen remembered the cold night-time boat trip across the North Sea to Scotland with several members of other cells, followed by a long drive to a secluded and enormous nineteenth century mansion, known only as the STS – Special Training School.

Jørgen had spent a grueling three weeks learning survival skills, unarmed combat, sabotage, and how to shoot the center out of a bull's eye. At the end of this first phase, several in the group were deemed inadequate and were politely asked to leave. In the next few weeks he learned parachute jumping and how to throw himself out of a truck doing thirty miles an hour by rolling on his shoulder.

When he entered the final phase, known as 'Finishing School,' he thought the worst was over because it began with radio operation, a skill he already knew. But then, reduced to a handful, the group was sent on a field trip for several days to execute a hazardous mission. On his return, he had fallen into his bed as though he were practicing jumping out of a moving truck. At three in the morning, he was yanked from his cot, marched off in the dark, and subjected to a seven-hour interrogation by men dressed in Gestapo uniforms.

After six weeks of training with the SOE he was parachuted back into Denmark. As his chute drifted down, he made three resolutions for the moment he landed: he would hold his legs together, he would roll on his shoulder, and he would kiss the blessed ground of Denmark. Whatever lay ahead of him in the Resistance, he knew it couldn't be as tough as dealing with the Brit trainers.

The door banged open and Marius strode in. He did not look impressive – he was of average height, his hairline had begun to recede, and his Van Dyke beard was gray in spots. But he commanded respect. Gunnar quickly whisked the red scarf off the skeleton's shoulders and replaced the skeleton's arms, which had been wrapped around his neck.

Marius took his seat in the doctor's leather chair that had been kept free for him. "Well, gentlemen; let's get started."

Stockholm.

C hristina stared at the phone. Ring, damn you, ring. She paced up and down her room at the Hotel Sturegatan, then stopped to light a cigarette. She drew heavily and looked down from her window onto the leafy Humlegården. Why she was so nervous, she didn't know. Everything had gone smoothly. After a bumpy flight, she had arrived in Sweden safely and had been unloaded with the diplomatic pouch.

Not much had changed in Sweden, still enjoying its neutrality from the war. Life went on much as she recalled it so many years ago. But she was edgy. She wanted the job to be finished. She wanted the German to call her. She wanted to deliver the package to the embassy and hightail it back to the United States. And the one thousand dollars.

But the thought of the money failed to steady her nerves. She ground out the cigarette and lit another as she continued to peer out the window. It was late afternoon on the eve of the midsummer holiday, and the Humlegården was bathed in brilliant light by a sun still high in the sky. Everything looked normal.

And yet she saw danger everywhere. The man sitting on the bench reading a newspaper – perhaps he was a Gestapo agent. Perhaps, despite all the major's assurances, her cover had been blown. Maybe there was someone downstairs in the lobby checking the hotel register at that moment. She felt flushed and opened the window.

The man on the bench in the square folded his newspaper, got up and walked in the direction of the broad boulevard of Karlavägen. Get a grip on yourself, an inner voice told Christina. He was just a Swede enjoying the summer evening. She stared at the phone, as if staring would make it ring. It remained silent.

Down in the Humlegården, another man sat on the bench. He took off his Homburg hat and opened a newspaper. She was sure he was looking up at her window. To hell with it, she thought. She grabbed her purse. She'd go to the embassy and tell them she couldn't go through with it. They could stick the thousand dollars—

The phone rang. She stared at it, shook her head and made for the door. Another ring. She picked up the receiver.

The voice was German. "The days are very long in summer." His prearranged password phrase.

She heard herself answer with a voice that did not seem to belong to her. "And we must enjoy them."

There was a pause as he recognized the correct response. "Berliner Restaurant. Seven-thirty."

The line went dead.

Reichminister Speer's Office. Berlin.

"Well, what do you think of my little project, Heldorf?" Speer spread his arms wide over the huge model that occupied the room next to his office. "I thought you'd like to see what Berlin will look like after the war."

"It's magnificent, sir." Heldorf raised his eyebrows as he looked over the model. "A masterpiece of architectural design."

"There, close by the Templehof airport," Speer's finger pointed to a huge building, "will be the new Reich Chancellery." He smiled proudly. "It will be over a million square feet in area, complete with cinema and banqueting hall where the Führer can entertain his friends.

"And here," Speer walked around to the other side of the model, "will be the *pièce de resistance*. The Volkshalle."

Heldorf's mouth was agape. Even on the model, the building based on the Pantheon looked gargantuan.

"The top of the dome will be over eight hundred feet high and the dome itself will be large enough to dwarf that of St. Peter's Basilica. It will accommodate a crowd of almost two hundred thousand to hear the Führer speak. And there will be an eagle seventy-five feet tall."

Heldorf clicked his heels and inclined his head. "You are to be congratulated, Herr Reichminister. The new city of Berlin—"

"Germania."

"—Germania will be a fitting capital for National Socialist Germany."

"For the world, Heldorf – for the world."

Heldorf pondered the seriousness of Speer's utterance and was surprised to see the Reichminister throw his head back and laugh.

"Do you know, Heldorf, how many tons of granite the project will need?"

"I have no idea, sir."

Speer laughed again. "Neither does the Führer. He just tells me to get it."

Speer's laughter died away, replaced by a serious expression.

"But I have other things to occupy me at the moment. Like building fifty new armament factories and doubling the output of aircraft. And winning the war."

He turned away and headed for his office, beckoning the Sturmbannführer to follow. "Which brings us to your project, Heldorf." He went behind his desk and planted himself in an amply-upholstered chair. "Of which, as you are aware, the Führer knows nothing. Please take a seat and give me the news."

Heldorf sensed the veiled menace in Speer's voice as he sat down. If anything went wrong, Speer would wash his hands of everything.

"Well," Speer fixed him with a stare, "is everything going according to plan? Are there any problems?"

Hannah Goldmann's face came to mind, but he pushed it swiftly aside. "The project team has been assembled and will shortly be making an initial survey."

"You mean to say," Speer was genuinely surprised, "that you have experienced no problems whatever?"

"A small one, but it has been overcome."

"Tell me."

"One of the Jews refused to cooperate." Heldorf allowed a half smile to his lips. "On, shall we say, moral grounds."

"And?" Speer half anticipated the answer.

"He and his wife are back in a camp contemplating the superiority of his moral position. But, I expect, not for long."

"There are no problems with the other scientists?"

Heldorf chuckled. "The incident had the effect of concentrating their minds wonderfully."

Speer slapped his hand on the desk. "Excellent. You have done well, Heldorf. Now give me the bad news. Tell me what resources you need."

The SS man pulled two sheets of paper from his pocket. "Here are the requirements for the first phase. Page one outlines the technical needs, and the other page the logistical requirements."

Speer scanned the first page quickly. "Mass spectrometer, something called a Van de Graff generator..." he glanced down the paper and then looked up with a frown. "I have no idea what all this stuff is, but it sounds expensive."

Heldorf cleared his throat. "I can assure you, Herr Reichminister—"

Speer waved the air impatiently to silence him. "I'm not questioning your need for all this equipment. The end product is too important to quibble about the reichsmarks. I was just considering how to pay for it." He thrummed the desk as he thought and then chuckled. "Hmm…perhaps we can borrow a little from the Führer's granite budget."

Speer turned to the second page. "Now, the logistical requirements." His eyes ran down the list. "A small camp…canteen…shower block." He threw his head back and laughed. "My dear Heldorf, you have no idea how to run a camp of prisoners. Where is the barbed wire? Where is the regiment of soldiers needed to guard the camp?"

Heldorf leaned forward and rested his finger on an item on the list.

"That's it?" Speer looked unbelievingly. "Three guards, three men for staff support, and half-a-dozen German Shepherd dogs? Perhaps you really are crazy, Heldorf."

"No one on the team will have any wish to escape, sir." The SS man spoke confidently. "They have their relatives to consider. The dogs are simply to keep nosey people out."

"Nosey people? But what about the Royal Air Force? They can be very nosey." Speer scowled as he slapped the paper. "Where in your plans are the anti-aircraft batteries to keep the RAF at bay? The expense doesn't matter. How many do you need?"

"With respect, sir, the RAF will never find the camp and even ordinary nosey people will never visit."

"But where in Germany can you put the camp away from the RAF's bombers?" Speer was on the edge of anger.

"The camp is not situated in Germany, sir." Heldorf pulled a map from his briefcase and unfolded it. "It will be here." His finger ran up the eastern coast of Denmark and came to rest on a small dot. "Mørkø. An uninhabited island in the northern waters of the Kattegat. Halfway between Denmark and Sweden."

Stockholm.

The man with the Homburg hat was following her. Christina quickened her step as she left the hotel and made her way to the restaurant.

She resisted the urge to run. He had got up from the bench as she had left the lobby. Don't panic, she thought. Don't look back. She saw the traffic lights at the intersection ahead. Timing her approach carefully, she hurried across as the lights changed and made a sharp turn down Linnegaten.

Her breath came easier. She was sure she had lost him. A brief glance over her shoulder. There was no Homburg hat. No one was following her.

She wondered if her mind was playing tricks. Was she paranoid? If she'd known the job was going to mess up her mind, she wouldn't have taken it. Not even for a thousand dollars.

Christina turned down Grevgaten. Her efforts to shake off her pursuer had taken her away from the restaurant where she was to meet the German. She thought about von Rastenberg. The major had shown her a photo back in New York. Mature, handsome, his dark hair flecked with gray at the temples. Appealing, in a way.

She looked up at the clock on the square. Seven twenty. Ten minutes to the meeting. She crossed her fingers for luck.

The restaurant was on the opposite corner of the intersection. Christina crossed the street and approached the door. Soon she would meet the mysterious von Rastenberg. And then a pleasant dinner, some idle conversation, and she would be away with the message. She glanced in the window hoping to get a view of the German.

She didn't see him. What she did see, as she reached for the doorknob, was a reflection in the glass. Behind her, across the street, was the man wearing a Homburg hat.

Special Quarters outside Berlin.

In the end, Max's evil ploy had not caused her to change her mind. It was something else.

Hannah Goldmann lay on the cot in her tiny room and watched a fly make its way in fits and starts across the ceiling. How dare it be alive when her family was dead? The fly disappeared from the ceiling and was replaced by faces she loved. She could see her sweet sister, Rachel, just having fallen in love and planning to get married. And there was her mother, standing in a kitchen filled with the aroma of baking bread, smiling and drying her hands on her apron. And she saw her father, tall and erect, his hands on her shoulders and his eyes locked on hers on the day she took her degree from the University of Leipzig.

Her father. She had been her father's favorite, just as Rachel had been her mother's. Although her father had been forced to drop out of school when he was only ten, he was a learned man, always reading, often regretting the lack of formal education which kept him employed as a watchmaker's bookkeeper.

When Hannah began doing well in mathematics and science at school, her father had seen the possibility of his dreams being realized through her. He arranged for Hannah's chores to be lighter than Rachel's to allow more time for her to study, and Hannah had paid him back by taking all the science prizes. When she went on to Leipzig University, her father toiled at two jobs to pay for her education.

The fly had buzzed to a window and was battering futilely against the glass. He, too, wanted his freedom.

On the day she graduated with top honors her father embraced her, put his hands upon her shoulders and, looking earnestly into her eyes, had said, "Hannah, you are my life. Through you, I live."

She rolled over and a tear raced out of the side of her eye and fell onto her hand. Papa, she thought, would you have wanted me to do this? Would you have wanted me to sell my soul to stay alive?

She could hear her father's deep voice almost as clearly as if he had been in the room. "You must live, Hannah," she heard him say. "You are the reason I was born."

Stockholm.

Franz von Rastenberg sipped his beer and looked out from the restaurant onto the square. His ramrod-straight back gave him a dignified and somewhat aloof air, although it was partly the legacy of a riding accident in his childhood. His elegant dress and impeccable grooming hinted at aristocratic roots. And dark hair graying at the temples together with brown eyes fringed with long lashes conspired to make him handsome despite a weak jaw and an aquiline nose.

He had taken a roundabout route to get to the restaurant and had made sure he arrived early. He didn't expect to be followed – after all, he was a regular visitor to Stockholm on his way to official business at the heavy water plant in Norway – but he wanted to play safe. There had been no tail.

"Are you ready to order, sir?" The waiter spoke German. The cuisine of the restaurant catered to the German taste and von Rastenberg always came when he was in Stockholm. The sauerbraten, pork loin with spaetzle, and roast goose stuffed with apples and prunes were all done to perfection.

"Not yet, Bjorn." He put down his glass. "I'm expecting a guest. Quite soon."

He glanced at his watch. Seven thirty-five. She was late. He hoped nothing had gone wrong.

A woman came down the street, but she walked past the restaurant. He looked again at his watch. Seven thirty-seven. Where was she?

And then he saw her, crossing the square. It was uncanny – the hair, the way she walked. For a moment, an irrational hope loomed in his heart; could it be? The woman approached the door of the restaurant and grasped the handle. He could see her eyes and mouth clearly now; they were the same as….

He forced his mind to think sanely as he watched her enter. It couldn't be. Elsa had been dead for six months.

Special Quarters outside Berlin.

He had not thought twice before accepting Heldorf's offer to work on the project.

Head bowed and shoulders hunched, Artur Steinitz sat on the edge of his cot and pushed his thick glasses back up the bridge of his nose with long, slender fingers. He recalled the day he had been declared an enemy of the people by virtue of having been born a Jew. The Nazi official pushed a form in front of him, a declaration of property, on which he dutifully recorded his meager bank balance and the few sticks of furniture in his apartment in Berlin. Then he came to the section labeled 'Art and Items of Value.' His violin; his beautiful old violin. His fingers begged him to stop as he entered it on the form.

In his early days at Auschwitz, he wept with his desire to play a Beethoven violin sonata. His fingers ached to hold his instrument again, cradle it under his chin, feel the pressure of the strings, draw the bow across it in a sweeping arc.

The image of his violin had faded as the months at Auschwitz ground him down and broke his spirit. He learned to submit, to grovel, to take gratuitous punishment, to endure without complaint, and, above all, to survive. It was a lesson he had learned well and he had carried it into his meeting with Heldorf.

"How would you like to see your—," Heldorf had put on his glasses and had read from a file, "—how would you like to see your beloved cousin, Hermann, released from camp?"

Hermann? Artur Steinitz had met him once, maybe twice in his life, and he had not liked him very much. But Hermann was his last surviving relative. He had never married and all the others – his aunts, uncles, brothers, sister, nephews – had been killed.

Obeying Nazi orders was now so programmed into Artur's psyche he did not hesitate to prostitute his physics skills. His moral backbone had been broken, his nerves shattered. He could no longer stand up for his beliefs, because he no longer believed in anything.

"Fine," he had said. "Fine. I'll work for you."

Stockholm.

Christina closed the restaurant door behind her. She didn't look back; she knew the man with the Homburg hat was there.

"*Guten Abend, Fräulein.*" The waiter's voice startled her; the German tongue was unexpected. She struggled to find her composure but replied fluently.

"I'm here as a guest of—"

"She's my guest, Bjorn."

Christina turned toward the voice that came from the window table. He looked different from the photographs she had been shown. Older, more rugged. But handsome. Yet it was the way he looked at her, as if he had seen a ghost, that unnerved her.

"Herr von Rastenberg?"

He got up from the table and approached her. "Franz, please, Fräulein Lindgren." A warm smile replaced the startled look. "Won't you join me at the table?"

She cast her eyes nervously around the restaurant. "Can we please sit somewhere else other than the window table?"

He saw her anxiety and the smile slipped from his face. "What's the matter? Is something wrong?"

She glanced briefly toward the window. "I think I'm being followed."

The smile returned to his face. "My dear Fräulein Lindgren, if you've been followed, it's better to behave normally, as if you've nothing to fear." He took her lightly by the upper arm and led her to the table by the window.

"But I *was* followed. I know it." Christina's mind raced as she tried to grasp the situation. Had she walked into a trap? Her eyes ran over von Rastenberg's face. There was no trace of alarm. She wondered why he didn't show any concern. If he was carrying the message, wasn't his own neck on the line?

He signaled to the waiter as he politely pulled back her chair and slid it under her as she sat down. "Please, Fräulein Lindgren—"

"Please call me Christina."

"Christina, it's important not to panic." He settled into his own seat and arranged his napkin over his lap. "I suggest we enjoy our meal and relax for a while." He took the menu from the waiter and ran his finger down the list of fare. "May I recommend the sauerbraten with red cabbage? Almost impossible to find in Germany nowadays. It's delicious."

"But how can you sit there so calmly?" Christina toyed nervously with her glass of water. "There's a Gestapo agent following me and he's right across the street."

"What if he is a Gestapo agent? What can he do?" Von Rastenberg ordered and handed the menu to the waiter. "He can't just walk in here and arrest you."

Christina blanched at the horrendous thought and he reached out and placed his hand gently on hers. "I'm sorry. I didn't mean to alarm you." The hand lingered. "But, truly, there's little he can do." He ordered the wine. "In Berlin, sadly, such things happen." He sighed. "Or even in Paris and Brussels. Anywhere the Nazis rule, people can vanish overnight. But this is Stockholm, and Sweden is a neutral country."

He didn't convince her. She still felt uneasy.

"Ah, here comes the wine. It's a good Gewürztraminer; I'm sure you'll enjoy it."

She sipped at the glass, but couldn't help but let her eyes wander to the bench across the square. The man in the Homburg hat was still there.

Special Quarters outside Berlin.

Ernst Schlegel and Georg Silberstein, bunking together, lay on their cots before the big meeting with Heldorf, each lost in thought.

The last time Ernst Schlegel and his brother, Aaron, had been to-gether – almost a year ago, just after Ernst's thirty-seventh birthday – they had made a pact. If either got out of camp alive and escaped from Germany, he would bear testimony to the unspeakable crimes against their people, would become a loud and eloquent voice for those who could not speak. Surely, the message could not fail to unleash the out-rage of the world. If the world would listen.

Ernst's scientific opinion was that Heldorf's bomb could not be built. It was a gamble, but he had agreed to work for Heldorf on a goal that was an anathema; thereby, he had gained Aaron's release. The al-ternative, both for himself and for Aaron, was death. Dead, they could not tell their story. Now Aaron was in Switzerland. With luck, he might get to the United States. He at least could bear testimony.

Compared to a few weeks before, life for Georg Silberstein was al-most perfect. Of course, he had wished that when Sturmbannführer Heldorf had released his daughter he would also release his son, but the Nazi had personally guaranteed his son's freedom at the conclusion of the project.

Apart from his family's release was the allure of the science. At forty-nine, ten years after being banned from the university laboratory, he could scarcely believe he was returning to the field of physics. He knew some of the others – including the Goldmann woman – thought along the same lines.

The extraction of the rare isotope from natural uranium posed a highly interesting problem. He had come up with three possible ways the problem could be approached; further analysis would have to wait until he had proper equipment.

He could hardly wait to get started. For the first time in years, he felt alive.

Stockholm.

"Are you finding our German food to your liking?" Von Rastenberg appeared relaxed, more as if he were enjoying a pre-theater dinner than delivering the message of a spy.

"It's truly wonderful," Christina felt the sauerbraten dissolve on her tongue, "but I must say it's difficult to enjoy a meal when a Gestapo agent is sitting on a bench across the street watching you."

Von Rastenberg patted his lips with his napkin. "Is he the short stocky man, wearing a Homburg hat?"

Christina forced herself not to look across the street. "Yes, that's him."

"My dear Christina, I can assure you that the man is not a Gestapo agent."

Christina felt a knot of foreboding. "How can you be so sure?"

Von Rastenberg looked at her and smiled. "Because I know every Gestapo agent in Stockholm."

Special Quarters outside Berlin.

Sol Friedberg fingered the fabric of his new suit. Not bad, he thought. Of course, it wouldn't be good enough for Helga. Nothing was ever good enough for Helga. He put on the shirt. The arms were a bit long, but he was in no position to complain.

As he buttoned the shirt, he chuckled as he thought about how the Sturmbannführer had said to him "Wouldn't you like to see your beloved wife, Helga, safe and sound in a neutral country?" His beloved wife? Helga the Horrible? Helga the Harridan? The neutral country could have her. For forty years she had made his life a living hell, always chiding him about how he didn't move up the ladder fast enough. Back in the days when there was a ladder.

He put on the trousers. Too big at the waist, but he could pull the belt tight. At sixty-two, Sol felt ancient. When they took him to the labor camp, he knew he would not last out the month. Then he had been given this second chance, a chance to make the best of what little time was left to him. Free of Helga. Away from the camp.

He sat on the edge of the cot tying his shoes; a bit tight in the toes, but they were nice and shiny. He sat up and blew through his teeth noisily. He knew he wasn't going to use his scientific background to find a cure for poverty and disease; he'd be using his talents to further death and destruction, and he'd have a lot to answer for in the hereafter. If there was a hereafter, which he doubted.

He stood up and looked at himself in the mirror. He could see the shine of his scalp through his thinning white hair, and his sagging face reminded him of melting wax running down a candle. His unruly eyebrows now resembled abandoned birds' nests.

He winced, looked away, and returned to his meditations. Using his talents for death and destruction was not a very nice thing. But what about the death and destruction of Albert Weiss's family, didn't that matter? They were his real family. During the times Helga had thrown him out of the house, Al and Rebecca had taken him in. And then, after Kristallnacht, they had risked their own lives to save his. Now he had a chance to pay them back. Al's family meant more to him than the faceless crowds a bomb might destroy.

He put on the jacket and adjusted the collar. Wasn't he only human? What did the deaths of fifty strangers on a speeding bus matter if he could save the life of the good friend standing next to him?

Stockholm.

Christina's fork fell with a clatter to her plate. "You know all the Gestapo agents in Stockholm?"

"Oh, my dear, I didn't mean to alarm you." Von Rastenberg patted her hand reassuringly. "I meant I know the *face* of every Gestapo agent here – I don't actually know them personally."

Relief swept through Christina as he continued. "You see, I make frequent visits to Norway – on business, of course – and I pass through Stockholm most of the time." He saw her look down at his hand resting on hers and he withdrew it.

"I get to know the faces of all the agents." He laughed. "They're always sticking their noses into other people's business. Of course, I have full security clearance – it's essential for my work in Norway – so they can't touch me." He glanced out of the window. "And I've never seen that fellow's face before." He pulled the bottle from the wine bucket. "More wine?"

"But that guy followed me!" She saw that the waiter had heard her raised voice.

"Perhaps he's the sort of man who follows pretty women." Von Rastenberg refilled her glass. "Come, Christina, let's enjoy our meal. Why don't you tell me about life in America?"

A Meeting Room. Special Quarters outside Berlin.

So I'm about to start a new career in physics, Albert Weiss thought as he glanced around the empty conference room. Who would have guessed it when I was emptying garbage cans at the university, when I had to sneak into the physics library after hours to check up on the latest developments? Now I'm about to lead perhaps the greatest enterprise in the history of physics.

He picked up a pencil and began to write down the agenda for the meeting. One: review Heisenberg's papers on thermal diffusion isotope separation. Two: consider the merits of other methods of separating out U-235. Three....

His mind drifted. Rebecca should be safe now, he thought. His wife and his daughters were all that mattered. Even so, he shuddered at the enormity of what he was being asked to do: produce fissile material for a device that could destroy cities and turn human beings into piles of ashes. And, if he and the other scientists did produce fuel for such a device, it would be placed in the hands of a madman. The proposition was ghastly, and every day since he had met with Heldorf, misgivings had troubled him.

But he had no choice. He loathed Hitler, but he couldn't afford the luxury of summoning up pity for his enemies. He remembered how, before the war, Hitler was applauded by some in Britain and the United States for crushing the workers' movements. How, long after Kristall-nacht screamed out to the world of the atrocities toward his people, American firms continued to help Hitler build his tanks.

Weiss's fists tightened as he remembered how his wife had fainted as they stood for endless hours in line at the American embassy desperately hoping for a visa. He had been offered an excellent position at an American university, but even so they were denied asylum; no reason was offered. And then there was his brother, Abe, who had had the sense to flee Germany in the early thirties and emigrate to England. But after the war broke out he was confined there as an 'enemy alien' because he was German. For the love of God, Abe was a Jew!

I'll work to produce the fissile material, he decided. It has bought freedom for Rebecca, and if it will buy the same for my daughters, I'll work hard.

Weiss was jolted out of his thoughts by Heldorf, who entered the room with a wide smile and a jaunty stride. "Good evening, Dr. Weiss. I have a very pleasant surprise for you." He pulled a letter out of his pocket and handed it to Weiss who immediately saw it was from Rebecca.

"I'll let you read it in private." Heldorf turned toward the door. "See you in half an hour for the meeting with the other scientists," he shouted over his shoulder as he closed the door behind him.

His hands trembling, Weiss carefully opened the letter.

My dearest husband,

After a long journey, I have at last arrived at my new home in Lisbon. My accommodations are not grand, but they are perfectly adequate.

I have enough.

I am very tired from the trip and I need to rest now, but, of course, I first wanted to write you this brief note. I count the days when you, Naomi, Miriam, and I can all be together again.

Your loving wife,
Rebecca

Something was wrong, very wrong. She had not mentioned their secret code, the number 82, to indicate that she had made it to Portugal. Weiss checked the back of the letter, held it up to the light, examined the envelope. The number 82 was nowhere to be found.

Rebecca had not made it out of Germany.

Stockholm.

The wine and small talk had eased Christina's fears and she felt comfortable in von Rastenberg's company. He was polite, charming, and he exuded confidence. But she kept glancing across the street to the man in the Homburg hat.

She turned her eyes back to the German and found him looking at her in the same dreamy way he had when she had first arrived. She saw a danger signal. Perhaps if she had met him in Providence, she might have considered.... But certainly not under these circumstances, certainly not when she had to get the package out and was being followed. Any flirtation with him had to be nipped in the bud.

"Is there something wrong? Why are you looking at me like that?" There was a sharp edge to her voice.

The look – and his self-confidence – fell away. "I'm so sorry – please forgive me." He blushed like a boy caught with his hand in the cookie jar.

"Look," Christina spoke bluntly, "I think we should do the business we have to do and get moving." She tossed her napkin onto the table.

His hand reached into his inside coat pocket, and she thought he was going to pass over the package she had to take to the embassy. Instead, he pulled out his wallet.

"Please, no, wait." His fingers dug into the wallet. "Let me explain." He took out an old photograph. As he pushed it across the table Christina saw that it was creased with the ravages of time. Then she caught her breath as she saw the face looking up at her: it was a photograph of her.

A Meeting Room. Special Quarters outside Berlin.

Albert Weiss felt great pain in his heart. He shuddered and thought he was going to be sick.

He'd been such a fool. The Nazis had tricked them all. And now Heldorf's treachery had been confirmed by Rebecca's letter: she had obviously been forced to write it. By not including their secret code, the number 82, she had signaled to him that Heldorf had not honored the deal. Tears came to his eyes. The tender moment when they reminisced about hearing the Bach cantata which became their code number – that was the last time he would ever see her.

He would tell the other scientists that they were all being duped, that their work for Heldorf must not go forward. Working for the Nazis was bad enough when they thought that by so doing they could buy freedom for their loved ones. Without that guarantee, there could be no deal. Of course, they would all be shipped back to the camps. And death.

Weiss picked up the letter and read again.

> …After a long journey, I have at last arrived at my new home in Lisbon. My accommodations are not grand, but they are perfectly adequate.
> <u>I have enough.</u>

'I have enough.' Why had Rebecca underlined 'I have enough'? Had she meant to say 'I've had enough'?

Suddenly he slapped his forehead. "Weiss, you *meshugener!*" His heart raced wildly. He brought the letter to his lips and kissed it. "Dear, sweet, Rebecca, you wonderful woman!" he said softly. "You never had a head for numbers, but you always, always remember a name."

I have enough. *Ich habe genug.* The name of Bach's Cantata 82.

Rebecca was in Lisbon.

Stockholm.

"Who is…who is she?" Christina picked up the photo to look at it more closely. The blue eyes, her cheeks dimpling as she grinned – the woman seemed her identical twin. Even the blond hair was done in the same upswept style. The hair was a little thicker than her own and the woman had earrings that were not to Christina's taste, but she felt an eerie sensation that she was looking at a picture of herself, yet knowing it could not be so.

"I hope now you will forgive me for staring at you." Von Rastenberg drank deeply from his glass. "Perhaps you can now understand why I looked at you so strangely."

"But who is she?" Christina's eyes remained fixed on the image.

"She's Elsa, my late wife. You can see a remarkable likeness."

"Your *late* wife?" The question came out before she had time to rein it in.

Christina flushed. She looked down at the picture of a vibrant young woman, a woman who looked like her. The smile, so like her own smile, was gone, gone forever.

"I'm so sorry." She reached out for his hand.

"It's alright. My work has eased the pain." His smile was uneasy.

She knew it was not the truth. Pain like that surely never went away.

He picked up the photo and looked at it for a few moments. "She was expecting a child. She was about—," he lifted his eyes and looked at her directly, "—she was about your age." He pushed the photo into his wallet and returned it to his pocket.

Christina fought for words, but none came. She squeezed his hand. He looked at her briefly, and then she was astonished to see the self-assured von Rastenberg reappear within moments.

"And now, Christina, we must attend to our business."

"You have the package for me?" The image of von Rastenberg's late wife hung heavy in Christina's mind, and the change of topic came as a relief.

"Yes, but I think it's too risky to give it to you here." He called the waiter and whispered at length in his ear. The waiter nodded and hurried away.

"Listen closely, Christina." He leant forward, speaking quickly. "At the back of the restaurant is a door leading to the restrooms. Beyond that is another door that opens onto a parking lot. A taxi will be there soon. Get in and I shall join you within a minute. We shall go to my hotel."

Christina was perplexed, flustered. "But what's the rush? You told me the guy out there wasn't a Gestapo agent. What's the problem?"

There was a signal from the waiter. "Go now." Von Rastenberg's voice was unusually anxious. He threw several bills onto the table to cover the check. "The man you pointed out is not a Gestapo agent." The waiter beckoned urgently. "But the man on the other corner of the street is."

Special Quarters outside Berlin.

Heldorf entered the meeting room where the scientists were assembled and strode to the head of the table.

"Good evening, everyone. I welcome you all to an elite team – a team that will do exciting research, a team that will push the boundaries of physics well beyond their present limits."

The Jews stared back at him, glassy-eyed.

"Most of you know each other personally. Many of you have worked together, written papers together. You each, I know, esteem the work and expertise of every other person in this room. Although I am well aware that, from time to time, friendly scientific squabbles over some abstruse point of physics are bound to arise even in the best of families." The sturmbannführer seemed amused at his remark, and a forced, weak laugh came from his audience.

"Fellow scientists, I leave you now in the capable hands of Dr. Weiss, who shall lead your efforts. In a few weeks, after our laboratories and other facilities are constructed, we shall move this scientific team to a new location. In the meantime, there is much you can do here, as you examine the papers of Professor Heisenberg – who failed where you shall succeed – and as, formula by formula, you uncover the theoretical flaws in his work. And so I bid you a good evening."

Eyes flitted discreetly about the room as they assessed each other. Was anyone in their number the eyes and ears of Heldorf? Who knew? It would be best to keep opinions about their unlikely mission to themselves. Heldorf had demanded that each of them keep their private agreement with him strictly confidential as a condition of the deal.

All eyes snapped to the other end of the table, which Weiss was slapping with the flat of his hand to bring the room to attention. "Well then, shall we get started?"

Stockholm.

Christina looked around carefully as she pushed on the hotel foyer door and stepped out onto the street. As she had expected, von Rastenberg had been the perfect gentleman, sleeping on the couch in his hotel room after offering her his bed. She had left early, before he had awakened, anxious to deliver the package.

She looked left and right and gave a small sigh of relief. There wasn't a Homburg hat in sight. Her watch showed seven o'clock, yet the sun had already climbed high into the sky as the long first day of the Swedish summer began to unfold. She checked again before setting out for the taxi stand at the end of the street, her hand clutching tightly at her purse. Inside was the package. Soon she would be home free, back in the United States. And with a thousand dollars to spend on a new sailboat.

There was no cab at the stand. Perhaps it would be better to wait in the hotel, she thought as she turned. And then she saw him. He was wearing a leather coat. It was the other man who had been outside the restaurant the previous night, the one Franz had spotted.

He stood one hundred yards away at the entrance to the hotel. There was no way back. She walked quickly away, her heels clicking on the sidewalk. She paused briefly to check a shop window. The leather coat was following her.

Her mind raced. Don't panic. But she couldn't help it. Perhaps what was in the package was so important that the Gestapo were prepared to flout the neutrality rules. What if they grabbed her and took her to the German embassy? She shivered and quickened her pace. The American embassy was about five minutes away.

Maybe her mind was playing tricks. She stopped again, pretending to window shop. The man stopped. Then she saw the other man. Ahead of her, about a block away. He was coming toward her. She tried to remain cool, but found that her feet hurried to a pace of their own. The man ahead was bearing down on her, an unsmiling mouth beneath unfriendly eyes. She looked behind her and saw his colleague. She was trapped.

Christina cast her eyes about frantically for a policeman, but saw nothing except an old man walking his dog. She turned down a side street and began to run. The embassy was only two blocks away. Her arms pumped as she picked up the pace. She rounded another corner and almost didn't see the newsstand. Her arm brushed against a rack of newspapers, bringing them clattering to the ground.

She began to fall, but recovered. The newsvendor shouted after her; she turned and saw the two men fifty yards behind. They spotted her and started to run. Her tired legs screamed at her as she tried to quicken her pace, her breast heaving as she gasped for air.

There was a narrow side street to her left; she didn't know where it led. She heard their shoes beating a steady staccato on the sidewalk behind, gaining on her. She turned into the side street. And ran straight into the man with the Homburg hat.

Her hands pummeled against his body as she sought to escape, but he knocked her arms aside and seized them in a bear hug. She kicked against his shins, but his grip held her helpless. She heard the shouts of her pursuers. She was lost.

"Calm down, miss, calm down!"

The American accent surprised her. She stopped struggling.

"The people at the embassy told me to make sure you didn't get into trouble." He pointed to a car parked at the curb. "Quick, get in!"

She no longer knew whom to trust. Breathless, she stumbled into the back seat as the man leapt behind the wheel. He gunned the engine and the tires squealed.

"We'll soon have you safe in the embassy."

Christina turned and looked through the rear window. The two Gestapo men were watching the escaping car.

"Go!" she screamed at the man in the Homburg hat. "Get me to the embassy!"

Never again, she thought. Not even for a thousand dollars.

PART TWO

*"If you gaze for long into an abyss,
the abyss gazes also into you."*

—Nietzsche, *Beyond Good and Evil*

SEPTEMBER 12, 1942

Mørkø Island. The Kattegat, between Denmark and Sweden

M ax Heldorf stood on the northern tip of the island and scanned his surroundings; the place was even more desolate than he had imagined. The wind was unrelenting; the tall yellow grass was doubled over as if pleading for mercy from the blast and the few bushes that eked out a stunted existence in the sandy soil clawed the air convulsively.

He was looking around the site, having arrived a few days before the Jews to make sure all was in order. The nuclear physics compound was completely satisfactory. His plans had been followed accurately, and the hastily-built wooden huts with pitched roofs, while far from handsome, were sturdy enough. His feet trod along the sandy path leading to the south of the island. The Jews' quarters on his left faced a fully-equipped laboratory to his right. Beyond these was his office. He peered inside; his aide-de-camp, whose living quarters were next door, was unpacking a typewriter from a box. Across the path from his office was the conference hut; there, to make sure progress was rapid, he would hold the Jews' feet to the fire in weekly meetings.

Continuing down the path, he came to his own quarters; that morning, he had carefully arranged a few cherished items around the room to make it appear more like home. On the wall he had hung a group photo of his old SS unit which featured Himmler in the front row. On his desk he had placed a cut glass ashtray with a swastika carved into the bottom. And atop a bookcase he had put a recent picture of his mother, from whom he had parted in Berlin only the day before.

He continued walking to the southern tip of the island and looked out over the Kattegat, the fifty-mile stretch of sea between Denmark and Sweden. Clouds, a shade of gray only slightly lighter than the slate of the water, scudded overhead. He took a deep breath; the vast dome of the sky met the endless plane of the sea and gave him a sense of limitless possibility. His heart leapt; he knew his plan would succeed.

He heard the barking of the dogs in their kennels on the western shore. The German Shepherds and the three guards stationed nearby were there to discourage the curious from landing on the only part of the island accessible to boats. The dogs and guards would not be needed to keep order among the Jews; it was the beauty of his plan: their community would be largely self-policing. To ensure that their individual interests – their loved ones in the camps – were protected, each Jew would help guarantee that all the other Jews behaved.

He picked his way northwest along the rocky shore and saw the supply boat tied up at the pier. The two men who manned it would manage the canteen and take care of general maintenance for the compound in addition to making trips into Frederikshavn for food and other essentials.

He looked out to sea again, marveling at the ingenuity of his plan. A large bird folded its wings back, dived into the water, and emerged with its prize. He admired the bird: it focused on what it wanted, made a plan to get it, and went after it. He would do the same. A time-tested recipe for success. He could not fail.

Frederikshavn, Denmark.

Jørgen reached nervously under the table for the toolbox; earlier, he had packed it with plastic explosives beneath a camouflage of small tools. When he brought his hand up, he ran his sweaty palms over his workpants and fought to hold back a wave of fear and nausea. It would be the biggest operation the Frederikshavn cell had ever undertaken. Marius had carefully planned and rehearsed all the details with them. If they succeeded, it would be a major step up from the small actions that had been merely annoyances to the Nazis; if they failed, they'd all land in Gestapo cells.

From the café window he had a clear view of their target across the street: the Frederikshavn Exhibition Hall. Or what used to be the Exhibition Hall – Danish workers were now hard at work inside transforming it into the new barracks for the Wehrmacht. Jørgen remembered going to livestock shows in the Hall with his father, and once one of his aunts had won a blue ribbon there in a quilting exhibition. He sipped his ersatz coffee and looked anxiously at his watch: in a few minutes the workmen would take their lunch break.

The noon whistle cracked the air and the workmen poured out of the building and headed off to their lunches. Jørgen watched as the exodus trickled to a few men, then no one. He looked at his watch: 12:06. Five minutes had to elapse after the last man left before they could begin. Five minutes to ensure no one else was inside.

At Marius's signal, Gunnar, wearing the white coat of a grocer, rode up to the building on his bicycle with a case of Tuborg beer strapped to the handlebars. As Gunnar approached one of the doors, Jørgen's stomach lurched as a German guard stepped out of the shadows and motioned for Gunnar to stop. Jørgen could see that the German wanted to look inside the case, and Gunnar took off the lid and showed him the bottles. The German smiled, cupped his hand and held it high, mouthed the word *Skål,* and waved Gunnar inside. Despite his fright, Jørgen chuckled at the incident; under the so-called peaceful occupation, some of the Germans were still trying hard to become the Danes' best friends.

Jørgen left the café with his toolbox and headed for a side door of the hall. He saw Marius and Erik, also dressed in workmen's clothes and carrying toolboxes, walking apart, converging on different doors. None of them acknowledged any of the others. Two German officers paused briefly and watched them, but then walked on.

Inside the empty hall, Gunnar had already taken out the beer and was unloading the plastic explosives that lay underneath. After the others had taken the explosives from their toolboxes, Marius directed them, referring to a marked-up blueprint of the Hall, on where to plant the explosives. They set the fuses, dashed out separate doors, jumped onto their bicycles, and disappeared down the maze of back lanes of Frederikshavn. The explosion rocked the entire city and beyond.

Later that afternoon, when Jørgen rode by on his bicycle, a crowd had gathered to watch the Germans comb through the debris; the Danes cheered as though they were at a soccer game. All that was left of the future Wehrmacht barracks were a few twisted ribs of metal framework that stabbed the gray afternoon sky like the frozen fingers of a giant corpse.

Frederikshavn, Denmark. Gronborg's Kosher Butcher Shop

"And then do you know what I said to her?" Gerda Rosenfeld warmed to her topic. Under the guise of begging a small quantity of offal for rendering, she had stopped in at Sara's shop to deliver the latest piece of gossip. "I said to her, 'Do you want I should—'"

As Sara finished wrapping the offal in brown paper, the doorbell jingled; two men wearing black uniforms and red armbands walked in. On each armband was a swastika within a white circle, but Sara knew the men were not German: they were members of the Danish Nazi Party. The party was small, but its members had a bad reputation. The taller of the two held up his hand and said with affected politeness, "Please, don't mind us. We'll just wait until you're done."

Sara tied a string around the package and handed the offal to Gerda, who hurriedly wished her a good day and, eyes cast down as she passed the two strangers, scurried out of the store.

"Good afternoon. May I help you?" Sara asked.

"Good afternoon," the tall one said. "Yes, we would like your best cut of meat. Let's take a look at what you have today." He leaned down and peered into the case; recent months had brought severe shortages and the selection was sparse and not of the best quality. "Hmm…Steffen, what do you think of that piece there? It looks like it came from an emaciated cow, but it might be edible."

"I'm sorry," Sara interjected, "but that piece is not for sale."

"Excuse me? You have meat on display that's not for sale?" The tall man stood up and frowned.

"I'm sorry. You see, the rabbi's wife already bought and paid for it, but she had to go somewhere and—"

"Do you take us for fools? And would you put a Jew ahead of us?" He turned to the other man. "Steffen, did you see what I saw? This woman didn't ask for the ration book of her last customer. Isn't that a reportable offense?"

The offal Sara had given Gerda was waste material not subject to rationing, but she sensed that the Nazis were out to make trouble. "Oh, please, please…" She grabbed the meat that she had promised to the

89

rabbi's wife – she'd understand – and frantically began wrapping it up. "Take it, please—"

"I'm no longer interested, Madam. And I'd watch my step if I were you." The tall man turned on his heel and left. The other man, who had said nothing the entire time, remained for a moment staring malevolently at Sara and shook his head before following.

Sara nervously busied herself tidying up the counter. She knew they could cause her trouble.

Peder, who had seen everything from a corner of the room, ran out a back door before his mama could notice. He had to get Jørgen.

Providence, Rhode Island. Army Translation Unit.

Christina read what she had just translated:

TOP SECRET

The British Special Operations Executive (SOE), which is now supplying weapons and ammunition to the Danish Resistance, has reported that forty new drop zones have been identified in Denmark.

While the German occupation of Denmark had been relatively peaceful, recent weeks have seen a marked increase in the number of strikes and acts of sabotage. Members of the Danish Resistance...

Christina looked out over the sea of desks, each with its clattering typewriter, but saw and heard nothing in the large room. She felt a strange kinship with the Danish Resistance. When she had been a small girl in Sweden, she and her family used to take trips there; her uncle had taught her to sail in the Kattegat off the coast of Jutland. And like the Danish Resistance, she, too had been in harm's way for her country. She shuddered as she remembered the Gestapo thugs chasing her down the Stockholm street the previous summer.

Suddenly all the desks in the room, along with their clattering typewriters, came back into sharp focus. It was good to be in Providence, good to be home: she had never realized what a luxury it was just to be able to feel safe every day. She reached over and patted her typewriter affectionately. "It's just you and me now, kiddo, doing our bit here in the good old USA. I promise I'll never leave you again."

Frederikshavn, Denmark. Sara's Butcher Shop.

As Peder squatted on the floor looking up at his mama, Jørgen put his arm around her, trying to calm her down. "Mrs. Gronborg, what's happened? Are you hurt?"

"He...He..." The memory of the incident made her cry. She took the handkerchief Jørgen offered, wiped her eyes, and tried again. "He wanted a certain piece of meat, but I'd already sold it to the rabbi's wife, so I told him—"

"Who wanted the meat, Mrs. Gronborg?"

"The tall one. There were two of them, both members of that horrible Nazi Party."

"What happened then?"

"He'd seen me give some discarded bits to Gerda." She blew her nose and looked up at him. "He said I had broken the law because I didn't stamp her ration book. Jørgen, I swear to you, the pieces I gave her weren't fit even for Peder's dog."

"Shh, it's okay." Jørgen rubbed her shoulder. "You did nothing wrong and they knew it. They were looking to cause trouble."

"Jørgen, I've heard they work with the Gestapo." She squeezed his arm tightly in panic. "I've heard that they rat on our own people."

"Shh," was the only response Jørgen could manage, but he knew that what Sara said was true. Danish Nazis acted as informers and were employed by the Gestapo to monitor radio messages. When a Resistance member was captured, they were only too eager to help out as translators during the interrogations. But Jørgen said nothing; he did not wish to upset Sara even more.

Sara looked at Jørgen and scowled. "Some people," there was an accusatory look in her eyes, and it was clear to Jørgen that the admonition was directed at him personally, "some people have not helped this situation, Jørgen. Some people feel they have to go around picking fights with the Germans – you know, staging strikes and bombing businesses that were forced to help the German army and all that. But what's the point? It only brings more trouble, and the trouble usually comes down on the heads of people who mean no harm. Like when the Germans blew up Mikkelsen's bakery after the exhibition hall was dynamited."

Jørgen suppressed his anger. "Mrs. Gronborg, the Nazis have robbed us of our country. If we have any self-respect, we've got to try to take it back."

"But we're such a tiny country, and they're so—"

"The important thing now is not to panic, Mrs. Gronborg. They left your shop peacefully and no harm was done. All I can do now is mention the incident to some friends of mine to see what they think."

"I've heard about those friends of yours." She wagged her finger at him. "I just hope they don't go making even more trouble for me."

Peder got up from the floor, went over to Sara, and took hold of her hand. "Mama," he said softly, "don't cry."

German Nuclear Physics Installation, Marka Island

The scientists filed in and took their seats in the cold, bare room that was used for meetings at their compound on the windswept island. All was silent save for an occasional cough, the shuffling of feet, the flipping of pages around the table as everyone studied their notes and pretended interest in the sorry results of their experiments.

Heldorf wanted to sigh with despair, but held himself in check. In earlier meetings, exasperated by their lack of success since their arrival on the island, he had tried both incentives and threats as goads. Neither was needed: the scientists had worked tirelessly, driven almost as much by their passion for the physics as by their zeal to see their families released from the camps. But they could not do what could not be done.

"Gentlemen," Heldorf affected a composed demeanor, "I bring this meeting to order. Dr. Weiss, we'll start with your report. What progress has the thermal diffusion team made over the past week?"

Notes in hand, Weiss cleared his throat and stood up. "Herr Sturmbannführer, so far we've been able to extract .09 milligrams of the rare uranium isotope…"

Point-zero-nine milligrams. They needed at least twenty pounds of the stuff. At this rate, it would take until the end of the century to produce what was needed. Heldorf let Weiss finish. "Thank you, Dr. Weiss, for that report. I hardly need to point out that your results, while interesting from a scientific perspective, do not lend themselves to any practical implementation."

"Herr Sturmbannführer, these are just lab results," Weiss countered. "If we built a separation plant—"

"I've seen your recommendations, Dr. Weiss, for such a plant. Germany is not large enough to house it, nor is the labor pool big enough to man it. Thank you, Dr. Weiss. Next we shall hear from you, Dr. Silberberg, on the electromagnetic approach to the separation of the fissionable isotope. What good news do you have for us today?"

Georg Silberberg's long, tedious report was as lacking in any cause for optimism as it was filled with copious data and detailed descriptions of blind alleys, and after a few minutes Heldorf's mind started to wander.

Speer was becoming increasingly impatient. He demanded to see results. Heldorf's written reports had glorified the few crumbs of success but had omitted any mention of failures, promising much more than he had any hope of delivering. But he could not string the Reichminister along forever, and very soon he would have to admit failure.

Silberberg sat down and was followed by Artur Steinitz. His hands trembled as he delivered his report in a low monotone without looking up from his notes. As he continued to mumble, Heldorf glanced around the room; his gaze caught Hannah's eyes, which quickly darted away. Despite his worsening mood, Heldorf could not help admiring her. Her black hair had grown back into a short, lustrous bob, the shadows under her eyes were almost gone, and her body was beginning to fill out pleasingly. He recalled the time in the laboratory when she had accidentally brushed against him, how he had felt…He had to stop thinking these thoughts. They would drive him insane.

Steinitz finished his report and sat down, his eyes still glued to his notes, their corners dog-eared with his nervous fingering. When Heldorf thanked him, he looked like a dog expecting to be whipped.

Heldorf felt sorry for Steinitz, who still could not shake off the bad effects of Auschwitz. He felt sorry for everyone sitting around the table, none more so than himself. They were all in the same boat. These scientists, who wanted so desperately to succeed for their own reasons, had failed to demonstrate that fissionable material could be separated out of natural uranium in sufficient quantity to fuel a bomb. Perhaps Heisenberg had been right. Now they would all share similar fates.

Heldorf felt drained. All he wanted was to retreat to his room, have a cognac, and think about what he should say to Speer in his next report. "And now, if no one has anything else to add, we'll adjourn this meeting." He rose; the scientists collected their papers.

"I have something to add." All eyes turned to the back of the room. Hannah rose from her chair.

Frederikshavn, Denmark. Danish Resistance Meeting.

The cell was meeting in the workroom behind the shop of Wilhelm's father, a shoemaker. Shoes in various stages of repair littered the table around which they sat; cigarette smoke hung in the air like a low-hanging cloud above their heads.

"I tell you, the secret to outsmarting the Germans is simple: just do the completely irrational thing, the exact opposite of what a logical minded Fritzie would do. Just look at how we outsmarted them last night when we collected that drop of guns." Gunnar, the comic of the group, loved to embellish his stories. "No sensible German would ever consider using a drop zone that had just been raided the week before. So which did we pick?" He paused to let the tension build. "The drop zone that had been raided the week before!" He flipped the end of his red scarf over his shoulder. "And you know what? It worked. Not a single Fritzie behind a tree when the RAF made the drop!"

Gunnar's report brought laughter around the table; it was welcome relief from the pain they felt upon hearing earlier that their friend, Svend Tormundsen, captured and tortured a month ago, had been put before a firing squad the previous day. The news had instantly quashed the high spirits that had fueled their missions ever since the destruction of the Frederikshavn Exhibition Hall.

Jørgen thought of Svend, a huge bear of a man with a ready smile and a hearty laugh. He had been a master mechanic at a factory making specialty parts for German aircraft which their cell had been ordered to target. Because of the tight security at the factory – workers were searched thoroughly on arrival each morning – it had seemed impossible to smuggle in the explosives needed to blow up the factory. Then Svend hit on the solution: each day, instead of his usual *smørrebrød* sandwiches in his lunchbox, he'd take explosives shaped like sandwiches wrapped in waxed paper, then store the explosives in his locker until there was enough to do the job. It had seemed foolproof: the Germans always checked inside the lunchboxes, but they never asked the men to open the waxed paper containing their lunch. Jørgen remembered with a pang how Svend had laughed and, patting his huge belly, had said, "Besides, this will be good for me – I could do without lunch for a few weeks."

At first, Svend's smuggling of the explosives into the factory went smoothly. Then on the third day he was asked by the German sentry to open the waxed paper. Never in the three years of German occupation had a worker been asked to unwrap his lunch. Was it just a coincidence? Or was there—

"Anyone have anything else to report?" asked Marius, the cell leader.

Jørgen put his thoughts about Svend aside. "There's something I'd like to raise," he said. "It's just a small thing..." Jørgen described the incident at Sara's butcher shop.

"It's probably nothing to worry about," Marius said. "Even if they reported your shopkeeper friend to the Gestapo, I doubt the Gestapo would pursue it. They've got bigger fish to fry."

"Like us," Erik said with a chuckle.

"But," added Gunnar, "they probably also don't want to rock the boat with, ahem, der Führer." He snapped two fingers over his upper lip with one hand, brandished his fist in the air with the other, and glowered menacingly.

"Gunnar's right," said Marius, ignoring the attempted impersonation. "There are a few advantages to being Hitler's 'model protectorate,'" he uttered the last two words with mock reverence, "the shining example of how rich life can be under Nazi rule."

Everyone understood what he was saying. Hitler liked the Danes, who therefore had it easy compared with people in other occupied countries. Not only were they considered Aryans by Nazi racial theories, but their official cooperation with their occupiers bought them relative freedom from German interference.

"So making trouble for little old Danish widows is not part of Hitler's master plan?" said Gunnar, feigning incredulity.

"Not yet, at least," said Marius. "In this case, I'm actually more concerned about the others."

"What others?" asked Jørgen.

"Our own home-grown Nazis. They're even worse than the Germans."

Mørkø Island, Denmark.

As Heldorf's eyes met those of Hannah he felt a frisson of hope, although he did not know why. "Please, gentlemen, return to your seats. Dr. Goldmann has something she wants to say." He took his place at the conference room table. "Dr. Goldmann, please proceed."

"Thank you, Herr Heldorf." Hannah rose from her chair. "I wanted to say, with all due respect, that I think we need a new approach."

Heldorf leaned forward and placed his elbows on the table. "A new approach? So far we've had progress reports on the thermal, electromagnetic, and gaseous diffusion methods of separating U-235 out of natural uranium. Is there a fourth separation method we should know about?"

"Perhaps, but that's not what I'm suggesting. May I?" She motioned to the blackboard.

"Of course." Heldorf shifted in his chair so he could see better.

"If this is natural uranium," Hannah took a broken piece of chalk and drew a large circle, "then this," she hit the board with the chalk, making a tiny dot within the circle, "is the rare uranium isotope we're seeking." She turned to face her audience. "But, as these gentlemen have proven today, separating it out is extremely difficult, next to impossible."

"Yes, I think we all know that, Dr. Goldmann. But what choice do we have if we need fissionable material?"

"I've been doing some experiments bombarding this," she shaded the large circle with the side of the chalk, "with neutrons. And I've found something very interesting. I've found that if the bombarding neutrons are slowed down with a moderator, they had a better chance of splitting the rare uranium isotope."

Weiss broke in. "Excuse me, but all our experiments have shown that, while you may split a few atoms that way, it's impossible to effect an uncontrolled chain reaction – a nuclear explosion, if you will – in such a manner."

"I agree, Dr. Weiss, but please bear with me," Hannah said.

Heldorf leaned back in his chair and frowned. Everyone around the table knew it was impossible to get a chain reaction out of raw uranium. Where was she headed?

Hannah persevered. "As the rare fissionable isotope is split, a few extra neutrons are created and thrown off, and these are absorbed by the abundant non-fissionable isotope." Hannah pummeled the shaded area of the blackboard with the chalk for emphasis. "And here's the key: over time, the non-fissionable isotope will transmute into a brand new element, following this sequence." On the blackboard she diagrammed the reactions that led to the creation of the new element.

Silberstein chuckled. "Transmutation. Alchemy. This is all very interesting, but how does it help us?"

Hannah put the chalk down and rubbed her hands to wipe off its residue. "Dr. Silberstein, my analysis shows that this new element will be as capable of sustaining a chain reaction as the fissionable uranium isotope, U-235. But it has an overwhelming advantage: it will be much easier to separate out of natural uranium."

"And does this new element have a name?" asked Heldorf.

"It's the second element on the periodic table after uranium, which was named for the planet Uranus. It seems appropriate to call this new element by the name of the second planet after Uranus."

"Uranus, Neptune...*Pluto?*"

Yes, Pluto. I believe we can create plutonium, a highly fissionable element."

"Hmm, plutonium." Heldorf made a steeple of his hands and smiled. "And what exactly do we need to produce this plutonium?"

"We need uranium, obviously."

"That is not a problem."

"And, for the moderator to slow down the neutrons, we need heavy water. Lots of heavy water."

Heldorf smiled. "That, also, should not be a problem. Our plant in Norway creates virtually all the heavy water that exists in the world."

Frederikshavn. A Bar.

"I went to see Svend's wife yesterday, Erik." Jørgen bit his lower lip and fought back tears as he nervously twisted his glass of akvavit around and around on the table. "I took the kids some wooden toys I carved."

Erik looked away. He knew there was nothing he could say that would relieve Jørgen's pain.

"Don't you think it's strange, Erik, that the one time, *the one time,* the Germans think of searching inside the wrapped sandwiches happens to be when Svend is carrying in the explosives?"

Erik shrugged. "Coincidences happen. The last time I was in Copenhagen I ran into my third-grade teacher on a bus. Hadn't seen him in fifteen years. How is Svend's wife?"

"Putting on a brave front. I don't think Svend's death has sunk in yet."

Erik shook his head and changed the subject. "At least you'll be happy to know that everyone was really generous when I passed the hat for Svend's family." He downed the last of his akvavit. "I know some of them really dug deep."

Jørgen continued to rotate his glass nervously. "Did that jerk Gunnar kick in?"

"Yeah."

"Much?"

Erik pushed his glass away. "I don't remember. Why do you ask?"

"I don't trust him. I don't like the way he's always making jokes out of everything."

"Oh, he's okay." Erik stuffed his hands in his pocket and sank down low in his chair. "Go a little bit easier on him, Jørgen. I think he's just nervous, that's all. Being a comedian is just a brave front he puts on."

"He told us he reused a drop zone that had been raided by the Germans on a previous drop. That took some guts, didn't it? If he's so damn nervous, why would he do that? A nervous man would surely have chosen a new drop zone, wouldn't he?"

"Surely it was Marius who chose the drop zone. Jørgen, what are you implying?"

"Only that—"

Several German soldiers walked into the bar and sat down. Jørgen and Erik threw some money down on the table and left.

Vemork Heavy Water Plant. Norway.

S hortly after midnight, a heavy boot dislodged a rock that clattered down the five hundred-foot gorge. The Norwegian commandos froze, clinging to the sheer granite walls of the bluff. They tried to stop their panting long enough to listen for the click of German rifles, but the howling wind and the hum of the turbines seemed to have masked all sounds of the small avalanche.

The commandos continued their climb to a ledge not far from the Vemork Heavy Water Plant, which sat isolated and protected atop a steep cliff overlooking the fast-moving and frigid stream they had earlier crossed. Threading their way through minefields, they cast their eyes about in the dark trying to pick out any German sentries who might be hiding in the shadows.

Two of the men entered the plant through a basement door and made their way into the factory through a cable duct before letting in the rest. Inside, they found only a single night watchman. They sent him to a place of safety and began laying the charges in the factory's high-concentration cells.

By the time the blast ripped through the heavy water plant and the sirens began to wail, the commandos had melted into the night to begin their two hundred and fifty mile trek back to Sweden.

Frederikshavn. A Resistance Meeting.

"This afternoon, I'd like you all to welcome someone I know only by his codename – Zebra." Marius was introducing a man at least ten years older than any of the men in the Frederikshavn cell; he had tobacco-stained fingers, an outcrop of stubbly beard, and silver-flecked hair.

"He and his cell in Copenhagen pulled off a spectacular raid last week against a heavily-guarded factory making ball bearings. Please give Zebra a warm Frederikshavn welcome."

The men slapped the table around which they sat with the flats of their hands.

As Zebra spoke, one man at the end of the table pretended rapt attention but was sunk in his own thoughts. He looked around at the members of the Frederikshavn cell. All were captivated by the grizzled activist from the capital city. He despised them. *Denmark hardly raised a finger of protest when the Führer's troops marched in. Now groups of amateurs like this one were banding together to perpetrate their boyish pranks.*

"First of all, I can tell you when it came to preparation we took great pains." A cigarette dangled from the side of Zebra's mouth. "We got hold of everything from the blueprints of the factory to details about the sentries and guard posts. Our weapons and explosives were transported to us inside the backpacks of a Boy Scout troop pretending to be out on a camping trip."

Zebra brushed off the ash that had fallen onto his flannel shirt. "We hid in the bushes that surrounded the factory and collected the weapons from the boys. An old grandfather," Zebra chuckled, exposing yellowed teeth, "saw us and came out of a nearby house to ask if we needed any help."

Grandfather. The man at the end of the table thought of his grandfather. He had owned a small shipyard in Bremerhaven, on the northwest coast of Germany, and he'd been rich. Until the Jewish industrialists came in with cheap labor and shoddy materials and undercut his prices. The Jews put his grandfather out of business. The profitable shipyard that should have been his father's legacy was sold for a song.

Zebra tapped the bottom of his cigarette pack, but nothing came out. Several hands bearing open packs shot up in front of him. Zebra helped himself to a cigarette out of one. "We rushed the guards with machine guns and tossed grenades at the sentry posts."

His father – he'd barely known him. Destitute, his father had come to Denmark to earn a living as a fisherman in a small village outside Copenhagen; he was only nine when his father died. His mother, a well-educated woman, had had to move to Frederikshavn because lodging was cheap. She made a subsistence living, cleaning the houses of rich people, and died just before the war. When the Germans invaded, he'd been pleased. So pleased, he had secretly approached the Danish Nazis to see if he could help.

"Then the arson squad did their work, and within minutes I can tell you the place was a wall of flames." Zebra plucked a piece of tobacco off his lower lip with his middle finger and his thumb.

Zebra's story enraged him, but he had to hide his anger. All his life he had kept his views and feelings hidden. At first, it was because he did not want to shock and alienate; he'd always been a private person. Now he was glad he had: it made his role as a spy for the Gestapo so much easier. Blending into the background was the best way to go undercover.

"In the whole operation, we lost only one man. Sad to say he was a friend of mine, but we all feared there'd be more casualties." Zebra stubbed out his cigarette and looked around the table for another. "Overall, we thought the operation – which completely destroyed the factory – came off well."

The men of the Frederikshavn cell jumped to their feet, cheered, and punched the air with their fists. The man at the end of the table joined in on the applause.

Perhaps they weren't small-time idiots, after all. He'd heard enough to realize that the Resistance movement in Denmark had come a long way since the high-spirited, hot-blooded high jinks of just a few months ago. They were now carrying out carefully-planned, meticulously-organized actions that struck at the heart of Nazi strategy.

They had to be stopped. And he knew how.

Laboratory in a Nuclear Physics Compound. Mørkø Island.

Hannah and Albert sat with Sol in the chilly, dimly-lit laboratory enjoying late-night cups of lukewarm tea. It had been a long day – they had spent sixteen hours working on a plan for the 'uranium machine' they would begin to build when the heavy water shipment arrived – but the work had been stimulating and the time had passed quickly.

"So, Hannah...." Albert began to speak and hesitated, reconsidering what he was about to say. "So, Hannah, it appears you've saved the project, and with it our skins. I congratulate you, but I confess I slept better when I thought we were failing than now, now that I think we may actually succeed."

As he took a sip of tea, he peeked over the top of the cup to gauge her reaction. Her eyebrows arched but she said nothing.

But Sol could not resist the bait. "I give up, Al: why were you sleeping better when we were failing?"

"Because when we were failing, the fate of my children was out of my hands – it was in the hands of whatever is controlling our destinies."

"The laws of physics is my guess," offered Sol.

"Probably," said Albert. "Anyway, I knew I couldn't stop doing everything in my power to save my girls, but at the same time the better man inside cried out to me to stop."

Sol narrowed his eyes as he considered Weiss's statement. "You couldn't stop, but at the same time you cried out to yourself to stop?"

"That's right. Every day I asked myself if I should throw in the towel." Weiss shrugged and tilted his head. "But every day I answered to myself, how could I do that to my girls?"

Hannah looked at Weiss sharply. "But you will continue to support the work?"

"Of course I will. As I say, I love my girls."

"Al's got a very good point, you know," Sol said. "How can we call ourselves sane when we're working to deliver the ultimate death machine to that *meshugener* whose mission in life is to kill us all?"

Hannah smiled. "I can assure you that Hitler wouldn't waste an atomic bomb on the Jews."

Sol swirled the light brown tepid water around in his cup and chuckled at the bitter irony. *"Oy gevalt,"* he said. "What we have here is the classic Faustian bargain."

"You're right," agreed Albert. "We've sold our souls to the devil to save the lives of our friends and families."

"Yeah, but in the case of Helga, the devil can keep her." Sol grinned mischievously. "But you wouldn't get an argument from any Jew still alive about the devil being our new employer." He snorted a half-laugh. "But his horns weren't scary enough, so he traded them in for a bad moustache."

Weiss leaned forward and put his elbows on his knees. "In the meantime, if we're lucky, maybe the war will end before we finish this dreadful work." He ran his fingers through his thick hair.

Sol banged down his tin cup on the table and pushed it away. "Of course we're not fools. I'm sure you both know that when we've finished our work, they'll have to—" He drew his finger across his neck suggestively and accompanied it with a guttural sound effect.

"Yeah, I realize that." Weiss sat up, frowning. "We'd know too much; we'd be too dangerous to keep around." His frown gradually softened into a wan smile. "Somehow, you know, that's actually a comforting thought for me." His smile broadened. "It's a lot easier for me to think about my own death than the deaths of my wife and girls."

Silence pervaded the room as they all pondered Albert's remark. But Hannah's thoughts voiced a different opinion. *Speak for yourself. I intend to stay alive.*

Hannah's Room. Mørkø,

H annah tossed on her cot in the hours before dawn as she wrestled
with a scientific problem. She couldn't sleep, but it was not the
physics keeping her awake. Indeed, physics was a safe harbor for her; it
helped keep her mind occupied, helped keep it away from the forbidden
thoughts that kept creeping in from the shadows like dangerous preda-
tors.

Concentrate on the basics, she told herself. Determine the critical
mass, the volume of natural uranium and heavy water that could sustain
a continuous chain reaction....

Her last year at Leipzig University in the autumn of 1931 forced its
way through the equations; it had been the best year of her life. Her
young and inexhaustible mind had been impatient to learn, impatient to
test its limits against some of the greatest intellects of Germany.
Werner Heisenberg, only thirty, was a professor of theoretical physics
at the university. Max Heldorf was also a student then; he had been part
of those years....

Focus, damn you, she told herself. To find the ideal quantity of
heavy water and uranium, we need to start with subcritical amounts and
gradually increase....

She had met Max outside Heisenberg's lecture hall. She had been
carrying an armload of books that slipped and fell to the floor, skidding
in all directions.

"Please," he had appeared at her side, "permit me." He dropped to
one knee with the grace of a dancer and began scooping up the books;
she looked down on the spun gold of his hair that caught the sunlight
coming through a window and beamed it back. His arms full, he shot to
his feet and smiled down on her. "I think I should walk with you back
to your lodgings so I can help you carry these."

Get back to the problem, she ordered herself. A self-sustaining
chain reaction will be achieved when, on average, one neutron splits
one U-235 isotope creating an additional neutron which, in turn....

What a beautiful fall it had been that year, the weather remaining
mild well into November. They studied together, took walks on the

banks of the Auer, listened to music, laughed and sang in the beer halls. She did not agree with his political views, but healthy debate was encouraged then, opposing views respected in the academic setting.

And then they had made love. She still remembered how it felt to rest her head on his bare chest, his arms wrapped around her, his soft lips lightly touching her hair with kisses…. Stop, she cried inwardly as she rolled over. The man works for the assassins who killed your family!

Again she willed her mind to think of physics. Some neutrons will be absorbed by U-238, forming the new isotope U-239, with a half-life of twenty-three and a half minutes….

After she had taken her degree, she had been offered a position as lecturer at the university. Max had headed off to the University of Göttingen. Then Hitler came to power….Why was she torturing herself? Wasn't there enough despair in her life without reliving the past?

Where was she? Oh, yes, U-239, formed by the resonance capture of slow neutrons, is beta-decaying and should decay to the next higher element, new element 93—

She was alive. She was flesh and blood. She was human. And she feared there was something within her not even her intellect could control.

Heldorf's Room.

Max Heldorf checked the luminous dial on his clock: three in the morning. He groaned and rolled over. He had to get some sleep, but he couldn't get her out of his mind. Damn her! Why had he allowed a Jew to torment him so? At times, she infuriated him. He tried to push his feelings aside. He should not have feelings of any sort for a Jew.

He forced his thoughts to Speer. By now, the Reichminister should have received his request, and soon there would be word of the shipment of heavy water. He looked forward to the work ahead….

But the memories of that time in Leipzig kept flooding back. He swung his legs out and sat on the edge of the bed, his mind agonizing as he reached for his cigarettes. Should he continue the course of action he had just set in motion?

He'd decided that morning. When he had made some inquiries in the afternoon, they said it would be very difficult. He lit the cigarette and took a long drag.

Perhaps he should give up on his inquiries. After all, she was only a Jew. It was wrong, he knew. He should just concentrate on the project. He had the uranium; all he needed now was the heavy water. The project was everything. Find out how to make fissile material, give the recipe to Speer, and take the plaudits.

Still, he was obsessed by this woman, this Jew. He wanted to find out everything he could about her background; it might be useful to him later. Specifically, he wanted to know what had happened to her sister. Was she dead? Or might she still be alive?

Frederikshavn, Denmark.

Peder heard it first. He scampered down the stairs in his pajamas and bare feet. Sara, who had not been sleeping well since her encounter with the Danish Nazis, had taken a sleeping draught before going to bed and was slower to respond. In the haze of waking, she wondered if the thud and sound of shattering glass was something she had dreamed.

She looked at the clock: people would not be up and about for another couple of hours. She often heard goings on in the street below her bedroom, but who would be out at this time of night? Pushing the blackout curtain aside and seeing nothing, she threw on her bathrobe, stepped into her slippers, and shuffled down the stairs.

At first she did not believe what she saw. Then her hands flew up to her face in horror. Peder, silhouetted against the moonlit buildings across the street, was standing barefoot in what looked like snow; the shop window had been smashed. Within its frame were only jagged shards of glass, like the menacing mouth of a gigantic shark.

"Peder, don't move!" Her first concern was for the boy's feet which might be cut. She gingerly made her way over to him through the broken glass, picked him up, and carried him upstairs to his little bedroom.

"Oh, Peder, what happened? How did the window break?" Had something got into the boy? She never knew what was going through Peder's head, but she had never known him to misbehave intentionally. Had he accidentally broken the window?

"Let me see your hands—are you hurt anywhere else?" She tweezed out several pieces of glass from Peder's left foot; the child didn't even wince. She realized she couldn't remove all the tiny fragments; she'd have to get Dr. Rasmussen in the morning.

"Sit still, Peder." She gave the boy a reassuring hug. "Wait here while I get something to put on your foot."

She went downstairs to retrieve the iodine from the medicine chest in the washroom, tears coming to her eyes as she once again saw the glass-littered store. Suddenly she stumbled as her foot caught against something on the floor.

Sara stooped and picked up what appeared to be a parcel. From its heft, she sensed it was a brick wrapped in brown paper secured by string. She reached for a butcher's knife and sliced through the string.

As she unfolded the paper, her heart raced. The words leapt up at her: *Now, Jewess, perhaps you will learn to obey the law. We shall be watching you.* Underneath the writing was a crudely-drawn swastika.

"I saw them, Mama." She turned. Peder, still barefoot, had padded his way downstairs. "Two men. The same men as the other day."

Berlin.

Reichminister Speer put down his pen and rubbed his eyes; he'd been at his desk since six and it was almost lunchtime, but there was still much to be done. He picked up the framed picture of his young daughter, Hilde, holding the hand of the Führer. The war was beginning to show on Hitler's face, he thought as he replaced the picture on his desk and reached for the next piece of mail. It was from Heldorf. He read it, frowned, then pulled out a sheet of his letterhead and wrote:

March 1, 1943

Dear Sturmbannführer Heldorf:

I am informed that our heavy water plant in Vemork, Norway has come under attack by saboteurs. Damage was serious.

While fully appreciating your needs, I most reluctantly must deny your request, both now and in the future.

Please provide me with a full report of the impact of my decision on your operation at once.

Heil Hitler
Speer

He pushed the paper away, put down his pen, and leaned back in his chair. He already knew what the impact of his decision would be. Heldorf had made it clear that heavy water was essential to his new plan.

Speer got up, moved to the room that contained the model of the new Berlin, and gazed down at it absentmindedly. It would have been excellent if Heldorf could have pulled it off, if he could have produced the ultimate weapon so desperately needed now to reverse Germany's declining fortunes. But Heldorf's reports of late did not inspire confidence. They seemed to pump up the same weak results as evidence of progress.

Of course, he hadn't told Heldorf that the heavy water plant would soon be repaired. Because there were even more important things at stake. He flicked a bit of dust off the dome of the *Volkshalle*. Reports said the enemy was watching the Vemork plant closely. What if the enemy were to attack a German ship carrying heavy water to Heldorf's island? That would certainly get Hitler's attention. And the Führer would not be pleased.

He moved over to the window and looked out. How bleak were the shades of gray that comprised the Berlin winter streetscape; as bleak as he felt at the prospect of abandoning the one project that might, had it been able to succeed, have saved Germany.

He walked back to his desk, marked the letter 'express,' and placed it in his out tray.

Mørkø Island.

It could be done. He knew it could be done. Germany could win the war. He was anxious to receive Speer's reply telling him when the shipment of heavy water would arrive. He could barely wait to get started.

Heldorf felt good as he looked out over the island's western beach. The weather was crisp, sharp; the sun shone brightly, trying to force its warmth through the wind that sought to bring the last cold of the dying winter.

A betting man would not gamble much on Germany's chances for victory. The Wehrmacht had been slaughtered on the eastern front, were on the run in Africa, and it was just a matter of time before they had to face the enemy in the west. But the war was not over, and Heldorf knew he had the secret to triumph within his grasp. A plutonium bomb. A carefully-chosen target. Germany would win the war.

He looked toward the horizon and saw the supply boat coming in from Frederikshavn: his larders would be replenished with Denmark's best. He rubbed his hands together as he thought of the excellent cheeses, fish and meat – much better than anything he would be able to get in Germany and a soul-warming consolation in such a frigid outpost as Mørkø. Perhaps the boat would also bring the dispatch from Speer.

Hannah had explained her theories and shown him the results of her experiments. The others had searched hard for flaws in her logic and had grilled her mercilessly. But in the end even the most skeptical admitted that her theory was sound: a new, highly fissile element – plutonium – could be created directly from natural uranium. Heldorf cupped his hands to light a cigarette in the wind and inhaled deeply. He smiled as he exhaled and ran his fingers through the blond hair beating a tattoo against his forehead in the wind.

Heldorf daydreamed of his success. Maybe he would be congratulated personally by the Führer, perhaps invited to share a meal with him. Perhaps even an invitation to Berchtesgaden. He pictured himself standing next to the Führer on the terrace of the Berghof taking in the glorious panorama, the Führer's hand resting amiably on his shoulder.

The view of the Bavarian Alps gave way to Hannah's image as she had looked when she led him through the logic. She had been sitting quite close to him, pointing to the formulas with her long, graceful fingers; as she looked down at her notes, her eyes were partly obscured by her hair, cascading around her face like a veil.

He tried to force his thoughts elsewhere. Why could he not shake this obsession? She was a Jew, but she was useful and was making a valuable contribution to the Third Reich and that was all. And perhaps he would try to see that she was rewarded as the others had been.

His luck was improving. Good luck seemed always to beget more good luck for him. Earlier in the day he had received a telephone call from Obersturmbannführer Eichmann's office: the records on Hannah's sister, Rachel, had been located, and she was alive at Treblinka! Because Treblinka was an extermination camp, she had been thought to be dead; most died within a few hours of arrival. But somehow Rachel Goldmann had been spared. She was alive! At last, after all the disappointments, the dice were falling his way.

He tossed his cigarette down on the sand and ground it out with his heel. If he could arrange to get Hannah's sister released from Treblinka, she could be used as a leverage, if ever needed – maybe even as a reward.

There were still problems. His ability to pull strings in the SS was not what it once had been and he might have problems getting the woman released. And it was becoming increasingly difficult to get Speer's authorization on anything. But that would change. The wind strengthened and he pulled up his collar.

"Excuse me, sir."

Heldorf was annoyed by the interruption of his thoughts; he turned abruptly. It was the corporal from the island's administration office. "Yes? What is it?"

"I thought you'd like to see this right away, sir." The corporal handed him a letter and saluted. "It just arrived on the boat from Frederikshavn. It's a dispatch from the Reichminister's office."

Frederikshavn, Denmark.

"Well, at least they didn't steal the meat."

"That's not funny." Jørgen shot Gunnar a withering look and felt his fists beginning to clench.

Gunnar put up both hands in a mock defensive pose. "Take it easy, Jørgen. What we've got to do is tough enough; we need a laugh now and then."

Tension in the Resistance cell meeting was high. One of their contacts – a farmer on the outskirts of town who was storing submachine guns for them in his shed – had just been arrested. Something – or someone – had inspired the Gestapo to raid his farm.

Marius intervened. "Okay, let's get back to the issue we were discussing. My guess is it was an isolated event. If we took any action against the Nazi creeps who threw the brick through Mrs. Gronborg's window we might have bigger problems."

"Bigger problems?" asked Jørgen. "What sort of problems? Our line of work isn't exactly problem-free. Every time we have an action, the Nazis retaliate with one of their own – like that pastry shop they blew up after our attack on the exhibition hall."

"Yeah, I know. Everyone loved Mikkelsen's Bakery, and the Nazis knew it. But the Jews are in an especially precarious position and need to keep a low profile. So far the Nazis have let them be, and the Jews want to keep it that way. The rabbi has asked that we do nothing on their behalf that would arouse the attention of the Germans."

Jørgen nodded. "I get the picture. They don't want to rock the boat. I think they're wrong but I understand."

"How's Mrs. Gronborg coping?" Erik always managed to see the human angle.

Jørgen smiled at his good friend. "She's doing very well; she should be back in business soon."

"Tell her that we all wish her well," said Marius. "Let's hope there's no more trouble."

Jørgen understood Marius's decision to take no action. But he promised himself that he would keep an eye on Sara Gronborg and Peder.

Frederikshavn, Denmark.

"It looks wonderful!" Sara admired the jury-rigged window Jørgen and Erik had installed in her butcher shop. "How can I ever thank you boys? Please stay and have some coffee and cake. Of course, it's the usual brewed chicory, and there's not much sugar in the cake—"

"I'm sure it tastes terrific, Mrs. Gronborg, but Erik and I have to be getting along." Jørgen looked over at their handiwork. "I guess it doesn't look too bad; we did the best we could."

Sara's neighbors had reacted with horror when her shop had been vandalized and several had pitched in to help her repair the damage. Into the empty space Jørgen and Erik had framed an old window donated by a neighbor; it was rough and ready, but it did the job.

Sara called to Peder, who was sitting in a corner stroking the sleeping Soldat. "Peder, come and say thank you to Jørgen and Erik."

"Thank you," Peder said softly without looking up.

"What do you think of your new window, Peder?" Erik asked.

Peder shot a sidelong glance at the window. "Good." He returned his attentions to his dog.

Erik chuckled. "Your Peder is a young man of few words, Mrs. Gronborg, but we know he's a sweet boy."

"Peder's my good friend down at the harbor," said Jørgen. "Mrs. Gronborg, I'll stop by tomorrow and give the frame another coat of paint."

"Thanks for all your help." Sara kissed Jørgen lightly on both cheeks and shook Erik's hand as they left.

The door's jingle caused Soldat to stir. He rose, padded to the door, pricked his ears back, and whimpered softly.

"Peder, perhaps you'd better take Soldat for a walk." Sara turned to rearrange some canned meats that had been moved during the repair work. "But don't be too long."

Peder opened the door and Soldat ran out, his tail wagging joyfully at the prospect of a walk. The boy beckoned with his hand and the dog obeyed instantly, following his master down the back alleys and past the half-timbered fishermen's cottages that lined the ancient streets of the Fiskerlyngen section of Frederikshavn.

Suddenly, Soldat crouched down and emitted a low growl. Peder looked up. Coming down the street were the two men who had thrown the brick through the shop window.

Mørkø Island.

Heldorf looked from his window at the bleak aspect of the island. Barely six in the afternoon but already it was dark. The snow had begun falling in late morning and by early afternoon had turned to freezing rain; to Heldorf, it sounded like the fingernails of demons clawing at his office window.

He sat down at his desk and read Speer's letter again, grimaced, and tossed it aside. "Bastard!" He spat out the oath as though it had the force to kill.

Heldorf pulled out a piece of stationery and tried to compose his thoughts in a response to Speer. A blank piece of paper stared back at him as he struggled to put his anger aside, to think clearly. Word had reached him that the heavy water plant was under repair. It was clear that the Reichminister had got cold feet after the enemy attacks on the plant, cold feet that made him prefer to save his own skin rather than help Germany win the war. But Speer was a powerful man and Heldorf had to frame his response carefully if he wanted to have a future when he returned to Berlin. He pushed the paper away; it would be better to work on it after his rage had cooled.

There was little hope of saving the project without the heavy water. He rose and paced the floor, thinking about how he should handle the Jews. At all costs, they must not be allowed to suspect the undertaking had failed; if they realized the project was coming to an end, they would know what was in store for them and he could have a rebellion on his hands. He would tell them about the enemy attack on the heavy water plant and would instruct them to return to their original experiments to find a way to separate out the fissile uranium isotope. While they toiled at this virtually impossible task, he would have time to work out the logistics for their departure.

Hannah would be his toughest audience. All the scientists knew that isotope separation was a lost cause, but, unlike the others, Hannah lacked the ability to lie to herself in order to live in hope. He needed to talk with her in private, isolate her from the rest of the team. He stuck his head out the door. "Corporal, please bring Dr. Goldmann to my office."

Frederikshavn, Denmark

"Well, what have we here, Steffen? Isn't this the little moron who lives with the Jewish bitch, the one who keeps breaking the law? Tell me, little Jew boy, how did your mother like the present we sent her?" The two men found this remark immensely amusing.

"Henrik, please tell me – if the little moron is a Jew, how did he come to have blond hair and blue eyes?"

"Good question, Steffen; I think he must be a bastard." They both laughed again. "His whore of a mother must have had it off with the village idiot, don't you think?"

Their laughter died away as Soldat, growling, darted for their heels.

"Get that mangy cur out of our way, you imbecile!"

Peder said nothing.

"I said get him out of the way!" The man's face had become red with shouting. Peder did not give way and Soldat continued to snap at their heels.

"You – you little bastard, your kike mother will be sorry she had you!"

Soldat barked loudly. Peder gestured to his pet and the dog stopped his attack but crouched on his haunches, baring his teeth and snarling.

The men backed up, turned a corner, and disappeared.

Mørkø Island.

Heldorf closed the door, sat down behind the desk, and pinched the bridge of his nose with his thumb and forefinger. It would not be an easy conversation. He could not tell her that her sister was alive; with the project virtually dead, it would be pointless.

After a few minutes there was a knock on the door. Heldorf assumed a relaxed attitude, leaning back in his chair and lighting a cigarette. "Come in."

She walked in and stared at him, a bemused look on her face.

"Please," he nodded toward the chair and she sat down.

"How are you, Hannah? Cigarette?"

She shook her head. "I'm well. Albert, Sol, and I were just working on the design for the uranium machine—"

"Hannah, that's what I wanted to talk to you about. Our plans have changed. We need to return to the original plan, the development of a method for separating out the rare fissile isotope. There can be no uranium machine; saboteurs have destroyed our supply of heavy water."

She frowned and shifted in her chair. "No heavy water?" She bit her lower lip and looked off to the side, as though studying something suspended in mid-air. She knows our work here is doomed, Heldorf thought; she's thinking about what will happen to her and her Jewish colleagues.

Hannah whispered something inaudible. He thought she was going to cry, like that time in Leipzig when…. Heldorf put the thought out of his mind. She muttered the words again, but he could not hear them.

"Hannah, what are you saying?"

She looked over at him, suddenly remembering he was in the room. "What? Oh yes, I was thinking about the capture cross section of carbon," she replied.

"You were thinking about what?"

"The size of the ideal neutron moderator's capture cross section. It's key. If it's too large, too many neutrons will be absorbed to sustain a chain reaction. A low capture cross section is what makes heavy water a good moderator." Her eyes grew large. "Can we get graphite?"

Heldorf still could not fathom her train of thought. "Yes, of course. Graphite is a common substance."

"Good!" A broad smile came to her face. "Carbon. In the form of graphite. If purified, it should work just as well as heavy water."

Frederikshavn, Denmark.

"There's just one little problem with the way we do this." Gunnar jerked a thumb at the pile of broken-down furniture in the back of the truck. "If the Fritzies stop us, they'll look at this load of crap and wonder who would pay a single krone to move it."

Jørgen, sitting at the wheel of the truck, bristled at Gunnar's remark. Gunnar had to make a wisecrack about everything. It didn't matter to Jørgen that perhaps Gunnar made jokes to relieve his tension, as Erik had once said; Jørgen just found it annoying.

Marius had asked Jørgen and Gunnar to move some boxes of explosives from the basement of a widow's house to the loft of a farmer's barn. To do this, they used an old moving van, donned workmen's uniforms and, as a disguise, had a supply of broken-down furniture. When they picked up the boxes of explosives from the lady's house, they wedged the furniture in front of them. If they were stopped, the Germans would have to unload a lot of rickety tables and stained armchairs if they were to discover the explosives. Relocating supplies the RAF was parachuting to the Resistance had become a routine task: their supply of ammunition was growing rapidly, but few Danes, however patriotic, wanted secret arsenals on their property.

"Come on, Gunnar," Jørgen said. "Let's go and get this done." Gunnar hopped in the truck as Jørgen started the motor and they headed north on the Danmarksgade. When they stopped to turn on the Vestergade, a pair of blue eyes beneath a mop of blond hair saw them from his hiding place in the shadows.

• • •

Peder saw Jørgen in the big truck. Jørgen was with another man. Peder did not know the other man. The other man wore a red scarf. Seeing Jørgen made Peder happy. Jørgen was a good man.

Peder had to protect his mama from the bad men. He saw the bad men the other day. They were in a parade. They were marching in black uniforms and had strange flags. He had followed one of the men home. He would watch the man from this spot and make sure he did not hurt his mama. His mama was good to him. He loved her.

117

He had been watching for a long time. He did not bring Soldat. Soldat was a good dog. He had left him to look after his mama.

But Soldat would have kept him warm. Peder was very cold.

Werner Heisenberg's Apartment. Berlin.

Franz von Rastenberg sipped his coffee as Heisenberg effortlessly coaxed a Mozart sonata out of his Blüthner grand piano. For Franz, the music was a remote background for his thoughts as he conjured up her hair, her eyes, the way she tilted her head as she spoke.

Elisabeth Heisenberg held out a tray of tiny tarts; he smiled, took one out of politeness, placed it on the edge of his saucer, and retreated back into his reverie. In his mind he could hear her voice and the way she spoke; how so very like—

Heisenberg finished the sonata and moved without stopping into a Granados waltz, an uncharacteristically romantic work in his mostly classical repertoire. The sumptuous beauty of the piece abruptly thrust von Rastenberg back to '39, the first time he had heard the waltz. It had been a warm evening. Elsa was in his arms on the dance floor, wearing a backless midnight blue satin dress; he could still feel the softness of her skin, could still smell the perfume of her hair—

Wolfgang, Heisenberg's five-year-old son, plopped down on the sofa beside him and handed him his scrapbook to admire. As von Rastenberg murmured appropriate reactions to the pictures of farm animals pasted on the pages, his memory continued to dance with Elsa. The waltz finished and von Rastenberg handed the album back to Wolfgang, who turned his attentions to begging his mother for another tart.

Heisenberg closed his eyes and began playing a Bach prelude from memory, and something in the cascading tones reminded von Rastenberg of the woman's voice. He wanted to see her again, to see the agent to whom he had delivered the message in Sweden.

The American agent. Christina. She was as close as he would ever get to his beloved wife, Elsa, in this life.

Frederikshavn.

Sleep began to overcome Peder. He had returned to watch the apartment building as he had for the past several days and, hiding in an alley across the street for over two hours, his eyelids were beginning to droop. He pinched himself to stay awake – he had to stay alert so he could find out what the bad men were doing and protect his mama. Suddenly he saw the door open. One of the bad men stepped out and walked quickly down the street. He wore street clothes, not the black uniform and red armband he had worn when Peder had seen him in his mama's shop.

As the man turned the corner, Peder jumped out of his hiding place and followed. After a few blocks, the man joined his friend. The two walked off briskly. It was Sunday afternoon, few were out on the street, and the sound of the men's shoes on the pavement echoed above their laughter.

Peder did not see the tin can on the sidewalk and his foot sent it rattling loudly down the street. He ducked into a doorway as the men whipped around.

"What the hell was that?" one of them asked. The other man pointed to where Peder was hiding. The boy, his heart beating wildly, pressed himself against the cold brick façade and tried to make himself as small as possible as he heard footsteps coming his way.

Mørkø Island.

Heldorf stared down at the unopened letter with the official stamp of the Reichminister for Arms and Munitions as though he could divine its contents from the outside. His heart beat wildly as he thought about what Speer's response to his request for a shipment of graphite meant to his career. He picked up the envelope, ran the swastika-embossed silver letter opener down its spine, and pulled out the sheet inside.

March 5, 1943

Dear Sturmbannführer Heldorf:

I have given your request for additional time and materials considerable thought. As you know, the Führer has mandated that all developmental projects produce results within nine months or be discontinued. Your project has been underway for that length of time, yet has shown no promise of bearing fruit. This would suggest immediate suspension of all work.

On the other hand, a substantial initial investment has already been made and cannot be reclaimed. In addition, your labor is free. These considerations, along with the potential, however remote, for your work to shorten the war, recast the situation in a different light.

I therefore approve your request and give you until mid-October to demonstrate results. If you are not successful by then, there will be no option but to terminate the project.

A shipment of purified graphite should arrive at your island shortly.

Heil Hitler.
Speer

Heldorf ran his fingers though his hair nervously. He had a reprieve but not much time. What could they get done by the middle of October? He picked up the phone. "Corporal, ask Dr. Goldmann to come to my office immediately."

At his desk he began jotting down the elements of a plan. There were three basic phases to making a plutonium bomb. The first, and most difficult, was the creation of plutonium using uranium surrounded by graphite bricks in a uranium machine. The second was the extraction of the plutonium out of the uranium using a chemical process. And the third phase was to design a gun-type bomb that would fire a subcritical bullet of plutonium at a plutonium target to create a critical mass yielding a runaway explosion.

He wrote down the three phases. If they could make it to the end of the first phase and develop a method to do the second, they could turn it over to the Wehrmacht engineers and the German armaments industry to do the rest. He was starting to write tasks beneath each phase when a knock on the door announced Hannah's arrival. He continued to write as she entered the room and stood before his desk.

He scribbled a last note and looked up. "Ah, yes, Hannah. Please sit down. I have some good news: our graphite should arrive in a few days."

Hannah was unfazed by this news. It never occurred to her that the graphite would not arrive.

Heldorf leaned back and made a steeple of his hands. He needed her help and decided to level with her. "Hannah, we have only until the middle of October to develop the uranium machine, so we have some work to do. In your opinion, can this be accomplished?"

Hannah grimaced. "I don't know. I doubt it. What we're attempting has never been done before. There are no precedents. We've got nothing to base any time estimates on."

Heldorf sighed. "Hannah, we can figure it all out. We need to develop a detailed plan. Look – I've already begun working on one."

Hannah ignored the piece of paper he held up. "Create a workable plan for something that's never been done before? How do you plan for all the things that will inevitably go wrong?"

Heldorf's rising temper battled with his sinking stomach to dominate his emotions. "We can build something into the plan for contingencies," he said with forced restraint.

"I don't know, Max. It's going to be a huge undertaking." Hannah didn't notice Heldorf's clenched jaw as he ground his teeth to control himself. "I just don't think we can get it done by October."

Frederikshavn.

"Someone threw something at us."

Peder trembled at the man's gruff voice and the sound of his approaching footsteps. He wondered if he should make a run for it but decided it was too late. He wished Soldat were with him; he always felt safe with Soldat around. Peder braced himself as he awaited discovery.

The footsteps got louder. "Henrik, where the hell are you going?"

"That piece of rubbish didn't throw itself; someone threw it at us, and I intend to find out who." The footsteps were only a few feet away from Peder, who held his breath and closed his eyes.

"We don't have time for that right now, Henrik. We're late."

The footsteps stopped. "Okay, but the next time someone throws something at me, I'll bust his head open."

"You've got a persecution complex, Henrik. It was probably just a cat jumping down from a trash can. Come on, let's go."

Peder heard the man grumble as his steps retreated. The two men strode off and turned into a busy street. Peder followed. A truck filled with German soldiers rattled by and the two men shouted and waved. After half a mile, they stopped at a house and knocked on the door. As they waited for the knock to be answered, Peder hid behind a garbage can directly across the street. The men knocked again, somewhat harder. Finally the door was opened and they went in.

The door had been ajar for only an instant, but Peder would never forget what he had seen. There could be no doubt. The man who had opened the door for the Danish Nazis was a man Peder had seen before. Peder had seen him with Jørgen.

Mørkø Island.

Max Heldorf and Hannah Goldmann spent the rest of the afternoon and most of the evening fleshing out the details of a plan to produce plutonium. They pored over her diagrams and formulas, calculated the amounts of materials they needed, worked out completion dates for major milestones, then filled in the detailed steps and assigned them to specific scientists. The first version of the plan took the completion date out to July of the following year, the second one ended in February.

Heldorf's temper had cooled earlier as Hannah had risen to the challenge. As he watched her refine the current version of the plan, he could almost hear her brain working. She looked at the plan as another problem to be solved, and her dedication to solving it gave him heart.

The corporal brought in a hastily-prepared supper and Hannah continued to study the plan as she ate her sausages and fried potatoes. "I think I've found a few more places where we can overlap the steps," she mumbled as she chewed, "and we can carve off a few more days if we lengthen the work hours a bit more. Can we get some carpenters to help us build the framework for the uranium machine?"

"I'm sure they can be provided."

"And we'll need goggles and lead sheathing for the scientists."

"How does that save time?"

"It doesn't, but I just thought of it."

At about one in the morning, Hannah put down her pencil. "What about the relatives you promised to release?"

Heldorf was taken aback by the abrupt change in focus; it was no longer Hannah the scientist speaking. "Yes? What about them? What does that have to do with our plan?"

"On the latest version of the plan everyone will have to work very hard in shifts around the clock, and they won't be doing it for the glory of the Third Reich. What can you promise them?"

"I can promise them that their relatives will be released as soon as the uranium machine is producing plutonium – if, that is, it can produce plutonium by the middle of October. Otherwise, the deal's off."

Hannah looked resigned and went back to her calculations.

At about three, as Heldorf dozed over the personnel assignments, Hannah put down her pencil. "Max, take a look."

Heldorf shook himself awake. "What?"

"I think we've done it, Max."

He rose from his chair and walked around the desk to look over Hannah's shoulder. She handed him the plan and he flipped to the last page: the final entry, the production of plutonium, had a date of October fifth, ten days ahead of schedule.

A rush of exhilaration overcame Heldorf's fatigue. "Hannah, this is wonderful. I'll tell you what – you must be director of the project."

"No, Max, no. Albert Weiss and I work well together, and there's no need to bruise his ego. Besides, I'm not sure the others would accept a woman as their director."

He looked at her with admiration. So brilliant, so beautiful, he thought. And she was saving his career. Yet she asked nothing for herself. He decided to tell her.

"Hannah, your valuable contributions shall not go unrewarded. I'm now in a position to give you some good news." He watched as she raised her eyebrows in curiosity. "Hannah, you, too, have a relative who shall be given the gift of freedom. Your sister is alive."

Hannah's face froze, then became spectral, drained of all its color. "Rachel? Alive?" She recalled with savage vividness the last time she had seen her sister. Rachel's soulful eyes taking one last brief look at her. Rachel heading into the house to be with their parents. Rachel in those last moments on the day the soldiers came. The day Hannah turned away and ran.

"Aren't you pleased?" Heldorf was dumbfounded by Hannah's reception of the news.

124

She doubled over in her chair, put her face in her hands, and began sobbing. Heldorf, shocked, dropped to one knee beside her. "Hannah, please don't cry. Your sister is alive – I thought you'd be pleased. Soon I'll get her released from the camp. I swear it." He patted her arm in an effort to comfort her.

"Oh, Max, Max!" Suddenly she felt her body slide out of the chair and into his arms. Her head rested on his shoulder. His arms hovered in the air for a few moments before resting lightly on her back. He kissed her hair, took her face in his hands, looked into the abyss of her eyes, and tried to brush away the tears from her cheeks with his fingers. His lips found hers and pressed gently at first, then harder. Hannah pulled him closer.

PART THREE

*"He who sups with the devil
should use a long spoon."*

—Old proverb

Mørkø Island.

"Slow down, Sol!" Hannah called to Sol Friedberg, as he struggled with a heavy block of graphite. "You're not a young man anymore. You've done enough for today; why don't you go take a rest?"

"Not on your life, Hannah." He carefully inserted the block into place. "I can't wait to see this beast take shape." His breath was labored as he stood back to admire his work.

Hannah nodded. They had six months to complete the uranium machine and start producing plutonium, and since the arrival of the graphite, the scientists had been doubling as laborers. She looked down at her plans: the uranium machine was being built to her specifications. Her designs showed a spherical structure consisting of purified graphite bricks surrounding lumps of uranium; it would sit in a deep well and would be supported by a wooden frame that would rise in step with the sphere. The machine was being housed in a specially-constructed building on the island.

Hannah watched as the backbreaking work went forward. Over the past month, the prospect of achieving ground-breaking science by building what they called 'the beast' had become disassociated from its ultimate and horrific purpose, and there was a sense of elation in the air. For all of them, life had settled into a routine that defined a new normality. Their basic needs were met – decent food, adequate shelter. Their work – grueling, but sometimes exhilarating – filled their days and a good part of their evenings. And for their free time they had cards, chess, and even a violin for Artur Steinitz, who entertained them with virtuoso skill.

The scientific work overwhelmed Hannah, but she couldn't deny her growing thoughts of Max. Her heart and mind screamed her dilemma. She should detest everything he stood for, but she could not deny that she savored their nights together. Their time was something to anticipate, an ecstasy at the end of the day, a drug to give her release from the demons that sought to capture her soul. She did not love Max, but she needed him.

In more ways than one. Hannah could now write to Rachel; perhaps Max could reunite her with her sister. Perhaps she could then explain to Rachel—

Sol's words broke into her thoughts.

"I wouldn't miss this for the world!" He raised his arm theatrically toward the burgeoning leviathan. "I'm fulfilling my boyhood dream."

Hannah made her way over to him. "Sol, you're the first person I've ever met whose childhood dream was to stack graphite bricks."

"You don't understand, Hannah. We're building nothing less than a giant Philosopher's Stone here." Sol took out a dirty handkerchief and wiped the sweat off his face. "Alchemy – the transmutation of base elements into gold – that was my childhood dream. That's why I went into chemistry in the first place."

Hannah laughed. Despite his years, Sol was in many ways younger than anyone else on the team.

Sol's bushy eyebrows descended like window shades over the tops of his rheumy eyes. "Tell me, Hannah, do you ever worry that this beast we're building will one day transmute the island – and us as well – into a heap of unsightly smoking cinders?"

"Sol, I'm more concerned about your sciatica." She smiled and reached over to rub him good-naturedly on his shoulder. "But so you'll sleep better, I'll tell you that Albert and I are designing control rods that will prevent that sort of thing."

"Control rods," Sol muttered. "I suppose these rods absorb neutrons?"

"That's exactly what they do, Sol. They can either be inserted into the uranium machine or pulled out, depending upon whether we want to slow down or speed up the rate of fission."

"So if the beast is getting ready to *plotz*, you push in a control rod to cool it off."

"Something like that, so not to worry." But Hannah did worry. She knew that even slow-neutron fission might get dangerously out of control and flash the uranium machine to dangerous levels of heat and radiation. The proper use of the control rods was critical.

She looked up to see a wry smile on Sol's face.

"Hannah, do you know who Pluto is, the god who is the namesake for our miraculous transuranic element, plutonium?"

Hannah shook her head. To her, Pluto was only the name of a planet.

130

"Pluto." Sol's eyebrows descended again. "In ancient mythology, he was the god of the underworld. Pluto, dear Hannah, was the god of death."

Providence, Rhode Island.

Christina was running. Her arms were pumping and her shoes were clipping on the wet cobbles. It was dark. She was sure they were closing in on her. Her breath came quickly; there was a pain in her side.

The bag was clutched under her arm as she ran. In it was a thousand dollars. The pursuing men came closer and she tried to quicken her pace. The agents could not have her money. The darkness pressed upon her, squeezing her breath from her. Where was von Rastenberg? He was supposed to help her. She could feel the growing weariness in her legs. Where was he?

The bag with the money felt heavier, dragging her back. Perhaps she should drop it so she could run faster. Where was he? Where was von Rastenberg? It was so dark.

Suddenly it was light. The sun came through the window and spilled over her bed. Christina started, sat up, and looked down at the pillow clutched securely under her arm. She cast the pillow aside. It had been the bag with the thousand dollars.

She breathed more easily as the nightmare subsided, but the memories of Stockholm and von Rastenberg kept coming back. She tried to banish them from her mind as she stretched and got out of bed. Through her apartment window, she could see the marina where her boat was moored. Göteborg was her pride and joy; she had named her boat after the city where she had been born.

Her nightmare and von Rastenberg's image came back briefly, but were soon dispelled by the sunlight. She'd be sailing that afternoon. Free. Von Rastenberg's image returned once again, and she shook herself. She got up, leapt into the shower, and felt the water cleanse away her fears. Free.

Morko.

Max Heldorf lit a cigarette to ease his frustration. His efforts to release Hannah's sister from Treblinka were going nowhere.

He ran his finger down the deckle edge of the photograph that had arrived in the mail pouch. The woman in the picture had hollows beneath her high cheek bones and darkness surrounded her large, frightened eyes.

Heldorf's long isolation on the island had cost him dearly: he had lost much of his power and influence within the SS. To get a favor, you had to be able to give a favor; that was how the system worked. But, away from the Berlin power centers for the past year and working on a project known only to Speer, he was in no position to provide a benefit to anyone's friends or pet projects. And he couldn't use Speer's name anymore; the Reichminister had bluntly said that he would deny all knowledge of him. A year ago, Heldorf had been able to use his own influence to arrange for the release of the Jews who now formed his project team. Now he found himself yearning for those good old days.

Heldorf had resorted to a base lie to get concessions for Rachel Goldmann. In his call to the administrative office at Treblinka, he suggested that Rachel was the cousin of a high-ranking Reich official. The officer on the other end of the line had sighed heavily and, perhaps swayed by Heldorf's story, perhaps just tired of arguing, had agreed to move Rachel to the camp infirmary. Heldorf made him swear that the infirmary would not simply be a way-station to the gas chamber as it was for many sick prisoners.

He looked at the woman in the photograph again. Her cropped black hair stuck out in short tufts beneath a gray scarf and her striped uniform was bunched around her meager frame as though her body were a pole. She looked very ill, maybe close to death. Her eyes were dark, wide-set. No one else had eyes like that. No one except Hannah. Heldorf could see that Rachel Goldmann had once been very beautiful. He didn't wish to consider the horrors she must have endured to became the skeletal creature in the photograph.

He had sent packages of food, clothing, and blankets. He had also sent her cigarettes, which were the coin of the realm in the camps and which she could trade for rations. That Rachel Goldmann had received at least some of these shipments had been confirmed. At least the guards had not played fast and loose with her packages, had not stolen them to distribute to their friends and family.

Now he despaired of getting Hannah's sister released from Treblinka. For the moment he was powerless. But it was essential that he not be seen as having lost power. The perception of power gave him his authority and propelled the entire operation; power kept the Jews motivated.

He had promised Hannah he would free Rachel by the spring. Now it was May and her frequent questions were annoying him. He needed to put an end to them immediately, and he would do that by showing her the picture. Clearly her sister couldn't be moved out – a glance at the photograph would convince anyone of that.

He looked down at the photo again and the dark eyes stared back at him in terror. She was a pitiful sight and Heldorf knew the picture would break Hannah's heart. He stubbed out his cigarette, poured a large brandy and drank deeply. An SS man shouldn't have such feelings.

Mørkø. Conference Room.

Like the ticking of a well-loved clock, the repetitive thwacks of the ping-pong ball were strangely comforting to the team. After their long days in the uranium machine room, those who were off-duty had congregated in the conference room to relax. The hoot of success that accompanied a change in the ball's rhythm was quickly followed by a grunt of disgust, and all eyes looked up to see Ernst Schlegel brandishing his paddle in triumph as Otto Weinstein laughed good-naturedly at his own incompetence.

In the corner, Artur Steinitz lovingly tuned his new violin. Heldorf had clearly not paid much for the poor instrument; it was hardly in a class with the violin they had taken from him. Nonetheless, all violins were beautiful, Steinitz thought, even if some were lovelier than others. He ran rosin over the bow, lifted the instrument to his chin, closed his eyes, and began to play a Bach Partita from memory.

At the end of the conference room table sat Georg Silberstein. Physics, itself, was his form of relaxation, and for the past week he had been working on a paper that considered whether the explosion of an atomic bomb could ignite the atmosphere. Most of the other physicists had ruled out this possibility, but Silberstein checked and rechecked his assumptions as he considered this grimmest of all horrors with the utter detachment of a scientist who was merely curious to see how the equations would work out.

At the other end of the table, Albert Weiss and Sol Friedberg sat huddled over a chess board. Sol moved his rook forward, pushed his chair back, and stretched out his legs. "Tell me, Al, why does Hitler put Jews in death camps?"

Weiss, cradling his chin in his hand as he pondered his next move, replied distractedly. "Because, according to him, the Jews are *Untermenschen.*"

"*Untermenschen.* Subhuman. Like animals. But if we're subhuman, why didn't he just put us in zoos? I hear the baboons at the Berlin Zoo are treated very well."

"Because no one would pay admission to see Jews." Weiss pushed his bishop to castle five with a flourish. "Besides, we're dangerous to the Reich."

"Ah, yes; that's right – we're dangerous." Sol had anticipated Weiss's move and quickly pulled his castle to the back rank. "Tell me, Al, what's the Yiddish word for 'weapons'?"

"Sol, you know there isn't one."

"And for 'ammunition'?"

"Doesn't exist."

What about the Yiddish term for 'military exercises'?"

"Come on, Sol, you know very well there's no Yiddish term for 'military exercises.' But *zol zein shtil* means keep quiet – you're disturbing my concentration." He smiled as he slid his queen to attack Sol's defenseless king. "Checkmate."

Sol cursed quietly as he lay down his king. "I don't get it, Al: why would Hitler be so afraid of the Jews?"

"Seems clear to me." Albert started setting up the pieces on the board for the next evening's game. "People who speak a language that excludes words for 'weapons' and 'ammunition' – well, they must have something pretty sinister up their sleeves."

Hannah, sitting nearby with a notebook in her lap, smiled at her friends' banter. She was about to take a break from her analysis of the day's results and indulge in the new-found pleasure of writing to her sister, Rachel. But the pleasure was bittersweet, and she often chided herself for once having taken for granted this rarest of all gifts, the one soul in all the world whose life was intertwined with her own as intricately as any filigree.

She sighed and picked up her pencil. *My dearest sister....*

Frederikshavn.

"Let's get out of the rain and I'll give you the full story." Lars ran in front of Jørgen as they raced through the sudden spring shower to the dentist's office where the Resistance cell meeting was planned for that afternoon.

Jørgen tried to concentrate on what Lars had said. Something he learned from his girlfriend, something about a couple of Danish Nazis snooping through official records in the government office in which she worked. They passed the Krudttårnet, the round, white-washed gunpowder tower that was Frederikshavn's beloved landmark. Jørgen thought about Peter Tordenskiold – Peter 'Thunder Shield' – the national hero who had used the tower in the seventeenth century as a base to fend off invaders. Jørgen sighed inwardly as he thought about how Denmark could use a Tordenskiold at that moment.

Their pace slowed as they turned the corner and saw a German patrol across the street. The soldiers eyed them suspiciously; gone were the days when the Germans had tried to be friendly. Some had seen their comrades blown to hell by the Danish Resistance's acts of sabotage. Now they saw danger on every corner; every young Dane was a threat. Jørgen pulled his raincoat tight about him and pushed up the high collar. The Germans' hobnailed boots crunched on the cobbles in a relentless cadence, a sound that Jørgen had learned to hate.

Jørgen looked at Lars, who nodded and picked up the pace again. As they crossed the square, Jørgen looked behind him quickly. Lars's information could be important, but he had other things on his mind. Three nights before, two of the Resistance group had gone out to pick up an RAF drop of submachine guns. The Germans had been waiting. It was the second such disaster in a month.

"Come on, Jørgen, we're late," Lars beckoned as they turned down the alley to the dentist's office. "Hey, look – the rain's stopped and the sun's coming out."

Jørgen wasn't paying attention. Something was wrong, he knew. How was it that the Germans knew the details of his cell's operations? He knew Marius was also worried. That was probably why he had called the meeting.

Mørkø.

"As you all know, the reason it's difficult to separate out fissionable isotopes from uranium is they're virtually identical to non-fissionable isotopes." Sol Friedberg was addressing a meeting of the scientific team to describe techniques he was investigating for extracting the plutonium they would soon be producing. "However, with plutonium, we can use a chemical process—"

"Excuse me, Dr. Goldmann," Heldorf's aide-de-camp whispered to Hannah, "the sturmbannführer would like to see you in his office." All of Heldorf's small staff treated the Jews with the utmost courtesy. Heldorf insisted upon it; it cost not a single reichsmark and went a long way toward keeping morale high.

As Hannah followed the corporal down the path to Heldorf's office, she wondered what could be so urgent that she had to be called out of an important meeting. The corporal opened the door, stood aside for Hannah to enter, and softly closed the door behind her. Heldorf stood in the middle of the room beaming; there was a strange basket on his desk.

"Hannah, look at this day." He motioned toward the open window. "After an endless winter, we can't waste this blue sky and warm sun."

Hannah scowled. "Max, Sol Friedberg was in the middle of a lecture on—"

"Hannah, you've been working twelve-hour shifts without any days off. The project won't collapse because you're away from it for a few hours. Come, see what I have over here."

As she peered into the basket, he embraced her with one arm while he pulled out delicacies with the other. "See, here's some fine Danish cheese. And some excellent pickled herring. And strawberries, Hannah, strawberries! Look at this good crusty bread. And wine, of course."

Like a schoolgirl, she clapped her hands together. "You even have some chocolate, Max!" The joy of a picnic – it would be like their student days when they took lunches on the banks of the Auer, although their fare had never been so grand.

"Let's go!' Heldorf picked up the basket and opened the door.

After they had eaten, Heldorf lay on the beach with his head propped on his arm as Hannah sat cross-legged watching the surf, the sea breezes playing with strands of her hair.

"You're so pensive, Hannah; what are you thinking about?" He reached over and tenderly ran his free hand down the length of her thigh.

"I was just wondering what one of our old professors would say about the lowly neutron, now that we know it can trigger power of immense magnitude. Professor—, oh, Max, what was his name? You remember, that professor who used to rail out against students who wanted a narrow specialty? What was his name, do you remember?"

"Professor Englesing I think is the professor you mean. He used to say 'You enter university as generalists and gradually narrow your field of study—'"

"'—learning more and more about less and less—'"

"'—until finally you know everything there is to know—'"

"'—about practically nothing at all!'"

He smiled as she threw her head back laughing. Eyes closed, she raised her face to enjoy the luxury of the sun's warmth on her skin, a joy she had missed during the long winter months.

"You're so beautiful when you laugh, Hannah. But you don't laugh enough. We need to do this more often."

"The afternoon was so enjoyable." She sifted some sand through her fingers. "Max, thank you. But—"

He braced himself; he knew what was coming.

"Max, please tell me you've brought me here today to give me some good news. Please tell me Rachel's on her way to Portugal or Sweden."

He had dreaded her question. He couldn't get Rachel released, not yet, but he couldn't tell Hannah. Above all, he couldn't let her or any of the other Jews know he had lost power within the SS.

"Hannah...," he reached into his pocket; his fingers felt the photograph. "Hannah..."

"Yes?"

Her smile was anxious, but warm. He could not break the heart of the woman he—

He pushed the photo deep into his pocket and sat up. He couldn't do it; he couldn't show her the photograph.

"Hannah," he got up and brushed the sand off his jacket, "these things take time. A number of complicated administrative details have to be dealt with first."

Subtle changes in her smile betrayed a deep but not unexpected disappointment. "I understand, Max. I know you're doing everything possible."

He offered her his hand. "Come, Hannah, we should be getting back to the laboratory."

Frederikshavn.

Jørgen looked around the room; there were only five left from the original Resistance cell. Svend had been executed, and Jan and Wilhelm, arrested during a recent RAF drop, were being held by the Gestapo. Except for Gunnar and the two new recruits, all had been friends since the cell had been formed in the early days of the occupation, when dangerous actions meant nothing more than beating up German patrols in dark alleys and stealing guns out of holsters. Jørgen knew Marius was worried about security and wondered if he was about to announce that he was dissolving the cell.

Marius called the meeting to order; the chatter around the table ceased and all eyes turned toward their leader. "In view of the recent arrests, we've got to tighten our security." Marius spoke with both urgency and sadness. "It's almost certain the Gestapo will torture our comrades, as they did Svend."

In the past, the mutual trust upon which the Frederikshavn cell was based had seemed to work; after all, Svend had been captured and tortured but as far as anyone knew hadn't given away any of the cell's secrets. But Jørgen knew that even the strongest of men caved in during torture. He'd heard that Resistance cells in Copenhagen had become so compromised they had to be reorganized under strict rules; names were never known and orders were passed on surreptitiously. Mutual trust had always worked for their cell, but now things were different.

"In the future, not only will we meet in different locations for every meeting," Marius's usually-stern face was particularly grave that day, "but I'll announce the venue through a chain of command."

Someone in the group couldn't be trusted, Jørgen thought. It couldn't be Karl or Johann. He looked at the fresh faces of the new recruits, tinged with fear as they realized it was no longer a game they were playing.

"I'll tell Jørgen," Marius began calling out the list and Jørgen was proud to hear his own name first, "who'll pass the message to Erik. Then Gunnar, then..." Marius ran down the names and adjourned the meeting, but Jørgen continued concentrating on his leader's logic. If the two new recruits were excluded, five were left. His mind tried to untangle the logic. There must be a common factor.

Lars's voice suddenly cut across his train of thought. "Please, Marius, I have something to report."

"Yes, Lars, what is it?" Marius looked at his watch impatiently.

"Sir, the Danish Nazis—they've been poking around official records."

"How do you know?"

"From my girlfriend." Lars looked around anxiously at the group. "She works at a government office."

"And what did she see?"

"The Nazis asked for records about orphans, adoptions, and dogs."

"Orphans, adoptions, and dogs?" Marius sighed with impatience.

"Specifically about Peder Gronborg and his mother, Sara."

Jørgen, who had continued to ponder Marius's security arrangements, suddenly focused on what Lars had said.

"There's been trouble with them before." Marius looked across at Jørgen. "They're friends of yours, Jørgen, aren't they?"

Jørgen looked around. "We all know Peder. Everyone knows Peder. Or of him, that is."

They all nodded. The small boy with the strange ways was part of the life of Frederikshavn.

"Wasn't his mother the one who pissed off the Danish Nazis when she wouldn't sell them some meat?" someone asked.

"Yes, and then they threw a brick through the window of her shop," added another.

Erik piped in. "Jørgen repaired her window."

"With your help, Erik," Jørgen nodded towards his friend.

"Okay, okay, I know," Marius snapped impatiently, "you're both good Boy Scouts. We've got enough on our plate now as it is," his fingers ran through his beard, "but we'll keep an eye on it to make sure there's no problem here." He smiled. "Peder's a sort of mascot. Jørgen, keep in touch with Mrs. Gronborg. Keep me informed if anything else happens."

Jørgen nodded. He saw Peder every day; he'd soon know if anything was wrong. But his mind returned to a more urgent problem. He looked around the room. One of the men at the meeting was a traitor.

Mørkø Island.

Hannah's evening walks were usually a welcome break in the long day of work. But that night she could almost hear and feel in the wind and the pounding of the surf the ghosts of the past keening and swirling around her. The white fingers of the sea pushed up onto the beach. The ghosts whispered that it was Rachel who had freed Hannah to devote herself to the study of science, Rachel who, when they were young, had done Hannah's chores. The fingers drew back and a roll of green sea menaced from behind. The ghosts chided that Rachel had run back to be with their parents the day the Gestapo came while Hannah had turned and run away. The waves thrust themselves onto a rock and shot up in wild frenzy. The ghosts moaned that Rachel now languished in a camp while Hannah enjoyed the bed of the enemy.

Hannah tried to shake the thoughts away. A cry came from a bird above; she sighed, envying the bird as it arched its wings and made its escape to the sinking western sun. There was no escape for her. Only the brief moments spent each evening looking out over the sea.

She was alone – that was her escape. Away from the team, away from Max. Alone, to try to conjure a dream of a future that would never be.

"Hannah, I thought I'd find you here." Albert's voice blew her thoughts to the corners of the world.

"Hello, Albert." Hannah's eyes fixed upon another gull flying from the island. How she wished she had wings.

"Hannah," Weiss drew alongside her, breathless from his run across the sand, "we have to talk."

"Talk, Albert?" Hannah's voice was world-weary. "Talk about what?" The image of her sister came to her mind; Rachel was the only person in the whole world she wanted to talk to at that moment. She wanted to tell Rachel—

"I think you know what we should talk about." Weiss's voice was embarrassed; he looked down at the sand.

"It's none of your business, Albert." She turned sharply on Weiss, anger in her voice.

Weiss flinched instinctively, but recovered quickly. "I've clearly touched a nerve. I'm sorry." He lifted his eyebrows.

"What I do in my own time is my business." There was still vehemence in Hannah's voice.

"The others are talking, Hannah."

"Then let them talk." She lit a cigarette and drew heavily. "What's it to you, anyway? Why do you even care?"

"Because you make me think of my daughters, Hannah." Weiss felt his eyes begin to well up; he cleared his throat and looked down at his feet to buy time to regain control. "Because, in a similar situation, I wouldn't want them to do what you're doing." He looked up, straight into her eyes. "And because I care about you. That's why."

Hannah looked away. Why was she doing it? It wasn't just the sex. Or was it? She could hardly deny that she was more than a little drawn to him. The faces of Max and Rachel came together in her mind, then dissolved, but fused once more.

"You have your family, but I have myself to consider." She gave a hardness to her voice to cover her confusion. "Max may be my ticket out of this place." She paused and fixed Weiss with a stare. "Tell the others to stick to the science and forget about moralizing. Their cant and hypocrisy disgust me."

Weiss winced and turned to walk back to the camp, but she pulled at his sleeve.

"Tell them that I, too, am flesh and blood. And for that I make no apology." She tossed her cigarette into the sand and ground it out with her heel.

Mørkø Island.

Perhaps it was the sherry spreading warmth throughout him, or perhaps it was Schnabel's ecstatic interpretation of Beethoven's Waldstein Sonata playing on the phonograph: Max Heldorf felt exuberant, almost euphoric. He stood up, loosened the top button of his shirt and began pumping his fist in the air in time with the music. This first movement exuded confidence, the confidence of a man who wrote music he could not hear, the confidence of a man achieving the unachievable.

Achieving the unachievable. The uranium machine was progressing well. That afternoon Hannah had shown him the emerging black monster that reminded him of a totem of some long-vanished culture. She was convinced it would yield the controlled chain reaction needed to produce plutonium, and her enthusiasm gave him confidence. She had not been wrong yet in any of her hypotheses.

He turned the record over and the sonata entered its haunting second movement. Heldorf sat down, rested his head on the back of the chair, and closed his eyes to listen. She was so beautiful, so intelligent. She seemed to prove the theory that excellence in the physical was a predictor of excellence in the mental. Even though her features did not conform to the Aryan standard, he thought her the most beautiful woman in the world. The music burgeoned, then softened, then swelled again.

Success was within his grasp. With a nuclear weapon, Germany could level cities, destroy military bases, wipe out invading armies. Germany would win the war and he would be a national hero, his reputation assured forever. He indulged himself with the thought of the glory that would be heaped upon him, the fame he'd achieve. Children would one day read his name in history books.

The movement started to slow, disturbing his mood, and he put the next record on the turntable; the needle complained with a screech as he roughly positioned it for the start of the Rondo movement. Of course, the war could go the other way if it ended before the weapon was completed. Ever since the Wehrmacht had been defeated at Stalingrad in February, Germany's fortunes had been on the wane. But even if the worst happened and Germany lost the war, he, Heldorf, could still win because he would have the recipe for plutonium. He wondered how much the Americans would be willing to pay him for the secret; whatever he could get, it would doubtless buy him a rich new life outside Germany. The sonata concluded with a flourish.

One problem nagged him like the whir-whir-whir of the needle that was now traveling endlessly in the final groove. The Jews' relatives. Soon they would expect him to start making good on his promises, and that would prove difficult. Although he was able to get packages of food and clothing through to some of them, he couldn't do much else. He had just learned that Naomi, Weiss's elder daughter, had died, how he did not know. It was a great pity; she was such a beautiful girl. Of course, Weiss could not be told.

His mother's smile beamed at him from the photo by the side of the phonograph. He wondered how she was coping in a Berlin ravaged by the thousands of tons of bombs the enemy had dropped since he had left nine months ago. Behind his mother's smile he knew fear was hidden. He hoped she was safe. He regretted not having visited her. Had he gone to Berlin to see her, he could also have tried to keep up his connections in the SS, the connections that might help him get the Jews out of the camps.

But there was one Jew he was desperate to get released, and that was Hannah's sister. That afternoon he had composed a letter to Speer asking for his help. It was a desperation move but one he had to make.

The mood had been lost, and he needed to recapture it. He turned the record over and began playing *Für Elise* on the other side. The lovely piece lifted him once more. He drained his glass. It was time to put work and the war aside. As he reached for the decanter, there was a soft knock on the door. Hannah. The anticipation was almost painful.

Frederikshavn.

Jørgen listened for the sound of aircraft engines overhead. He had taken part in many RAF drops, but he still felt afraid, the familiar tightening in his gut, as he stood in the dark field. Despite his fear, he was always awed by the sight of parachutes floating down like huge spent dandelions wafting in on a breeze. After the crates landed, there was no time for fear; only the usual scramble to collect the supplies and hide them before the Germans arrived.

He glanced at his watch; twelve past midnight. The RAF plane wasn't due until one, but they had arrived beforehand to listen and watch the full moon sky in case the plane arrived early. Waiting for the drop was the worst part, waiting and wondering if anything would go wrong. He remembered the time one of the parachutes collapsed; a crate had split open, strewing hand grenades all over a newly-plowed field. It had been almost dawn, but the locals had come out to help collect the grenades.

He looked at the bleak midnight landscape and pulled his jacket tighter around his body; it was chilly and he could see the others by the small clouds of breath that hung in the moonlight. He checked his pistol and hoped he would have no use for it. It was a three-man operation, just he and Lars and Karl, one of the new guys. He blew on his hands for warmth; he was bone weary and longed to go home and fall into his bed.

They all heard the plane before they could see it. It was early. They flashed the recognition signal and the plane flew nearer until it was overhead. Soon the parachutes would come drifting down.

Suddenly the night sky was ripped apart by tracer bullets. Jørgen looked up in fear – and glimpsed a Luftwaffe night fighter diving low and firing on them. He scrambled for shelter underneath a wagon parked by the side of the road and watched as one of the men was shot and spiraled slowly to the ground. Lars struggled to his knees and then fell forward on his face.

The plane flew off. Jørgen rushed over to Lars, gently rolled him over, and put his jacket under his head. Despite the darkness, he could see the blood bubbling from Lars's mouth. "Don't worry, Lars – Karl is running to fetch the doctor." He motioned to Karl, who raced off the field toward the road.

He held Lars's hand and watched as he tried to say something, but only incoherent guttural sounds emerged from his throat as his eyes darted back and forth. Slowly the sounds died away and Lars's eyes froze into glassy fixtures staring at some invisible point midway between the earth and the sky.

Jørgen squeezed Lars's hand. "Lars, goddamn you! Goddamn you, Lars! Lars, please come back!" he screamed. Then he heard a plane overhead. Probably the RAF plane, but he withheld the recognition signal – the German pilot would have radioed an alert to the local foot patrols who were probably on their way. But despite the danger, he couldn't stop squeezing Lars's hand; he couldn't stop sobbing his name.

He wondered if the appearance of the German plane had been a coincidence. There had been too many coincidences.

Berlin.

Albert Speer pushed back from his desk, took a deep breath, and looked up at the clock on the office wall. Almost seven; he planned to break for dinner soon, then come back and work a little more. His sixteen-hour days seemed normal to him now, and he often thought of the irony that the reward for his efficiency was more responsibility. But he was proud of having been able to improve war production despite dwindling supplies and manpower.

He had spent a bleak day reading reports of the Hamburg bombings. The enemy had essentially accomplished what the Führer had tried to do in London: burn down an entire city. The first attacks on Hamburg had put the water pipes out of action, giving the emergency workers little with which to battle the inferno, and Speer could only wonder at the Führer's refusal to receive a delegation from the brave rescue crews.

He pulled out a sheet of paper to jot down some notes for a meeting with Hitler the following day. The human cost of the firestorm had been terrible, but the impact on war production worried him more. The Führer had to be told that any future attacks like the bombing of Hamburg on half a dozen or more major cities would bring armaments production – and consequently the war – to a hasty conclusion. Speer closed his eyes and pinched the bridge of his nose. He did not relish the prospect of the meeting; the Führer did not receive bad news with good grace.

Speer picked up the next report – an inventory of Tiger Tank spare parts manufactured in Hamburg – and pushed it aside. He had to get Hamburg out of his mind or his appetite for dinner would be ruined. He thumbed through the remaining stack of work, looking for something that might bring good – or at least neutral – news, and settled on a letter from Sturmbannführer Heldorf.

Speer broke the seal on the envelope, pulled out Heldorf's letter, read it and frowned. Heldorf was requesting – practically begging for – his intercession on obtaining the release of the sister, a Rachel Goldmann, of one of the Jewish scientists. Speer tossed the letter aside as though it were unclean.

The letter angered him, and he regretted having endorsed Heldorf's project. Had Heldorf forgotten the terms of their deal? The relatives of the Jews were to be released only after they produced results, not before. That was the agreement. Not a single Jew was to be released before that time.

Heldorf's letter reported some progress in the project. Speer's mind tried to find a balance. On the one hand, Heldorf might yet come up with the weapon to win the war for Germany; on the other, the whole scheme might collapse in failure, and if the Führer got to know—

Speer knew he was sailing a tight line between success and disaster. Heldorf had another three months, no more. If he didn't succeed by the middle of October....

He glanced at his watch; it was time for dinner.

Frederikshavn.

"Gentlemen, yesterday the madman in Berlin presented Denmark with a series of demands." Marius had called a special meeting of the Frederikshavn cell, which sat around a polished mahogany table in the conference room of a law practice.

"We all heard about them." Karl thumped his fist on the table in disgust. "The bastards wanted the government to ban public meetings and put gun owners in front of firing squads."

"They also wanted permission to fiddle with the truth in our pressrooms," added Gunnar. "If we want fiction in our newspapers, why don't we just reprint the fairytales of Hans Christian Andersen?"

"What about the curfew they demanded? How can you tell a farmer when he's allowed to go out and milk his cows?"

Erik's rhetorical question was about to be answered by Gunnar when Marius held up his hand. "I know everyone has an opinion about the demands that were made, but I didn't bring you here to debate them. I think all of us were delighted to hear that yesterday afternoon the government finally demonstrated it has a backbone by rejecting Hitler's ultimatum."

"Does this mean we're not going to be his model protectorate anymore?"

Gunnar's quip brought a few chuckles but Marius ignored it. "This morning, we woke up to find German guards stationed at Frederikshavn's key facilities – the railroad station, the power plant, the radio transmitter. I hear that in Copenhagen the bastards even posted guards at the Amalienborg Palace. And to make life even less pleasant, they've shut off the telephones."

"Excuse me, Marius, but I think the important question is what can we do about it?" Jørgen asked.

"Nothing right now. The reason I called you here is to tell you that the Nazis will be making an important announcement today. They're putting Denmark under martial law." Marius held up a piece of paper. "The Resistance has obtained a copy of their proclamation, which will be read over the radio later this afternoon. I'll pass this around. For the most part, it's a tougher version of the ultimatum, and any unfortunate Dane who runs afoul of it will be tried in a German military court."

A hush fell over the room. Denmark was about to get a taste of what other occupied countries had suffered for years.

Marius continued. "It's obvious that our job is now about to get more difficult. It was never easy, but in the past we were able to count on ordinary citizens for help. Now if those people shy away from sticking their necks out, who can blame them? But at least no one can call Denmark Hitler's pet canary anymore." Marius's face broke into a rare smile and there was nervous laughter around the table.

"I'm proud to report to you that our leaders have responded to this outrageous proclamation of martial law with courage and dignity." Marius stroked his beard as he considered his next piece of news. "The entire government has just resigned in protest. What's more, our navy has scuttled its fleet; or at least most of it – I understand that a few ships have escaped to Sweden."

There were intakes of breath and amazed expressions at the news. A country without a government. Who would run it? A navy without ships; it was sad beyond measure.

"Clearly," Marius said, "the German actions show we have the Nazis on the defensive. And Denmark's reactions show that we will not tolerate being bullied. Gentlemen, our strategy is working."

Although a cheer went up, Jørgen wondered about Marius's conclusion. How could the strategy be working? Had the harsh conditions the Nazis were about to impose been brought on by the Resistance's actions? And if so, would the people turn against the Resistance for having irritated the monster?

He looked around the room. The others were pumping up their courage with brave words, gesticulating with bravado. Jørgen was less hopeful. The government was gone. The Danish navy had been scuttled. Now everyone would be waiting for Hitler's other jackboot to fall.

Only time would tell how the devil would get his revenge.

PART FOUR

"If the devil doesn't exist and man has created him,
he has created him in his own image and likeness."

— Dostoevsky
The Brothers Karamazov

Berlin.

"Do you have a moment, Werner?" Franz von Rastenberg stood in the doorway of Heisenberg's study. Heisenberg nodded and his junior associate entered, quietly closing the door behind him. "Werner, I've just learned something extremely disturbing."

Heisenberg raised his eyebrows. "Yes, Franz? What is it you find disturbing?"

"I've just received a message through the grapevine." He pulled a piece of paper from his pocket. "It says that all the Jews of Denmark are to be rounded up and shipped off to the camps."

Heisenberg sighed and shook his head. "About that, my friend, I can do nothing. I'm not happy with the policy of *Judenrein* – I've lost a number of excellent colleagues to it – but what can I do? What can any of us do? We're powerless."

"Please let me finish, Werner; there's more. The plan is for the Gestapo to sweep through Denmark on the second day of Rosh Hashanah arresting all the Jews. My informant says that Niels Bohr is to be taken, as well."

Heisenberg pushed his chair back and stood up abruptly. "What? Niels? I knew his mother was Jewish, but *Niels?*" His face was red with anger. "How can those idiots dream of arresting a Nobel laureate?"

Heisenberg paced the floor before sitting down on the edge of his desk. "Franz, we have to get word to the Americans that Niels is in trouble. Surely you need to visit the heavy water plant in Norway to assess the repairs again?"

"No, Werner, I was just—"

"Then make some pretext for going back. I want you to stop in Sweden on your way and alert the Americans. I'll arrange for you to make contact with an American agent there."

American agent. The image of Christina came into von Rastenberg's mind. How much she looked like Elsa. He wanted to see her again. "I'll do it, Werner, but...," von Rastenberg hesitated as he considered the insanity of what he was about to ask, "but..."

"Out with it, Franz, we've got no time to lose. But what?"

"But there's one thing I'd like…" Von Rastenberg cast his eyes down in an unfocused stare.

"If it can be arranged, you shall have it, dear Franz."

Von Rastenberg's eyes shot up. "No, Werner, it's not a request, it's a condition I must insist upon. The American agent I met last year, she must be my contact."

Frederikshavn.

P eder had gone out; Soldat was snoring in a corner of the shop. Sara wondered what had got into Peder lately – in the past, the boy never went out without Soldat. She shook her head and smiled; she never would figure out his strange ways.

She picked up the mail that had just been delivered and set it on the counter. It was mid-morning and so far there had been only one customer. There wasn't much business lately; Sara's meat selection had never been so poor – she was embarrassed by the grisly cuts and organ meats that now dominated her meager offerings. It was the Germans' fault, and everyone cursed them; they were helping themselves to more and more of Denmark's bounty. She busied herself trying to arrange the pieces in the display case in the vain hope they would appear more attractive.

She made herself a cup of tea, set it on the counter to cool, and began to open the mail. There were three letters. The first was from a friend in Copenhagen; her migraines were getting worse and the Jewish community there was worried because things were getting tense. She ripped open a bill; surely that amount could not be right – she made a mental note to look into it. The last piece of mail came in a long official envelope with her name and address typed. She opened it and read:

North Jutland Office of Child Welfare

Please be advised that a complaint has been lodged against you with respect to the following.

It has been alleged that:

1. You have assumed illegal custody of a child not related to you by blood, marriage, or adoption.
2. Said child is mentally defective, possibly requiring institutionalization for the wellbeing of himself and of others.

3. You are harboring a vicious dog; furthermore, said dog is in the charge of the aforementioned mentally defective child.

Verification of these charges will result in severe penalties in addition to the removal of the child and the destruction of the dog.

Sara's hand flew up to her mouth catching her teacup, which fell off the counter to the floor. The sound of the shattering crockery awoke Soldat, who sat up, looked at her through half-closed lids, and yawned. Sara wrapped her arms around herself and shook uncontrollably.

Providence, Rhode Island.

Christina felt the sun on her face, the salt spray on her skin, the tug as the sail caught the wind – even though she was still taking the vinyl cover off her typewriter. The weather was forecast to be perfect for sailing, and in just eight hours she'd be out on the harbor, padding around barefoot on her boat and—

"You're wanted in the conference room, Christina. Immediately." The pinched face and squeaky voice of her boss's assistant brought Christina back to solid ground and into the workaday world of Army translations. Christina stored her typewriter cover in a desk drawer and checked her hair in her compact mirror before grabbing a pad and pencil and heading over to the conference room. She had been inside the room only once – for an orientation session when she was first hired – and could not imagine why she had been summoned there that morning. She hoped that she would not have to work late that evening and miss her sail. Anything but that.

She opened the door and was startled to see the man who was seated alone at the conference room table. "Major Stevens?" Christina held onto the doorknob with a hand that was suddenly clammy; the last time she had seen this man he had talked her into going to Sweden on a mission that had almost cost her life.

"Come in, Private Lindgren. Very nice to see you again." The major was removing the tinfoil from one end of a roll of LifeSavers. "Care for a Wint-O-Green? I've given up smoking."

Christina shook her head.

"Private Lindgren, we need you for another special assignment in Sweden." Stevens popped a mint into his mouth.

Christina felt as though she'd just been shot in the chest. The trip over in the tiny plane, the Gestapo agents chasing her down the streets of Stockholm – the frightening memories all returned. She wouldn't go back. She just wouldn't.

"You'll be happy to know the stipend has been increased. It will be twelve hundred dollars this time."

Stipend or no stipend, she wouldn't go. The reports she translated had taught her more than she ever wanted to know about what horrible things the Nazis were capable of. Christina coughed nervously. She wouldn't go back, she wouldn't do it.

The major leaned forward and clasped his hands. "You'd be making a big contribution to the war effort, Private Lindgren."

Christina looked down at her lap. She knew there were a lot of brave Americans out there giving their all, risking their lives for the country they loved. But she couldn't face it again.

Stevens raised his eyebrows. "You're scared, aren't you, Private Lindgren?"

Christina nodded. "I'll be honest, Major Stevens, I just don't have the courage for this sort of thing. Last time—"

"You know, Private Lindgren, my mother was a volunteer ambulance driver during the last war and she knew all about courage. She gave me some good advice. She told me never to confuse courage with not being afraid. Being unaware of danger and rushing in without fear, that's not courage – that's stupidity." Major Stevens crunched the remains of his LifeSaver. "Courage, my mother used to say, is appreciating what you're up against and feeling real fear, but – if it's something that really needs to be done – going ahead with it anyway."

"Well, then," Christina's voice cracked, "I guess I qualify."

"Sure you don't want a LifeSaver?"

"Yes, I think I could use one." Christina reached for the candy. "When do I leave? I was hoping to go sailing tonight."

"You need to be in Sweden in two days. You'll meet your contact in Gothenburg this time. Say, weren't you born in Gothenburg?"

"Yes." Christina smiled. The mention of Gothenburg – Göteborg in Swedish – brought her some comfort.

"That's all I can tell you now. I'm still working out the rest of the details. Meet me at this address at eight tonight," Stevens handed Christina a scrap of paper, "and I'll give you a full briefing."

He paused as Christina made a note on her pad. "Look, why don't you take the rest of the day off and go out for that sail? I'll fix it with your superiors. Love sailing myself. I always say if you're lucky enough to be out on the water, you're lucky enough."

"Thanks, I'd like to. Sailing always helps me get my wits back in place."

Stevens nodded. "I know what you mean. And look, it'll be a short mission – you'll be back home in about a week."

"You might remember, Major Stevens," Christina smiled archly, "that I've heard that line before."

Frederikshavn.

S ara pulled the letter out from beneath the cash register. Her tired eyes betrayed a loss of sleep and her hands trembled. *Verification of these charges will result in severe penalties in addition to the removal of the child.* All night long the words had interrupted her fitful sleep. How could they take Peder from her? It was true she hadn't gone through any formal adoption procedures, but perhaps she could still do that.

All was quiet upstairs; Peder was taking his afternoon nap. She remembered with tenderness how she and the little boy had become a family. Peder, tired and hungry, had been found wandering the streets of Frederikshavn when she'd taken him into her home. It had seemed the natural thing to do, and the neighbors had all praised her for her kind deed. No one knew where he had come from, and Peder had not been able to tell them. If he had had a home, she certainly would have taken him back there.

She read the letter once more. Surely there had been a misunderstanding. She'd sent a message to Jørgen; he was a brash young man, she knew, but he'd been kind to her when the shop window had been smashed. Perhaps he could help. She had nowhere else to turn; the leaders of the Jewish community didn't want to be mixed up in legal matters that might jeopardize the Jews' position.

Sara recalled the early days with Peder. He'd been a difficult child, and the school had given up on him, saying he sat silent in class and refused to play with other children. The head mistress had shaken her head. It was, she had said, impossible to teach Peder anything.

A sob racked Sara's body as she remembered the hours she had labored to teach him to recite the alphabet, read basic words, and recognize numbers. He wasn't like other young people. He could recite the names of all the ships in the harbor but had little aptitude for what was taught from books.

Soldat's growl cut across her thoughts: someone was coming. She remembered when Soldat had come into her house, when Peder had brought him home. Like Peder, the dog was an orphan, a stray. Peder had said simply, 'This is Soldat. He's my friend.' And the two had become inseparable. Peder was a good boy. He loved his dog. He loved his mama. He meant no harm to anyone. How could they take him from her and put him in an institution?

The dog growled again. Had they come already? Perhaps they were here to blow up her shop, like Mikkelsen's Bakery. The bell rang as the shop door opened and Sara looked up. Soldat rose and wagged his tail at the man who stood in the doorway, then yawned and padded into the back room.

Sara ran to Jørgen and grasped both of his hands. "Thank God you've come, Jørgen."

"What's the matter, Mrs. Gronborg?" Jørgen took the arm of the sobbing woman and eased her into a chair.

"They're going to take Peder." She thrust the letter into his hand.

Jørgen read it quickly and knew the situation was serious. He recalled Lars saying at the meeting that his girlfriend had seen Danish Nazis prying into official files. The letter was without doubt the result of their vile handiwork. For a moment Jørgen felt shame that Denmark, his country, could produce such foul creatures.

"Don't worry, Mrs. Gronborg, we'll soon sort this out," Jørgen said reassuringly, although he was by no means sure there was anything he could do.

"But what can we do?" Sara wrung her hands, her eyes wide with fear. "They even want to take the dog. Dear God, that would break Peder's heart." Her eyes glistened with tears. "But to take Peder would break my own heart. Please help us, Jørgen."

A pair of blue eyes looked out from the back room. His mama was crying because of him. And someone wanted to take Soldat. He was unhappy.

Jørgen realized that reassuring words would not work. "Mrs. Gronborg, I don't think you should stay here." He knew the immediate job was to get her and Peder out of danger. "Perhaps you could spend the night with your friend, Mrs. Rosenfeld."

"Why should I leave? I've got to be here to open the shop tomorrow."

"Mrs. Gronborg, I don't mean to scare you, but we don't know when the Gestapo might knock on your door."

"Dear God, dear God…"

"Please, Mrs. Gronborg, please get a hold of yourself. Where's Peder?"

"He's upstairs taking his nap."

"We've got no time to lose. Go put some things in a suitcase for yourself and Peder and come back with him as soon as you can."

Sara nervously wrung her hands as she disappeared through the back room and went up the stairs that led to their living quarters.

Jørgen's mind reeled. He had to talk to Marius, they had to get Sara and Peder away from danger, they needed a plan—

He jumped as Sara screamed from the top of the stairs.

"Peder's not here! He'd never go out without telling me first – something's happened to him!"

Frederikshavn.

Peder had slipped out the back door and run away to the harbor with Soldat.

He had to run away. He would get his mama into trouble if he went home. Soldat would be in danger if he went home. But where could he go? He reached down and rubbed the back of Soldat's head. It made Soldat feel good. It made him feel good.

The harbor was almost empty. The eleven trawlers that had left at dawn would not return until dusk. He knew there were eleven. He counted them every day. Seahawk… Porpoise…Black Cat… His tidy mind automatically ran down the list. He knew them all and could draw them from memory.

He reached down to rub Soldat's head again but Soldat was not there. Where was Soldat? The boy's keen eyes cast about the harbor. Where was his friend? The dog had been by his side while he was counting the boats, but now he was gone. Where was Soldat?

There was a splash in the water. Peder started, but saw quickly that it was only a flurry of gulls plunging down for a dead fish.

The boy's eyes scanned the wharf side again. His face showed not a trace of emotion, but his heart beat quickly as he fretted for his friend. His eyes searched the long groyne that stretched out to form the northern harbor wall. Where was Soldat? His friend could not be hungry. Peder had given him the pieces of fat his mama had trimmed off the meat in her butcher shop. It was not like Soldat to run away. Soldat was his friend. Soldat would always sit by him quietly, unless someone he didn't know approached Peder. Then he would growl and snarl until Peder stroked and reassured him.

But where was he? Peder pursed his lips and whistled. It was a strange whistle, very high-pitched. Most people could not hear it. But Peder could, and he knew that Soldat would hear it. Peder became agitated when there was no response. His body hopped from foot to foot in a weird dance he did when upset.

He looked out over the harbor again from underneath the shock of blond hair that hung into his eyes. Nothing. Perhaps Soldat had gone home. No, his dog never did that, not without him. Soldat would push his wet nose against him first, asking to go home. Peder hopped again from foot to foot.

And then he saw his dog. Soldat was half-hidden by the strange boat, his tail just visible. Peder had seen the strange boat many times before. It was not a fishing boat. There were no nets. It had a funny name he didn't understand. The men on the boat spoke differently, not like his mama and Jørgen.

Peder whistled again, but Soldat did not respond. Why didn't he hear? Peder picked up his backpack and began running toward the boat. Then the boy heard the barking of another dog on the boat. That was why Soldat had run to the boat: he wanted to join the other dog.

His arms pumped, his thick blond hair tossed from side to side as he raced for the boat. No, Soldat, no. But the dog leapt from the quay, his legs flailing and claws scratching as he hauled himself to the deck. Peder came to a halt on the quayside by the boat. He whistled again. Soldat stopped and looked at him, panting. There was nobody on the boat, no sound except the barking of another dog below the deck. He looked around him. There was no one. He hesitated. Maybe he should go home. But he jumped onto the deck. He could not leave Soldat. Soldat was his friend.

Soldat's tail disappeared down a stairway. Peder moved quickly toward the stern of the boat, his backpack bouncing on his upper back. His feet scurried over the ropes on the deck. Where was Soldat? He looked down the stairway, down into the bottom of the boat. Then he heard Soldat. He knew Soldat's voice. He looked back at the pier. No strange men. No one. Then another bark. Not Soldat. Another dog voice.

He skipped down the steep stairs. It was dark. "Soldat!" he called softly. His friend heard his voice and barked a reply. Then came the voice of the other dog. "Soldat." Peder felt the brush of his friend's tail against his leg. His eyes began to see through the darkness. There was another dog, like Soldat. The dog was in a cage. Why was it in a cage? The dog barked. Soldat barked.

"No, Soldat, no." His friend settled at his feet, quiet.

Suddenly, Peder felt the boat rock. He heard the footsteps and the voices of the strange men, the voices he didn't understand.

"Let's get to the island before dark, Hans. Offload the stores and have a drink in the mess."

Peder heard the engines start. He was frightened. Perhaps they were the men Jørgen had said would come to get him and Soldat. Peder saw a closet. He opened it and climbed inside. He called quietly to Soldat. The dog followed him and lay beside him. On his leg he could feel the warm breath of his friend as he panted. The other dog barked.

One of the strange voices spoke again.

"Go and see what's upsetting the new guard dog for the Jewish camp."

Peder heard the feet come down the steps. He looked through a crack of the door of the closet. He forced his breath through clenched teeth. He knew the men couldn't hear the sound of the high-pitched whistle. But the other dog could. She stopped barking and lay down in her cage. Peder pulled the closet door shut.

"The bitch is quiet now." Peder heard the feet climb back up the steps. "Let's cast off."

Peder ran his hand gently over Soldat's head. He would not let them take his friend.

Frederikshavn.

"There's no trace of the boy?" Marius looked at the clock on the wall of his apartment. "It's almost six o'clock. Two hours since he vanished."

"Nothing." Jørgen stubbed out his cigarette. "I've searched everywhere – the harbor, all the places Peder usually goes."

"And nobody's seen him?" Marius narrowed his eyes skeptically. "Strange. Everyone knows Peder, and his routine is so predictable – someone should have seen him by now."

"No, no one's seen him." Jørgen shook his head and frowned. "And the really weird thing is there's no trace of Soldat, either."

"If you don't find the dog, you won't find the boy. They're insepa-rable." Marius rapped on the table with his knuckles. "Come back and see me in an hour. I'll see what I can find out in the meantime."

Mørkø Island.

Peder felt the boat jolt. The engine stopped. He was frightened. He had been in the closet a long time. It was dark and hot. He heard Soldat pant beside him. His friend's tongue licked at his hand.

The strange voices came from above. "Just get the dog, Hans. Put it in the compound with the rest of the dogs. We'll unload the other sup-plies in the morning. Jesus, I'd murder my grandmother for a beer."

Peder heard the footsteps coming down the stairs. The dog in the cage began to bark. Soldat moved. Peder's hand felt for his friend's ear. "Hush, Soldat!" His voice was a whisper. Soldat lay down.

Peder heard the man open the cage. "What's up with you, you mangy mutt?" The strange voice spoke gruffly. "Shut up while I get this leash on you."

Peder could hardly breathe. He ran his hand gently over Soldat's head. The man and the other dog were close to the closet door.

"Come on, you stupid bitch!"

Peder heard the dog yelp. Peder winced. The man had hit the dog. He was not a good man. Peder listened as the man stomped up the stairs, dragging the dog behind.

The boat rocked as the man got off the boat, throwing Peder against the wall of the closet. The men's voices and the dog's bark became muffled. They were walking away from the boat.

Peder, gasping for fresh air, opened the closet door. "Come, Soldat." The boy and his dog raced up the steps. His hands shielded his eyes as the light blinded him. He looked out over the deck. He was frightened. It was a flat place with some huts. There were no people in this flat place. There were no trees. Just grass and sand.

Soldat brushed against his leg. Peder looked down. Soldat needed water badly. He leapt from the boat onto the jetty. Peder could hear more dogs barking. He had to take Soldat away from them. He beck-oned to his dog and they walked along a beach. Peder looked behind him. The other dogs had stopped barking.

• • •

A sudden barking had startled Hannah, but the dogs soon became silent and she returned her attention to the notebook in her lap. She enjoyed coming to the edge of the camp at the end of the day, away from the rest of the team and their petty jealousies, away from Heldorf's demands. It was a time when she could be alone with her ideas, alone with the science, the science that captured her mind and thrust aside the pain of her life.

She looked at the diagram on her pad: the uranium machine. She felt a surge of pride as her pencil made a few final notes. She knew how to build a device that could create a new and powerful element – not even Heisenberg had been able—

The whimpering of a dog caused her to look up. Startled, she dropped her notebook. Beside the large dog stood a small boy, scruffy, unkempt, with a pair of blue eyes beneath a tousled mop of blond hair. How on earth had he got onto the island? There had never been children on the island. Hannah quickly looked around the camp; there was no one about.

"Where have you come from, little boy?" She spoke softly, reaching out for him.

He jumped away from her hand and stared at his feet. "Soldat." He pointed to the dog. *"Vand."*

The boy didn't speak German; he was Danish, she guessed. But with the dog's tongue hanging out one side of his mouth his meaning was clear: his dog needed water, and he probably did, as well. She picked up her notebook. "Come with me." The boy frowned. He didn't understand.

She looked back to the camp; still no one. The boy couldn't belong to anyone on the island. He must have been a stowaway on the supply boat, she reasoned. But how? Why had no one seen him and the dog? She had to hide the boy. He would be in great danger if he were left to roam around. She thought quickly and decided on the one place no one would look. She gathered up the boy in her arms.

The dog's bark made her jump and almost drop the child. The boy raised his hand and the dog fell silent, following Hannah as she hurried to the building housing the uranium machine.

The room was dark. Almost as dark as the closet on the boat. There were only two red lights. But there was something very large and strange in the middle of the room.

Peder watched as Soldat lapped at the bowl. The lady was kind, but he could not understand what she said. She had brought water for his friend. And for him. Peder gulped noisily at the glass.

"Wait here – I'll get some food." Again the lady spoke words Peder did not understand, but her eyes were kind. She went away. The room was quiet. The only sound was Soldat lapping thirstily at the bowl of water.

Peder picked up the lady's notebook. It was like his sketchbook. Perhaps she, too, drew birds and animals. Peder opened the notebook and stared. There were drawings only of strange things. His eyes lingered on the page for a few moments, noting the curious shapes. He turned to another page. It was full of letters and numbers.

Hannah hurried along the path between the huts of the camp, a heel of bread, some cheese, and an apple in the pocket of her laboratory coat. Her mind worked feverishly. What was she going to do with the boy? One of the guard dogs barked in the distance; she stopped, waiting for the creature to settle. She was touched by the boy. He wasn't like normal children of his age. She had never seen a child so withdrawn. Whenever his eyes met hers, he looked away. Where had he come from? The barking died away and she hurried toward the hut.

She glanced up at the darkening sky and remembered all the work she had to do that evening. An idea, born of fatigue, that she should get him off her hands by turning him over to the guards was instantly dismissed. She was getting a headache: too many things were colliding in her mind. She'd worry about what to do in the morning.

Hannah looked around once more. The camp was quiet. She reached the uranium machine building and pushed open the door. The boy was already asleep, his arms wrapped around his dog, which lifted its head and looked at her briefly before dropping its snout to its paws. As she put the food by his side, she saw that she had left her notebook – it was lying open on the floor next to the sleeping boy. She picked it up and looked tenderly at the child.

"So, little fellow, are you here to steal our secrets?" she whispered. She studied the boy for a few more moments – it had been so long since she had last seen a healthy child – then left, quietly closing the door behind her.

Frederikshavn.

"I'm afraid it's bad news." Marius pushed his unfinished dinner aside, "I found out that the Gestapo could come calling at any time. How's Mrs. Gronborg?"

"She's distraught, of course." Jørgen looked at his watch. "But I think she's safe now. I've moved her to her friend Gerda Rosenfeld's house. Unfortunately, her place is only across the street from the butcher shop, but I had to act quickly."

"And you'll have to move quickly tomorrow." Marius rose from the table and shoved his hands in his pockets. "You're going to have to take Mrs. Gronborg to her relatives in Sweden. In your boat, early tomorrow. At first light."

"But I'll never get her to go without Peder."

"Well, if she doesn't, I'm afraid she's in big trouble." After a moment's silence, the Resistance leader pulled his hands from his pockets and slapped them together lightly. "And now I've got other matters to deal with – there's another RAF drop next week. And I'll be needing you back here for that."

Jørgen pulled on his cap and began to leave.

"Oh, and Jørgen —"

"Yes?"

"You'll be sailing through the mine-swept channel, so be careful." Marius reached for his bottle of Carlsberg and drained it. "The Germans worked hard, but their sweepers didn't find every last mine."

"I'll do my best."

"You know, Jørgen," Marius followed Jørgen to the door, "blowing up Nazis with bombs is tough," he grinned, "but dealing with an old Jewish lady and her little boy is more difficult."

Frederikshavn. Gerda Rosenfeld's Parlor.

"Sara, I honestly don't know what to tell you. You're lucky to have a cousin in Sweden who'll take you in. We should all be so lucky if, God forbid, the need should arise."

Gerda Rosenfeld sat on the threadbare divan in her tiny parlor, her arm wrapped around Sara, who sobbed silently. On the floor by Sara's feet was a battered suitcase containing clothes and a few cherished possessions. A smaller suitcase with Peder's things sat next to it. Warm coats for the sea voyage lay atop the suitcases.

"But where is Peder? I won't go without Peder. I just won't go."

"Listen to me, Sara." Gerda looked into Sara's red-rimmed eyes. "Jørgen and his friends will find him. They're combing the town. They'll find him tonight; you'll see."

Sara blotted her eyes with her embroidered handkerchief. Gerda's words brought some comfort. "Perhaps you're right, Gerda, they'll find him tonight, I'm sure, and then we'll leave tomorrow." She blew her nose. "It will be good to see my cousin Ben and his family after all these years. Who cares about an old butcher shop, anyway?" Tears slid down her cheeks. "Oh, Gerda, Jacob and I worked so hard to set up that shop. Jacob toiled night and day – he made it so nice, and built up the business. That shop was our life together."

Gerda rubbed Sara's hand, as if she could knead out all of Sara's troubles. But Gerda was also worried about herself. What if the Gestapo tracked Sara down to her house? What would happen to her? One way or another, Sara would have to leave in the morning.

Sara sniffed and regained her composure. "The one thing I don't understand is why me? I understand the Nazis hate the Jews, but why did they pick on me? And why Peder, my innocent little boy?"

Gerda heaved a sigh. "Sara, perhaps it's not for me to say…."

"Not for you to say what, Gerda?"

"I've heard tell…," she bit her lip and hesitated, "I've heard tell it might have been Peder who brought this terrible trouble down on your head."

Sara pulled her hand away from Gerda and scowled. "What are you saying?"

"Oh, I don't mean Peder's responsible, mind you." Gerda could not resist passing on the gossip. "It's not Peder's fault, and it's not yours, either. It's those *meshugah* Nazis."

"I realize that. But why me?"

Gerda heaved a loud sigh. "Anna Epstein explained it to me. According to the Nazis, we Jews are subhuman. She heard it from her husband, who heard it from—"

"And I've heard it before, as well. What are you trying to say, Gerda?"

"Sara, I tell you it makes me sick to my stomach." Gerda closed her eyes and shook her head. "While we're supposed to be like garbage, the Nazis in the meantime are God's gift to the world, some sort of superior race."

"I've heard those lies before, as well, Gerda. What on earth are you driving at?"

"Well, it's just that, if Peder's not Jewish, he must be one of them. Technically speaking, that is."

"So you're saying…"

"Yes, Sara. What I heard is the Nazis are claiming that you, a Jew, took in a child of their race, and they're saying that somehow being in a Jew's house made Peder, well, strange."

"But Peder's always been different. And besides, he's not strange – he's a wonderful little boy."

Gerda's hands flew up in the air. "I know, I know. You don't have to tell me, Sara. I'm just saying that that's what someone said that someone else heard the Nazis, with their twisted minds, were saying."

Sara frowned. "I can't believe that's why they're after me."

Gerda glanced at the clock on the mantel. "Oy, look at the time – it's past ten. We'd better get some sleep. Look Sara, when they find Peder, I'll wake you up and let you know."

Mørkø Island.

Peder edged open the door of the building and peered out. Although the sun had not yet risen, he could see the boat in the pre-dawn light. The boat would take him back home. There was no sign of the kind lady. He slung his backpack across his shoulders.

Soldat pushed his wet nose against Peder's hand; the fast-pumping bellows of his lungs sounded like laughter. Peder stroked his head, caressed his ears. Soldat, his friend.

Peder knew he should not have run away. He should have stayed with his mama. She would be unhappy. She would not be smiling with the smile that made him happy. But they could not take Soldat. When he had heard his mama say they were going to take him and Soldat, he thought he had to run away. Now he knew he had to get back to his mama. But he had to keep Soldat away from the bad people.

There were voices around the boat, men speaking in that strange way the kind lady had spoken. The men jumped down from the boat and walked back to the buildings on the island. He leapt up from behind the bushes. He would hide in the same cupboard on the boat; they would not find him.

He ran toward the boat and suddenly stopped. Soldat was following him. "No, Soldat, no!" The dog's eyes fixed him, then looked from side to side.

"Stay!" Peder raised his finger. "Stay!"

He ran toward the deserted boat and leapt aboard. As he scurried down to his hiding place, tears ran down from his eyes. They would not take Soldat. The kind lady would look after him.

Frederikshavn, Denmark.

Jørgen moved quietly along the street as the first fingers of dawn clawed at the night sky. He'd received a message from Marius: the Resistance had found out the Gestapo would come for Sara Gronborg soon after sunrise. He glanced at the faint light in the eastern sky and

170

hurried his steps toward Mrs. Rosenfeld's house. He was late. He had spent fruitless hours dodging German patrols after curfew looking for Peder. None of the fishing boat skippers had seen the boy. He had vanished, along with his dog.

Sara had slept little. Her thoughts were mostly of Peder. Where was he? Was he dressed warmly? Was he able to get something to eat? Perhaps the Resistance had found him. But what if the authorities had already taken him? Or what if he had become sick or had had an accident? She wouldn't go without him. She had to find Peder and know he was all right. Surely Jørgen had exaggerated the risks of staying to her. In Frederikshavn, she had always been safe.

Jørgen saw that the town was beginning to come to life to go about a new day. The first bus lumbered down the main street. Small groups of fishermen were making for the harbor to catch the tide for their day's work, a tide he knew he, too, had to catch.

Sara got up and paced the floor. Her head ached and she couldn't sleep. She didn't want to leave her friends; Frederikshavn was her home. Peder and the snug little rooms upstairs from the shop were her life. How could she leave? How could she go and live in someone else's house? It would never be her home. And the butcher shop – tending it gave her purpose when she got up each morning.

Jørgen pulled up his collar as a shower drifted across the sky. What was he going to tell Mrs. Gronborg? She'd never leave without Peder. The boy and her shop were her life, and now she was deprived of both. He turned the corner onto the street where Gerda Rosenfeld's house stood, almost opposite Sara Gronborg's butcher shop.

Suddenly, Sara recalled the little bell on the shop door. How she wished she had taken it down and packed it as a keepsake. Perhaps she still could – the shop was just across the street. Jørgen had told her not to stay there, but she could still get the doorbell and leave; it wouldn't take long. She dressed quickly, stole downstairs, and opened the door a crack. What she saw made her cover her mouth with both hands to suppress a scream. German soldiers were outside her shop.

Jørgen's eyes narrowed as he saw the truck. There was a screeching of tires and the clatter of hobnailed boots as soldiers leapt down onto the cobbles.

Sara's body shook as she quickly closed the door. They were out there. They had come for her, just as Jørgen had said they might. She had seen three armed men heading toward her shop. And now she could hear them banging on the door.

Jørgen stopped and pressed himself into a doorway. Shouts broke the stillness of the early morning air as an officer hammered on the shop door. Jørgen slipped into an alley leading to the back of Gerda Rosenfeld's house. He prayed that Sara Gronborg was ready, that she'd come with him. Where was Peder, damn him? His knuckles rapped urgently on the back door. The curtain on the door parted and an eye peeped through the crack.

"It's me, Mrs. Rosenfeld. Jørgen." He heard the bolt on the door slide back and the door was opened.

"Thank heavens it's you, Jørgen." Gerda Rosenfeld closed her eyes as she breathed her relief. "I thought you might be a German soldier. They're all outside Sara's shop."

"I know – I saw them." Sounds of barked orders and frustrated voices echoed along the alley. Jørgen moved quickly through the kitchen and into the parlor, the anxiety on his face caught by the feeble light of the oil lamp hanging from the wall. "Mrs. Gronborg – is she ready? We've got to get going."

"I think she's ready. She's scared to death, the poor thing." Gerda Rosenfeld's hands wrung nervously at her apron. "But then we all are."

Jørgen tried not to show the fear that was also twisting his own gut. "She's got to come now. Once the Germans find she's missing, they'll start a house-to-house search. Where is she?"

"Have you found Peder?" The voice came from a dark corner of the room. Jørgen could barely make out the figure caught by the dim but growing light that struggled through the small window.

"No." Jørgen saw no point in lying. "But we will. However, you've got to come with me. Now!"

"I won't go without Peder." There were no longer any tears but Sara seemed to have aged ten years.

172

"You've got to!" Jørgen spoke sharply, his fear turning to anger. "Do you realize what will happen to you if you fall into the Nazis' hands?"

Sara slowly lifted her reddened eyes. "It doesn't matter. Life without my little boy has no meaning."

Although Jørgen struggled to control his anger, his voice was sharp. "It's not just a question of your life, Mrs. Gronborg. If you stay here, your friend's life is at risk. If the Nazis find you here, what do you think will happen to Mrs. Rosenfeld?"

Gerda began to whimper. "Sara, I'm an old woman and I live alone. I have no one to protect me." She braced herself against a chair so she wouldn't fall from her violent trembling. "I'd do anything for you, you know that, but I can't keep you here, I just can't."

Sara pondered for a few moments before walking over and wrapping her arm around her friend. "I understand, Gerda." She forced a smile. "Thanks for all you've done."

Gerda's lips brushed Sara's cheek. "Once they find Peder, I'll look after him until you come back."

"Alright, Jørgen, let's go." Sara's voice was soft, resigned.

She picked up her old suitcase, bruised with time, containing the small vestiges of her life. Jørgen took the suitcase from her, put his other arm around her shoulders, and led her to the back door. He looked at his watch. There was less than an hour to make the tide.

Göteborg, Sweden.

Christina put down the phone in her hotel room and smiled: her uncle's voice brought pleasant memories of her childhood. She had called to try and meet him after she had delivered von Rastenberg's message, but he was leaving for a week-long business conference in Stockholm.

He had urged her to visit his summer cottage on the headland at Särö, some twenty miles from Göteborg. They had reminisced about the times she had spent at the cottage, walking on the deserted headland, sailing in his ketch, the Sofia. "Pay a visit to the old place," he had said. "The key's still in the usual place. And Sofia's still moored in the harbor, so take a sail. Like the old times."

She had smiled wistfully at the thought of seeing the little cottage again, but dismissed the dream. It would be too sad to be alone in a place whose walls had once rung with the laughter of people she loved and missed so much.

Her reverie ended when she looked at the clock. There would be time enough for sailing when she got back to Providence. She went to the bathroom and turned on the faucets in the tub. It would soon be time for her meeting with von Rastenberg.

Off the coast of Göteborg, Sweden.

Jørgen raised the mainsail as his boat, Beatrice, cleared the Göteborg harbor wall. He had to get back to Frederikshavn as soon as he could. Peder, whose mama was now in Sweden, had to be found.

He shortened the sail to make sure he could maintain control. The wind plucked at the canvas and filled the small jib. Beatrice responded at once, her stem cleaving the waves. He pulled on the tiller, eased the mainsheet, and cast a glance at the sky. Wisps of cloud raced across the sun. The ship's clock in the cockpit showed four-thirty – the sun still had several hours to run. He cut the motor and Beatrice, the wind clutching her sails, pulled away from the Swedish coast.

Jørgen braced his foot on the empty bench where Sara Gronborg had sat on the long trip over. Pallid, sitting quietly with her hands in her lap and her eyes cast down, she had shed no tears and had said nothing.

With luck, he would be back in Frederikshavn before midnight. Jørgen wasn't worried about sailing at night, even though rip tides and currents could catch a sailor unawares in the Kattegat, the sea that lay between Sweden and Denmark. The wind was fair, from the southwest, coming off the port quarter. He was sailing close-hauled, and Beatrice responded well.

Once he sailed clear of the neutrality exclusion zone – thirty miles from the Swedish coast – he'd have to look out for German patrol boats. And mines. The Germans had been ruthlessly efficient at clearing the mines that had been laid by the British in the Kattegat before the invasion. Still, he needed to keep a wary eye. Even though he and Beatrice had not done the sail too often since the start of the war, he felt confident.

Mrs. Gronborg's cousin, Ben, had been at the dock to meet her when they had arrived and she had managed a wan smile as he greeted her. Then Jørgen told her he had to go. When he promised to find Peder, she had taken his hand and had held it tightly as she looked earnestly into his eyes. "You must," she had said. "Please, please find my little boy."

Göteborg, Sweden.

Christina sat in the lobby of the hotel. There was an evening newspaper on her lap, but it scarcely held her attention. Her eyes darted from her paper, catching quick glimpses of the people in the other lounge chairs. They all seemed normal, but she knew from her previous visit that she could not be sure. She looked at her watch: ten to six; von Rastenberg was due to arrive shortly. Her glance caught the eye of the man opposite; he held his stare for a few moments before returning his attention to his newspaper. Was he a Gestapo agent?

She tried to calm her fears, but her last visit had left her wary and suspicious of everyone. That's why the small Browning 6.35mm pistol sat at the bottom of her purse. To allay her fears, Stevens had insisted that she be trained to use it.

She forced herself to concentrate on the newspaper. German troops were now occupying Rome while the Americans and British had just joined forces south of Salerno. She wondered how her native Sweden could remain neutral while the rest of the world battled the Nazi scourge.

Her eyes kept looking to the hotel forecourt, willing von Rastenberg to arrive. Why had the German specifically requested her to receive the message? The thought that he might have transferred to her feelings he had for his dead wife gave him an eerie sensation. She needed to keep the relationship on a business level. To get the message and go – that was all that mattered to her.

She had insisted that he pick her up in a car. She never again wanted to run the gauntlet of Nazi agents on the streets. The man opposite was watching her again. She was relieved to hear him call for a waiter and order a drink in her native tongue. But where was von Rastenberg? She looked at her watch anxiously. If he didn't arrive on time, she'd go back to her room, call a taxi and head for the consulate to—

"Message for Herr Schlossberg!" The bellhop's shout made her jump. The uniformed young man circled the lobby. "Message for Herr

Schlossberg!" The sound of a German name alarmed Christina. A man at the back of the lobby raised his hand. Christina looked up briefly from the paper. The man was nondescript: fat, balding, like a hundred other businessmen in the city.

She was relieved to see a Volvo with von Rastenberg at the wheel drawing into the forecourt. He saw her, smiled, and waved. She tried to appear unhurried as she made for the door, but she felt tense. She couldn't resist a glance over her shoulder. The fat man's eyes quickly scanned the message and then fixed on her. He turned and nodded to a younger man who stood by the reception desk. Christina pushed on the hotel door and ran to von Rastenberg's car.

At sea in the Kattegat.

Beatrice cut through the waves. Jørgen reached in his breast pocket for a pack of cigarettes. Perhaps Peder had already been found. He began thinking what he would say to the boy – it would be difficult to explain why his mother was no longer at home. Jørgen shielded the lighter with his hand, but the wind snatched at the flame. He needed three spins of the flint wheel before it sparked a flame.

He looked up at Beatrice's sails and felt her roll slightly. The wind was getting stronger. And turning. There had been nothing amiss in the weather forecast. His eyes scanned Beatrice's weather side. Black clouds were gathering on the southern horizon. He took the measure of the wind. The storm would probably run away to the north. The image of Peder's face came to his mind. He decided to push on.

Göteborg.

Christina's fears lessened as she left the hotel and got into the car.

Von Rastenberg, still smiling warmly, reached for her hand and gave it a squeeze. "It's good to see you again, Christina. How are you?"

Christina returned his smile. "I'm fine, Franz. And you?"

Von Rastenberg pulled out into traffic but didn't answer her question; his smile dropped to a frown as he checked the rearview mirror. He made a sharp turn down a side street and Christina was thrown against the back of the seat as von Rastenberg snatched at the clutch and gunned the motor.

"What's wrong, Franz? Are you lost?" she shouted as the car swung around another tight corner, tires screaming

"I'm afraid we have a small problem." His voice was even and calm, but Christina could sense his anxiety. He looked in the mirror and pulled on the wheel. "We're being followed." Another glance in the mirror. "And they're about a block behind us now."

Christina turned her head to look through the rear window. A squat black Saab. Two men.

"That explains it then." She lurched against the door as von Rastenberg swung around another corner.

"Explains what?"

"The men in the hotel lobby. I thought they might be tailing me."

"Damn!" He hammered at the wheel angrily. "I'm so sorry, Christina; the last thing I wanted was to expose you to danger." His scowl deepened. "I'd hoped this meeting would be so different."

"So did I." Christina knew what he meant, but her train of thought was different. "So where's the message, the message that's so important that we have Gestapo agents on our tail?" There was an angry impatience in her voice, fueled by the danger.

"The message is in my briefcase," he dropped down a gear as he veered left, "which is in the trunk of the car. I don't think it would be a good idea to stop right now."

Christina leaned forward to look again in the mirror. The Saab was closing in on them.

At sea in the Kattegat.

The wind had veered and was growing stronger. Jørgen heaved on the tiller, trying to bring Beatrice as close to the wind as possible, but he could sense that the boat was beginning to struggle, making slow headway against the gusts that now came over the port bow.

Jørgen cursed his luck. The weather had been fine when he had brought Mrs. Gronborg across, and there had been no hint of a storm in the weather forecast. But he knew that storms could come from nowhere in the Kattegat. He and Beatrice had seen their fair share. She had always brought him through safely.

He checked the wind again as he pulled on his weatherproof coat and leggings. It was now coming from the west and was beginning to blow even harder. The sky had lowered and dark clouds were scudding toward them. The sea was becoming choppy; Beatrice pitched as she fought her way through the waves. He knew he would soon have to reduce sail again to enable Beatrice to cope.

Jørgen checked the cockpit clock. There was no chance he would make Frederikshavn before dark. He lashed the tiller to the guardrail and made his way forward to take in another reef of the mainsail. His feet struggled on the wet deck and twice he had to clutch at the ratlines to hold his footing.

He took in a reef, but then the wind gusted, plucking violently at the canvas, making it impossible to reduce sail further. Beatrice pitched sharply and heeled alarmingly. Jørgen knew he had to turn the boat. He realized that Frederikshavn was beyond them.

He unlashed the tiller and looked up. The dark clouds now enveloped the sky around them, blotting out the sun and turning the day into night. Beatrice could not ride out the storm. He had to return to Göteborg. He pushed the tiller over, slowly, carefully. Now, another danger threatened. He had to run before the wind.

Göteborg.

"Make a left here." Christina spoke quickly, fear in her voice.

Von Rastenberg spun the wheel around, glancing quizzically from the corner of his eye.

"Göteborg is my old stomping ground." She looked over her shoulder as the Saab behind them careened around the corner. "I grew up here." She sighed, but the pressures of the moment quickly doused the flickering memories of long ago. "I have an uncle who has a summer house twenty miles away. Perhaps we could go there."

"Do you think we can shake them off?"

"Maybe." She looked in the mirror. "Depends how well those goons behind know the city." A plan began to form in her mind, but she was distracted as von Rastenberg took a corner too tightly and clipped the curb.

"Where is everybody?" A finger of his right hand pulled away from the wheel and pointed at the empty streets. "The place is deserted. Where are the police?"

"Big celebrations yesterday. Gunder Haegg, our local track star, broke his fifth world record." She checked anxiously in the mirror. "Everyone's probably sleeping it off today. Turn right here. You'll be on the main highway out of the city."

Von Rastenberg gunned the motor as the car hit the open road.

Perhaps, she thought, if they could give the Gestapo agents the slip, they could get to her uncle's house in Särö. It was in a secluded location down a road even the locals had trouble finding. So remote that—

"Damn!" Von Rastenberg's shout cut across her thoughts.

"What's the matter?"

"I didn't fill the tank. We're running low on gas."

At sea in the Kattegat.

There was only the darkness of the sky and the howling of the wind.

Jørgen knew the danger of running before the wind. Control of the boat was difficult. The near-gale coming from astern could bring the mast down or turn the boom into a lethal weapon. He could barely feel his fingers on the tiller as the rain lashed down. He had been through many storms in the Kattegat, but none that had battered a boat so heavily.

The compass spun wildly, offering little help. Jørgen knew he was steering by instinct, relying on his long experience. He looked at his watch, trying to estimate when he would regain the Swedish coast. He had to find a safe inlet, although he knew it would be difficult in the storm. The situation was deteriorating. He was caught on a lee shore in a gale.

Even with reduced sail, Beatrice pitched heavily as she ran before the wind that screamed through the rigging. Jørgen tried to haul in the boom, but the wind caught at the canvas and the line ran away through his wet hand. The wind came from astern, causing the mast timber to groan. Beatrice pitched awkwardly, clawing her way to a foam-tossed crest, before plunging down, down into the next trough.

"Come on, Beatrice, you can make it." His voice was swallowed by the wind. He ran his hand across his face and peered ahead, over the bow, but saw nothing except the raging spray that lashed his face and blinded him again.

The tiller tugged at his arm, threatening to break away from his grasp. He heard a sudden flapping, like a thousand birds in flight. Jørgen looked up and saw the foresail in tatters, torn to shreds by the gale.

He tried to view it as good fortune; he had needed to reduce sail. But he wondered if Beatrice would make it. Fear reached for him, and he tried to shrug it off with laughter. "Come on, Beatrice, you can't miss Sweden." His maniacal laugh was snatched from his lips, lost at once to the wind that whistled through the strained rigging.

Göteborg.

Christina glanced quickly at the dashboard. The fuel gauge was leaning toward empty.

"I'm sorry," von Rastenberg checked the mirror anxiously for the pursuing car, "but I wasn't planning to drive very far. I thought I was going to give you the message and then drive to the port for my ferry back to Germany."

"It doesn't matter. What matters is that we have to get out of this mess now." She checked the gauge again. How much? Twenty miles? Thirty?

"Perhaps we could lose them if we got off the main road?" Von Rastenberg asked hopefully.

"No, keep going." Twenty miles would get them to Särö, her uncle's home town on the coast. Maybe they could shake off the pursuers there.

She peered over her shoulder and was alarmed to see the Saab begin to pull alongside. When she looked across through the driver's window, the Saab was abreast, the man in the passenger seat waving at von Rastenberg to pull over.

"Franz, look out!" Christina shouted as the driver of the Saab pulled on the wheel, trying to drive the Volvo off the road. Von Rastenberg gunned the motor, but the Saab had the edge on speed. She heard a grating sound as the fenders touched. Despite his efforts, the steering wheel spun through von Rastenberg's hand and he was forced to hit the brakes. The Saab pulled over in front of them.

Von Rastenberg pushed open the driver's door. "Try to get out of here while I stall them. Remember – the message is in my briefcase in the trunk."

"Franz, no—" Christina's shout went unheeded. Von Rastenberg slammed the door and ran toward the Saab.

Christina was transfixed. Events unfolded over which she had no control. Franz confronted the Gestapo agents as they got out of the car. The driver was a small man; for some reason, she noticed that his hat was a size too big. There was shouting, in German. She thought she heard the word 'spy.'

The other man was tall, lean, wiry. He moved around the front of the Saab and tried to push Franz toward the rear door. The small man grabbed Franz's lapels.

Christina pulled the pistol out of her bag and lowered the window. There was no clear shot. Just a melee of bodies. She might hit Franz. Then Franz broke away from his captors and ran from the two cars. Perhaps she could get a better angle from the driver's side. Christina moved quickly to the driver's seat, cursing as she caught her knee on the gear shift. The engine was still running.

She tried to take aim, but the two Gestapo men were running after Franz. Suddenly the tall man pointed toward her; the other stopped and turned toward the Volvo.

Christina struggled with the gear lever. She looked up and saw the other man running in her direction. At last she found the reverse gear, but she snatched at the clutch and the engine stalled. Then she heard the shot.

She looked up and saw Franz's hands flailing in the air. There was another shot. Franz's head jolted as the bullet found its mark. He crumpled and fell, his body lifeless before it hit the road.

Everything stopped. For a moment, the man stopped running toward the car and turned to see what had happened. Christina sat motionless in shock. Then the Gestapo man came toward her again. Her hand turned the key and the starter fired at once. She pushed the stick into reverse and the car began to edge backwards.

Suddenly, the man was at the open window, desperately reaching inside the car to pull up the button that would unlock the door. She leveled the pistol and fired. His face convulsed and he slid to the ground. Christina pushed the shift into first and ran through the gears as she sped past the other Gestapo agent and the body of Franz lying in the road.

She heard a shot and there was a ping as the bullet ricocheted off a fender. Christina looked in the mirror and saw the agent rush to the Saab. She looked anxiously at the gas gauge, but had no option. She pushed the pedal to the floor.

At sea in the Kattegat.

He wiped the spray from his face as Beatrice plunged down into another bottomless trough. Then up, up she came, grudgingly, the wind toying with the tattered foresail, as she battled to face the next challenge.

And then he thought he saw a light as the wind tore a brief gap in the clouds. The ship heeled over sharply, distracting him as he hauled vainly on the tiller. An illusion, he thought; you're fooling yourself. He screwed up his eyes and peered through the spray. Beatrice rolled heavily and the illusion was gone, lost in the wind and the lashing rain.

He saw it too late. Beatrice was carried high on a crest and it was there before her. The monstrous rock towered over them as an ugly sentinel of doom; at the base, the waves tossed and churned, white with fury. Beatrice shuddered as the wave threw her into the maelstrom. He pulled madly on the tiller, a vain gesture that could not save the boat from her fate.

Beatrice seemed to groan above the wind as her beam crashed onto the rock. Jørgen heard the mortal blow as the hull splintered. The timbers moaned as Beatrice wallowed in her death throes. Above the wind, Jørgen heard a loud crack. He looked up and saw the mainmast come crashing down. The boom swung wildly, hitting his head and plunging him into the roiling sea.

Outskirts of Särö, Sweden.

The wipers beat a hasty staccato on the windshield. The rain teemed down, driven sideways by the wind. The storm had come from nowhere, and the daylight was now fading.

Although she was sure she had lost him, Christina peered anxiously in the rearview mirror. The circuitous route down which she had led him when she had turned off the highway – a route on the back roads and country lanes she remembered from her youth – seemed to have worked. She had given him the slip.

Only the sound of the rain pelting on the roof of the car disturbed the eerie stillness when she pulled over and turned off the engine, a stillness that invited in the memories she had held at bay. Franz frozen in the air as the bullet ripped through him. The Gestapo man's face convulsing when she pulled the trigger. Pent-up tears began to flow and she pummeled the wheel in frustration, anger, grief.

Stop it! she screamed at herself. She grabbed the wheel and squeezed it tightly, seeking a control of her body that was eluding her mind. Make a plan, she told herself. Her uncle's house on the headland. It was about two miles away. She had to get there. She breathed deeply in an effort to clear her head. She had to find shelter and a safe place.

Rain washed over the windshield, but she had to press on. Her fingers found the ignition key and turned. The engine fired, but a glance at the gas gauge showed the needle stuck on empty. Please, just two more miles, please, she prayed.

Then she saw it: headlights in her rearview mirror. They were not bright – the car was perhaps a half-mile down the road – but they were there.

Christina slipped the shift and gunned the engine. The car lurched forward a few yards and then stopped as the engine died. Frantically she turned the ignition key. No response, just the futile coughing of the starter motor. The lights were coming closer. She grabbed the pistol from the passenger seat; the cold steel felt both frightening and reassuring. She had used it before and she would not hesitate to use it again.

Be calm, she told herself. You have the advantage. You know the surroundings – the schoolhouse on the left, the path beyond to the headland. But she could not shake the fear as she leapt out of the car into the driving rain. She began to run toward the schoolhouse, steadying herself as she slipped on leaves.

She stopped. She had forgotten the briefcase.

The other car was about a hundred yards away. It looked like the Gestapo's Saab. She ran back to the Volvo, yanked the trunk open, snatched the briefcase, and cradled it in her arms. The car was getting closer. She turned to run and caught a glimpse of the driver – it was the man who had shot Franz. Her legs raced toward the school gates.

Crack! She heard the whine of the bullet as it ricocheted off the road. She spun around, leveled the pistol in her right hand and pulled the trigger. She heard a groan as she began to run again. Perhaps she had hit him, but there was no time to stop and check. She ran into the schoolyard.

The wind clutched at her as if trying to snatch the briefcase away, but she clung to it tightly, carrying it as she would a baby. She prayed that there had been no changes to the layout of the buildings since she had played in the schoolyard as a child. There should be a path between them, behind the bicycle sheds. Her feet slipped on the mud and she almost went down. If she could get to the far side of the school before him, she would be on the path through the trees that led down to the headland. He would never find her once she made that path.

A shaft of lightning lit up the school, but she saw nobody in its brief stark light. Boom! The thunderclap startled her, but she ducked quickly behind the schoolhouse wall. Her eyes peered through the teeming rain, but she saw nothing. Her breath came quickly as she held the gun in front of her, backing along the wall. She reached the end of the wall and saw the path leading through the trees.

She waited a moment, listening. There was only the wind and the rain. She took a deep breath and ran for her life.

Mørkø Island, Denmark.

The scientists gathered around the mail pouch as Heldorf's corporal called out names.

"Rosen."

"Siegel."

"Ziegler."

In a circle around the corporal, desperate to hear their names called, to Hannah they seemed like pathetic schoolchildren surrounding a teacher, not knowing if they'd be punished with a cane or rewarded with a piece of candy.

"Weiss."

184

Hannah hoped Albert's letter would be from one of his daughters. For a long time, there had been no news from either. Hannah could see from the shake of his head as he glanced at the handwriting on the envelope that it was from his wife, Rebecca. The letter probably brought good news – Hannah knew that Rebecca, despite scant resources, was managing well in Lisbon, welcomed and helped by the Jewish community there. But she also knew that Albert yearned for news about his daughters.

Hannah's heart sank as the corporal closed up the mail pouch and left the room: nothing for her that day. Hannah's perpetual worry for Rachel surrounded her like a fog she could not escape; it was worst during mail delivery, when her heart beat quickly each time the corporal reached into the mail pouch. But her sister's letters came in fits and starts, an unpredictability Max attributed to the hammering the British and Americans were giving Germany in their bombing raids.

To ease the ache she went to her room, pulled Rachel's last letter out of a drawer, and sat down to read it again.

Dearest Hannah,

How happy I was to receive your last letter! It brings me great joy to know you are well. I hope the farm work you do is not too taxing.

After I was released from the camp infirmary, I was given a job in the laundry washing and ironing the shirts of the officers. It's not so very bad, and I'm now eating much better, thanks to your packages!

I cherish your words – I feel sad because the others here get no mail – and I greatly look forward to your next letter.

With all my love,
Rachel

She carefully folded the letter, returned it to the envelope, and put it away. Her father's words came to her again. *You must survive, Hannah.* But mere survival was not enough; there must be something more. There must be love. Without it, she now realized, survival meant nothing.

Särö, Sweden.

Christina nervously looked out through the kitchen window. The darkness of night had closed in and she could see little. She peered out again. Nothing. Only the sedge grass dancing wildly in the wind as the abating storm dragged itself inland.

She drew the curtains and lit the oil lamp that hung from the wall. She shivered, not only from the sodden clothes that clung to her body, but from fear, from the horror the day had brought. Scenes came to her mind, scenes she didn't want to remember but knew she would never forget. The man in the hotel, the chasing car, the look on the face of the Gestapo agent as she shot him. But above all, Franz's arms, high, lingering in the air for the briefest of moments before he fell, dead.

Christina grabbed a bucket and her hands frantically worked the water pump. She tore off her clothes, lifted the bucket, and poured the water over her body. But she could not wash the memories away.

Her uncle's dressing gown was large, enveloping her slender frame. The pale light of the lamp flickered over the room that looked over the bay through windows streaked with rain. The small room appeared much as it had so many years ago: the whitewashed walls, starched curtains, wide floorboards, corner fireplace with decorative tiles – all so familiar to her. From where she stood she could see into the bedroom, the same pink chenille spread still gracing the large bed, the same worn ship's chest at its foot. And then her eyes fell upon Franz's briefcase; it lay on her uncle's easy chair, where she had tossed it. In the case was the reason she had come to Sweden.

Her hand shook as she reached for the briefcase, her fingers running nervously over the soft leather. The catch snapped open easily at her touch and she tipped the contents onto the sofa. The mundane things surprised her: a bag of coffee, a box of chocolates, a pack of American cigarettes – small creature comforts he had bought in Sweden because he could no longer get them in Germany.

There was a leather-bound business diary. She flipped through pages that were filled with the once-important details of a life that was no more. Somehow reading it seemed an invasion of his privacy and she was about to close it when she noticed the photograph of his late wife tucked into the inside cover. She pulled it out; again she had the eerie sensation that she was looking into a mirror. He must have loved his wife very much if he sought solace with someone who resembled her.

The envelope pushed the thought from her mind. She pulled it out from under the pack of cigarettes. Brown, stiff, formal. She turned it in her hand. It bore no inscription.

She felt a chill and pulled her uncle's dressing gown tightly around her. For what was inside this envelope Franz had given his life. She saw again the look on his face before he had fallen. The envelope fell from her hand. A weariness consumed her; her body and mind screamed for release from the foul day. She went into the bedroom and fell upon the chenille spread, begging sleep to claim her.

The noise thrust her need for sleep aside. She leapt off the bed; there was somebody outside.

Treblinka, Poland. Three weeks earlier.

Rachel's sunken eyes looked out over the camp as she hurried to the laundry. There was no color – buildings, watchtowers, barbed wire, uniforms, faces – all were limned in shades of mud brown, ash gray, death black.

She'd become inured to the horrors of the camp, living through the nightmare with a dull day-to-day acceptance – the only way she could preserve her sanity. That, and reading the letters of her sister, Hannah. She felt the packet of letters nestling in the pocket of her apron.

Rachel felt fortunate to be employed in the laundry ironing officer uniforms. Many of the other prisoners had jobs clearing out the gas chambers and burning bodies; they often wondered if the people whose remains they hauled away were the lucky ones. Still, something deep within the living clung to life. When the number of new arrivals into the camp dropped off, they became alarmed. One of Rachel's friends, a woman who cleaned out the ovens, spelled out her fear: if there were no more bodies to be cremated, she'd be out of work, and if she was out of work, she'd be next in the gas chamber. Such was the horrendous logic that governed life in the camp. More victims were needed for others to survive. Rachel shuddered.

She pushed open the door to the laundry. She had heard that some of the inmates were planning an uprising. As she worked, the stifling heat of the steam made her sweat; the tattered blouse clung to the sparse flesh that hung feebly on her bones.

They were fools. The SS would kill them all – a point she tried to make with one of the hotheads. She picked up a tunic from the basket and put it on the ironing board.

She recalled the words of the would-be rebel: "Rachel, we have nothing to lose. Whatever we do, we're all dead anyway."

Rachel ran the iron over the collar, taking care that the creases were pressed away.

Särö, Sweden.

Christina heard the noise again. A scratching at the front door. She picked up her pistol and checked the chamber: two bullets. She moved swiftly and quietly to the lamp, lifted the glass, and blew out the flame. Her free hand felt the way – along the wall, across the back of her uncle's chair. The noise came again, a barely discernable tap on the front door. She held her breath and her heart raced.

She edged herself to the window that overlooked the bay; from there, she'd be able to see the doorstep. A wave crashed over the headland, but she heard something else: another feeble tap. She tightened her grip on the gun, reached for the curtain with her free hand, and slowly pushed it aside. The rain was still falling; the drops trickled randomly down the glass, distorting her vision.

She could see little in the darkness. There was something on the doorstep, but she couldn't see clearly. It looked like a bundle of rags someone had carelessly tossed aside. Then she saw the hand. The fingers reached for the door and she heard the noise once more: tap...tap.

For a brief moment, the moon found a gap in the clouds. She saw a man on his hands and knees crouched before the door. He had no shoes and there seemed to be a wound on his head.

Christina lowered the pistol, her breast heaving. Who was it? She retraced her steps in the dark and put the pistol back on the table. Her hands shook as she relit the lamp. After the happenings of the day she felt exhausted, drained of all emotion except fear. She began to sob. She didn't know what to do. She picked up the pistol and went to the door.

Treblinka, Poland. Three weeks earlier.

Rachel sat on the floor of the hut, spooning the watery gruel into her hungry mouth. She knew how the rebels planned to get weapons for the uprising. An SS guard had brought a lock to one of the prisoners to be fixed, and he had recognized it as the lock to the arsenal door. He had made a key from the lock, a key that would enable them to raid the arsenal.

Rachel wanted nothing of such madness and made her own plan: she'd hide in the laundry under one of the tubs when the uprising began. If she didn't take part, she might escape the death squads that would inevitably follow. She put down the bowl and fell exhausted to the floor.

It began in the late afternoon. Rachel was carrying a basket of freshly-laundered officers' uniforms across the courtyard when she saw prisoners heading in the direction of the arsenal. The uprising was about to start; it was time for her to head for the laundry. An SS officer appeared unexpectedly in the midst of the rebels; there was a look of panic in the eyes of a prisoner who had just been given a gun. The sound of the shot he fired into the officer's chest was taken by the others as a signal and there was a sudden descent into chaos, with noise and confusion everywhere. She had to get to the laundry, had to get to safety.

As she ran across the courtyard she saw prisoners fighting with guards as others headed for the gates. Still carrying the basket, she tried to make her legs move faster. Suddenly most of the prisoners began running in aimless terror as the guards in the watchtowers fired down with machine guns. Her legs felt like lead weights, her lungs felt close to bursting, but the laundry building was just a few strides away. She was almost there—

Särö, Sweden.

The gun shook in her hand as she approached the front door. Her free hand wiped the tears from her eyes and reached slowly for the big brass key in the lock.

There was a muffled cry from the porch. She leapt back, fearful. It sounded like a man's voice.

"Who are you?" she shouted through the door in Swedish.

There was no response. She repeated the question in German. Silence.

She heard his hands claw their way up the door. The knob on the door turned, then rattled as he struggled against the lock. Christina raised the pistol but her hand was stayed by his voice.

"Help me, help me, please."

She recognized the tongue from her childhood when she used to sail across the Kattegat with her uncle. He was Danish. Her hand turned the key and the door flew open.

With great effort the man managed to get up and stand, unsteady, in the doorway before staggering into the room.

"Thank God. Thank God." He fell onto her and she grasped him, the pistol tumbling to the floor. She felt the wetness of his clothes and smelled the brine in his hair. In an ungainly dance they teetered into the bedroom. She pushed him onto the bed.

"Thank you. Thank you." His blue-green eyes looked at her briefly before closing with exhaustion.

Christina fought her own fatigue as she pulled the dripping clothes from the unconscious man's body. She struggled with his belt, wrenched it free, then pulled his pants from his legs. She was weary, exhausted from a day that had drained her.

Her exhaustion carried her beyond the point of considering the propriety of undressing a man who had just shown up on her doorstep. She knew it had to be done, one last ordeal for a mind and body fatigued beyond comprehension. She tossed his sodden clothes aside, covered him with a blanket, and fell onto the bed alongside him.

Treblinka, Poland. Three weeks earlier.

Pistol cocked, the SS man moved slowly through the courtyard looking for signs of life among the corpses. "Hey, Otto, look at this one." The SS man guffawed. "She looks like she's still trying to run away." He pointed to the frail body of a young woman lying in a corner near the camp laundry among a pile of other bodies; one of her legs was straight, the other bent at the knee.

190

The woman's face stared back at the laundry hut, a look of surprise in her large, unmoving dark eyes, a trickle of black dried blood winding its way down her chin from a corner of her mouth. One of her arms pointed gracefully in the direction of the laundry hut; the other still firmly grasped the handle of the basket she had been carrying, its contents draped like funeral palls over the bodies that surrounded her.

By her side lay a packet of letters, neatly tied up with string. In her pocket was a letter she had written that morning.

Särö, Sweden.

Christina tried to resist the early morning light that beat upon her eyelids, insisting on a new day. She begged sleep to reclaim her, to push back the memories that sought to remind her of the day before. But they were insistent, forcing their way into her mind with the dawn. Göteborg, the car, Franz's hands in the air.

She flung her arm out and awoke with a start when she touched his warm body. She quickly pulled her hand away and swung her legs from the bed as further memories flooded into her mind. He lay there, still asleep, his head cushioned in the cradle of his arm, a thick growth of beard on his face. His fingers were bruised and cut and there was a wound near his temple. Some of his light brown hair was matted with dried blood. But he was breathing deeply, easily.

Who was he? She knew he was Danish, but how had he turned up half-drowned on the doorstep of her uncle's house?

Christina cast her uncle's dressing gown aside and dressed quickly. She would try to get answers when he awakened. She tied her hair up into a bun and went into the parlor. The curtains, parting at her touch, revealed a sun climbing into a cloudless sky and a sea that was calm, without memory of yesterday's storm.

Yesterday would not let go of her so easily. She glanced in the mirror over the mantelpiece; she didn't look different from the day before, but she felt older, as if one day had added years to her life.

In the mirror her eyes caught Franz's briefcase and the envelope lying beside it on the sofa. She grabbed the envelope, tore it open, and pulled out a page filled with typewritten script in German. Someone called Niels Bohr was to be seized by the Nazis. She looked up from the letter – the name was familiar; she remembered it from her translations back in Providence. He was a leading Danish scientist. Her eyes returned to the letter. The seizure of Bohr was to be part of a roundup of all Danish Jews on the night of October first, the second day of Rosh Hashanah. Further details about Bohr followed.

So this was what she had been sent half-way around the world to get, this was the message Franz had risked – and given – his life to pass on. Now she and the message were trapped on a remote headland in Sweden.

Jørgen's eyes would not focus. He could see only dim shapes. The blankets hugged him, seeking to drag him back into the comfort of sleep. Suddenly he sat up in the bed. Where was he? The pain hit him. The pain in his head and his limbs drove the memories of the previous day into his mind. Beatrice, the rocks, the falling mast. He groaned.

Christina heard a noise in the bedroom. The young Dane was awake. Christina read the document again. The closely-typed German script swam before her eyes and she let the paper slip from her fingers, the paper for which Franz had died. She saw yet again his lifeless body fall to the road. Her spirit was heavy, unrefreshed by sleep. As she put the message back in the briefcase, she heard another groan from the bedroom. Her head buzzed; she had a vital message and an injured man in the next room, and she didn't know what to do with either.

She walked to the bedroom and pushed the door open. "Would you like some breakfast?" she asked him in Danish with forced cheerfulness.

Mørkø Island.

As Hannah opened her notebook from her perch on a rock by the sea, a gust of wind alarmed the pages. She snapped the covers of the notebook shut and pushed it aside; she had other things on her mind.

She wondered what had happened to the little boy with the blond hair: he had disappeared as mysteriously as he had appeared. She missed him. How incongruous was his innocent presence on the island that housed the devil's workshop. Why had the boy left his dog behind? She had fed the dog the previous morning when she found the boy gone but, like the boy, the animal, too, had disappeared.

The wind blew her hair into her eyes and she felt a few drops of cold rain on her face. But for the dog, she might have believed she had imagined the child. Now, she worried about him. Like her sister, Rachel, he had a trusting nature – a trait that was not well-suited for survival in a malevolent and conniving world.

Hannah opened her notebook and tried to force herself to concentrate on the diagrams. Again she closed it and looked out to sea. Despite her success with the uranium machine, physics was no longer enough to sustain her.

People, like her sister, Rachel, and the unknown boy, were beginning to matter more.

Mørkø Island. Heldorf's office.

"Are you *certain* she's dead? Do you have actual proof?" Heldorf screamed the words into the receiver, which he squeezed as though he were trying to strangle it. "Have you checked the infirm—"

The officer at Treblinka cut him off, saying he had pressing duties and hanging up. Heldorf slammed the receiver into its cradle and dropped into his desk chair. The week before, he had learned that there had been some sort of riot at Treblinka and he'd been trying to get through to the camp commandant ever since. And now this. He propped his head on his arms and raked his fingers through his blond hair roughly as he tried to grasp the situation. She was dead. Hannah's sister was dead.

His mind raced. He picked up his fountain pen and rapped it on his desk rhythmically. Hannah must not be told about her sister's death. The feelings she had for her sister – love, maybe even guilt – were powerful and complex, and he was certain that the death of her sister would send her into a tailspin. Her remorse could impair her zeal for the project, even kill her passion for his bed.

But what if they had made a mistake at Treblinka? What actual proof did they have that Rachel had been killed?

Heldorf barked through the doorway to summon the corporal. "Contact the Treblinka camp commandant's office. I need official written confirmation that Rachel Goldmann, a prisoner of Treblinka, died in a camp uprising. Do you understand?"

"Yes, sir."

"And I need it as soon as possible."

"I'll make sure they know it's urgent, sir."

Heldorf hit the desk with his fist in anger. There was probably not the remotest chance they would find Rachel Goldmann alive. He was grasping at straws.

Särö, Sweden.

The bacon and eggs sizzled in the pan, filling the kitchen with an aroma that maddened hunger.

"I can't thank you enough for opening the door last night." He sat at the kitchen table wrapped in her uncle's dressing gown. His clothes hung over the kitchen chairs, still drying. "You probably saved my life."

Christina's Danish was still coming back to her and she struggled with the words. "How on earth did you end up here on the headland?" She slid the bacon and eggs out of the pan onto plates and took them to the table.

His story came slowly, interrupted by the food he devoured greedily. Göteborg. Storm. Shipwreck. Shipwreck: her thoughts turned to her uncle's beautiful boat, the Sofia, moored safely in Särö's small harbor.

She listened, but her mind drifted elsewhere. The message. The message that had to be delivered, the message that had cost Franz his life. A leading scientist to be seized in Copenhagen by the Nazis. Jews to be deported.

Her mind pondered these thoughts as she half-listened to his story about how he had clung to rocks, clambered ashore, dragged himself to the light in the house.

How was she to deliver the message? She dared not go back to Göteborg. The Gestapo agents would be covering every approach to the American Consulate, waiting for her to show her face.

"My God, this bacon is delicious." He smiled at her across the table. A plaintive smile.

She couldn't ask her uncle to take the message. He wouldn't be back for a week. The message couldn't wait a week.

"But at least Mrs. Gronborg is safe. Fortunately, I got her to safety before the storm hit." His knife and fork clattered on the plate as he pushed it aside.

"Who's Mrs. Gronborg?"

"She's a Jewish woman who—" He stopped suddenly.

Christina could see he had something to hide. "A Jewish woman who what?"

He squirmed on his chair, enduring a moment of indecision as he tried to decide if he could trust her. "She was being harassed by the Nazis. They'd come to arrest her."

So, he was opposed to the Nazis.

"Listen, I have to get back to Denmark fast." His blue-green eyes looked up from beneath a lock of brown hair. "I know…I know you've already done a lot for me, but I'm wondering, I'm wondering if there's any way you can help me."

She thought again of her uncle's boat, a fifty-five foot ketch. It would serve this purpose well.

"Perhaps." An idea began to form in her mind. She went to the desk, pulled out a sheet of paper, and wrote a note to her uncle. Perhaps, with the young Dane's help, she could deliver the message.

Jørgen cleared his throat nervously. "Can I ask you a question?" He looked sheepishly at her, then dropped his eyes to the table.

"Sure."

"Last night, did you, did you—" He couldn't get the words out. "Last night, did you—"

She laughed. "Did I take off your clothes?" Christina put the note to her uncle in an envelope, sealed it, and placed it on the mantelpiece. "Well, of course I did. It was a cold night; you didn't want to catch pneumonia, did you?

"And as for helping you, perhaps there's a way. Maybe we could sail to Denmark today."

Frederikshavn Harbor.

Jørgen clambered onto the jetty, caught the ropes thrown by Christina, and secured the vessel in the fading light. Barely had he finished when he felt a hand grasp his arm.

"Jørgen, what happened?" Marius was frowning and his voice was stern. "Where's your boat?"

The pain rushed back to Jørgen with a force that was physical; he swallowed hard and looked down at the harbor flagstones. "After I dropped off Mrs. Gronborg, there was a storm. I lost my boat."

"Rotten luck." Marius patted Jørgen's upper arm to show sympathy. "But where did you get this one?"

"Are you all right, Jørgen?" Christina called from the deck.

Marius started at the voice. "And who the hell is she?"

Jørgen wondered how Marius could shrug off his feelings of sympathy for his misfortune so quickly. He had always been distant and formal, but now, after a year and a half of leading the Resistance cell, he was cold, barely capable of emotion.

"Jørgen, is everything okay?" Christina's voice came again, more insistent.

"Yes, come ashore."

"Who is she?" Marius demanded, looking around at Christina and poking a thumb over his shoulder.

"To be honest, I'm not sure. She saved my life." He saw her hands grasp at the metal rungs that led up to the harbor wall. "She say's she's an American agent and that she's got a message for Niels Bohr."

"Niel's Bohr? Are you crazy or is she?" Marius raised his eyebrows and shook his head as Christina emerged onto the harbor wall. "I think we need to sort this out. Bring her to my place in half an hour." He checked himself as he started to turn. "And make sure you avoid the German patrols. They're crawling like cockroaches all over town right now."

Jørgen reached down to help Christina onto the jetty. He turned his head as Marius spoke again. "Oh, and by the way, we found your little friend Peder. He's fine. I told him you took his mother to safety. He seemed happy, but you never can tell with that child."

Christina jumped onto the jetty, stumbled, and fell into Jørgen's arms. She looked up into his eyes. "And just why might you be smiling?"

Frederikshavn. Marius's Apartment.

"Please sit down." Marius offered her a chair. "I'm sorry, I don't know your name."

"Christina." She glanced around the room; it was untidy, littered with a bachelor's existence. She placed von Rastenberg's briefcase at the foot of the chair and looked anxiously at Jørgen, who gave her a reassuring smile.

"Jørgen tells me you're an American agent." Marius's voice was gruff.

She shot Jørgen an accusing look.

"I'm sorry, Christina." Jørgen flushed with embarrassment. "I had to tell him if we're to act on the message. Marius is—"

"I'm a fisherman." Marius cut Jørgen short without removing his gaze from Christina. "You speak Danish rather well for an American."

"I was born in Sweden. My family used to vacation in Denmark—" She stopped suddenly. "Say, what is this? I came here to bring an important message and the next thing I know is I'm being subjected to an interrogation!"

"Sorry, Christina. No offence meant." Marius's voice was still cold. "Can I see the message?"

Christina's hand plunged into the briefcase and emerged with a piece of paper that she thrust at him.

"Hmm, it's in German." Marius lit a cigarette as his eyes ran over the message. "I can make some of it out, but—"

"Of course it's in German, you fool." Christina's temper snapped. "It was written by a German." Her face flushed with rage. "Look, Marius, I'm here to help you. Your leading scientist is about to be snatched by the Nazis and Danish Jews are going to be rounded up and sent to concentration camps." She breathed deeply trying to contain her temper. "If you don't want my help, I'll just sail back to Göteborg tomorrow and—"

She was startled as the door flew open.

"Jørgen! Jørgen!" The boy bounded into the room, his straight blond hair dancing on his head. He ran to Jørgen and clutched him around his thighs.

Jørgen reached down, picked the boy up, and lifted him above his head, a broad smile on his face. "Good to see you, little man!" He held him in the crook of his arm and ruffled his hair; the boy smiled, but his eyes never met Jørgen's. Jørgen looked across at Christina. "Christina, I'd like you to meet Peder."

"What a beautiful boy!" Christina, charmed by Peder, felt her anger ebb away.

Jørgen's voice hardened as he spoke to Marius. "Look, we have to trust her. Why should she lie to us? The message is clear: our top scientist is to be seized by the Nazis and the Danish Jews are to be shipped to the camps in the east."

He lowered Peder gently to the floor. Christina reached out for the boy, but he ignored her, scampering to a corner of the room where he pulled his sketchpad from his backpack.

Marius sat impassively at the table, saying nothing.

"For God's sake, Marius," Jørgen erupted, thumping on the table, "the Gestapo tried to kill her! Do you have to have a letter signed by Roosevelt before you'll believe her?"

Marius drew heavily on his cigarette and looked intently at Christina. For a few moments there was no sound in the room except the scratching of Peder's pencil on his sketchpad.

Marius slowly stubbed out his cigarette. "Okay, I guess I'll have to trust you, Christina."

His doubt and indecision cast aside, Marius rose from his chair. "If we hurry, we might be able to catch the train that gets into Copenhagen in the early evening. I know people in the capital who can arrange a meeting with Niels Bohr. We'll see what he thinks of your message."

Jørgen felt a tug at his pant leg and looked down. Peder thrust his sketchpad into his hand; Jørgen's eyes widened as he looked at the drawing. "Christina, take a look at this." He handed her the sketchpad.

"My God, it's me!" She ran her fingers over the drawing – the hair, the eyes, the pouting of her lips were all true to life. Or was it Franz's wife? She shook the thought aside.

"Peder will have to come with us." Marius reached for his jacket. "If the Germans find him wandering around Frederikshavn, they might start asking awkward questions about Mrs. Gronborg's disappearance. Come on, let's go." He headed for the door.

"Wait a minute!" Jørgen knelt down next to Peder. "Something's wrong!"

"What the hell's wrong now?" Marius's voice was brusque with impatience.

Jørgen grasped the boy's face and turned it toward him. "Peder, where's Soldat?"

The boy's chin fell to his chest. "Soldat. Lost." He spoke almost in a whisper. "Lost." His cheeks were moist with tears.

Copenhagen.

Niels Bohr showed them into his study and eased his tall, angular frame into his leather club chair. Marius, Jørgen, and Christina took places around him, remaining silent, in awe of the great man who pondered what

199

Marius had told him. Peder climbed into a wing chair and began sketching Bohr's cocker spaniel, Lulu, who lay curled up by the fire.

"I still can't believe it," said Bohr at long last. "Even though in my heart I always knew it would happen. How could it not? How could the fiends resist taking Denmark's Jews when they've wreaked havoc in all the other countries they've sullied with their presence?"

"Dr. Bohr," Marius said softly, "we must get you and your family out of Denmark as soon as possible."

"Absolutely not!" Bohr said emphatically. "How could I desert my fellow Danes when I might be of some help here?"

"Dr. Bohr," Marius cleared his throat, intimidated by the Nobel laureate's outburst, "Jørgen and I thought of a plan on the train down from Frederikshavn, and we'd like to get your advice on it. You're part of the plan, but the part you play is in Sweden."

Bohr scowled but said nothing. He picked up his pipe and tamped some tobacco into the bowl.

"First, we need to get word out to rabbis all over Denmark. We need to ask them to tell their congregations that the Nazis are planning a mass roundup of all Danish Jews on the second day of Rosh Hashanah. They should instruct them to go into hiding immediately."

"But where would they hide?"

"With non-Jewish friends, if possible. We can arrange for safe houses and hiding places in public buildings. We know quite a few doctors who are sympathetic to the Resistance; perhaps they could find places in hospitals."

Bohr caught the gist. "Yes. Perhaps they might even use ambulances to move people to the hospitals." He lit his pipe as his mind began turning over ideas.

Peder worked quietly on his portrait of Lulu as Bohr embellished and fine-tuned the resistants' plan. From his address book, Bohr compiled a list of names and addresses of people who could help.

Marius saw a new problem. When the Jews were hidden, the Resistance would have to acquire a fleet of boats to ferry them to Sweden, arrange for the Jews to be transported safely to the boats, and coordinate the departures. He made a mental list of fishermen who would help.

Christina felt anxious as the others talked. The plan was a huge undertaking, a colossal gamble. And she was part of that gamble. She prayed that luck would be on their side.

They finally convinced Bohr that he had to go to Sweden as soon as possible and pave the way for the arrival of so many refugees. "Gentlemen, your plan is a good one," said Bohr. "I'll go to Sweden. And the first thing I'll do when I get there is visit the foreign minister, maybe even the king. Sweden must accept Danish Jews into her country. Besides sanctuary, the refugees will need food, shelter, jobs."

"Dr. Bohr, I hope you can persuade them; it's critical to the plan." Jørgen leaned forward, resting his elbows on his knees and lacing his fingers.

Bohr nodded. "I hope so, too. I think I can. Sweden's neutrality is rather pragmatic: they seem to prefer whichever side seems to be winning. Now, with Germany's defeats continuing to mount, I think they may want to do something to please the Allies in an attempt to offset the many favors they've done for the Germans in the past. But the main issue is that it's a matter of simple human decency."

"Amen," nodded Marius.

"Amen," Jørgen echoed.

Marius looked at his watch. "Sir, it's nearly two in the morning; why don't we sleep on these ideas and discuss them in the morning over coffee? We'll accept your offer to stay the night, Dr. Bohr; Jørgen's little friend over there seems to be all tuckered out."

Everyone chuckled at the sight of Peder, sprawled in the chair with his mouth slightly open, his eyes firmly shut, and his sketchpad under his knee.

Jørgen stood up. "Come on, big boy – it's way past your bedtime." He picked Peder up and the sleeping boy instinctively wrapped his arms and legs around him. As his body left the chair his foot dragged against his sketchpad, kicking it to the floor.

"Good night, everybody," Jørgen said as he ascended the stairs with Peder, followed by Marius.

Christina bent down to pick up the sketchpad, which had landed open to the just-drawn picture of Lulu. "Oh, do take a look, Dr. Bohr," she said, standing up; "Peder's done a wonderful picture of your dog."

She held up the book up for the scientist to see, but noticed that his eyes drifted to the opposite page.

"May I see that for a moment?" A frown came to his face as he put down his pipe and reached for the sketchpad.

Christina watched the scientist closely. He was looking at the curious drawing with the circles and arrows that Peder had made on the opposite page. Christina could make no sense of it.

"Is Peder a particularly bright child?" he asked.

"I really don't know. Why do you ask?"

"Because…," the scientist looked at the sketchbook and shook his head, "because on the page opposite this very fine drawing of Lulu, he's sketched a diagram for a nuclear reactor."

Mørkø Island.

Everyone was there, even Sol Friedberg, whose worsening sciatica had made the walk to the meeting difficult. All were wearing their best clothes, such as they had, for the historic occasion. The room, gray with graphite dust, housed an object that looked like the small moon of an unknown planet that had somehow strayed to earth. The object was a black squashed sphere, about twenty feet high and twenty-five feet wide; it sat in a deep well and was supported by a wooden frame. They were about to commission the uranium machine.

Heldorf entered and sat down on the room's only chair, facing the uranium machine. He said nothing, trying to hide his anxiety. He hoped to God that the damned thing worked. If it didn't....

Albert Weiss walked to the front of the room and cleared his throat.

"Sturmbannführer Heldorf and fellow scientists, I hardly need tell you that we expect this day to be a watershed in the history of science and, indeed, perhaps in the history of the world, which—" he held up his hand to quell the scattered applause, "which all of you here today have toiled to make possible. But before we begin the demonstration, I thought it might be useful to start with a reiteration of the basic scientific principles involved."

Heldorf bristled at Weiss's pomposity. "Get to the point, Weiss."

"What we're going to demonstrate here today is the self-sustaining chain reaction needed to manufacture plutonium. The key measurement we're using to determine our success is the average number of secondary neutrons produced during fission. If, for a single original neutron, this average is less than one, the chain reaction will die out; if it's greater than one, the chain reaction will get out of control."

"When you say the chain reaction will get out of control, what do you mean?" Weiss's comments were beginning to interest Heldorf. "Do you mean that a nuclear explosion would take place within the uranium machine?"

"Mein Herr, we're quite sure that a nuclear explosion could not occur in the uranium machine under any circumstances." Weiss watched Heldorf's eyebrows rise; the statement seemed to take him by surprise.

"More likely, the uranium machine would produce lots of radioactive material and would intensify to perhaps a million kilowatts; in the process it would destroy itself."

Heldorf leaned back in his chair and smiled. "So we'll have to wait for the uranium machine to produce the plutonium that will fuel the nuclear weapon."

"Yes, *mein Herr;* the uranium machine, by itself, will never explode like a nuclear bomb." Weiss could not prevent the wave of nausea he felt as he looked at the machine; what were they about to unleash upon the world? "And now, if there are no further questions, we'll begin the demonstration. Dr. Goldmann, will you please take over as I demonstrate?"

Heldorf watched as Hannah walked to the front of the room, as calm as if she were about to demonstrate how to ice a cake. Everyone knew she was the real brains behind the operation and that Weiss, while a competent physicist, was merely a figurehead.

"Thank you, Dr. Weiss. As you all know, the graphite in the uranium machine slows the neutrons and enables them to do their work in the uranium that's embedded in the graphite. In order to control the rate of neutron generation, long control rods made of cadmium are inserted in slits and passed through the machine. Cadmium, as you know, is capable of absorbing large quantities of neutrons. Thus, when the rods are inserted, neutron production slows; when they're pulled, it increases. At the moment, all of the control rods are fully in place. Dr. Weiss, if you'd be so kind as to move a control rod to a position about half-way out of the uranium machine."

Heldorf rested his elbows on his knees and leaned forward as he watched with keen interest.

Click. Click click click. Click click click click. Click click. Click.

The clicks on the neutron counter rose, became steady, and subsided. In the corner a recording device flipped its pen in time with the clicks as it measured neutron intensity.

"Dr. Weiss, will you now please move the rod out another six inches." They all listened to the clicking, the sound of neutrons being counted, that again built to a crescendo, leveled off, and died away. "As you can see, gentlemen, the chain reaction has not been sustained. The uranium machine is still subcritical."

Twenty minutes later, after adjustments had been made to the control rods, the sound of the clicks became constant and the average number of secondary neutrons now hovered at a stable level.

"Gentlemen," Hannah scanned the room briefly, catching Holdorf's eyes for a second, "I am pleased to announce that the uranium machine has gone critical. A self-sustaining chain reaction had been achieved."

As applause and cheers broke out, Hannah held up her hand. "There's one more thing I'd like to show you. Dr. Weiss, please pull the third control rod out another six inches."

Weiss's eyes became large. He held his breath as he followed her instruction. The clicks of the neutron counter began again, but this time they continued until they were almost a roar. The pen on the recorder went wild.

"That's enough, Dr. Weiss," Hannah turned to him, "you may replace the rods."

Weiss slammed all the rods back into the uranium machine as fast as he could and wiped his brow with the back of his hand.

"Gentleman," Hannah said coolly, "you have just witnessed the beginning of an uncontrolled chain reaction, in which the neutrons are increasing exponentially. If it had been allowed to continue, in about two hours the machine would begin to melt down. And no one in this room would be alive."

There was a loud exhalation of relief when the neutron counter finally stopped clicking.

Heldorf gazed with admiration at his handiwork. It was a great black giant, a machine that made no sound, a machine that had no moving parts. And, if not treated with respect, it could reap a harvest of death.

Copenhagen.

Silence, broken only by the ticking of a clock and the clinking of silverware against china, pervaded the Bohr's dining room as Jørgen, Christina, and Marius sat eating their breakfasts. Despite the early hour and their lack of sleep, each had an air of nervous anticipation.

Christina looked fretful, worried about all that had to be done and hoping that she could be of some help. Jørgen gave her a reassuring grin as he reached for a pastry on the plate the maid placed on the table.

Christina returned a wan smile, a little afraid of the attraction she felt for him. Marius's pencil moved rapidly over the notebook open before him at the table.

The aroma of baking wafted into the room. From the hall came the indistinct voice of Niels Bohr as he spoke on the telephone.

Margrethe Bohr bustled in from the kitchen. "The coffee's almost ready," she said. "I'm afraid it's ersatz – we haven't had any real coffee for six months."

"Maybe I can help." Christina leapt up from the table and retrieved Franz's briefcase from a chair. Her hand plunged in and emerged with a treasure.

Mrs. Bohr's jaw dropped. "Real coffee?" The others looked at the packet in her hand as if it were the Holy Grail. Even Marius looked up in surprise. "Where did you get that?" asked Mrs. Bohr.

Christina saw Franz's face. "From a friend." She thrust the packet into the hands of Mrs. Bohr, who took it with a barely-suppressed whoop of delight and rushed into the kitchen.

"I've sent out the warnings." All eyes turned to the imposing figure of Niels Bohr as he appeared in the doorway. "The Chief Rabbi of Copenhagen knows of the danger and will pass the message on to the other rabbis. At the Rosh Hashanah services, they'll tell their congregations to go into hiding immediately." He pulled back a chair and sat at the table. "I've also spoken to some friends and they've agreed to raise money. The fishermen who are willing to ferry the Jews across to Sweden – they'll be risking their lives and are entitled to some remuneration. We can't expect them to do it for nothing."

"But what of yourself, Dr. Bohr?" For Marius, the key to the whole plan was to get the scientist to Sweden before the Nazis came to arrest him. "You've got to get out now, before the Nazis come banging on your door. Surely you realize you're in danger."

The scientist nodded, then put his nose in the air. "Is that real coffee I smell?"

Marius cut across the laughter. "Early tomorrow, someone will come here to arrange for your immediate transfer to Sweden. Trust him. Do as he says, and you and Mrs. Bohr will soon be safe in Sweden."

"It's all so very hurried – my head's spinning." The Nobel laureate smiled as his wife deposited the coffee urn on the table. "Let's enjoy the coffee first."

Marius drained his coffee cup. "I've got to leave soon to make the arrangements for your journey."

"Are there many Jews in Frederikshavn?" Bohr's question stunned them; while thinking about his safety, they had forgotten about their own neighbors.

"Not many – perhaps a dozen or so." Jørgen put down his cup and pushed it away. "There's Mrs. Gronborg's friend, Gerda Rosenfeld, and there's Mr. and Mrs. Abramowitz, and—" He jumped to his feet. "We'd better get right back."

Marius was unperturbed. "We'll go as soon as I make arrangements for Dr. Bohr's departure. Don't worry; we'll make sure our friends back home are safe. Now I've got to go. Jørgen and Christina will wait until I come back. Then we'll return to Frederikshavn." He picked up his notebook and left.

The maid was clearing away the dishes when the door flew open. Peder raced across the room to Jørgen and clutched his knees.

"Ah!" Bohr smiled. "The young man who knows how to build a nuclear reactor." He looked across at Jørgen. "May I take another look at his sketchpad?"

Jørgen dug the pad out of Peder's backpack and handed it to the scientist.

Bohr studied it intently. "Without a doubt, this is a diagram for a nuclear reactor. Interesting design; no one's ever actually built one, as far as I know. I wonder if it works." He looked over at Peder and spoke in a louder voice. "Where did you get this, young man?"

Peder tried to hide by burying his face in Jørgen's lap.

Bohr flipped a page. "Heavens, this drawing is a remarkable likeness of you, Christina."

He turned another page and gasped. "My God, I don't believe it! It's Hannah Goldmann, the expert on beta decay. She was taken by the Nazis last year; I thought she was dead." He put down the pad. "Where did you see this woman, Peder?"

Peder buried his head deeper in Jørgen's lap, but Jørgen gently pulled it up by the chin. "Peder, tell Mr. Bohr where you saw the woman you drew; he needs to know."

Peder stared at the floor. "Soldat. With Soldat. Soldat lost."

• • •

Jørgen brushed away some leaves, sat down on a bench in Bohr's garden, and looked across the flower beds at Peder. The boy was sitting on a wall, his attention locked onto his sketchpad as his pencil stroked across the paper sketching a house martin that perched on the branch of a linden tree.

Jørgen got up and approached the boy, his feet shuffling through early fallen leaves. He would try once more. Since Bohr had spotted them in Peder's sketchpad, Jørgen had tried to ask the boy about the reactor diagram and the sketch of the woman. Peder had said little, averting his eyes, retreating into his own world.

"Peder, tell me where Soldat is."

There was no response. The boy's eyes flitted from the bird on the tree to the flowing pencil in his hand.

"Peder, where is Soldat?"

The pencil paused. "Soldat lost." The boy looked at the bird and his fingers began to run across the paper again.

Jørgen's temper snapped. "Peder, stop that!" He reached down and pulled the sketchbook from the boy's hands.

The hurt in Peder's eyes stabbed at Jørgen's heart. He should not have snatched the book from the boy; Peder did not expect a friend to do what he had done.

Jørgen turned the pages of the book. "This diagram, Peder." He thrust the book in front of Peder. "Where did you see it?"

"Lady. Lady's drawing."

Peder reached for the book but Jørgen moved away and turned the page. He showed the page to the boy. "Is this the lady? Where is she?"

"With Soldat. Lady with Soldat."

Jørgen sighed. The same answers as before. He flipped through the sketchbook. The usual birds, precise in every detail. He was about to hand the book back when he saw a drawing of his friend, Erik; Peder must have drawn it the day Erik had helped fix Mrs. Gronborg's shop window. The likeness was remarkable.

"Very good, Peder."

The boy seized the book. Peder lifted his pencil and drew a large 'X' over his drawing. "Bad."

"Jørgen, we need to get back to Frederikshavn now." Marius had come into the garden. "I've fixed everything for Bohr's transit to Sweden. Now we've got to arrange for the escape of our own Jews."

Jørgen nodded. He'd begun to formulate plans in his mind.

"And we have to arrange for the drop from the RAF next Tuesday." Marius blew through his teeth. "Goddamn, we've got a lot to do."

Jørgen lifted Peder off the wall and set him down. Why did the boy think his drawing of Erik was bad? It was a perfect likeness. He shook his head; he'd never figure out his little friend.

PART FIVE

"*There is in every man, at every hour, two simultaneous postulations, one towards God, the other towards the devil.*"

—Baudelaire, *Nouvelles Fleurs du Mal*

Frederikshavn.

"My friends, I have a very grave announcement." After opening with prayers, the rabbi of Temple Emanuel went straight into his terrible news. "Tomorrow begins Rosh Hashanah, a time when we're all home with our families. I'm sorry to have to tell you, but, on the second day of this high holiday, the Nazis plan to come to our homes, arrest us, and ship us to their concentration camps in the east."

The voices of the small congregation rose up in a chorus of shock and disbelief. Gerda felt faint and gripped the seat in front of her to keep from falling.

"There will be no service today. You must go home now, pack a few essentials, and leave your homes immediately. Seek shelter wherever you can."

Where could she seek shelter? Gerda had no living relatives nearby, only a brother and sister-in-law in Copenhagen, and they were Jews, too.

"Now go – go into hiding as soon as you can, and may God be with you."

The score or so members of the congregation sat silently for a while as the rabbi's words sank in. Gradually they got up to leave, their voices swelling, but in moments the synagogue was quiet and empty. Except for Gerda, who remained rooted to her chair, her arms wrapped around her shaking body. She was alone. Where was a poor old Jewish lady supposed to go?

Gerda felt a hand on her shoulder; it was the rabbi's wife. "Gerda, can you make it home on your own?"

Gerda was about to say no, she could not, she was an old lady and she needed help – but then she looked up at the kind face of the rabbi's wife and remembered that she, too, was a Jew, and, with three children, would have her own problems and plans to make.

"Thank you, Frida, I'll be fine." Gerda braced herself to help her arthritic knees rise from the seat. "You be safe, too. Look after the little ones."

Gerda struggled on the walk back home. Before going in, she stopped and took a long look at her little house. Years ago its walls had

213

echoed with the beloved voices of friends and family. Now many, like her husband, were dead; others, like Sara, were gone. Soon she'd never see her house again. Where would she go?

"I'll take ten thousand a head and not a krone less." Captain Jacobsen, the skipper of the Kestrel with whom Jørgen was trying to negotiate, shrugged his shoulders. "I have to think of the risk. If I was caught, I'd really be in hot water with the Germans."

"Look, have a little heart, for God's sake." Jørgen's upturned palms and imploring tone sought to appeal to the better nature of Jacobsen, the good man he'd known all his life. "The Copenhagen fishermen are charging only four thousand kroner."

"Hah! They don't have to make a trip across the Kattegat!"

"Yeah, but they've got a lot more patrol boats to dodge."

In the end, Jørgen had managed to get the price down to eight thousand kroner for each Jew ferried to safety. He knew it was not an unfair price for Jacobsen to risk his life and his livelihood, but it would quickly begin to eat up the hundred thousand kroner the Resistance had managed to raise so far from Frederikshavn citizens.

Jørgen left the wharf and boarded a streetcar to head for his next stop, the hospital. The Resistance couldn't move all of Frederikshavn's Jews out at once, so they would have to hide them for a few days. The head doctor at the hospital had promised to hide them in beds there – maybe even in the hospital morgue, if need be – and Jørgen wanted to make sure that he knew the plan.

The streetcar made a stop and three German soldiers got on. Jørgen and the other five Danes inside the cabin got up and moved to the outside platform.

Gerda sat on her divan watching the hours spin away on the mantelpiece clock, frozen with bewilderment about where to go and what to take with her. Eventually she got up with a sigh and went upstairs to her closet. She put on her best dress over the top of the dress she was wearing – who would ever notice it on a fat old lady? – and stuffed some clothes into a pillowcase. She came downstairs and looked again at the mantelpiece clock – it was a wedding gift from her parents so many years ago; it was part of her life, full of precious memories. Her hands reached out and clutched it gently to her bosom as she slipped out the door, terrified of staying in her house any longer.

Outside, she looked up at the front door of her neighbor, Kirsten Ekblad. Unlike her, Kirsten had nothing to fear – she was not Jewish. Kirsten was a much younger woman; it was Wednesday, and her two children would be in school now, her husband at work. Already weary of her burdens and feeling hot and pinched by the two dresses, Gerda knocked on Kirsten's door.

The smiled that graced Kirsten's face as she opened the door vanished as she ran her eyes over her bedraggled neighbor. "Oh, Mrs. Rosenfeld, it's you."

"Please, Mrs. Ekblad, please, may I come in?"

"Actually, Mrs. Rosenfeld, I was just about to go out this very second—"

"Mrs. Ekblad, I need your help. The rabbi announced at the morning services that the Nazis are coming to take all the Jews in Denmark—"

"Oh, surely not, Mrs. Rosenfeld. The Jews have been quite safe under German occupation for three and a half years, why should they—," Kirsten Ekblad suddenly pulled Gerda by the arm into the house and slammed the door. "I just saw a German truck heading down the street."

Kirsten went to a window and edged the curtain aside. "They're stopping at your house, Gerda! Quick, in here." Kirsten opened the door to a closet in the hall.

The darkness of the closet frightened Gerda. She could hear men shouting "Open up! Open up!" Then came the sound of a boot kicking in her door, then muffled voices. Gerda trembled uncontrollably and slid to the closet floor, unable to stand. If only Sara Gronborg could be with her, she thought. But what kind of friend was she to wish Sara into the middle of this hell? Her friend had gone through her own hell. One hell was enough.

Her heart pounded. There was a hard knocking on the door of Kirsten's house, and she heard Kirsten open the door. "Good afternoon, officers. What can I do for you?" Her voice was calm and unhurried.

"Do you know where the Jew Gerda Rosenfeld is?" a voice thundered.

"No."

"Is she a friend of yours?"

"No."

"Just to be on the safe side, I think we should take a look around."

Gerda bit her hand in fear. They would find her, drag her out, and send her to a camp.

The boots clunked through Kirsten's hallway toward the closet.

Jørgen returned to his apartment for lunch and found Christina watching as Peder hastily sketched a street map of Frederikshavn.

"He's drawing the map from memory," Christina whispered. "Will it be accurate?"

Jørgen grinned and whispered back. "Peder's a strange child. There's a lot he can't do, but what he can do, he does perfectly."

Christina stopped whispering and raised her voice to a normal conversational tone. "Look, Jørgen, I've got a list of all the Jews in Frederikshavn; Marius got it for me from a woman who works in some government office."

"I know the woman you mean, Christina. She used to be the girlfriend of one of my friends." A memory of Lars flashed through his mind. Jørgen took the list and studied it. "I'm relieved to see I was right – the number of Frederikshavn Jews we have to evacuate is pretty small. I don't envy the Copenhagen cells. They've got to take care of thousands."

"I wish Peder could guide me around the town," Christina frowned as she studied the list and the map Peder had drawn, "but I understand why he has to lie low."

Jørgen made a sandwich and dropped into a chair. He was exhausted but felt revitalized by Christina's presence, admiring the way she had selflessly thrown herself into the task of saving the Jews of Frederikshavn. But other things drew him to her. His eyes wandered to the stray lock of blond hair hanging over her forehead.

"You know what to do?" He took another bite of his sandwich.

Christina's eyes scanned the list. "I'll knock on these doors and try to get a warning to those Jews who may not have heard about the Nazi raid. Marius thought a young woman would attract less attention knocking on doors than one of you firebrands."

Jørgen glanced at his watch. "Damn, I'd better get going – I've still got a lot left to do today." He gulped down the remains of his *smørrebrød,* pushed his plate away, and jumped up. "Christina…"

216

"Yes?"

"Please be careful out there when you go knocking on doors. The wrong people might see you and find it suspicious." He gazed at her, then impulsively leaned down and kissed her quickly before grabbing his cap and running out the door.

"Excuse me, but what do you take me for?" As Kirsten addressed the soldiers in an offended voice, Gerda trembled in the dark closet. "Do you really think I'd harbor a dirty Jew in my house?"

There was a long pause, then a gruff voice. "Okay, let's move on, boys. But we'll be back." Gerda heard the door slam and began breathing again.

She blinked at the light as Kirsten opened the closet door and helped her to her feet. "Mrs. Rosenfeld, please don't be offended at what I said. I had to say it – the brute was headed straight into the hall." Gerda crept out.

"I understand. Thank you, Mrs. Ekblad, thank you." Gerda's body continued to shake.

"Well, I couldn't let them find you on my doorstep, could I?"

Gerda puzzled over Kirsten's remark as she struggled to stop shuddering. "I feel faint, Mrs. Ekblad. May I please sit down?"

"Oh, yes – please do. But just for a moment – my children will be home in just a short while. It would be better if they don't find you here." Kirsten ushered Gerda into the kitchen and the two women sat at the table. "Tell me, Mrs. Rosenfeld, what do you plan to do?"

"Do?" Gerda had no plans. She didn't know how to plan, where to start.

"Yes, where will you go?"

"Go? I was hoping maybe I could stay here for just a little while, until—"

"Mrs. Rosenfeld, I'm sure you know I'd like to help you, but how could I?" She looked down at the floor. "There'd be too many problems. What would you eat? They'll be checking ration cards, and yours are probably no longer valid. And where would we put you? And what if the neighbors saw you and reported you? If the Nazis ever found you here – well, I just can't put my children in danger." She looked at Gerda and shrugged. "Would you like a cup of tea before you go?"

Gerda rose from the chair. "No thank you, I don't think I would." She pulled the curtain aside and peeked out. "There's no sign of them. I'll be going back home now."

"Do you think that's wise?"

"Wise?" Gerda furrowed her brow as she considered the question. "I don't know if it's wise, but that's my plan. Good day, Mrs. Ekblad."

Gerda, her stuffed pillowcase under one arm and her clock under the other, headed for the front door, but Kirsten intercepted her. "Mrs. Rosenfeld, perhaps it would be better if you used the back door. Just in case." She escorted Gerda to the back door and held it open as the old lady trudged through. "Goodbye, Mrs. Rosenfeld. "Look after yourself."

Look after myself. Easy for you to say, thought Gerda.

Gerda's home was a shambles. Closet doors hung open, furniture was overturned, a favorite figurine lay smashed on the floor. The locks on both her front and back doors had been broken; she went to each and drove home the inside bolts. She looked around at the mess and began to clean it up, then shook her head, sat on her divan, and whimpered. She wondered how much food there was in the house, how long she could hold out, how soon they'd return—

She froze when she heard the knock at her back door. The knocking continued, only louder, and then there was the sound of breaking glass. From her place on the divan she watched in terror as a hand reached through the smashed window and pulled back the bolt.

Mørkø Island.

As he stared out the window, Max Heldorf absentmindedly toyed with the cream-colored piece of stationery bearing the neat handwriting. This latest letter from his mother, the one he'd received that day, was particularly disturbing. He unfolded it and read it again, searching for a buried note of hope that perhaps he'd somehow overlooked.

Dear Son,

There's no way I can describe the horror Berlin has become. The English are here every night to bomb us without

218

letup, then the Americans come in to torture us during the day. I haven't slept properly in weeks and my nerves are frayed to snapping point. I don't know how much longer I can take this dreadful punishment.

But I want you to know that I think of you every day....

He folded the letter and returned it to the envelope. Under the best of circumstances, his mother was highly strung; under the worst, there was no telling how long her fragile state of mind could hold up. If she survived the bombing.

The completion of the project had now become an intensely personal mission. Germany *must* have an atomic weapon to counter these hideous attacks on innocent civilians like his mother; he wanted the bomb with an intensity that made him angry.

He rubbed his eyes with the flat of his palms and opened his desk drawer to put his mother's letter away. He was about to lay it on top of an envelope, one he had received the previous day. Inside was a letter from the camp commandant at Treblinka confirming Rachel Goldmann's death. Attached to the official letter was an unposted letter to Hannah from Rachel, found in the dead woman's apron pocket.

He took the envelope out of the drawer. Should he detach the unmailed letter from the commandant's correspondence and pass it off to Hannah as a piece of new mail from her sister? He had been telling her that mail had been disrupted because of the bombing, and her sister's letter would seem to prove his point. He fanned the air with the envelope as he thought.

The knock on the door startled him: he was interrupted only for matters of urgency. He thought of his mother. Had the bombing...? He quickly dismissed the idea of giving Rachel's letter to Hannah, returning the envelope to the desk and slamming the drawer.

"Yes, what is it?" He barked the words with irritation. Whatever it was, the chances were that it was something he did not want to hear.

The door opened and the corporal's head popped around the side. "Dr. Goldmann would like to see you, sir."

Heldorf grimaced. Something was wrong. Hannah had never come to his office unbidden. He collected his thoughts; he did not wish to betray to her his frame of mind. "Show Dr. Goldmann in."

He relaxed when he saw her radiant smile. She waited for the door to close before she spoke. "Max, we've done it!"

"Done it?"

"We've detected plutonium in the uranium machine!"

Heldorf beamed. He had emerged from a dark cell into the bright sunlight. "Detected plutonium?" He had often wondered if this moment would ever come. He rose from his chair and walked over to her.

"It's just a small amount, but—Max!" Hannah squealed as Heldorf lifted her high into the air and swung her around. She threw her head back and laughed like a child being tickled.

He put her down and kissed her forehead, her nose, her chin. "We've got to celebrate." He stuck his head out the door. "Corporal, bring me the 1934 Château Haut-Brion. And two glasses!" Heldorf closed the door, took Hannah in his arms, and held her tight. "I've been saving this bottle for a special occasion." He kissed her hair. "It's time to open it. But it's hardly enough; how else can we celebrate?"

He stepped back and smiled at her, his arms still planted on her shoulders. Succumbing to the exuberance of the moment he said, almost without thinking, "It's here, Hannah. A letter. I was going to give it to you later."

Almost as soon as the words were out of his mouth he regretted them, but he went to his desk and took the letter from the Treblinka camp commandant out of its envelope. He carefully detached Rachel's unposted letter and brought it to Hannah, stuffing the official letter from the camp commandant in his jacket pocket. "Here, *Liebchen*. This letter from your sister arrived just this afternoon."

"Oh, Max," Hannah's eyes glistened as she studied Rachel's handwriting. "This is wonderful beyond words – much better than finding the plutonium!" She clutched the letter to her breast.

"I know you were worried, Hannah." He stroked her cheek. "The letter took a long time to get here – look, she wrote it on August thirty-first – a month ago. I'm just glad it got here at all." He shook his head and scowled. "With all the bombings, one never knows."

Hannah looked up at him with grateful eyes and planted another kiss of thanks on his cheek. Her lips seemed to sting his skin; of all the bad things he had ever done in his life, he had never done anything shabbier. He smiled to hide his guilt.

Frederikshavn.

Jørgen pushed open Gerda Rosenfeld's back door and looked around: a kettle lay on the floor, the kitchen table lay on its side, the rod of a ripped curtain hung on the diagonal. He righted the table, sat down at it, and held his head in his hands. He was too late; the Nazis had beaten him there. But how? Christina's message said that the raid on the Jews would take place on the night of October first. Had it been wrong? Or had the Nazis come early for Mrs. Rosenfeld because she was a friend of Mrs. Gronborg, who had managed to evade their filthy clutches?

"Damn!" Jørgen struck the table with his fist. "To hell with it all!" He struck the table again.

He jumped at the noise, a curious low moan that came from the parlor like the cry of a wounded animal. But when he looked in the parlor, all he could see was mayhem. It wasn't enough for the Nazi bastards to stomp in and look around, they had to strike, throw, smash.

"Jørgen, is that you?" In the gloom, he could just make out the small round figure clutching what looked like an overstuffed pillow. "Mrs. Rosenfeld?"

"Oh, Jørgen, thank God it's you! I'm scared – I don't know what to do."

"Mrs. Rosenfeld, how did you manage—oh, never mind now." Jørgen put his arms around the old lady and held her tight, as much for his own comfort as for hers. "We've got to get you out of here. First, you need to pack a few things."

"I've already done that." She pointed to the stuffed pillowcase. "Here's my luggage."

"You'll need to take a warm coat, as well."

"That I didn't think of. I'll just go get one now."

His mind raced. He needed to hide Mrs. Rosenfeld for about a week. Not only could they not move the Jews out all at one time, but he needed to see if he could arrange for a place for her to stay in Sweden.

Gerda returned carrying an old worn winter coat. "I decided to leave my mink behind for Hitler." She chuckled and gave Jørgen a wink. The closest she'd ever come to a mink was at the zoo.

"How're you feeling, Mrs. Rosenfeld?"

"How am I feeling, the man asks. So how should I feel? I can tell you I've had a lot better days."

"Mrs. Rosenfeld, you're suffering from severe stomach ulcers. And your name's not Mrs. Rosenfeld, it's Ingrid Petersen. Come on, we've got to get you to the hospital."

"Stomach ulcers? What *meshugas* is this you're talking?"

"Mrs. Rosenfeld, in the hospital you'll be safe."

Mørkø Island.

Heldorf was breathless with excitement as he sat at his desk pondering his magnificent achievement. Out of habit he reached for the schnapps he kept in his desk drawer, then pulled his hand away. He hardly needed spirits out of a bottle to raise his own.

He had to get word of his success to Speer as soon as possible. The Reichminister had given him until the middle of October; he had finished two weeks early. Speer would want to plan when and how to tell the Führer that he would soon have a weapon that would guarantee victory for the Reich; the Führer would want to begin building the weapon into his overall plan for the conduct of the war. The words came easily:

> Dear Reichminister Speer:
>
> I am pleased to inform you that success is now ours.
> We are now able to produce the fuel for the new weapon you and I have discussed. All that remains to be done, apart from the manufacture of a sufficient quantity, is to engineer a relatively simple mechanical device for detonation. This device would bring two masses of the material together in such a way that the resulting mass would become supercritical; I envision a gun-type device, with one of the masses acting as the bullet and the other the target. In any event, the runaway explosion so created should be equivalent to at least ten kilotons of TNT.
> I look forward to discussing this exciting development with you in further detail at your earliest convenience.
>
> Heil Hitler.
> Sturmbannführer M. Heldorf

His pen scratched a few changes. He didn't want to sound too self-congratulatory or to wax eloquent on the staggering implications of his achievement – he would let the Führer do that. He sealed the letter in a brown envelope; it would go out in the morning

Heldorf had never felt so alive, so euphoric. He looked at the clock, eagerly wishing away the hours before Hannah would come to share his bed.

Mørkø Island.

"**M**ay I please have your attention, gentlemen." Hannah's soft voice could not carry over the hubbub. The meeting was abuzz with talk of the latest development – the beast was now producing plutonium – and everyone was excited. Only Albert Weiss, brooding in a corner, was unable to share the excitement. Some of the team said he was nursing a bruised ego, resentful that Hannah had assumed virtual leadership of the project.

Sol Friedberg slowly hauled himself to his feet and held up his hands, demanding silence. "Dr. Goldmann needs to bring this meeting to order!" The room became still. All eyes turned toward Hannah standing at the head of the table.

Hannah smiled at Sol and turned back toward the scientists. "I appreciate your enthusiasm over the detection of plutonium in the uranium machine—"

The scientists' fists beat upon the wooden table in applause. Some stood and clapped. "Bravo!"

Hannah held up her hand. "—but we have no time to waste. The second part of our endeavor – the extraction of the plutonium from the uranium – promises to be almost as challenging an effort as the first part. However, I'm delighted to announce to you today that Dr. Friedberg has developed a technique that is both ingenious and feasible."

The hut rang to renewed shouting. All except Weiss stood and applauded; not only had they breached the frontiers of science, but their success had moved them closer to securing freedom for their loved ones. Weinstein beamed a smile: his wife was already safe; perhaps soon his son would follow.

Sol Friedberg stood and rearranged his notes for the talk he was about to deliver. "Thank you, Dr. Goldmann. Gentlemen, our ability to extract plutonium rests on a peculiar property of the element that I recently discovered accidentally. Let me begin."

He raised a piece of chalk to the blackboard and began to write. Through formulas and diagrams, he described an elaborate process in which plutonium precipitated into insoluble crystals, enabling it to be extracted from the uranium in a chemical process. Although the explanation took half an hour to deliver, all, save Weiss, sat in rapt attention.

"And, to conclude, when the precipitate is dissolved in nitric acid and oxidized, pure plutonium is left behind. Using this process, we should be able to extract enough plutonium to create two sub-critical masses that, combined, will produce a chain reaction of a magnitude few can imagine." The scientists leapt to their feet once more and applauded, drunk at the thought of their amazing achievement.

"Don't you understand what you're doing?" The angry voice silenced the euphoria. All eyes turned to Albert Weiss.

Frederikshavn.

"So what's the plan for tomorrow?" Erik yawned as he watched Jørgen eat his breakfast. "Mind if I have a piece of bread?"

"The plan?" Jørgen sawed off a slab of bread and held the bread tray out. "Here. Help yourself."

Erik took the bread. "Yes, the plan. Tomorrow's the big day for moving the Jews out to Sweden, isn't it?"

Jørgen wondered where Erik had heard that; who was the leak? "Come on, Erik, you know I can't discuss any plans with you unless I get the go-ahead from Marius."

Erik broke his piece of bread in two. "For Christ's sake, Jørgen, we've been friends most of our lives. If you can't trust me, who can you trust?"

"Why do you want to know the plan, anyway? What's it to you?"

"Just thought I might be of use. Sometimes it's helpful to run things by someone else – I might just spot a flaw you missed. Good bread." Erik tore off another bite with his teeth. "But, if you don't trust me, Jørgen, don't tell me."

Marius's rules were a pain in the ass, Jørgen thought. He could see Erik's feelings were hurt. Why shouldn't he review the plan with his good friend? As Erik said, he might spot something they'd overlooked. But there was no way Jørgen would go back on his word to Marius.

They continued to eat in silence. Jørgen sliced a wedge of cheese and laid it on his bread as he thought over the plan. Christina's boat, the Sofia, would go out at dawn the following day carrying seven Jews.

Christina would captain the boat and Jørgen would be crewing for her. "Want some cheese with your bread?" Jørgen held out the plate.

"Yeah, that looks good. Thanks."

The four Jews who had been hiding out in hospital beds would leave the hospital under the guise of a small funeral procession. Jørgen would escort them to the church near the harbor where they'd hide overnight. The few possessions they had selected to take with them would be hidden under bouquets of crepe paper flowers piled up in a hearse Jørgen would drive.

"Did you hear that Svend's wife is moving back to Copenhagen?" Erik's words, muffled as he munched on his bread and cheese, cut through Jørgen's thoughts.

"Yeah, I did. I think she's got family there. It's been really tough going for her without Svend."

A Jewish family of three was to be collected before dawn from the private home in which they were now hiding by someone driving the Resistance moving van; with the Jews from the church, they would be loaded in Christina's boat for a dawn departure. The Kestrel, captained by Jacobsen, would by then be gone – he was to leave two hours before dawn with his refugees.

Jørgen scooped up bread crumbs from the table and tossed them on his empty plate. "Say, Erik, how'd you know the evacuation of the Jews is going to be tomorrow?"

"I didn't – it was just a guess." Erik smiled as he shrugged. "But I think you just told me."

Jørgen's heart sank. Was it so easy to leak information without realizing it? Thank God it was only Erik who had found out or the whole plan could be in real trouble.

Jørgen remembered the van that was picking up the Jews the next day; he didn't think Marius had assigned a driver yet. It would be reassuring to know Erik was at the wheel. "I'm going over the plan with Marius later this morning, Erik. I'll ask him if there's anything he wants you to do."

Erik bowed theatrically from his chair. "Glad to be of service in any way possible."

"It would be good if you were in on the plan, Erik. I don't trust some of the others." He recalled his doubts about Gunnar. "We need people we can trust."

"You worry too much." Erik looked at his watch. "Must go – there's something I have to do." He stood up. "Listen, good luck tomorrow."

Jørgen frowned. He remembered that there had been other well-planned actions in the past that had ended in disaster. Dear God, if anything happened to Christina—

"Hey, look," Erik gave Jørgen a friendly cuff on the shoulder, "you take care, you hear?"

"You too, Erik."

Erik reached for the doorknob, gave Jørgen a jaunty salute, and left.

Mørkø Island.

"Don't you see what we're doing here?" Albert Weiss's face was red with anger as he rose to his feet. "We're trying to make Adolf Hitler the conqueror of the world." He raised an accusatory finger and pointed it at each scientist in the room. "Shame on you! Shame on all of us! We all know what we're doing, and we should all be ashamed."

Sol Friedberg raised his hands to try to quell the commotion in the room. "Al, we know what we're doing." Friedberg spoke softly. "We're saving loved ones." There was a murmur of agreement from the others. "I have no relatives in the camps. Maybe I should be ashamed. But, Al, you can't blame the others."

"I blame all of us." Weiss scowled and shoved his chair under the table. "Think about it: if Hitler rules the world, there will be no place left on earth where Jews will be safe." Weiss's knuckles turned white as he tightened his grip on the back of his chair.

"We're scientists, not oracles," said Georg Silberstein. "We can't predict what will happen if we continue, but we know with grim certainty what will happen if we stop: we'll doom our families in the camps. Weiss, you have two daughters. Have you thought about them?"

Weiss closed his eyes, fighting to control his temper. "I think about them all the time. "I haven't had a letter from Naomi, my oldest daughter, in over two months, and now my youngest daughter's letters have stopped." He bit his lip; his chin trembled.

The room fell silent as the scientists considered the significance of Weiss's words. Weinstein jumped up. "I know how Albert feels. I ha-

ven't heard from my son, Morry, in six weeks. I'm concerned that…"
He sat back down without completing the sentence.

"And my sister's letters have stopped, as well," another added.

Nervous glances were exchanged. Until that moment, they had kept their worries hidden. Heldorf had warned them to keep silent about the deals he had made with each of them or risk losing their loved ones. Now, finding they were not alone, they could not help but share their worst fears. The room swelled with the sound of anxious voices.

Frederikshavn.

"You don't have to do this, Christina. There are safer ways for you to get back to Sweden; I still might be able to find another boat." Jørgen knew it wasn't true; he'd never be able to find another boat to ferry the Jews across to Sweden now. But as the day of the mission had drawn closer, his fears for Christina's safety had grown. She would refuse his offer to bow out of danger, and he admired her for her courage.

They sat by the window of a small pastry shop near the harbor, sipping their ersatz coffee and nibbling on a shared pastry. It was the first time they had been able to relax together since they had met. Rain spattered the befogged window and the outside world reminded Jørgen of an unfocused movie, of reflections on water.

"I have to go tomorrow – how else am I going to get my uncle's boat back to him?" Christina held up her hands in a display of mock umbrage. "I only borrowed my uncle's boat, I didn't intend to steal it." She grinned. "Besides, if I sail back tomorrow, I get a crew." She winked at him.

He smiled and took another bite of the pastry. He was glad to have time alone with her, glad to be taking dessert with her as though they were a normal couple, unscathed by the war that, unwelcome, had thrust itself into their lives. "Christina…." There was much he wanted to say and to do, and there wasn't time. He wanted to tell her she was as brave as she was beautiful; he wanted to caress her cheek, smooth back the stray lock on her forehead, kiss the nape of her neck…

"Say, this pastry is delicious." She took a sip of the warm brown liquid to wash it down. "Ugh, I wish I could say the same for the coffee." She put down her nearly-full cup and pushed it away. "When I get back to the United States, I'll send you some real coffee."

Back to the United States. The thought of her leaving made his heart sink. He had no doubt; a rip current was pulling him into waters far deeper than he had ever known.

"Weren't you about to say something?" she asked.

"Oh, yes. Christina...." He coughed nervously; there was so much he wanted to say, so little time.

Christina smiled and tilted her head. "Yes?"

"Christina...thanks for what you're doing for us." He pushed his hand across the table, placed it on hers, then self-consciously withdrew it and turned his attention to the crumbs on the plate.

"You're welcome." Christina hoped the wide smile she flashed at Jørgen would hide her disappointment. When he had taken her hand, she had hoped he might say more. Hoped he might, but had no reason to suspect he might. Since they'd met, he'd hardly touched her. While she slept in the bed in his apartment, he had made do with the floor of his tiny living room.

Jørgen glanced at his watch. "Well, if you're through, I guess we'd better get going. We've got a big day tomorrow."

Mørkø Island.

The chorus of voices had risen to a din when Hannah tugged on Sol's sleeve. "Sol, please ask them to be quiet. I have something I want to say."

Sol raised his arms. "Silence!"

Hannah faced the crowded room. "Gentlemen, I can well understand how you all feel, but I think I can shed some light on what's happening." She could see the resentment in their eyes; they did not trust her. "You may not know that I have a sister in Treblinka, a sister from whom I had not heard in over a month. I asked Sturmbannführer Heldorf," at his name, brows were raised and eyes were cast down, "for information about my sister." She looked around the room. "I was relieved to hear his explanation. He said that increased bombing raids by the Americans and British in recent months have disrupted mail delivery."

Stunned silence was broken by mumblings of doubt. "Of course he'd say that," a voice from the end of the table shouted, "it would be hardly in his interest to tell you that she's—"

"Please let Dr. Goldmann finish!" Sol shouted. "Hear her out!"

"Why should we?" another voice shouted. "We all know what's going on between her and Heldorf."

Hannah shook the accusation aside. "I know we're all worried about our loved ones, and with good reason." Hannah dug her nails into her hands in frustration. "But I believe what Heldorf told me." She heard more mutterings as she reached into the folder with her notes and pulled out an envelope. "Here's a letter I received from my sister just a few days ago."

"So how does this prove anything?" Weiss asked.

Hannah held up the letter for all to see. "Look at the date she put on it. My sister wrote this letter well over a month ago, but I just received it."

Hannah glanced around the room; a few heads shook in doubt but some showed relief, hoping that letters from living, breathing family members were simply delayed or lost in the bombings. She knew they believed because they wanted to believe.

She looked at Albert Weiss. He averted his eyes. He no longer believed.

Berlin.

As Albert Speer walked down the marble gallery of the Reich Chancellery toward Hitler's office, he admired his own handiwork. He remembered with some nostalgia the monumental effort of designing and building the Chancellery back in '38, a feat that had won him Hitler's admiration and made him one of the most powerful men in the Reich.

He found the Führer in an expansive mood, having just returned from inspecting the rocket program at Peenemünde. Hitler sat at the small table set with silver, china, and linen to partake of his vegetarian lunch; he motioned for Speer to join him.

"When I saw the rockets fired," Hitler cut into a tomato that sat atop a mass of spinach, "I felt the awesome power of the new weapons." As he chewed, he seemed to relive that moment of glory, his glowing eyes taking on a faraway look.

Speer could understand his enthusiasm with the V-1 and V-2 unmanned flying bombs; both delivered a ton of high explosives. The V-1 had a jet engine and could outstrip most Allied aircraft. The rocket-propelled V-2 travelled at twenty-five hundred miles an hour and was undetectable in flight.

"All we have to do now," the Führer mashed a turnip with his fork, "is hold out, because by the end of the year, when the rockets are in full production, London will be completely leveled. Even the rubble will be ground into dust." He brought the napkin to his mouth and delicately ran it downward over his moustache. "The enemy will come groveling and beg to surrender. Have some more Savoy cabbage, Speer."

Speer held up his hand to indicate to the waiter that he had eaten his fill of cabbage. "Mein Führer, it is my belief that the V-1 and V-2 rockets could very well win us the war."

Hitler peered out at Speer above his glass of Fachinger mineral water. "You're so very right, Speer. You know, appointing you as my armaments chief was a masterstroke on my part. You never cease to amaze me; I wish I could say the same for my other ministers."

Hitler pushed his plate away. "The reason I invited you here today, Speer, was to talk about the allocation of resources toward new munitions projects."

The waiter cleared the dishes and set the dessert of baked apples before them.

"Mein Führer, it is a matter of the utmost concern to me." Speer glanced at the wrinkled brown apple on the plate before him; it looked like the face of a wizened crone.

Hitler cut into his baked apple with gusto. "The secret to winning the war is to focus on new development that is truly strategic. We must ignore everything else."

"I quite agree. Resources are exceedingly scarce these days. We must use them wisely."

"Exactly. As a result, effective immediately, I want all developmental resources directed exclusively to the V-1 and V-2 rocket programs. Outside of these, not a single reichsmark is to be spent on any other new munitions project." Hitler's plate clanged as he dropped his knife and fork and slapped the table for emphasis. "Make sure everyone understands this. Not a single reichsmark!"

• • •

The afternoon had been a success. Speer dropped, exhausted, into the desk chair in his office. His good feelings vanished as he spotted the brown envelope bearing Heldorf's latest report lying on his desk. 'Not a single reichsmark is to be spent on any other munitions project,' the Führer's order, rang in his mind.

Speer picked up the unopened envelope and tossed it aside. No doubt it was filled with the usual meaningless data, empty promises, and lack of practical results. But whether Heldorf ever had any chance of success was no longer the question; Speer could hardly run the risk of violating the Führer's mandate with a dubious initiative like Heldorf's. He cursed himself for ever having endorsed the project.

He took out his fountain pen and reached for a sheet of stationery. Heldorf was to take immediate steps to terminate his project. The Jewish scientists were to be returned to the death camps.

PART SIX

"The stars move still, time runs, the clock will strike,
The Devil will come and Faustus must be damned."

—Christopher Marlowe,
The Tragical History of Doctor Faustus

Frederikshavn.

T he early morning light caressed the tall stained-glass window at the eastern end of the Lutheran church. The mock funeral the night before that brought the four Jews to the church had proceeded without incident, and as soon as the other three arrived in the Resistance moving van, it would be time to set sail. Jørgen cast his eyes over the sad group huddled on the pews. They had been hidden when the Gestapo had made their fruitless raids two nights before, but were still afraid. During the night a few had slept fitfully, stretched out on the benches. Others had fretted with their solitary suitcases in which they had crammed a few meager possessions. Now, most stared blankly into space.

Jørgen could feel their fear, almost tangible in the cool air. In the third pew was Mr. Abramowitz, the greengrocer in Frederikshavn for over two decades; his hand shook as he helped his wife put on a sweater. The baker, Mr. Schiller, sat behind him, nervously readjusting the pince-nez glasses perched on the bridge of his nose. Jørgen remembered how, as a young boy, he had hung around Mr. Schiller's shop knowing that, on occasion, he would be rewarded with a smile and an éclair.

Gerda Rosenfeld sat in the front pew, quietly twisting a handkerchief in her hands, her stuffed pillowcase and her clock by her side. That morning, Jørgen had received word that Sara Gronborg's cousin in Sweden would welcome Gerda into his home, and when she heard the news, Gerda had clapped her hands and cried with joy. But now there was no smile. Only fear and a mute acceptance of her fate.

Peder, soon to be on a voyage that would reunite him with his mama in Sweden, sat blithely in the back pew. His fingers sailed rapidly across a page in his sketchbook, leaving in their wake a perfect representation of the church and its occupants.

The young boy was oblivious to the sense of dread that pervaded the place, but Jørgen felt the tension. He still didn't know who would be driving the Resistance van that would bring the rest of the Jews. When he had asked Marius, the cell leader had looked at him coldly and said that, under the new security rules, it was not essential that he know.

Jørgen glanced at his watch: it would soon be high tide. Marius and Christina had the job of getting her boat, the Sofia, ready. The minutes dragged by; all were anxious to depart.

The door at the back of the church opened. All eyes swung to the figure in the door as Pastor Magnussen swept in with a smile, proffering a plate of pastries to the Jews. Considering religion a waste of time, Jørgen had never been a churchgoer. Yet when he had approached the pastor the day before, he had unhesitatingly offered his church as a way station, a last hiding place before the Jews made the dangerous trip across the water to Sweden.

The door flew open again. "We're ready!" Jørgen looked up and saw Christina's face. The Jews reached for their bundles and suitcases. He took Peder's hand and followed their procession as they half ran, half stumbled down the stone steps toward the harbor.

Mørkø Island. Heldorf's Quarters.

Hannah pushed the sheets aside and swung her legs from Heldorf's bed. The window of his room offered little light in the dull day, and dark clouds scudded across the sky. Yet she felt a sense of elation.

Her eyes fell upon the depression in the pillow where Max's head had lain, and she ran her fingers over it lightly, remembering with tenderness the night before. He had left earlier; the corporal had called and said something about some important message from Speer.

She poured water from the jug into the basin and splashed her face. When she had asked him about her sister, he had told her Rachel would soon be released from Treblinka. A great weight had been lifted from her: the worry, the fear, the torment – all had fallen away. Gone was the guilt, the guilt that had caused her to relive, over and over again, the moment she saw Rachel's parting glance, the glance that said goodbye to Hannah. The day the soldiers came. The day Hannah ran away. Now Hannah felt a surge of joy. Someday, somewhere, she and Rachel would be together again. As family; Rachel was her family. Hannah would no longer be alone in the world. The thought made her giddy with happiness.

As she patted her face dry, she smiled at herself in the mirror. Through the reflection of the window she could see the building that held the uranium machine. Her machine. The others had played a part, but she had been the prime mover; without her, the beast would not exist. She had built it. No one, not even Heisenberg, had been able to build such a machine.

She dressed quickly; she had a full day ahead of her. She needed to review Sol's work to see if she could speed the process of extracting two masses of plutonium that, combined, would become critical. Then a meeting with Albert on the control rods. They needed a way to make the rods' manipulation, the key to controlling the beast, less of an art and more of a science. Pushed in too far and the chain reaction would begin to falter. Too far out and the machine would begin to get hot. Then the beast would start producing dangerous radiation and would eventually melt down, taking all their hard work with it.

She dabbed on some lipstick and ran a brush through her hair. She hoped she'd find Albert in a better mood. She could understand his concerns of the day before, but he was wrong to insinuate that not hearing from family members meant they were dead. Rachel's letter proved he was wrong. Now was hardly the time for him to start dragging his feet – they were within reach of their goal, and that goal had not changed. They were still working to free their families, and they would soon gain that freedom now they were succeeding. Max had assured her.

Hannah sat at the small desk beneath the window, opened her notebook, and began reviewing her notes of Sol's experiments. As she looked at the page, she thought of the formulas and diagrams that had run across the blackboard of her mind back in the dark cell of the camp, back when she had first postulated her theory. She reached for her pack of cigarettes, found it empty, and tossed the wrapper in the wastebasket. If she could only have known, back in the camp when everything seemed hopeless, that she'd be able one day to prove her theory.

She wanted a cigarette and got up to head for the closet – there were sure to be some in Max's jacket. She glanced at her watch; Albert would be expecting her in his room to discuss the control rods soon. Hannah reached into Max's jacket and pulled out a cigarette pack. As she took one, she noticed a letter sticking up out of the pocket. Her eye caught the official stamp on the envelope – Camp Commandant's Office, Treblinka, Poland – and through the window of the envelope she could make out 'achel Goldma.' The cigarette pack dropped from her fingers as she pulled the letter out.

Dear Sturmbannführer Heldorf:

As you requested, we are providing written confirmation
of the Treblinka prisoner Rachel Goldmann's death. Said
prisoner died on August 31 while taking part in an insurrec-
tion. As there is no tattoo identification system at Treblinka,
positive identification of the deceased was achieved by
means of the enclosed letter, dated on the day of her death
and found in her pocket. It is signed by Rachel Goldmann
and addressed to a Hannah Goldmann …

Hannah dropped the letter onto the bed as though it had burst
into flames. Time stopped; the world stood still. She could hear her
blood rushing, could feel her heart pounding; her legs buckled,
barely able to support her. It was all a big lie; Max had fed her a tis-
sue of lies.

Through welling tears she saw the key to the uranium machine
building hanging on the door. She breathed deeply, trying to rid the images of her sister from her mind. Her shaking hand snatched the key
from the hook. The door slammed behind her as she ran from Heldorf's
quarters.

Frederikshavn Harbor.

The jetty bustled with action as the Frederikshavn fishing fleet prepared for another day. Gear was loaded onto boats rocking gently at
their moorings. Hands reached for ropes, sails were prepared. For the
fishermen, it would be just another day at sea.

But not for Jørgen. He lit a cigarette. He – and Christina – had the
fates of seven Jewish refugees and a little boy entrusted to them. Still,
he was relieved that so far all had gone well. Jacobsen, the skipper of
the Kestrel, had left two hours earlier with eight Jews, and those who
had spent the night in the church had already boarded the Sofia. He cast
his eyes to the street, begging to see the Resistance truck bringing the
rest.

"Where are they?" Christina drew anxiously on her cigarette. As
much to calm his own nerves as to comfort her, Jørgen ran a hand over
her shoulder.

The noise of the truck answered the question. Jørgen, relieved, looked around and pointed to the Resistance van coming down the road. Marius, at the entrance to the pier, waved to flag it down.

But something was wrong. Jørgen looked again. It was not Erik who was driving. The van was tearing down the road at a dangerous speed, and Gunnar was behind the wheel. Gestapo sirens screamed in the distance and grew louder by the moment. Jørgen felt the stab of fear: they'd been betrayed. And Gunnar was the Judas.

"We've got to cast off!" shouted Jørgen. "Untie the lines!"

He watched in horror as Gunnar jumped out of the truck and ran around to the back. The Jews would be easy targets for the Germans. Gunnar had done a good job for his task masters.

Mørkø Island. Heldorf's Office.

Heldorf's head fell to his chest as he tossed Speer's letter aside. He was on the cusp of success – about to provide Germany with a weapon to win the war – and now Speer was pulling the chain on the whole project. He picked up the bottle of schnapps from his desk, filled his glass, and drank. Success was within his grasp, but Speer was abandoning the project, and he could sense there was a revolt brewing among the Jews. He lit a cigarette and drew deeply. And he couldn't deliver Hannah's sister. Nor any of the other relatives.

Surely Speer couldn't be such a fool. Perhaps the man didn't understand. Heldorf read the letter again. "Place a call to Reichminister Speer's office," he shouted to the corporal. There was desperation in his voice.

He feared Hannah's reaction the most. It wasn't for his lack of trying that her sister hadn't been released, and now she was dead. On impulse, he'd given Hannah Rachel's last letter, but he couldn't stall her forever and before long he'd have to tell her the truth. He poured some more schnapps into his glass and threw it down his throat. Everything was falling apart.

The jingle of the phone made him jump. He put down the glass and picked up the receiver. Heldorf found himself speaking to an aide, some minor functionary.

"Sturmbannführer Heldorf here." He tried to keep the edge from his voice. "I need to speak with Reichminister Speer."

"I'm afraid the Reichminister is extremely busy." The voice almost purred with the delight of being unhelpful. "He has a meeting with the Führer in half an hour."

"Tell him it's a matter of extreme urgency!" Heldorf screamed into the telephone.

Frederikshavn Harbor.

Jørgen saw Gunnar jump down from the truck; a knot of hatred twisted his stomach as he pulled the sten gun from his shoulder. Gunnar, the traitor. His eyes peered along the gun sight and he placed his finger on the trigger. Slowly, he eased it away. Gunnar was urging the Jews to run down to the pier, down to the rescue boat.

Stunned, Jørgen lowered his weapon as Gunnar leapt back into the truck, reversed it, and positioned it to form a barrier between the stone walls at the entrance to the harbor. Behind it, the German truck's tires screeched, but the crump of the collision rang around the dock.

The chatter of Marius's sten gun forced his attention to the back of the truck. German soldiers, rifles in hand, were jumping down, shouting, preparing to fire.

"Get the people on board fast, Jørgen!" Marius's voice carried over the noise of the chaos. Jørgen ran forward, his gun held waist high, protecting the Jews as they scrambled on the boat. He saw Christina help an elderly woman aboard and then run along the dock to release the mooring line.

The Germans were pinned down by Marius's fire, but Jørgen saw two crouching on the blind side of the truck. He fired a quick burst that had them scampering for cover.

"Jørgen! Jørgen!" He turned in the direction of the shout. Gunnar was running towards him, the ends of his red scarf flying behind him. "Jørgen, we made it!"

There was a burst of fire from the Germans. Jørgen watched helplessly as Gunnar stumbled. He fell to his knees, a puzzled look on his face before he crumpled to the ground.

"Bastards!" Marius yelled as his fire cut down the two Germans. "Bastards!"

Jørgen was snapped from his momentary paralysis. "Get on board, Christina! For God's sake, get on board!" He ran toward the boat as Marius continued to spray the German truck.

Suddenly, there was a blaze of light as the gas tank of the German truck exploded. For a moment, the scene was frozen as the noise of the explosion died away.

"Look out, Jørgen!" Marius called. "There's another one!"

Jørgen turned and looked back past Gunnar's fallen body. Out of the back of the German truck, a man jumped from the flames. Jørgen saw that it was Erik. Erik? A traitor? As Jørgen watched his lifelong friend begin to run away, confusion gave way to rage and he raised his gun. His hand shook as his finger met the trigger.

With a groan, Erik fell to the ground. Jørgen was stunned; he hadn't fired. "Get on the boat, Jørgen." He turned to see Marius lower his weapon. "I've got to get out of here."

Jørgen ran to the boat and leapt aboard.

Mørkø Island. Heldorf's Office.

Heldorf hung onto the phone and used his free hand to pour another drink. When he told Speer about the breakthrough – that they were already manufacturing plutonium, the fuel for an atomic weapon – he'd change his tune.

"I'm sorry, Sturmbannführer," it was not Speer's voice, "but the Reichminister says he explained everything in his letter to you and has nothing further to add." The voice was smug. "Do you have a message for the Reichminister?"

"Yes." Heldorf emptied his glass and slammed it on the desk. "Please tell the Reichminister that he has lost Germany the war."

"Is that your message, Sturmbannführer?" The voice sounded perplexed.

"No, there's more," Heldorf shouted. "Kindly tell the Reichminister that he can go to hell!" He slammed the receiver down onto the cradle.

Heldorf lit a cigarette and drew deeply. They could all go to hell – Hitler, Speer, and all the fools who surrounded them. He now had to shift for himself. He had the secret of an atomic bomb. And he had Hannah, the author of the secret. If he could get her off the island, he'd have a huge bargaining card. He could make a deal with the Americans. Even the Russians.

He crumpled Speer's letter and tossed it into the wastebasket.

Morko Island. Albert Weiss's Quarters.

"My God, Hannah, what's wrong?" Albert Weiss was stunned at the sight of the dazed, ashen-faced woman framed in his doorway.

"You were right, Albert." Hannah raised both her hands to her mouth and shuddered with a violence that alarmed him. He reached out to her and she stumbled forward, half falling into his arms, unable to stay the tears. "We've all…we've all been betrayed," she stammered, her voice choking.

Weiss clutched her to him, his arms feeling the grief wracking her slender frame, as if all the torments of hell were lodged there. He stroked her hair in a futile gesture of comfort and eased her gently onto the edge of his cot.

Willing herself to stop crying, she took the handkerchief he offered. Her reddened eyes looked briefly into his, then fell, heavy with remorse. "I've been a fool, Albert." Haltingly, Hannah told him of the letter she had found in Heldorf's pocket.

"We've all been fools, Hannah. None more so than I." He lit a cigarette, passed it over to her, and watched as her hollow cheeks sucked greedily. "I was the first to make a pact with the devil. I remember it well, that first meeting with Heldorf."

He lit a cigarette for himself and inhaled deeply. "I remember thinking that all I had to do was buy some time. If I could buy enough time for my family, I thought, somehow matters might resolve themselves – maybe the war would end and they'd be free. If I could buy time, all of us would be off the hook."

Leaning forward, he rested his arms on his knees and looked earnestly at the cigarette in his hand. "At the time it didn't seem a bad bargain; after all, the alternative was death for all of us." He tapped the cigarette and ash fell on the wooden floor. "But now it seems that the devil has come to collect his due."

"You only worked for the devil, but I slept with him, Albert." Her voice was angry, and he knew that the anger was turned upon herself.

Weiss sat up and fixed her with a compassionate look. "Hannah, you're not to blame." He weighed his own guilt. But for him, none of this would have happened. But for him, Hannah, Sol, and all the others would not be there. It was true that his wife, his beloved Rebecca, was safe, and that was a comfort. But he knew he would never see his daughters again.

He stood up abruptly and reached for his jacket.

"Albert, where are you going?"

"I've got to tell the others they're being betrayed. They need to know."

"Albert, please don't leave me." The terror in her eyes made him stop short. "Please, Albert, please stay with me. I don't want to be alone."

He looked at her with sadness and gently pressed her back on the cot. "Lie down and rest, Hannah. Try to get some sleep, if you can." She lifted her feet into the bed and he arranged a thin blanket over her. "I'll be back as soon as I can, Hannah." He leaned over and kissed her on the forehead. "But right now I've got to tell the others about Heldorf's treachery."

Hannah heard the sound of Albert's footsteps die away. She reached into her pocket for her handkerchief and found the key to the building that housed the uranium machine. The cold metal burned the palm of her hand. She got up, opened the door, and looked at the dull day. She knew what she had to do.

Mørkø Island. Heldorf's Quarters.

Heldorf still seethed at Speer's treachery as he left his office and made his way unsteadily to his quarters, his anger fueled by the schnapps that fired his stomach. Hannah was now his only hope; the rest of the Jews could go to hell. If he could get Hannah off the island, there was the possibility of selling her secrets and her expertise. To whom? The Russians? The Americans? He wasn't sure; he had no clear-cut plan and his head ached as he grappled with a course of action.

His feet stumbled on the gravel path. He wished he hadn't drunk so much; he needed to think clearly, needed to devise a plan to get away from the island with Hannah. He would have a bargaining chip, a means of survival. Then he'd work out his next step. It was a long shot, but he had no other option.

He took a deep breath, trying to clear his mind. Hannah would come with him; he was certain of it. After all, she seemed to be in love with him. He would promise to reunite her with her sister in Lisbon. It was a lie which she'd eventually discover, but it was a ploy he had to use if there was to be any escape.

Heldorf looked at the gathering clouds darkening the sky and hoped they were not an omen. Lying to Hannah was not something he enjoyed. He was fond of her. Fond of her – he knew he was lying to himself. He felt more than fondness for her, much more. Perhaps they could find a life together.

"Hannah!" he called as he pushed opened the door to his quarters. "Hannah!" There was no answer; she was not there.

Heldorf unstrapped the holster holding his pistol and hung it over the chair. He was about to take off his tunic when he saw the letter lying on the bed. For a moment, he thought it was a note from Hannah. His stomach sank as he picked up the letter bearing the stamp of the Treblinka camp commandant.

Mørkø Island. Conference Room.

The room was in tumult. Albert Weiss held up his hands, calling for order. "Listen to what I have to say!" he shouted. The noise fell away to a hubbub of chatter; the scientists exchanged anxious looks.

"It gives me no pleasure to say that I was right," Weiss's voice was soft, resigned, "but what Hannah told me proves we've been betrayed."

"It proves nothing of the sort," Weinstein snapped back. "It merely proves *she* was betrayed. Of course Heldorf wouldn't tell his whore about her sister; it would spoil the sex."

"And where is she now?" The voice came from the back of the room. "Why isn't she here to tell us herself?" The clamor returned, the noise swelling.

"Because," Weiss shouted above the racket, "because she's resting in my room. She's naturally distraught with the grief of losing her sister."

"But what about my son? How does this prove he's lost?" Weinstein persisted.

"And my sister? She could still be safe."

Weiss waited for the shouting to stop. "You're angry with me because you don't want to stop clutching at straws of hope. That's only natural. I, too, would like to believe my daughters are safe." Weiss looked self-possessed, but no one could see the struggle in his heart. "I've worked here for the past year and a half, hoping I could get Miriam and Naomi released from Auschwitz," a slight tremor of his lips was the only evidence of his deep pain, "but the time has come for me to face the reality that I'll never see them again. If Heldorf can betray Hannah, he certainly wouldn't make any concessions for the likes of me. And—"

A scientist by the door cut in. "It's convenient that you waited until you thought your daughters were dead," he poked the air with his finger, "to find your high moral ground. And now, while the rest of us are still working toward the freedom of our families, you come preaching to us."

"Yes, that's right," Gerhard Ziegler shouted, "and you're forgetting about the project. We're on the brink of success. If we deliver, Heldorf will deliver. He said he would."

"Do you realize what you're on the point of delivering?" Weiss's sorrow changed to anger. "You're about to deliver the ultimate death machine into the hands of the man who's murdering our people!"

The room became subdued. Guilt fought with hope in every mind.

Artur Steinitz stepped forward and addressed Weiss in a soft voice. "Look, Albert, these men, your colleagues, your friends – they're not proud of the bargain they struck." He put his hand on Albert's arm. "They understood what they were getting into from the start, and nothing's really changed. Now they've kept their end of the deal. Would you expect them to give up just as they're about to get what they worked for?"

"Don't you understand what I'm trying to tell you?" Weiss shot back. "Heldorf won't honor his end of the deal. If Heldorf would betray Hannah, he wouldn't stop at betraying anyone else in this room!"

"Why don't we go and ask Heldorf?" Otto Weinstein's suggestion brought nods and murmurs of agreement, and the men began making for the door.

"Yes, by all means – go and ask the devil." Weiss shook his head in frustration as they filed out. "Surely, the devil would never lie to us," he muttered sarcastically as he followed.

Morko Island.

Hannah ran through the camp, the world around her a haze. She'd been betrayed. Max had lied to her; he had lied to all of them. The letter was proof of his treachery – he'd given her Rachel's last letter pretending she was still alive, then invented a story about delays in the mail to hide that there would be no more mail, that her sister was dead.

She stubbed her toe on a rock and almost fell but didn't slow her pace. The one thing she wanted above all else – to see her sister once more – was gone. Her chance for redemption, her chance to repay Rachel for her sacrifices – gone. Sacrifices Rachel had made so she could study physics, so that she could—

Hannah's whole life had been a lie.

Brambles along the path caught her leg and tore into her flesh, but she kept running. Guilt clutched at her every fiber, engulfing her. Anger came to drive the guilt away – rage at her sister for dying, rage at Max, rage at the Nazis. And, above all, rage at herself, at her naïve foolishness.

She ran on, gasping for air. Rachel's sacrifices had enabled her to crash through the barriers of nuclear physics, and Hannah had felt pride in her achievement. It was foolish pride. How could any sane human being be proud of working to put an instrument of unspeakable destruction into the hands of a madman? How could she have fooled herself that she was doing so to save her sister, when all the while she had been driven by her pride, her overbearing pride?

The lowering clouds cast their gloom upon her. Her father's words came back to haunt her. "You must live, Hannah, you must live." The words that had driven her all her life were now hollow. They had no meaning.

As she reached the edge of the camp and approached the uranium machine building, she stopped to catch her breath. The dogs were barking in their compound near the beach and jetty, but there was not a soul in sight.

Her lungs struggled for air and she was cold. Not just her body, chilled by the wind driving the scudding clouds across the gloomy sky – she was cold within. Now she felt nothing but an empty void. The horror of discovering the letter, the grief over her sister, the rage at Heldorf's betrayal – these no longer tore her apart. All she felt was an aching emptiness at knowing that everything she had worked for over the last year – the realization of all her dreams – was for nothing. Her life had no purpose. Save one.

That which she had created she must destroy.

Mørkø Island. Heldorf's Quarters.

The letter fluttered to the floor as it slipped through Heldorf's fingers. Hannah knew.

His heart raced and the dulling effects of the schnapps began to lift from his mind as he quickly thought of excuses. He had been powerless to get Rachel released. The responsibility for Rachel's death was not his. He had hidden Rachel's death to spare her.

Snatching the phone from its cradle, he drummed his fingers on the desk impatiently as he awaited the response from the office. "Have the boat ready to sail in an hour!" he shouted into the mouthpiece. "They're in Frederikshavn picking up supplies? When will they be back?....Three hours? That long?....Well, make sure they're ready to go out again as soon as they arrive!"

As he replaced the receiver, he realized how futile his action was. Where was he going? Certainly not back to Berlin. Speer would hand him over to the Gestapo; his death would preserve the Reichminister's secret.

He paced the floor. Only if he took Hannah and her secrets with him could he survive. But what could he offer her? Her life and a chance to work on physics somewhere else. There was nothing else. He could offer her life – or death.

He still felt uneasy as he buttoned up his tunic and prepared to leave. Where was she? The empty hook on the wall caught his eye: she had taken the key to the uranium machine building. He had to go there without delay.

He could not suppress a gasp as he opened the front door: coming down the path en masse were the Jews, looking determined and disgruntled. The warmth of the schnapps in Heldorf's stomach brought a foolish wry smile to his lips. Every man marching toward his hut would be dead or dying but for him. He slammed the door, turned the key in the lock and ran to the phone.

"Tell the guards to release the dogs. Now!"

Mørkø Island. Uranium Machine Room.

She was surprised to find the door to the uranium machine building unlocked. As it closed behind her, her eyes fought to adjust to the darkness of the room. Two pale red lights were the only illumination afforded the beast of her creation lying in the recessed floor that was its lair. Hannah listened as it purred gently, tamed by the cage of cadmium rods that held it captive. She made her way to the steps that led down to the pit.

"Everything's fine, Hannah." The voice startled her. She saw Sol's smiling face looking down on her from the control desk.

"Sol, I didn't realize it was your watch."

"Everything's okay. The reaction continues to remain controlled." His finger pointed to the needle of the neutron counter, which held steady in the safety zone. Only an occasional blip disturbed the heavy darkness of the room.

"You must be very proud of your baby, Hannah."

Pride. Her pride had caused this disaster. "Sol, you've got to get out of here. Now."

"Huh? What's going on?" Sol stood up, a stunned look on his face.

"We've been betrayed, Sol." Hannah reached down, pulled one of the cadmium rods from its bed, and bent it over her knee. "Heldorf's been lying to us." The needle on the neutron counter flickered.

"My God, Hannah!" Sol clambered down into the pit. "Stop! Even if Heldorf is a lying bastard, there's no reason to blow us all to kingdom come!"

"Get out of here, Sol." Hannah reached for another cadmium rod. "Please, just get out of here!"

"Hannah, you're out of your mind!" he shouted as he struggled up the stairs and out of the building, slamming the door behind him.

Hannah pulled another rod; the neutron counter registered its alarm. Her beast was beginning to wake up. It would soon be set free.

Mørkø Island. Heldorf's Quarters.

There was a knock on the front door. "Go away!" Heldorf screamed at the door.

"We need to speak to you, Sturmbannführer Heldorf! Please—"

"Go away!"

"Please—"

"I said go away! Are you all deaf?"

Heldorf leapt back as the doorknob rattled against the lock. The voices became more agitated, the shouts louder.

"We have to talk to you about our families!"

"Tell us when they'll be set free."

"What's happened to my mother?"

"When will my sister be released from Auschwitz?"

Heldorf fought hard against the alcohol that clouded his judgment; he could not afford to panic. He had to buy time for the dogs to arrive. "Don't be fools. Go back to your quarters," Heldorf shouted from behind the door. The voices, cowed by his authority, fell to a murmur.

"You need to complete the project before we can discuss anything." He cast a glance through the window, anxious for the arrival of the dogs. "Then we'll talk about releasing your relatives." His voice cracked, betraying his desperation.

"We demand answers, Heldorf." Weiss's voice was quiet and composed. "If you can't produce our family members, we intend to hold you hostage against our own safety and freedom."

The shouts of the other scientists rose to a clamor, drowning out Weiss. "When will you honor your promise to free our families?"

"Open up and talk to us – we need to know your plans. Open up!"

"Open up! Open up!"

Heldorf felt a chill of fear as the others took up the call.

"Open up! Open up!" The call became a piercing chant as Heldorf watched the doorknob turn back and forth. The door shook in its frame as shoulders crashed into it, trying to break it down.

"Open up! Open up!"

Sweat poured from Heldorf's brow. The wood surrounding the hinges splintered and split.

"Open up! Open up!"

Heldorf yanked his pistol from his holster and fired several shots pointblank through the door. The fusillade halted the clamor, and for a few moments there was a silence broken only by gulls alarmed by the pistol's report. Then came a muffled groan.

"My God! He shot Weinstein!"

The banging and shouting began again. "You shot Weinstein!"

"Open up! Open up!"

"Listen, you fools," Heldorf shouted, "do you think you can escape from here? This is the end of the road for you all. There's no hope for you!" He snorted in a half-laugh as he realized that he might also share their fate. "And as for your miserable family members—," his laugh became maniacal, "the ones who're not already dead are doomed!" He heard the roar of rage heave out of their throats and prayed for the dogs to arrive.

"Come on, he can't get all of us." The door groaned under the renewed assault. Heldorf raised his pistol and pulled the trigger, but the hammer clicked against the empty chamber. He threw the useless weapon at the door and ran to the back of his quarters, his heart racing, his mouth dry as cotton.

He was surprised to find no one as he stepped through the rear doorway. Behind him, the sound of the Jews pounding and yelling became more frantic. He looked nervously about, forcing his eyes to focus as he tore down the path that led to the headland. In the distance was the uranium machine building. He ran toward it.

Hannah. He knew Hannah would be there. She was his only hope.

The noise of the Jews breaking into his quarters cut across his thoughts. He ran faster.

Morko Island. Heldorf's Quarters.

The door gave way and crashed to the floor. Some of the scientists rushed in, others lagged behind helping Otto Weinstein, who grimaced in pain as he held the bloody arm that had taken Heldorf's bullet.

"He's gone!" Steinitz shouted. "The filthy bastard's gone!"

"Look – there's a back door!" A cry rang out. There was a trampling of feet as several made their way through Heldorf's quarters.

"Wait!" Weiss shouted. Through the shattered doorway he saw Sol limping down the path, his white coat flapping in the wind, his legs defying their age and infirmity. A hundred yards behind him was the lead guard dog, his muscled legs driving him in pursuit of his prey; a few yards behind him came the rest of the pack.

"Sol, over here! We're in Heldorf's quarters! Over here!" Weiss's cry was taken up by the others, "Come on, Sol! Come on!"

Driven as much by his own fear as his friends' encouragement, Sol, his face flushed, lumbered awkwardly toward the doorway. The lead dog was gaining on him.

"Josef, Dietrich, pick up the door," Weiss barked. "As soon as Sol comes through, push it back into position." Willing hands lifted the door from the floor. "The rest of you, pull the desk over to make a buttress."

Weiss felt he was watching a slow-motion film. Sol was but five yards away, but it seemed like a mile, even though Weiss was close enough to see the panic in the old man's eyes. The lead dog was barking, his teeth bared as he anticipated the capture of his prey. Sol fell through the doorway. Hands grasped his flailing arms and dragged him inside.

"Now! Now!" Weiss called impatiently. Josef and Dietrich picked up the fallen door and slammed it upright. They braced themselves as the dog hurled itself forward, his claws scratching frantically at the wood.

Weiss leapt forward to add his weight. "The desk! For God's sake, the desk! Turn it upright!" The upended desk was slammed against the door. The lead dog, now joined by the rest of the pack, barked in frustration.

Weiss rushed to where Sol lay on the floor, surrounded by his colleagues. "Back, back, give him air." Weiss thrust his way through the press of bodies. "Are you all right, Sol?" He dropped to his knee and took his friend's hand.

Sol's chest heaved and his eyes were wild with fear. "Al," Sol spoke haltingly as he gasped for air, "Al...."

"You're safe now, Sol." Weiss spoke reassuringly despite doubting his own words. The barking of the dogs reached a crescendo of frustration.

"Al," there was terror in Sol's eyes, "something terrible has happened."

A shout came from Artur Steinitz, kneeling at the window. "Three guards coming this way!"

Sol reached up and pulled Albert's head down to his mouth. He could only manage a whisper from his voice, still raspy from his frantic run. "Al, I don't want the others to hear this, but—"

"The guards are armed!" Steinitz screamed.

"Later, Sol, later." As Albert jumped up, his foot kicked something and he looked down. He saw a pistol spinning on the floor.

At Sea in the Kattegat.

Christina checked the compass and pulled on the wheel, holding onto the course for Göteborg. "Tighten the foresail, Jørgen."

Jørgen's muscles bulged as he worked the winch; he was relieved to be on the open sea. The wind was set fair, although there was a chop on the water with occasional whitecaps.

When Christina told him to take a rest, the bloody scene on the dock flooded back. As he stood next to her in the cockpit watching the water, the memory pulled his spirit down with the force of an iron anchor. Erik, his best friend, was a traitor. He clenched his fists as he thought of the men Erik had murdered: Svend, Lars, Gunnar. Gunnar, who had sought his friendship, the comedian who had annoyed him, was a true hero. Jørgen remembered a book he'd read when he was a child about a topsy-turvy world where nothing was as it appeared to be. That's what the world felt like now. He'd gone through the looking glass.

The hurt in his heart grew when he realized that he could not return to Denmark. As long as the Germans were in his country he would be a wanted man. Like the Jews in the cabin below, he was now a fugitive.

But at least he was still alive. He felt a tightening in his throat, a prickling in the back of his neck as he remembered Gunnar. Why couldn't he just once have said to Gunnar, 'well done, pal'? Why couldn't he have laughed at just one of his silly jokes?

Christina seemed to read his mind. "The man who was driving the Resistance truck," she said, scanning the horizon, "the one who got shot, you knew him, didn't you?"

"Yes." Jørgen remained stiff-jawed as he blinked away the tears. "His name was Gunnar, and he was a good friend of mine."

Christina could see that Jørgen struggled with his emotions. He would tell her more when he was ready, she thought. If he wanted to.

For the moment, she needed to distract him from his thoughts, to keep him busy. "Jørgen, please raise the Swedish flag. It's time to declare our neutrality."

Mørkø Island. Heldorf's Quarters.

"The guards are getting closer!" Artur Steinitz shouted from the window. "Three of them."

Weiss stooped down, picked up the pistol, and opened the magazine: it was empty. "Quick, search all the drawers, look everywhere – there must be a box of ammunition somewhere!"

The barking of the dogs increased in frenzy. The blockaded door shook as the dogs' claws scratched frantically at the wood. "You, Gerhard, push against the desk – make sure the dogs can't get in!" Weiss joined Steinitz at the window. The guards were fifty yards away.

"Why don't we just give up?" The plaintive voice came from Georg Silberstein, who had slumped to the floor on his knees. "There's no way out."

Artur Steinitz answered his question. "If we surrender now, Georg, Heldorf will shoot us out of hand." Steinitz spoke without looking away from the window. "He doesn't need us anymore – we know too much."

Weiss was surprised at Steinitz's support. He'd always been a quiet one, bowing and scraping to Heldorf. The Nazi's bullets had clearly given him a different perspective.

"Is this what you're after, Albert?" Ernst Schlegel appeared holding a cardboard box. Weiss opened it and cursed as the half dozen bullets inside tumbled through his hand.

"You'd better load fast, Albert," Steinitz shouted. "The guards will be upon us in moments."

Mørkø Island. Uranium Machine Room.

Hannah pulled another cadmium control rod. There was no rage in her action, no fear – only sorrow and a conviction that it was something she had to do. She raised her knee and bent the soft metal rod on her thigh, then tossed it down. The neutron counter sputtered its annoyance. She pulled another rod and bent that, too; the counter chattered in surprise. As she pulled another, the door flew open and Heldorf burst in.

"Hannah, thank God I've found you!" He slammed the door. "Listen, I know you saw the letter from the camp commandant, I realize that you know all about your sister, but I can explain—"

"There's nothing to explain, Max," her voice was quiet, without anger, "I understand. I understand everything." She smiled at him and brought the rod down heavily upon her thigh. The neutron counter pattered like rain on a tin roof during a heavy storm.

"Hannah, I've got to talk—in God's name, what are you doing? Stop, for Christ's sake! You'll blow us up!" He rushed over, grabbed her by the upper arms, tossed her roughly aside, and scooped up one of the bent rods. He tried to straighten it, his face red with exertion.

Hannah pulled another rod. The neutron counter no longer produced discrete clicks; a loud buzz filled the room.

"Stop!" Heldorf struck Hannah hard on the face with the back of his hand, sending her flying to the floor. He tried to jam the bent rod back into the machine, but the more force he applied, the more deformed the rod became. Sweat poured from his brow as his desperation forced him to try another rod, and another. The neutron counter roared its rage. Heldorf swore and tossed the rod aside; the uranium machine was already out of control. The beast was snapping its chains.

Mørkø Island. Heldorf's Quarters.

Weiss's fingers trembled as he thrust the bullets into the magazine. "Get away from the window, Artur." He slammed home the magazine and smashed a pane with the barrel. The foremost guard was at the edge of the path, clutching his rifle across his chest as he ran toward him.

Weiss took careful aim and squeezed the trigger. The soldier's face twisted with pain as the bullet slammed into his chest. His arms flew upward; his rifle spun through the air and came clattering down to the ground. The other guards looked at each other, turned, and ran. Weiss shot hurriedly but they disappeared behind Heldorf's office.

The barking stopped, reduced to a whimpering. Weiss looked at the soldier's body. All was quiet.

"Albert!" The silence was broken by Steinitz's urgent voice. "There's a sailboat off the head of the island!"

At Sea in the Kattegat.

"Oy, vey, can't you stop the rocking?" The voice came from the small cabin below, behind the mainmast.

Christina gave Jørgen an embarrassed grin as he made his way aft. "Uh-oh, someone's seasick."

He peered down into the cabin where the Jews were huddled on the bench seats. "Is everything all right, Mrs. Abramowitz?"

"No, everything is not all right. I'm sick. I wish I'd never come!" Her pale face looked up at him. "I never felt so bad, even when I was giving birth to Moishe."

"Stop your kvetching!" Gerda Rosenfeld wagged her finger at Mrs. Abramowitz. "You don't know from bad. You want bad? I'll give you bad. The Nazis arresting you and sending you to a camp, now that's bad. How can you kvetch when these young people are risking their lives to save yours?"

Mrs. Abramowitz pressed a handkerchief to her lips. "What a *yenta,*" she muttered under her breath.

Jørgen turned away and looked at his watch. "About eight hours, Christina?"

She looked up, casting her eyes about the sky. "Maybe less with this wind."

Jørgen knew that when they arrived in Sweden the Jews were likely to receive a warm welcome – Marius had told him Niels Bohr was in Stockholm arranging for the Jews' safe conduct.

Jørgen's thoughts wandered as he admired the graceful curve of Christina's neck. Then his eyes caught Peder. The boy sat at the back of the boat, his eyes scouring the horizon. Jørgen was happy to see a broad smile back on Peder's face; the boy knew he was to be reunited with his mama. When Jørgen had told him, Peder had jumped from foot to foot in the strange way he had when he was excited.

But Jørgen could detect a wistfulness in Peder's eyes that dulled the effect of his smile. He knew what was amiss. Peder, without Soldat, his good friend, was inconsolable. The boy seemed to be taking the dog's absence bravely, but no one knew what feelings were in his heart.

Christina pulled on the wheel, her free hand reaching out to clutch Jørgen's arm for balance. He jumped at her touch and looked at her. If things were different, he thought. If only there were no war—

"Soldat! Soldat!" Peder leapt up, his finger pointing to an island to starboard.

Mørkø Island. Uranium Machine Room.

The uranium machine was now in the throes of an uncontrolled chain reaction; Heldorf knew they had to get out quickly. His mind raced: if he could save the specifications – the diagrams, formulas, and processes that would enable the machine to be built elsewhere – all might not be lost. He glanced at his watch – the boat would be back in two hours, maybe less. But the machine could blow in two hours. Their one chance was to get off the island as soon as the boat arrived.

He shoved the notebooks with the specifications under one arm and grabbed Hannah's hand with the other. "Come on, Hannah; we've got to get out of here."

He yanked her to the door and tried to open it. It was stuck. He pushed harder. Still it would not yield. He threw the notebooks on the floor and shoved and twisted fiercely with both hands. The heavy door refused to budge.

"Damn. I think the door's locked." He reached for his gun to shoot the lock and cursed when he remembered he'd left it in his quarters.

"Hannah, hand me the key."

"I can't, Max."

"You have the key! I know you have the key! It was missing from the hook in my room. You were the only one who could have taken it."

"I can't give it to you, Max. I swallowed it."

Everything in the room became frozen to Heldorf; even the roar of the neutron counter seemed to have disappeared.

Hannah watched in silence as Heldorf's face contorted grotesquely with a mixture of rage and fear. His voice started with a low moan and grew to a roar of terror. He leapt at her and she felt his hands around her throat.

"You bitch! You miserable Jewish bitch! I tried to help you, to help your sister, and this is the thanks I get!" He threw her aside in disgust. "Strangling is too good for you, you filthy whore!"

He tried the door again, desperate to find a way to open it. He pushed and twisted the doorknob until the veins in his forehead bulged. He slammed the door with his body, kicking and banging it with his fists. He screamed through the door, trying to alert a guard. Finally, exhausted, he sank slowly down the wall to the floor and covered his face with his hands.

Mørkø Island. Heldorf's Quarters.

Weiss looked over Steinitz's shoulder. The boat was about half a mile offshore on an easterly course. The sails were full with wind. Weiss squinted and looked again.

"Artur, can you see the flag at the masthead?"

Steinitz pushed his glasses up the bridge of his nose. "Barely. I think it's blue. Yes, blue, with a yellow cross."

"Swedish!" Weiss leapt up from the window. Maybe they could get a signal to the boat. "Helmut! Gerhard!" He ran into the bedroom and pulled the sheets from the bed. "I want you to get onto the roof and wave these sheets to attract the boat's attention."

"But Albert," Gerhard looked stunned, "the guards – they'll shoot at us."

Weiss pushed the sheet into his hand. "Stay at the back of the hut, behind the roof's peak. I'll keep you covered." He waved the pistol.

"But the dogs—"

"They're out in the front." Weiss's words were confirmed by the renewed barking around the door. He ran back to the front window and thrust the pistol into Steinitz's hand. "When I say, fire a shot at the dogs." He returned quickly to the rear of Heldorf's quarters. "Kurt, open the window. Get ready to give Gerhard and Helmut a leg up to the roof."

Crack! The pistol shot echoed around the hut.

"Not yet, Artur!" Weiss shouted angrily. "We've only a few bullets left!"

"A guard stuck his head out." Steinitz's eyes did not turn from the window.

A scratch of wood against wood came as the window was opened.

"Al, I have to talk to you!" Sol had limped across the room and put his hand on Albert's shoulder.

"Later, Sol." Weiss turned to see Helmut push Gerhard's leg up to the roof. He felt in his pocket and pulled out his matches, pushing the box into Helmut's hand. "Here, before you wave the sheet, set fire to it."

Helmut clambered through the window. Kurt took his heel in his hand and thrust him up to the roof.

"Now, Artur, now!"

At Sea in the Kattegat.

Jørgen moved swiftly to the stern and sat beside Peder, still pointing at the island. "Soldat! Soldat!"

Jørgen reached out and held the boy firmly by his upper arms. "Is that where Soldat is, Peder?"

The boy became alarmed and dropped his head; his friend seemed angry. Jørgen relaxed his grip and spoke more softly. "Please tell me, Peder, is Soldat there?" There was a nod of the blond crop.

"What's going on?" Christina held the helm steady as she called over her shoulder.

Jørgen braced himself against the roll of the boat in the swell and crossed to her side. "Peder says that's where his dog, Soldat, is – on that island." He pointed off the starboard bow.

"But that's impossible." She looked at him incredulously. "What on earth would the dog be doing there?"

"I don't know." Jørgen shook his head. "But I do know that Peder is incapable of telling a lie."

"What is that place?" Christina kept her hands firm on the wheel as the boat rolled.

"It's Mørkø."

"Mørkø," Christina repeated, mulling over the Danish translation. *"Bleak Island."*

Mørkø Island. Heldorf's Quarters.

The footsteps pounded on the roof overhead. Weiss rejoined Steinitz at the front window. The dogs had become agitated again after

Steinitz's gunfire, barking incessantly. Now they milled around, lacking direction.

Weiss looked out. The dead guard lay nearby, his body sprawled awkwardly on the ground. One of the dogs sniffed over the corpse, licking the dead man's face, seeking a response that would never come. Beyond, Weiss saw the shore and the boat, still holding its course.

"The other guards are over there." Steinitz motioned with his pistol toward Heldorf's office. "One stuck his head out, but disappeared fast when I shot at him."

"Perhaps they don't want to be dead heroes," Weiss nodded toward the body, "like their friend. But I don't like it. Keep an eye on the windows."

Shouts came from above. Helmut and Gerhard's feet crashed against the roof. "Albert," Helmut called down. "We can't set the damned sheet on fire."

Mørkø Island. Uranium Machine Room.

Hannah felt pity for Heldorf as he kneeled on the floor by the unyielding door. She could hear little because of the relentless whine of the neutron counter, but she could see that his body was wracked with piteous sobs. She kneeled down and pulled him to her. His arms reached up to her and he rested his face, ghoulish in the red light, on her breast like a child. His violently quivering body shook her own.

"We're doomed, Hannah, doomed," he whimpered. "There's no way out."

"I know, Max."

They were two of a kind, she thought. He had been selfish, but so had she. He had been misguided, but so had she. He had been the unwitting accomplice of the devil, and so had she. 'Was it really so wrong to want to save your country at any price?' the devil had asked him. 'Was it really so wrong to want to save yourself at any price?' the devil had asked her.

At Sea in the Kattegat.

"The island's uninhabited," Jørgen said. "Just sand dunes and sedge grass. My friends and I used to sail out here in the summer before the war."

259

Christine squinted. "It's not uninhabited now. I can see buildings."

"That's impossible."

She reached into a storage box, pulled out a pair of binoculars, and handed them to him.

When his fingers adjusted the focus, he could see the huts clearly. "Incredible! There's never been anyone—" Jørgen felt a tug at his trousers and looked down to see Peder turning the pages of his sketchpad. He put down the binoculars and moved to look over the boy's shoulder. "What is it, Peder?"

The boy pointed to a drawing he had done in his sketchbook. It was of a boat. "Strange men. Not speak like you."

Jørgen understood what Peder was trying to say. The boat was German. It came several times a week into Frederikshavn, loaded up with provisions, and sailed away. Everybody thought they were taking the best of Denmark's bounty to smuggle back to Germany. He raised the binoculars again and scanned the island. But what if it was a provision boat for the island? Was it possible that Peder had been on the boat? The time he had disappeared?

Jørgen reached for a ratline as the boat lurched. Peder's sketchbook fell from his fingers, the pages flipping in the wind. The boy grabbed the book, found another page, and held it up for Jørgen to see.

"Peder, did you go—" The question died on Jørgen's lips as he looked at the page Peder held up. It was the drawing of the woman whom Niels Bohr had recognized. He could not recall her name. A Jewish scientist who was an expert in—

Peder's finger jabbed at the drawing. "Lady! Lady!" He hopped from foot to foot in his excitement. "With Soldat! With Soldat!"

Soldat. The woman who was a scientist. Jørgen felt there was an important connection he was missing. If they were able to land on the island to look for Soldat, perhaps they could also—

"I'm sorry, Jørgen, but landing on the island is out of the question." It was as if Christina had again read his thoughts. "I know how much the dog means to Peder, but we can't put our passengers in any further danger. After all our efforts, we can't jeopardize them for a dog."

Jørgen sighed. "I guess you're right – our main responsibility right now is to our friends below deck."

Mørkø Island. Heldorf's Quarters.

"Keep trying to set the sheet on fire! Keep trying!" Weiss shouted back at the men on the roof without taking his eyes from the window. The boat still held its course. He called out to the others. "Shout! Scream! Make as much damned noise as possible!"

Pandemonium rang within the hut. Some pummeled on the walls, others stamped the floor, all yelled as loudly as they could. Weiss doubted that the noise would carry to the boat, but he knew it would encourage them all.

"We've done it!" Even through the din Weiss heard the cry from the roof above. "The sheet's burning!" At the sound of Helmut and Gerhard's shoes jumping up and down on the roof in jubilation, the cacophony inside the hut intensified.

But as Weiss watched the boat, his heart sank – the vessel continued to plow its course. Were they blind? Or suspicious? Perhaps they just didn't want to get involved.

He was aware that everyone's eyes were upon him. There was no escape.

Mørkø Island. Uranium Machine Room.

Max Heldorf's head ached, he felt sick to his stomach, and he was burning up with the heat. He sobbed unashamedly on Hannah's breast.

He didn't want to die; he knew he didn't deserve to die. He had done nothing wrong. He had been loyal to the Führer and to Germany and had made the Jews – who owed their lives to him – comfortable in his camp.

Why had Hannah done this to him? For reasons of misguided morality? Nothing was moral in war, on either side. Was it moral for the enemy to bomb Berlin night and day? Wouldn't they gladly save the lives of their own men if they could drop a single bomb and wipe out the entire city? There was no morality in war.

He began to vomit. Oh, God, why had she done it? Why? Why?

At Sea in the Kattegat.

Jørgen scanned the horizon. He adjusted his stance to the pitch of the boat. "Peder's going to be upset when he realizes that we're abandoning Soldat." He looked sadly at the boy, perched at the stern, his eyes fixed on the island that held his beloved friend. "I'm not looking forward to the moment when he sees we're leaving the island behind."

"Jørgen, please take the helm." Christina turned, the wind from the starboard beam raising her hair to dance across her face. She brushed it aside and took Peder's sketchpad from Jørgen as his hand gripped the wheel. He checked the compass. On course for Göteborg.

Christina flipped through the drawings and found what she was seeking. "Jørgen, if the woman Peder drew – the scientist Dr. Bohr recognized – is on that island, then maybe so is this." She held up Peder's diagram of the uranium machine. "Remember what Niels Bohr said? He said this thing was some sort of—"

Jørgen completed her sentence. "Nuclear reactor."

A cry of alarm came from behind them. "Soldat! Soldat!" The boy ran across the deck, tears streaming down his face. He could see that the boat was heading away from the island and he threw himself at Jørgen, clutching his legs.

"Christina, could you take the wheel? I need to calm down my friend here; he's upset."

"Just a moment." Christina picked up the binoculars and scanned the island. "My God, Jørgen, I think there are people on the roof of one of those buildings." With the roll of the boat, she lost her sighting. She steadied herself and tried again. "Yes, there are two people, and they're waving something that's burning – I can see flames." She fine-tuned the focus. "I think it's a distress signal – I think they're trying to get our attention."

Christina thrust the binoculars into Jørgen's hands and seized the helm. "Prepare to come about." The wheel spun in her hands as the boat heeled over to starboard, toward the island.

Mørko Island. Heldorf's Quarters.

The boat was not going to change course. Everyone in the room knew it was not going to come to their rescue. Still the scientists continued to shout and wave. The boat was their only hope.

A shot rang out, silencing the tumult. There was a cry from the roof.

"It came from the office window." Steinitz raised the pistol.

"Shoot! Shoot!" Weiss shouted, "Aim at the window. Force the guard to keep his head down."

"Gerhard's been hit in the arm," Helmut cried from above. "The sheet's now completely ashes – we've got to come down!"

Willing hands helped them down from the roof. Helmut swung through the window, but Gerhard had to be carefully lifted through the frame. His face was white, his bloodied arm hanging useless at his side.

"Quick, Kurt," Weiss picked up a towel from the washstand, "bind up Gerhard's wound."

"Over here, Albert! Take a look over here!" Steinitz called from the window.

Weiss rushed over, looked out, and smiled. "Listen, everyone! The Swedish boat – it's turned around and heading for the pier!"

There was a crash of glass as a bullet smashed through the window. "Get down, all of you!" His shout was needless; everyone was already lying on the floor. Weiss scrambled on his hands and knees across to the window. "Artur, are you alright?"

"A few cuts from the broken glass." Steinitz wiped away the blood that ran down his face from his brow. "But what are we going to do now? How're we going to warn the boat that there are armed guards?"

Weiss did not answer. He did not know what to do. He peered cautiously from a corner of the window and saw that the boat was nearing the jetty. He forced his eyes to focus: a man was standing on the prow.

Weiss laughed and slapped Steinitz on the back. "We don't need to warn them."

"What—?"

The unmistakable chatter of a submachine gun carried to their ears.

"Our visitors need no warning."

Mørkø Island. Uranium Machine Room.

Exhaustion and nausea wracked Hannah's body. Her feeble arms were barely able to clasp Max to her breast. But it was not Max whom she comforted.

Rachel, I love you, my sweet sister. I'm not afraid to die; my one regret is that when I'm gone there will be no one left on earth who will remember you. Yet all the world should honor you: because of you, the world has been spared the catastrophic consequences of my pride.

Mørkø Island. Heldorf's Quarters.

"Kurt, pull the desk away from the door."

They crouched on their knees, worry writ large on their faces.

"Yes, move it!" Weiss moved away from the window and stood up. "Listen, everybody," he looked down at his colleagues, cowering on the floor, "we have to make a run for it. We have to try to make it to that boat!"

"But the guards," an anxious voice muttered.

"And the dogs—"

"It's too risky. I'm staying here." Georg Silberstein spoke from his position on the bed.

Weiss rushed across the room and grabbed the lapels of Silberstein's lab coat. "Listen, you fool!" He spat out the words. "Anyone who stays here will die. The boat is our only hope!"

"But Georg has a point. The dogs—"

"We have to take the chance. Pull down the desk. Let's go!" He turned to see Sol still sitting in his chair.

"I don't think I can make it, Al."

"Don't worry, Sol, I'll help—" Weiss slapped his forehead. "Dear God, I've got to go and get Hannah! She's still in my quarters—"

Sol shot up with surprising briskness. "That's what I keep trying to tell you, Al." He leaned over and whispered in Weiss's ear.

"Dear God, no, Sol, no!" Nothing in that terror-filled day had struck Weiss with the force of Sol's whispered message.

There was a shout. The desk fell with a crash and they all ran out, screaming at the top of their lungs to summon up their courage.

Mørkø Island. Uranium Machine Room.

Vomit spewed from Max Heldorf's mouth, dribbling down his tunic onto Hannah. The radiation was eating at his soft tissues. The machine

264

was now emitting blue flashes and such oppressive heat his lungs could barely catch the air. The counters were driving him mad. They were no longer tallying neutrons – they were counting the seconds remaining in his life.

Why had Hannah done this monstrous thing?
After he had told her Rachel was alive, she had changed. The locus of her life was no longer the project, no longer him – it was her sister.
But he had searched and found her sister. He had tried to get her sister out of the camp. It wasn't his fault that he had failed. The irony made him want to laugh. By trying to prove his love, he had caused his own downfall.

Max Heldorf gagged as his body tried to void an already-empty stomach.

Mørkø Island.

Weiss felt Sol's hand clutch tightly at his arm. The old man could do no better than a shambling gait. Weiss fixed his eyes on the boat at the jetty, two hundred yards ahead. Crouching on the prow of the boat was a young man firing his machine gun at the guards' position in the camp office.

Weiss saw Steinitz running ahead. He was almost at the jetty, his arms pumping, his white coat flapping behind him as one of the dogs chased him, snapping at his heels. Weiss gasped as the dog leapt; its teeth sought flesh but bit instead into Steinitz's white coat, bringing him to his knees. A young woman emerged on the boat, a pistol in her hand. The dog fell as the bullet hit him, his teeth locked on Steinitz's coat in his death throes. Steinitz slipped his arms from the sleeves and jumped up, his feet flying as he ran to the boat and leapt onto the deck.

Another dog went down. The rest of the pack backed off, barking their rage.

Weiss felt the grip on his arm relax. Sol fell to his knees. "I'll never make it, Al," the old man gasped. "I'm slowing you down; go on without me."

"Not on your life, Sol." Weiss reached down and hauled his friend to his feet, bracing Sol's arm around his neck.

"But Al," Sol spoke haltingly, fighting for breath, "Hannah's pulled the control rods. Surely you understand what that means."

"Let's keep going, Sol. Just put one foot in front of the other, one at a time." Weiss pretended calm but had no illusions about the danger. At any moment the uranium machine could begin melting down and shower them all with radioactive dust. To escape, they needed to be at least half a mile away.

But he could only worry about the imminent danger. He saw that some had made the boat and from the safety of the deck were shouting, waving their arms, urging them on. The young man and woman were still firing their weapons, holding the dogs at bay.

"We're almost there, Sol," Weiss shouted above the uproar. "We're going to make it."

As he uttered the words, out of the corner of his eye he caught a glimpse of a dark shape moving toward them. A hundred yards away, one of the dogs had come forward and was bounding in their direction, teeth bared, eyes set like fiery coals in its huge head.

"I have to stop and rest, Al." Sol gasped for breath. "It's my sciatica; if I take more than a few steps, my old legs just won't work anymore."

The dog was closing on them. "Come on, Sol, just a few more yards. You can do it." They had reached the edge of the jetty. Only thirty yards to the boat. The last of the team was scrambling on board. Steinitz stood on the deck waving, frantically urging on his colleagues. The young man stood on the prow, firing sporadically at the office, pinning down the guards.

Weiss heard the barking of the dog behind them. Sol tried to move, but stumbled, pulling at Weiss's arm.

"Get down!" The cry came from the young woman, now standing on the jetty. In one hand she held a rope, securing the boat; in the other was a pistol. "Get down! Let me get a clear shot at the dog!"

Weiss went to the ground, his arm embracing Sol in a protective gesture. His chin dug into the gravel as he saw the woman raise her pistol and take aim. Suddenly, a young boy raced along the deck of the boat, his blond hair streaming out behind him.

266

"No! No!" he screamed as he jumped down from the boat. He leapt at the young woman, his hands clutching at her arm. "Let go, Peder, let go!" As she struggled to free her arm, the woman dropped the gun.

The ferocious bark told Weiss the dog would soon be upon them. "Put your face down flat, Sol!" he said, putting his own down as well. He wrapped one arm around his own neck, the other around Sol's, and closed his eyes.

Mørkø Island. Uranium Machine Room.

The noise of the neutron counter had become strangely comforting to Max Heldorf. Had a thousand crickets crept inside the room? The crickets – the noise reminded him of the sounds on the sweet starry nights in Lierstedt when he was a boy and used to lie for hours out on the grass, gazing at the star-studded skies.

His mother – where was his mother?

He lay in the grass on that star-filled night and could see his mother standing in her dressing gown, a dark silhouette in the doorway against the golden light from within their home.

"I thought I'd find you here, Max," she said. "Still dreaming, are you? You were always a dreamer. The world was never big enough for you – you always had to reach for the stars, as well."

She was now in the light and he could see her clearly. He knew he had to hold onto her, because when she was gone, he would be gone as well.

"I always said that someday you'd go on to do great things, Max, my beautiful boy. I always said that the world would take notice of what you did."

The door closed, the golden light was snuffed out, and his mother vanished, leaving Max Heldorf alone in a great void.

Mørkø Island.

Weiss lay next to Sol on the jetty, every muscle in body tensed for the attack of the dog. He could feel Sol's body trembling violently under his protective arm as they braced themselves.

Then he heard the boy shout something in Danish.

"Soldat, no! No, Soldat!"

Weiss knew the dog was upon them because he could hear it panting, could feel hot drops of saliva on the back of his hand. But the dog did not attack.

Again the boy shouted Danish words Weiss could not understand.

"Go, Soldat! Go! Go!"

Weiss felt gravel hit his body; he sensed that it had been kicked up by the dog's retreating feet. He raised his head and looked around: the dog was running off to join the rest of the pack. The boy, whom the woman held close to her, was looking off into the distance where the dog had run. His lips were pursed, as though he were whistling. But Sol heard nothing.

Weiss helped Sol to his feet, hobbling the remaining few yards to the cheers of their colleagues. The young man, his machine gun slung across his back, grasped Sol's arms and pulled him up. Weiss jumped on behind him.

Weiss caught his breath before shouting at the man, "Quick, there's going to be an explosion! We're all in danger! We've got to get away fast!" The man looked at Weiss and frowned.

"Dear God, he doesn't speak German!" Weiss ran his fingers through his hair in frustration.

The woman shouted from the jetty in Danish to the man, then turned to Weiss and said in German, "What sort of explosion?"

A shot came from the guards. The young man turned and fired a burst at the hut.

"Poison gas." It was not true, but Weiss had no time to explain nuclear physics.

The young woman nodded. "Jørgen, we need to cast off. Now!"

Mørko Island. Uranium Machine Room.

Max was gone. Hannah let his body slip to the floor; her fingers ran over his face and closed his eyes. She was sorry for him; she was sorry for all the others, too. It wasn't their fault. But her thoughts were not of Max, nor of the other scientists. Her thoughts were still of Rachel.

A moment from the past flooded her drowning mind – a dolls' tea party when she was nine and Rachel was seven.

They sat around a tiny table with their dolls, drinking tea from tiny china cups and nibbling on rugelach their mother had made for the party.

"What special thing do you want to do when you grow up?" she asked Rachel. Rachel bit her lip and looked up at the ceiling as she pondered the question. Her short bobbed hair was done up with a large pink bow at the top of her head.

"Umm...when I grow up I want to do good things for people," Rachel said, nodding her head emphatically. "What about you? What special thing do you want to do?"

Hannah's answer came quickly. "I want to discover a secret no one knows."

"And use the secret to do good things for people?"

"Yes, and use it to do good things."

"Promise?"

"Cross my heart."

She had not kept her promise to Rachel. She had discovered her secret, but she wondered where the devil would have unleashed the hounds of hell imprisoned in plutonium, the great secret Hannah had discovered. England? Russia? The United States?

Wherever lived the nameless, faceless people who would escape death, they would never know the name of Hannah Goldmann, the woman who had saved their lives by destroying her own creation.

Mørkø Island.

Christina snatched up Peder. "Here, take the boy." Jørgen grabbed Peder and pulled him inboard.

"Casting off!" Christina unwound the rope from the bollard.

"No! No! Soldat! Soldat!" Peder struggled in Jørgen's arms, pointing at the dog pack.

As Christina jumped on deck, Weiss ran to her. "The explosion will produce a poisonous cloud that could kill us all!"

"Jørgen, he says there's going to be an explosion that could kill everybody! We've got to get out of here now!"

Jørgen began to spin the wheel.

"No! No! Soldat! Soldat!" As Peder clutched at Jørgen's legs, he pursed his lips and whistled with all his might.

The bow of the boat swung away from the pier. A dog separated from the pack and stood looking at the boat.

"Soldat!" Peder jumped up and down on the deck, his arms waving frantically. The dog began running, his ears pricked. The wind plucked at the foresail.

"Wait, wait for Soldat!" There was panic in the boy's voice.

Weiss shouted at Christina "Tell him we've got to get out of here! Now!"

"Jørgen, he says we've got to push off fast!"

Jørgen nodded and looked at Peder, the boy's arms waving as he called to Soldat, bounding towards the jetty. Jørgen's hand steadied the wheel, holding the boat to the wind. The foresail fluttered; the boat swung slowly back to the pier. Soldat bounded onto the jetty, his tongue lolling.

"Quick, Soldat!" The boy leapt up and down.

The dog sized up the increasing gap and jumped, his paws flailing at the deck. Christina bent down, grabbed his collar, and helped him on board.

"Soldat." Peder ran forward and threw his arms around the dog's neck. "Soldat." He ruffled the dog's ears. "Friend."

Jørgen pulled the helm to starboard. The wind filled the sails and the boat swung out to sea.

At Sea on the Kattegat.

As the Sofia's bow plowed through the waves, Albert sat in the cockpit, his eyes fixed on the island, their home for the past year and a half, now a mere smudge on the horizon with a plume of black smoke wafting skyward. At his side sat Sol, wrapped in a blanket and looking like his Biblical namesake dressed in his royal robes. Sol shivered and pulled the blanket tight to his body as the wind blew through his thinning white hair; he briefly considered the irony of surviving a pack of vicious dogs and a hail of bullets only to expire from a chill caught on the rescue boat. The two men lingered without speaking, lost in their own thoughts.

Albert shook his head and turned to Sol. "What a waste her death was, Sol, a dreadful waste." He blinked hard to stem the tears forming in his eyes.

"Yes, Al, I know. She was brilliant – her insights into physics were nothing short of phenomenal."

"I didn't mean a waste in that sense. I meant a waste of a human being. She had a good heart. All she really wanted was to love and be loved. Physics was what she hid behind when the love wasn't there."

Sol pondered his friend's words as he looked at the clearing sky; the sun, nearing the horizon, was now splashing golden nuggets on the water. "You may be right, Al."

Albert wiped the corners of his eyes. "I loved her, Sol. I loved her as I would have loved a younger sister. She was always kind to me. Everyone knew she was masterminding the show, but she always deferred to me as the team leader." Albert returned his gaze to the sea. As the sun painted the clouds, it struck him that the splendid hues, unknown to any artist's palette, were an irreverent contrast to the black fate of the tiny island, now just a dot. "What a waste."

"Not a total waste, Al. She did save our souls from the devil."

Albert frowned at his friend. "I don't believe we have any souls, Sol."

"No, maybe not." Sol sighed and squinted toward the setting sun. "But, in this *meshugah* world, there's one thing you've got to admit, Al."

"What's that, Sol?"

"You've got to admit there's a devil."

Albert guffawed and put his arm around his friend. "I won't argue with you on that, Sol. No question about it – look at the grim harvest he's been reaping."

"Yeah. Lately, he's been doing exceptionally well at doing ill. You, me, and everyone else on this boat – we've all seen some terrible things." Sol watched as the sun touched the sea and bled into the water. "There's really only one hope for this *meshugah* world."

"What would that be, Sol?"

"Him." Sol pointed at the little blond boy who sat cross-legged on the deck drawing a picture.

Albert grasped Sol's meaning and nodded sadly. The mess created by one generation always fell upon the next to clean up. Albert hoped that the little blond boy's generation would not make the same mistakes.

Peder sat quietly on the starboard side sketching, his good friend curled up at his feet. Soldat, sleeping on his side with his back arched, wore a contented smile. His nose rested on his bent forelegs which met his hind legs, and his tail came forward to complete the circle.

Gerda Rosenfeld stuck her head out of the cramped cabin for a breath of fresh air. "May I see your drawing, Peder?" The boy handed his sketchpad to her over his shoulder without taking his eyes off his dog.

Gerda looked at the drawing and, with a sudden intake of breath, brought her hand up to her mouth. "Oh, my, Peder – this is wonderful!"

The boy stroked his sleeping dog, her voice unheeded.

Gerda traced the outlines of the drawing with her fingers. From the sketchpad she held in her hand, the kind eyes of Sara Gronborg smiled up at her.

"We'll soon see your mother, Peder."

A smile came to Peder's lips.

In the cabin below deck, a dozen passengers jammed onto the two benches on either side of the table on which Artur Steinitz perched. He reached up and touched the bandage on his head and felt proud: it was a memento of his courage.

From the moment they had broken the door down and Albert pushed Artur's trembling frame into Heldorf's quarters, he had been convinced that they were all dead men. Even if the Nazis took them alive, he'd rather be dead; he had seen what they did to those who tried to escape at Auschwitz. When he had taken the gun and sat down at the window, his one desire had been that his death would be quick.

But when he began firing, he forgot his fear and wanted only to live. He still thought he would die, but the terror had left him. As he fought on for his self-respect as a human being, euphoria mixed with rage rose up within him, born of the sudden realization that life, no matter how brutish, was worth fighting for, and that no man had the right to take it from him.

Ernst Schlegel, sitting at the end of the bench, caught his eye. "Artur, I'd like to add my congratulations to all the others. You were wonderful this afternoon; you helped save our lives. What you did at the window – that really took guts."

Artur smiled and nodded at Ernst. Guts. He had guts. Maybe now he'd have the guts to throw off the shroud of constant fear that had been Auschwitz's legacy.

Jørgen finished tightening the foresail and called to Christina. "Anything else you want me to do, Captain?"

"Yes – take a rest, why don't you? You've had quite a day. We've all had quite a day." She edged the wheel to port.

Jørgen looked over his shoulder. "Sun's going down. Say, Christina, I suppose—," he hesitated as his eyes met hers, "I suppose you're looking forward to getting back to the States."

"Am I ever! The sooner the better. I'll report to the American Consulate as soon as I get to Göteborg and let them know I'm still alive." Christina checked the compass. "What will you do, Jørgen? You can't go back to Denmark, can you?"

"No. Not until the Nazis are forced out."

She bit her lip and looked up at him. "I'm sorry, Jørgen. That must be very hard for you."

"I'll be all right. There's a Danish Brigade forming in Sweden – I'm going to try to join that."

Christina tried to hide her concern. She had already lost one friend to the war; a memory of Franz von Rastenberg smiling at her in the Stockholm restaurant came and went. Now she'd have to worry about Jørgen, to whom she felt a good deal closer. "Say, look – when we get to Sweden I'll give you my address back in the USA. Let's keep in touch."

"Yes, let's." Jørgen looked down shyly at his feet.

"Brrrr, it's chilly." Christina took a hand off the wheel and blew on it. "Once the sun goes down, the temperature out on the water really drops fast, doesn't it?" She reached into her pocket for her gloves; as she pulled them out, one dropped to the deck.

Jørgen dipped and picked it up, but as he gave it to her, his hand lingered; he squeezed her fingers before pulling his back. He stuffed his hands into his pocket and looked self-consciously off to sea. He could face the Nazis, but he was suddenly terrified of the woman standing next to him.

Christina broke the long silence that followed. "Jørgen, if you do join the Danish Brigade, you'll be careful, won't you?"

He smiled at her. "Sure I will. The Allies are winning; this lousy war won't last forever."

"It can't last forever." She raised an eyebrow and looked up at him with a coy smile. "I have to come back to Frederikshavn – you owe me a decent cup of coffee."

Jørgen's face lit up in an immense grin. "It's a deal."

Author's Afterword

The Devil's Alchemists, like my other novels, *The Sobs of Autumn's Violins* and *The Mirror of Diana,* is a work of fiction based on historical fact. My book revolves around three major themes: the possible development of a German atomic bomb during World War II, the heroic actions of the Danish Resistance during the German occupation, and the nearly-miraculous rescue of almost all of Denmark's Jews. As readers often like to know fact from fiction, I shall summarize some of the less well-known history that readers might consider fictitious in my novel.

Much mystery surrounds the German World War II atomic weapons program, and whether Germany could have built an atomic weapon before the end of the war is still the subject of much speculation. At the outbreak of the war, Germany seemed poised to be the first to develop an atomic bomb. German physicists had been the first to split the uranium atom. The Blitzkrieg had given Germany the world's richest supplies of uranium and heavy water. And Germany's 'Uranium Club' was engaged in military research at the Kaiser Wilhelm Institute in Berlin, a circumstance of such grave concern it prompted Albert Einstein to write a series of warning letters to President Roosevelt.

Prominent in the Uranium Club was Werner Heisenberg – Germany's leading nuclear physicist, Nobel Laureate, and director of the Kaiser Wilhelm Institute. In March of 1941, German physicist Fritz Houtermans, a good friend of Heisenberg, sent a secret message to the United States. In his message, passed on by an emigrating German-Jewish scientist, Houtermans alerted American scientists to the existence of the German atomic bomb program, in full swing at the time with investigations into reactors, isotope separation, and nuclear explosives.

In September of 1941, Werner Heisenberg visited his old friend and mentor, the Danish Nobel laureate Niels Bohr, who was living and working under German occupation in Copenhagen. In a private conversation with Bohr, Heisenberg implied that Germany was working on an atomic bomb and asked Bohr whether he thought physicists should engage in such an undertaking. The purpose of Heisenberg's visit – whether it was to inform, warn, or seek moral advice – is still the subject of much heated debate, and after the war the recollection of the conversation was different for both scientists. In any event, Bohr became convinced that Germany was working on an atomic bomb and so informed the Allies.

Indeed, Heisenberg and other German scientists recognized the potential of atomic weapons and understood the scientific principles of building them, but the Uranium Club was unsuccessful in discovering a means of separating out uranium-235, the fissionable uranium isotope, in quantities required for a bomb. In a meeting in June of 1942 with Reichminister Albert Speer and his military advisors, Heisenberg suggested that developing an atomic weapon would be an undertaking of such magnitude that its funding would be prohibitive and its realization too late to affect the outcome of the war. He requested only modest funding from Speer, thus effectively ending Germany's official nuclear weapons program.

Plutonium was known to German physicists as a result of research done by Fritz Houtermans, the scientist who sent the secret message to the United States. Evidence that German scientists understood that plutonium is as fissionable as uranium-235 came to light recently when a German patent application from 1941 was discovered for what amounted to a plutonium bomb. Some historians have speculated that Heisenberg was part of a pact to suppress information about plutonium; it is interesting to note that the patent application for the plutonium bomb was withdrawn the same year and resubmitted on behalf of the entire Kaiser Wilhelm Institute with every mention of a nuclear weapon removed.

Albert Speer was one of only two of Hitler's high-ranking officials to escape a death sentence at the Nuremberg trials, although he spent twenty years in Spandau Prison. As Minister of Arms and Munitions, Speer used forced labor but claimed later not to have known about the extermination camps. Many historians view it unlikely that a top official so close to Hitler would have been unaware of the Holocaust.

The raid in Vemork, Norway depicted in the novel is based on an attack on the hydroelectric plant that produced most of the world's supply of heavy water, then thought essential as a moderator in the construction of a nuclear reactor. During the war the plant was the target of several daring raids by the Allies, who understood its strategic significance. Although Heisenberg did not think that graphite could be used as a substitute for heavy water as a moderator in a nuclear reactor, graphite was used by Enrico Fermi in the "Chicago Pile," the first nuclear reactor to sustain a chain reaction, built in 1942 in Stagg Field at the University of Chicago.

An uprising at Treblinka occurred in August, 1943, much as described in the novel. Of the eight hundred prisoners in the camp at the time, most were killed during or shortly after the uprising. Of those who managed to escape, only a few dozen survived the war.

Many of the resistance actions portrayed in the novel are based on real operations of the Danish Resistance. However, most did not occur in Frederikshavn; for example, the destruction of the exhibition hall took place in Frederiksberg, a town in southeast Denmark.

In August, 1943, after the Danish government refused to impose the death penalty on citizens for anti-German sabotage, Germany declared martial law in Denmark. Soon after, the Danish Resistance learned that Germany had decided to deport all of Denmark's eight thousand Jews, rounding them up from their homes on the second day of Rosh Hashanah. Aided by the Resistance, almost all of Denmark's Jews went into hiding overnight and eventually were evacuated to Sweden on fishing boats; only a few hundred were captured.

Niels Bohr and his wife were among those who made their way by boat to Sweden. There Bohr met with members of the Swedish government and the King of Sweden to discuss helping the Danish Jews after their arrival in Sweden. Eventually, Bohr went to Los Alamos, New Mexico, to advise the Manhattan Project scientists, although his primary concern during and after the war was the prevention of a nuclear arms race.

To all who find themselves in Copenhagen, I heartily recommend a visit to the Museum of Danish Resistance. The rescue of Denmark's Jewish citizens is one of the most extraordinary events of World War II, for which the people of Denmark are justifiably proud.

Finally, you will not find Mørkø on any map. The island and those who toiled on it – the reluctant alchemists of a human devil – are the product of my imagination.

Printed in the United States
127598LV00004B/154/P

9 781595 265036